SUNWARD I'VE CLIMBED

**Book One
of
The Sunlit Silence Series
of
World War II in the Air**

Frank A. Mason

For Deri, Always...

Copyright © 2023 Frank A. Mason

First paperback edition April 2023

Book design by AmazonProHub

ISBN 978-1-962621-42-7 (paperback)
ISBN 978-1-962621-41-0 (ebook)

www.frankamason.com
www.thejourneymanchronicles.com

Table of Contents

High Flight

Oh! I have slipped the surly bonds of Earth
And danced the skies on laughter-silvered wings;
Sunward I've climbed, and joined the tumbling mirth
of sun-split clouds—and done a hundred things
You have not dreamed of—wheeled and soared and swung
High in the sunlit silence. Hov'ring there,
I've chased the shouting wind along, and flung
My eager craft through footless halls of air ....

Up, up the long, delirious, burning blue
I've topped the wind-swept heights with easy grace
Where never lark nor ever eagle flew—
And, while with silent lifting mind I've trod
The high untrespassed sanctity of space,
Put out my hand, and touched the face of God.

John Gillespie McGee, Jr.

1

Map of Europe

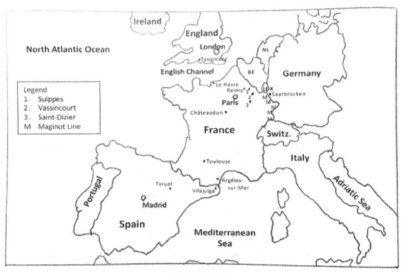

Europe - 1940

Chapter 1 – Spain, February 1939

A burst of 7.92-millimeter bullets rattled across the left wing and shattered the windscreen frame, spraying fragments in all directions. Trip Gibson stomped hard left rudder and wrenched the spade-grip control column hard to the right. The little *Mosca* snap rolled right so suddenly that Trip's head was pinned to the cockpit sill.

Rolling out of the frantic maneuver, Trip shoved the control column hard forward, putting the Polikarpov I-16 into a near-vertical dive. The negative g-forces threatened to throw Trip clear of the airplane and would have done so had he not brutally tightened his harness before takeoff. As it was, blood rushed to Trip's head, making things turn a strange red as his eyes attempted to compensate.

As the little airplane went through the vertical, Trip relaxed the pressure on the control column and jerked the throttle to idle. Pulling out of the dive, he frantically swiveled his head left and right, searching the airspace around him for the Bf-109 that had come within an instant of killing him.

There! The grey Messerschmitt was perched 3000 feet above him. It was rolled up on its starboard wing like a falcon watching its prey. Trip fleetingly thought such an image was appropriate, given that the Nationalist nickname for his little fighter was *Rata*, meaning 'rat.'

There was no time to consider ironies as Trip's unpleasant situation worsened. The Bf-109 rolled on its back, and Trip watched as its nose swung through the horizon to point at his airplane. The German pilot was now in a dive with Trip's dark green Russian-supplied plane as its target.

Trip jammed the throttle as far forward as it would go and wrenched the controls to haul the *Mosca* into a climb. Trip had plenty of airspeed from the dive, making the little plane zoom skyward. He pointed his nose directly at the German. This time, the positive G-forces as he pulled the airplane into a near-vertical climb crushed

Trip into the seat, dragging his oxygen mask down and making him grunt as he strained to keep from blacking out. With luck, Trip would get a shot in before the German closed the half-mile gap. If not, Robert Harney Gibson, III, called Trip by family and friends, would die in a pile of Russian metal on a hard piece of Spanish dirt.

Trip Gibson knew the Bf-109's 100 kph speed advantage over the *Mosca* in level flight. Trip knew he could not escape by diving, so the audacious, head-on climbing pass was his only chance. But now, Trip's *Mosca* was slowly bleeding off airspeed. This engagement must end quickly. If Trip stalled and fell off on a wing, the German would shred his little airplane into confetti.

The distance closed quickly. In seconds the two airplanes would flash past one another. The German was diving and picking up speed. Trip saw a puff of black smoke from his exhausts as the Messerschmitt throttled back to moderate the dive. It was no use. Ten heartbeats later, the two aircraft were nose to nose.

Trip nudged a little right rudder, pushed the control column a tiny bit to lead the German, and hit the trigger. The *Mosca* shuddered as all four 7.62-millimeter ShKAS machine guns rattled. Trip held the trigger for a long three seconds. He saw the Messerschmitt's nose and wings flash white as the German fired back.

Bang! Clang!

Trip swiveled his head to see long tears in both wings. The license-built Wright Cyclone Engine banged as a 20-millimeter shell hit a cylinder. Loud pops and rumbles erupted from the cowling area. Oil spurted and coated the windscreen, blotting out Trip's view.

The Bf-109 flashed past to port. Trip rolled left and lowered the nose. Jerking the throttle to idle to keep the engine from tearing itself apart, Trip turned his head to watch the German. Flames squirted from the enemy's engine. A fine mist of coolant spewed from the enemy airplane.

"Damn! I think I hit him."

Clunnnk....clank, clank, clang! Chug, chug...Silence.

Trip quickly returned to reality as he realized his *Mosca* was badly damaged. Worse, the huge radial engine in front of him had stopped. Its two-bladed propellor was frozen vertically. Reality dawned that the bang Trip heard precipitated the oil on the windscreen and warned that his engine was hit.

A quick glance told Trip the German was still trailing black smoke and disengaging from the fight. Trip scanned the sky for other Nationalist planes. Seeing none, he turned his attention to keeping the damaged *Mosca* airborne. His airspeed was alarmingly low, so he put the nose down and gained enough airspeed to avoid the incipient stall. With the dead engine, the silence was disturbing.

Trip looked around to get his bearings. He was either going to have to bail out or crash land. Pulling off the suffocating oxygen mask, Trip gently turned the airplane to a northerly heading and quickly set up the *Mosca* on its best glide airspeed. He looked for where he might land.

~~<>~~

Robert Harney Gibson, III. – Trip – was an accidental soldier of fortune. This was not by design but because he was touring Europe in early 1938 when the allure of adventure drew him into the Spanish Civil War. A novelist friend in Paris, André Malraux, told Trip about the excitement of flying for the Republican Air Force in Spain. The idea of combat in the skies was appealing. Even more attractive was the opportunity to fly one of the world's first high-power monoplane fighters – the Polikarpov I-16 – was too good to ignore.

In the summer of 1938 Trip ambled south from Paris, crossed the Spanish frontier, and found Andrés Garcia La Calle, squadron leader of the Republican 1st Fighter Squadron. The squadron was well respected, and La Calle was reputed to be a fine leader. La Calle was impressed with Trip's willingness and logbook documenting over 500 hours in the air. La Calle sent him aloft, where Trip demonstrated excellent flying skills. More importantly, Trip's aggressiveness in the air impressed La Calle. In no time, he was issued a uniform, flying clothes, boots, and a helmet. Trip became a member of the Republican Air Force. Well, more of a contractor, really. Trip Gibson was at war.

Flying the *Mosca*, the Polikarpov I-16 Type 10, was certainly exciting. The airplane had an impossible center of gravity, making it treacherous if ignored even for a moment. Overpowered, the diminutive airplane was quick in a climb and would turn on a dime. The Type 10 was armed with four 7.62 mm machine guns, which suggested to Trip that the machine would be devastating in a fight. Trip loved the idea that the barrel-chested little airplane had retractable landing gear, a feature he had never experienced and one that promised a sleek, uncluttered silhouette in the air.

Back in his native Atlanta, Trip owned a Curtiss JN-4D Jenny. A First World War training plane, the Jenny was somewhat more docile than other airplanes, but it could be temperamental. Trip kept his airplane at the Atlanta Municipal Airport, a field that was once an auto racetrack on the south side of the growing Southern city.

Trip's parents were well off. His father, R. H. Gibson, Jr., was an engineer at Westinghouse. Trip's mother was Edith Burke Gibson, a member of the Daughters of the American Revolution and President of the Garden Club. Both R.H. and Edith were from old Atlanta money. Their home off Paces Ferry Road was a mansion, but they considered it modest.

A student at the Georgia School of Technology – Georgia Tech – in downtown Atlanta, Trip was a rising Junior in 1936. He decided a year on the Grand Tour of Europe would be good fun – and educational. He took a year off from school. The year turned into two, and then the civil war in Spain took an especially vicious turn. The Nationalists, Nazis to Trip's way of thinking, seemed to be winning. Certainly, the Communists and Soviets from Russia were no better, but they supported the Anti-Nazi Republicans.

None of that history mattered just now. Neither did it matter that Trip was an American. If the Nationalists captured him, a death sentence was likely. Trip was, therefore, motivated to land the *Mosca* somewhere friendly. Best outcome: land the airplane in France, get out of the cockpit, remove his flight coverall, adjust his tie, collect his small suitcase from behind the pilot's seat, and walk quietly away.

Trip scanned around as he gently maneuvered his stricken airplane. No sense in loading up the airplane with G-forces; that would merely bleed off airspeed and the remaining energy of his 2000 meters of diminishing altitude. Trip nudged the stick rather than pulling it with authority.

Ahead were the Pyrenees Mountains dividing Spain and France. Behind him lay the dun-colored coastal plain and the small town of Vilajuïga, Spain. Vilajuïga was located on the extreme north coast of Spain near the French frontier. La Calle's Republican squadron left there this morning for France.

The Nationalists were pressing in on every front, and fighting was fierce. Just before takeoff, La Calle told his pilots that the Spanish government had fled to France on February 6th. Trip was disgusted. That was almost three weeks past, and no one had said a word.

Equally disgusting to Trip was the cold. The chill of February 1939 penetrated everywhere, especially at altitude. The pilots needed heavier coats, gloves, and boots, but none were available.

La Calle and the squadron had taken off from Vilajuïga, heading Northwest toward Francazal, a French aerodrome south of Toulouse. If the government had fled, there was no point in further fighting. The Spaniards would deliver the Republican air arm's remaining fighter aircraft to the French to prevent the Nationalists from having them. The Spanish Civil War was coming to a sputtering conclusion, and Francisco Franco's Nationalists had won.

Trip's engine was balky on the pre-takeoff run-up, coughing and sputtering. The few remaining mechanics quickly changed out the magnetos that fired the sparkplugs, and Trip took off to chase the rest of the squadron. Alone, he ran into the Nationalist Air Force, leading to the current situation.

Carefully stretching his glide, Trip thought, *I think I shot down that Messerschmitt, but I hope the pilot lived.*

The Pyrenees were too high for Trip to fly over. Despite stretching his glide as much as possible, Trip was already at 1000 meters and descending. He was trading altitude for distance, but soon he would run out of altitude.

The oil covering the windscreen made forward visibility impossible. Leaning out from side to side, Trip saw a small plain and valley under the bulbous nose. The heights on either side of the valley were threatening. Landing in the valley was tempting.

But was it France?

Chapter 2 – France

Trip looked at the altimeter with rising alarm. He was now at 500 meters, he quickly converted that to about 1500 feet. Some mental arithmetic told Trip he could glide another couple of miles but would have no remaining airspeed for maneuvering. He could still bail out, but things would have to go perfectly at this altitude, or he would be a corpse wrapped in silk in some French orchard. *Easy to bury me, already neatly wrapped in a shroud.*

Nope, a forced dead-stick landing it would be. And soon.

Trip swiveled his head. Although this was probably the French countryside, Trip still worried about dealing with officialdom should he be detained. *The hell with that, first job is to survive the landing!*

Praying that this part of France – if it was France – had few power wires, Trip picked out a flat-looking stretch of farmland, dropped the nose slightly, and set up on a base leg. He kept the *Mosca* at 100 kph, 20 kph above the stall speed with flaps.

Before committing to the final turn, a descending left 180° maneuver that would result in landing regardless of the terrain, Trip looked over the field. He considered that the *Mosca* was excellent at landing on rough ground. Should he lower the landing gear? He had no idea if the landing gear would come down after the battle damage. His stall speed was about 80 kph – 52 miles per hour – so he would keep the landing gear up and hope to slide on smooth ground. He worried he would hit a swale and get flipped on his back.

Dropping his feet out of the leather straps on the rudder pedals, he thought, *What the hell, it's now or never. At least my feet won't get caught in the straps.*

Trip rolled off his 200-meter-high perch and lowered the nose of the little airplane. He had no throttle to control speed, so it was simply nose up/nose down to maintain speed just above a stall. One wrong move and the airplane would stall, roll over and crash.

Trip lowered the nose a touch to pick up 10 kph. *I'd rather be slightly fast than slightly dead.*

The 30 seconds of the final turn seemed to last for hours. Trip's teeth hurt from clenching his jaw. He felt one eye flutter from a tic he had when under stress. The golden grain of the farmer's field flashed below him. *This is it!*

The *Mosca* made a *wuhfff* sound as it settled into the long grass. *Wheat?* Trip dismissed that thought instantly as he danced on the rudder bar. At 70 kph indicated airspeed, he hauled the stick into his lap. He had no brakes. Hauling on the stick was merely a nod to the possibility that putting up the elevators might keep the little airplane on the ground now that it was sliding through the grass below flying airspeed. The ailerons had no control authority.

The airplane seemed to slide forever before slowly nosing to the right and then sliding down a gentle embankment at the edge of the field. The Mosca stopped, leaving a trail of flattened grass about 150 meters long. Trip breathed for the first time since rolling off the perch to land. That was only about one minute ago, but it seemed a lifetime.

Not waiting for any bad things to happen – fire, explosion, police – Trip Gibson snatched his harness lock, flicked the cockpit entry door latch, and stood up. His legs shook, and his mouth was dry. His eye still fluttered. He avoided putting a hand on any of the oil-smeared parts of the windscreen or fuselage. He snatched his small valise from behind the seat and flung it into the wheat. Grabbing a shoulder strap as an escape rope, Trip quickly stepped onto the wing.

The wing was slick with oil, and Trip painfully landed on his rear on the metal wing. He was fortunate to miss the sharp metal where the Messerschmitt's shells had torn gouges.

Since he was already sitting on his butt, Trip scooted off the rear of the wing and landed in the soft grass. He thought, *Best part of my day.*

Trip picked up his valise and hurried away from the airplane. He heard ticking noises from the hot engine as the airframe settled. Trip trotted upwind and turned to see the little fighter looking forlorn, its red, yellow, and purple Republican-flag-striped rudder erect above the rest, a defiant gesture to the last. A tendril of smoke wafted from the cowling.

Stripping off his flying helmet, gloves, and oil-soaked flight coverall, Trip turned the coverall inside out and used it to wipe the oil off his face as best he could. He pulled out his comb and ran it through his thick, dark, wavy hair. Something stung his scalp, and the comb came away with a smear of blood. He gingerly felt his face and scalp and noted a few painful spots.

Damn! Not good, not good at all. Must have been hit with some fragments. What do I look like? This will get attention. Must wash and be presentable.

Trip adjusted his tie, smoothed his shirt and pants, and started walking, his small suitcase banging his leg with every step. The landing had been on a northerly heading, so he walked, putting the landing streak in the farm field to his back.

Two hundred yards and a loud pop made Trip turn. The *Mosca* had burst into flames.

Shit! That will bring the Gendarmes, border guards, and whichever authorities are hereabouts.

Trip started to run toward the trees about a quarter mile north. He would hide there and see what happened.

~~<>~~

The cell door slammed behind him as the guard roughly shoved Trip into the dank, tiny room with bars on the windows. His eyes adjusted to the gloom, and he saw Major La Calle sitting on the single bunk in the room.

"Ah, *Teniente* Gibson! Welcome to my humble abode."

"Buenos tardes, Mi Mayor." That was almost all the Spanish that Trip knew. Fortunately, La Calle spoke excellent English.

"I see you must have contacted the enemy. You have some nicks and cuts on your face."

"Si, Mi Mayor. I was jumped by a 109 a few miles south of the French border."

"Ah. Probably from the same group that bounced the rest of the *esquadrón. Alemanes* fly those 109s. Most dangerous. I see you survived."

"Si, Mi Mayor. We ended up in a head-on pass. He shot out my engine, but I hit him and last saw him smoking and streaming coolant as he disengaged."

"Bueno!" La Calle snorted, *"Bastardos."*

Trip looked around the miserable cell. "What now?"

"Oh, *Mi Amigo*, eventually they will let us go."

"You think?"

"Oh, *sí.* We are refugees, former military officers, from a friendly nation. They will not want to create an international incident by abusing us or sending us back to be shot by the Nationalists. I think I will go to the concentration camp at *Argelès-sur-Mer.* You, as an Americano, will be quickly released."

Trip said, "Oh, God! A concentration camp?"

"Sí...but not terrible, I hear."

~~<>~~

The French Army trucks ground through the mountains and rumbled along, hitting one pothole after the other. Several hours of this jarring, pounding misery ended abruptly at the gates of the *Argelès* concentration camp.

12

Trip and the others quickly disembarked from the back of the trucks. Their first sight of the concentration camp was disheartening and only worsened as La Calle and Trip were roughly shoved through the gate along with about thirty Republican compatriots.

There were no shelters. Everyone sat in the open. A few men had dug shelters into the ground, but the wet, dank dugouts were only slightly better than being fully exposed. There were no latrines, and the entire compound stank of human feces and urine. Dysentery was rampant, but since there was no food and little water, the griping bowels of the internees ached for relief. As Trip stood inside the gate, a man twenty feet away vomited, spasmed, and died. No one even looked a second time.

Trip looked toward the wire, wondering if there was a possibility of escape. He saw the main form of escape – death – in a pile near the wire. Corpses were stacked, bloating in the sun, the stink of death wafting when the wind shifted.

Trip glanced at La Calle, "Jesus! I think it would be better to be repatriated to the Nationalists. At least being shot is quicker and more dignified."

La Calle snorted, "I was wrong about this place. This is hell, and it will only get worse, *mi amigo*. The dying man by the gate told me they throw food over the fence, and if you get it, you eat. If not, you die."

~~<>~~

Four hellish days later, a French soldier – a *poilu* – armed with a rifle and fixed bayonet marched through the gate. He trod around the camp, calling out something indistinguishable. Trip squatted on his haunches, watching with vague interest.

The *poilu* came closer, and Trip thought he heard his name. He stood and looked intently toward the *poilu*, who stopped every few feet and demanded a response. In a moment, the French soldier marched up to Trip and La Calle and said, "Gibson? Gibson?"

Trip said, "I'm Gibson."

"Come." The Frenchman turned on his heel and walked with a purpose toward the gate.

Trip looked toward La Calle, his eyebrows arched.

La Calle said, "Either they shoot you, they send you to the Nationalists, or they let you go."

Trip said, "Farewell, *Mí Mayor*."

"Adios, mí amigo. Vaya con Dios."

Trip said, "I hope we meet again."

He turned and hurried after the French soldier who was fifty feet away, waiting impatiently.

Trip and his personal French *poilu* escort reached the gate where a French officer in a stiff kepi waited with a disdainful look. "You are Monsieur Robert Gibson, *Etats Unis*?"

Trip said, *"Oui."*

"Come."

The French *poilu* turned away, and Trip followed the French officer who led the way to a waiting car. The officer beckoned Trip to get into the car. Trip was not fully seated beside the French officer when the car roared away, banging through potholes and mud puddles at a rapid clip.

"Where are we going?"

"Toulouse."

Chapter 3 – Paris

Trip Gibson stank of sweat, human feces, urine, petroleum, raw gasoline, and dirt. He was tired but fortunately not sick. At least, not yet. He sat, face in his hands, on the hard bunk in a gray jail cell in Toulouse, France. His nicks and cuts from last week's shattered windscreen frame shell no longer bled. One was deeper than the others, and Trip feared it was infected. The conditions in the *Argelès* Concentration Camp certainly did not help.

The tramp of hard boots preceded a jailer and a nattily dressed Frenchman who appeared at Trip's door.

The jailer barked, *"Allez!"*

Trip wearily stood and faced the door. *What now?*

The well-dressed man – clearly an official - said, "Monsieur Gibson, you are to have a *douche* – a shower. New clothing will be provided. I hope they fit. This man will escort you. I will meet you after."

Trip grinned as he walked down the corridor. *Will I have to use Aunt Sally's douchebag? She called it a hot water bottle.*

Trip stood in a tepid shower scrubbing with a bar of rough soap. *I doubt I'll ever get the dirt and stink off!* But he scrubbed every inch of his body three times.

The jailer looked pointedly at his watch, and Trip said, *"Fin."*

The jailer snatched a threadbare towel from a hook and threw it to Trip. The jailer's lip curled in apparent disgust at having to attend to another man's ablutions.

Trip scrubbed dry and looked at the towel to discover it was mostly clean. *Guess I got most of it off.*

The jailer jerked his head at a stack of clothing on a bench. *"S'habiller! Allez!"*

Trip took this to mean, "get moving," so he took his time about carefully dressing, boxers, vest, shirt, pants, socks, shoes. There was even a nice belt of decent leather. The shoes fit and were new. Trip was not sure about the provenance of the other clothing.

The jailer's frustration was at a boil. He spat, *"Allez! Allez! Allons-y!"*

Trip muttered, "I reckon if you bastards were gonna guillotine me, you wouldn't have given me a bath and clothes. I guess you're going to shoot me."

The jailer paled, and in a softer tone, said, *"Non! Non! No guillotine! Non! Allez, Allez."*

"Shooting it is, then."

The jailer said, "Eh?"

Trip mimed a rifle and himself dying.

"Non! Mon Dieu. Allez! Allons-y!"

The jailer turned to lead the way, and Trip grinned at the jailer's back. *Gotcha, you jerk.*

They walked quickly until the jailer reached a large, heavy door which he opened with an oversized key to reveal a courtyard.

My God, I am going to be shot!

A dark maroon Cadillac 452 V-16 pulled up, and the man in the passenger seat jumped out to open the door for Trip. Trip noticed that the driver was wearing a gray livery. The man holding his door wore a cheap American-cut suit.

The well-dressed Frenchman was standing by the door. *"Bon chance, Monsieur* Gibson. Please leave France and do not return."

As he turned to get into the car, Trip muttered, "I think that can be arranged."

The Cadillac roared out of the prison compound and onto the street. A few turns and the car glided down the road. Trip saw a sign: *Paris – 680.*

Trip asked the driver and passenger, "We going to Paris?"

"Yep. Might want to rest some; you got a long trip."

Trip took a long, silent breath and settled in for the ride.

~~<>~~

Eleven hours and two piss stops later, the maroon Cadillac drew up at a gate protecting a large home in the center of Paris. Trip tried to get his bearings. He knew the city well from past visits, and escaping might be necessary.

This worry was alleviated when Trip saw a brass plaque on the gated wall beside the gatehouse. The plaque was engraved *Embassy of the United States of America.* Just inside the gate stood a United States Marine in his dress uniform. Trip breathed a sigh of relief at this sight.

The car ghosted around the drive to stop at the steps to the house. Looking straight ahead, the man in the cheap suit said, "Here you are, Sir. Please give the guard your name."

Trip stepped out of the limousine and turned to thank the two men, but the car instantly drove off. Trip shrugged and turned to the gate. A second Marine guard said, "Mr. Gibson?"

Trip nodded, "Yes, I'm Gibson."

"Welcome home, Sir. Please step inside and report to Room 107, just inside the main door."

"Thanks. Good to be back."

The Marine nodded, "Combat's not what it's cracked up to be, eh?"

Trip briefly touched his face, "No, not by a long shot."

The Marine grinned, one warrior to another. Trip was flattered by this small but significant courtesy.

Before he walked up the steps, Trip looked around. 2 Avenue Gabriel was a large corner lot, perhaps an acre. The wall enclosing the imposing, new-looking mansion was at least six feet high. *Guess that makes them feel safe.*

~~<>~~

Trip walked through the large doors and checked in at Room 107. An officious French woman at a desk noted his name on her list and beckoned him to a seat. Trip waited patiently on an uncomfortable seat in the hallway.

A slight, balding man wearing a suit and tie came from an internal room and stopped before Trip. "Come. The doctor will see you."

Trip wondered exactly what the plan was, but he rose and followed the small man to a door down the hall. There a woman behind a desk said, "Name?"

Trip told her. She rose and led him into an examining room. Moments later, a man in a white coat stepped into the room and said, "Disrobe, please. How are your wounds?"

As Trip removed his clothing, he said, "I think they are healing. This one seems deeper than the others, and I am concerned it may be infected. My scalp has some nicks, but I think they are also healing."

The doctor examined Trip from head to foot. "Aside from the nicks, which are healing, as you say, I see no infirmities. You should be able to go without any concerns. I'll give you some salve for the one cut that concerns you."

Trip asked, "Go where?"

The doctor looked surprised, "Why, to New York, of course."

Trip said, "I had no idea."

The doctor said, "I fear I have spoken out of turn, but the Ambassador will certainly explain the plan to ensure you leave France."

~~<>~~

The man in the cheap suit from the car ride was waiting in the hall when Trip emerged from the doctor. Cheap Suit showed Trip to a small but comfortable room on the second floor. He escorted Trip to the bathroom at the end of the hall and acquainted him with the general layout of the Embassy.

Turning to leave, Cheap Suit said, "Please don't leave the building, Mr. Gibson. Your life is in danger on the streets of Paris. Your presence here at the embassy is protected because this is American soil. The Spanish government fell days before you flew into France. The leaders fled to France. On the 27th of February, the British and French governments recognized the Franco regime as the legitimate government of Spain. Spain now seeks to prosecute mercenary flyers for the Republicans as war criminals. You, Sir, are technically an international fugitive from justice. Moreover, you are in violation of the U.S. Neutrality Acts for being a member of another nation's military. You may be arrested when you reach New York."

Cheap Suit continued, "Exactly how we got you here is not to be discussed among others. It required considerable diplomacy. Ambassador Bullitt will not meet with you because to do so would expose him to criticism from Spain and, frankly, France. The ambassador wishes me to say you will leave for Le Havre at the end of the month, where you will board the *SS Normandie* bound for New York. Please comport yourself as a guest and avoid exposing your host to criticism."

Trip nodded. "I understand completely. May I have visitors?"

Cheap Suit said, "It is not advisable."

Trip knocked around the Embassy for several days. He examined most of the books in the library, but none interested him enough to commit to reading. Some week-old newspapers from the U.S. provided a distraction.

He carefully read the Atlanta Journal. The March 15 edition screamed, "Hitler Swallows All of Czecho-Slovakia." Of course, there was local news of his hometown, which he read with interest. Miss Eleanor Crawford Peabody was visiting relations in Miami, Florida. Miss Peabody was a teacher at Druid Hills School.

Trip and Ellie dated until he left for the Continent. Ellie had not been pleased with Trip's leaving. *Guess she finished her degree at Georgia.*

Trip grinned at Ellie's success, but the Czecho-Slovakia headline was disturbing. *Damned if we won't be in a war sooner or later.*

~~<>~~

On March 25, 1939, Trip was roused at 1 a.m. and escorted to the same Cadillac limousine. The car was idling at the door of the Embassy Mansion. Same grey-liveried driver accompanied by Cheap Suit, the taciturn demi-official.

The Cadillac rolled in near complete silence through the sleeping streets of the 8th Arrondissement, past the Arc de Triomphe, and headed out of the city. Trip's flying experience told him they were on a Northwesterly heading. Having looked at a map Trip knew that Le Havre lay some 280 kilometers away on this heading. The roads would be narrow, and the car would be restricted to 40 kph. The journey promised to take about seven hours.

Trip asked, "Wouldn't it be easier to take the train?"

Cheap Suit replied, "Faster, not easier. The railway people would demand papers and that would not be good."

"Won't the people from the ship ask for papers, as well?"

Cheap suit looked around from the front seat. His face said, *Stop asking questions.* He said, "We have made arrangements. Please enjoy the ride."

Trip shrugged and stretched out across the roomy back seat. At least he would arrive rested.

Chapter 4 – *Normandie*

It was cold in Le Havre, France, on March 25, 1939. Trip stood at the rail of the SS *Normandie* as the ship's horn blared its departure from the dock at 8 a.m. Trip felt no emotion at leaving France. After the past few weeks, Trip looked forward to going home.

A few feet down the rail stood a dark-haired woman with notable features and distinctive heavy brows. She looked both sad and bored. Trip searched his memory and realized this was a Mexican artist named Frida Kahlo. While idling at the Embassy, he had read that *Señorita* Kahlo was in Paris this past month and that she had sold a painting to the Louvre.

Trip watched the tugboats pushing *Normandie* out into the channel. He looked at the French harbor and the town beyond. He was disappointed to be leaving France without seeing his friends. He had made good friends in Paris. He had some fond memories of nights in the salons and jazz clubs.

Trip smiled at the memories of searching out this or that club where Django Reinhardt, Stéphane Grappelli, and others from the *Hot Club du France* group were playing. The sensuous rhythms and driving melody lines from Django's gypsy guitar and Grappelli's violin were intoxicating. Never mind the kick from drinking French 75's at Harry's New York Bar at 5 Rue Daunou. Everybody called it Roooo Danooooo. The bar was a legend, and so were some legendary Trip Gibson hangovers from the gin and champagne mixture in the French 75.

Then, there were the women. Trip's good looks – tall, handsome, thick wavy hair parted near the center. He had steel gray eyes and a ready smile that drew the French ladies like bees to a flower.

One motivation for Trip to go to Spain had been Madame Allard, a sultry blonde of indeterminate age but certain marriage to a French officer. Commandant Marcel Allard frequently toured units at the Maginot Line, and Louise Allard just as frequently toured Trip's bed.

When Mme Allard began to talk about divorcing Marcel and taking up full-time with Trip, Spain beckoned with more urgency.

Trip was incensed by the bombing of Barcelona in March 1938 and said so to his drinking companion Marcel Roche, a serious wine aficionado and jazz lover. Roche introduced Trip to André Malraux, a writer, and supporter of the Republican cause in Spain.

Malraux was commander of the *Espaná* Squadron, a unit comprising poorly performing French Potez Po-540 bombers flown by aviators from a variety of backgrounds. After flying on some 60 bombing missions – and losing half his force – Malraux left Spain in 1937. This did not stop him from regaling Trip with stories of the glory of fighting against the fascist Nationalists. The romance of flying fast airplanes and avoiding Commandant Allard convinced Trip to go. Malraux facilitated Trip's travel to Spain and introduction to La Calle. Malraux also facilitated a munificent contract for Trip specifying $1500 per month pay and a $1000 bounty for every enemy airplane shot down.

As Trip settled into the life of a fighter pilot at war, the Nationalists were driving the Republican forces southward along the Ebro River. The Republicans staged a counterattack in July 1938. Although the squadron flew several times trying to protect the ground forces from Nationalist air attack, little could be done. The Republican's final major offensive against the fascist rebels ended in defeat after four months.

Toward the end of November, Trip flew almost daily, often in the morning and afternoon. It was exhausting. The Nationalists were pushing the Republicans into an ever-decreasing semicircular section of Spain. Trip came to realize that steady nerves were required to penetrate the airspace. Surviving and escaping that same airspace required luck and lots of it.

Twice during the Ebro offensive, Trip got into dogfights with Bf-109s. The 109s were faster and more heavily armed, carrying 20-millimeter cannons and machine guns. But the *Mosca* was nimble and held its own against the 109s. The first of these fights resulted in Trip diving away from the fight when he realized he was alone against four 109s.

The second fight had developed into a twisting, turning dogfight between Trip and a highly skilled opponent. Trip used the superior climbing ability of the *Mosca* to force the German to fight on his terms. Fighting in the vertical – climb and dive versus turning in the horizontal plane – was difficult because the airplanes would ultimately run out of airspeed. The first one to stall would be killed. This day, the German was late to apply throttle and start the climb. Trip was well established in his climb with the German offset, cockpit to cockpit. If the German tried to pull the lead required to shoot at Trip, he would stall and fall off on a wing. The same applied to Trip. But Trip had more energy from having higher speed entering the climb.

The German could have stayed in the climb longer, but he made the critical mistake of impatience and jerked the airplane in a wild attempt to end the fight. The 109 wobbled, seemed to sag in the air, and then fell off on its starboard wing. Trip snatched the *Mosca* around in a dive to follow the 109 as the German tried to regain flying airspeed. Trip did not need to aim. The gray Messerschmitt filled his windscreen, and Trip held the gun button down for four seconds. Trip saw bullet strikes all over the square-winged enemy.

Already in a dive, the Messerschmitt never attempted a pull-out. It dove into the ground at more than 500 kph airspeed. Trip pulled out of his dive and observed that there was no fire from the downed 109. The Messerschmitt was buried in a blackened crater sprinkled with aluminum confetti that was once an airplane.

Trip landed at that day's airfield. Tomorrow would bring more combat and another airfield. He climbed out of the *Mosca*, staggered to the left wingtip, and vomited. He retched until he was empty. Then, he walked to the operations tents to report.

~~<>~~

As the *Normandie* picked up a couple of knots on its own, Trip reflected that he wished Spain had been as easy to get out of as it was to get in.

As the last rays of the late-March sun illuminated the bow and forward superstructure on the world's most luxurious ship, Trip smiled. When the Embassy announced to him that he would be booked on the *Normandie*, he immediately asked to visit the Banque du Nord du Paris to withdraw his funds on deposit from Spain. This was denied. Trip was restricted to the compound. Period...end of discussion.

Trip then asked the Embassy to wire his parents for sufficient funds to pay for first-class passage. The Embassy staff were only too happy to do this. Otherwise, the limited funds for such repatriations of American citizens would have been depleted, even for a Third-Class ticket. Thus, Robert H. Gibson, III., was living like a grandee on the most beautiful ship in the world. He soon would join the other well-off passengers in the First Class Salon. Drinks were certainly in order!

Trip wondered if some young, attractive heiress might be looking for adventure on the high seas. His idea of adventure was taking said heiress to his beautifully paneled cabin and vigorously trying to put the last several months into perspective. He smiled at the thought.

Trip paused as he turned to walk toward the gangway and the First-Class salon beyond. The plight of La Calle and the other Spanish internees at the *Argelès* Concentration Camp briefly spoiled his mood. He said a silent prayer for their survival. More, he hoped one day to see La Calle. He thought, *War is not what it's cracked up to be.*

Trip walked into the salon. The money wired from his parents had covered the ticket and a small wardrobe. The French confiscated his battered valise when he was arrested. It was never returned.

The Embassy arranged for a haberdasher and a tailor to visit. Now he had a new leather suitcase, two suits, a tuxedo, a pair of everyday brown shoes, and a pair of black evening shoes. Modest, plain studs adorned one of two formal, pleated shirts. His other shirts were conservative white cotton, starched to perfection. A brown-felt fedora completed his new ensemble. Trip thought, *Not bad for a guy who was in a concentration camp less than a month ago.*

He entered the salon and quickly found several guests had already located the bar. An hour of pleasant conversation followed. Trip initially considered he should be reticent about his recent past of flying for the Republicans. After a drink and being pressed for information by a couple of the younger passengers, Trip quietly told his story in brief.

He left out the concentration camp and the forced repatriation by the U.S. Government. Trip smiled to himself, *No need to offend their tender sensibilities.*

~~<>~~

The dining room was spectacular, and Trip was pleased to be seated with Monsieur and Madame Boucher from Lyon. M Boucher was an investment banker connected to J.P. Morgan, Jr. Trip thought the Bouchers were delightful dinner companions.

M. Boucher explained that the *Normandie* was called the Ship of Light in honor of its beautiful Lalique glass. Of course, the French origins of *Normandie* and Paris, being the City of Light, all seemed to fit together.

Another guest at Trip's table was Frida Kahlo. Trip found her interesting but not terribly attractive. Her features seemed coarse. Harsh, even.

Madame Boucher asked Frida, "What did you do in Paris?"

Frida Kahlo said, "I brought a collection of my paintings at the behest of Marcel Duchamp. When I arrived, I learned that half of the paintings had not cleared customs, so my exhibition failed. Of course, it did not help that Marcel had sold his gallery, and the new owners had the taste of maggots! They love sugar but not the spice of my work."

Madame Boucher said, "Oh, my! That must have been quite upsetting."

Frida continued, "They only exhibited two of my paintings. They put my work next to the photographs of Manuel Bravo and cluttered the entire gallery with pre-Columbian sculptures. The final straw was the inclusion of junk! Toys and sugar skulls that the lower classes enjoy on *El Día Del Muertos* – the Day of the Dead."

Trip said, "I hope you let them have it."

"Let them have it?"

"You know, told them off?"

"Ah, *Sí*. I did 'let them have it,' as you say."

Trip grinned his most friendly grin, "Good. They had it coming!"

M. Boucher said, "I understand you have a piece in the Louvre now?"

Frida brightened, "Oh, yes. They bought my *El Marco*. In English, it is called *The Frame*."

Trip said, "Then, your trip was a success!"

Frida said, "Perhaps that is true. I was privileged to meet Picasso and Miró. They received me considerably better than those pigs at the gallery."

M. Boucher asked, "What did you think of the surrealists?"

Frida's face changed to a smirk, "That bunch of coo-coo lunatics and very stupid surrealists? They are crazed intellectuals. Their philosophy is rotten, and I couldn't stand them anymore."

Madame Boucher turned pink. "My dear, these are among the world's greatest artists."

Frida Kahlo snorted, "I hope not. *Díos Mío!* They are scribblers who need lessons."

Trip said brightly, "Does anyone know if there's dancing in the Salon?"

Chapter 5 – Voyage

Trip stood at the rail, breathing the frigid morning air of the North Atlantic in early March. He looked forward toward the bow. The small nicks on his face had mostly healed, but scars remained. The air stung, but Trip relished the freedom of the fresh air; it helped with the hangover. He lit a cigarette and smiled at the way the smoke was instantly whipped away.

The rushing wind reminded Trip of flying in the semi-open cockpit of the I-16. Breathing through his nose, Trip enjoyed the cold burst of air against his sinuses. His eyes watered a bit, and he used his handkerchief to blot away the moisture. Trip reflected that flying combat had made him feel more alive than at any other time in his 23 years. He wondered if he would ever have that feeling again.

Mildred Wright came out of the main entrance to the First-Class Deck and languidly walked out into the bracing wind. While Trip had on one of his new suits and no overcoat, Mildred wore full-length fur over a relaxed wool dress. Mildred wore a white fur hat that was shaped like a beret. The brim of Trip's fedora fluttered in the wind. Mildred held the rail as she squinted in the morning sun.

Trip said, "Good morning. Miss…"

Mildred raised her voice to be heard over the wind, "Mildred Wright. Good morning, Mr. Gibson."

Trip said, "Ah, I regret not remembering your name."

Mildred waved her hand, a dismissive gesture. "Never mind. We all had a good bit to drink last night. The marks on your face tell me you have been through quite an experience."

Trip nodded. "Yes, I could use some coffee. Would you like some?"

"Yes. Can we take the air for a few minutes first?"

Trip nodded. "Of course."

They stood in companionable silence.

Trip observed her out of the corner of his eye. She was pretty. Her dark hair streamed below her fur beret, and the cold naturally rouged the skin of her cheeks. Dark eyes danced as she took in the uniqueness of an ocean voyage on such a beautiful ship. Two tiny acne scars on her right temple emphasized the beauty of the rest of her face.

Trip recalled her laughing and dancing the night before. Trip thought about Mildred relaxing in the salon's soft smoky light, her bare shoulders and long gloves accentuating her lissome figure. She smoked without the benefit of a cigarette holder. Her head swayed to the rhythm of the music.

The jazz quintet music moved everyone to tap feet, snap fingers, and dance with abandon when a partner was available. A couple of the women danced alone.

Trip danced with Mildred twice. She was lithe on the dance floor and did a credible version of the Lindy Hop to Big Joe Turner's *Roll 'em Pete*. She snapped and twirled, expertly following Trip's competent lead. She mouthed the words, "I've got a gal. She lives up on the hill..."

The quintet did good renditions of several popular songs. *Moonlight Serenade* and *In the Mood,* both Glenn Miller hits, were very popular. Not quite jitterbug numbers, these two tunes inspired a fun shag dance. The evening was great fun, and the quintet was quite good.

The second set started with the quintet ripping into Count Basie's *Lester Leaps In*. The pianist hit the rolling piano notes in tinkling runs, and the guitarist chummed along, laying down an excellent jazz rhythm backing for the saxophonist. The saxophonist was the star of the moment as he cruised through the long lead lines that made the song such a hit.

The quintet next jumped to Coleman Hawkins' *Body and Soul*. The piano and sax picked up their counterpoint, but this time with a more languid tempo and easier rhythm. Trip enjoyed Mildred's smooth, rhythmic sway in his arms. She smiled at him as he led her expertly in the complex dance.

Duke Ellington's *Caravan* rounded out the set. It was another jazz number with a relaxed but mysterious and driving tempo.

In their third set, the quintet did passible renditions of Django Reinhardt's version of *I'll See You in My Dreams, Sweet Georgia Brown,* and *I Got Rhythm.* Trip tapped his foot and grinned, remembering his time following Django's Hot Club around Paris.

The jazz guitar made Trip nostalgic for last year before he learned how harsh the world is. It also made him drink another bourbon on the rocks. He smiled that the French had stocked the lounge with the American whiskey, all the better to wipe away the past few months.

~~<>~~

Trip's head still pounded when the steward served coffee to Trip and Mildred in the main First-Class Lounge. The coffee was the strong French brew that reminded Trip of his first days in Paris. The bright light of the morning made the elegant furnishings seem slightly garish.

The lounge had red marble columns and lighted glass sculptures resembling stacked tulips flowing from floor to ceiling. Low tables and comfortable, red velvet embroidered chairs surrounded the sculptures.

Mildred asked, "Was it terrible?"

Trip said, "What?"

"Was the war terrible?"

Trip said, "How do you know I was in a war?"

Mildred lowered her eyes, "You have that look. My uncle was in the Great War. He had that look. So did my friend's father. Daddy didn't go. He has a bad back. They wouldn't take him. He doesn't have that look."

Trip nodded. "I wasn't aware I had some kind of look."

Mildred said, "You look a bit haunted. Was it terrible?"

Trip said, "The war was not so terrible. It was the days after."

Mildred asked, "What happened?"

After a moment's hesitation, Trip told her.

Mildred said, "My God! That's inhuman. How did you get out?"

Trip said, "The American embassy learned that Republican Air Force units were flying into Southern France, and the pilots were being interned. They inquired about me with the French and got no answer."

Mildred said, "So the Embassy got you out?"

Trip said, "I am not entirely sure. Someone got me out. Maybe it was Ambassador Bullitt himself. Regardless, the Embassy transported me to Paris. No one would tell me much while I stayed at the Embassy. The Ambassador refused to meet with me. He didn't want to create a diplomatic problem with Spain and France. I guess I'm what they might call *untouchable*. The Embassy staff refused to let me leave the compound. Then, they put me on this ship."

"In First-Class?"

Trip laughed, "No, no. I had to wire my parents for funds to make this trip tolerable, else I probably would have been in steerage. Of course, I'll have to pay them back when I get home."

Mildred smiled enigmatically, "Your parents must be well off."

Trip smiled, "I suppose they do all right. Dad's an engineer with Westinghouse. Mom's quite the socialite in Atlanta. Tell me about yourself, Mildred."

Mildred said, "Daddy is a merchant. He owns a chain of dime stores in smaller New York and Pennsylvania towns. He also owns a dozen small-town telephone exchanges. Mama is a homemaker.

Granddaddy left me some money that sent me to Vassar. The trip to France was a graduation gift."

Trip said, "Quite a good school and a nice gift."

Mildred smiled more to herself than to Trip, "Would you like a stroll around the deck?"

~~<>~~

They walked through the vestibule into the main entrance hall and up the stairs to the sundeck. The wind was still brisk as they walked around the sundeck.

Mildred asked, "What do you do when you are not touring the continent and fighting a war, Trip?"

"I'm a mechanical engineering student at Georgia School of Technology."

"My, my. Georgia Tech. That is a most difficult school, my friend."

Trip grinned, "I'm fortunate to have a knack for mathematics, so that reduces the difficulty somewhat."

Mildred said, "Vassar requires arts, languages, natural sciences, and Social Sciences courses. I pursued the required hours in languages – chiefly French – and Social Sciences. I love history."

Trip smiled, "I enjoy history. I even managed Gibbon."

She looked at Trip with respect. "All six volumes?"

Trip grinned, "As difficult as *The Decline and Fall of the Roman Empire* was to read, I stayed with it to the bitter end."

Mildred said, "Then you must have enjoyed visiting Rome."

"Yes, but I expected so much more after the picture that Gibbon and my high-school history teacher painted. Sadly, the Forum was overgrown with weeds. Fallen columns were everywhere, making it dangerous to walk. Worse, the grandeur of the marble on the columns was gone. Mussolini stole the white marble to build his garish white building on that highway right through the middle of the ancient part of the city."

Mildred said, "Mussolini is a pig. He looks like he would have body odor!"

Trip laughed out loud. "Thanks for that image!"

Mildred turned a little pink. "Are you mocking me?"

Trip's face became serious, "I would never mock a beautiful woman like you."

Mildred said, "Oh, look. Here we are at the entrance to the First-Class cabins. Would you like to see my little nook?"

Trip said, "Sure."

~~<>~~

It was almost one in the afternoon when Trip Gibson paused, hand on Mildred Wright's doorknob. He smiled at Mildred as he was about to step out her door. He was fully dressed as he had been when they met on the sundeck at 8 a.m.

On the other hand, Mildred was languidly lying on her bed, a sheet covering most – but not quite all – of her nude body. Her hair was disheveled, and her makeup needed a touch-up.

Mildred sighed, "Hail the conquering hero."

Trip said, "Are we dancing tonight?"

"Have you not had enough dancing this morning?"

Trip smirked, "I meant standing up."

Mildred said, "Are you Baptist?"

34

"Episcopalian, why do you ask."

"I understand that Baptists don't make love standing up. Looks too much like dancing."

Trip snorted, trying to suppress a loud laugh. He did not wish to compromise the beautiful woman who had helped him return to the world of the living.

"See you at dinner?"

"Hell, I'm going to dress and fix my wrecked hair. Then, I'm going to lunch. I could eat a horse!"

Grinning, Trip quietly opened the cabin door and, checking that the corridor was empty, stepped out to walk with great nonchalance down the passageway to his own room. There, he collapsed onto the bed.

His hangover was long gone.

Chapter 6 – New York

Trip rose from the bed. His knees were weak from the morning's excess and a ravenous appetite that reminded him he had not eaten breakfast. He combed his hair and used a warm, wet cloth to wipe his face. He carefully removed the remnants of Mildred Wright's lipstick from the corners of his mouth. He smiled at himself in the mirror. The passionate kisses with Mildred were indelibly etched into his memory.

Trip tottered out into the corridor. The heavy feeling in his groin was a pleasant reminder of his morning of reawakened libido. He made his way to the First-Class Dining Room. The sculpted bronze doors to the dining room had a riot of scenes from French history and contemporary France.

As he entered the dining room, Mildred was walking out. She had a spring in her step, and she smiled broadly at Trip as she stepped out the door. He smiled back. Mildred had renewed him.

He liked her very much.

~~<>~~

Trip just caught the end of luncheon. The dining room would close in a few minutes to prepare for the evening meal.

Trip started with the *Mayonnaise of Salmon à la Russe*. It was a wonderful small plate of salmon rolls with a mayonnaise sauce. He delighted in the light flavor. But it was not enough.

Trip had enjoyed quite a workout this morning, so he ordered the *Cassoulet a la Mode de Castelnaudary*. The cassoulet was a brilliantly slow-cooked, heavy mixture of dark duck meat, beans, sausage, pork hock, onions, and other ingredients simmered in duck fat. It was a perfect follow-up to the light first course of fish. He enjoyed it with a baguette and cold, salted butter. A Grand Vin Rouge offered a gentle complement to the meal.

Trip pushed back from the table and ordered a second glass of Grand Vin Rouge to follow the cassoulet. He savored the wine.

He thought, *Jesus! Less than a month ago, I was living in a dirt hovel, wondering how long I would survive.*

~~<>~~

Trip spent the afternoon sitting in the grill room watching the North Atlantic crash by the wall of windows. He shared a bottle of champagne and chatted with other passengers. Señorita Frida Kahlo spent a pleasant hour at Trip's table. They chatted about various topics, including a renewed discussion of Frida's views on the surrealists.

"Insane! Every one of them!" she declared. "They're coo-coo. They think I'm a surrealist. Bah! I never painted dreams. I paint my own reality. I tried to drown my sorrows, but the little bastards swam to the surface."

Trip commented, "The luncheon menu today had Mexican Eggs. Did you try it?"

Frida snorted, "Shit! Mexican Eggs. *Díos mío!* Every egg I eat is a Mexican egg. But no. I expect the Frogs merely threw some kind of spice on some eggs and claimed it to be Mexican. Come to Mexico City, my darling man, and I will show you *Huevos a la Mexicana*. It will make you cry."

Trip smiled at Frida's passion.

She looked at him. "Have you never made love with a Latina?"

Trip was surprised at her frank approach. "No. Well, twice in Spain, but I think you refer to women from Latin America."

"*Sí! Las Mujeres de España* are not the same hot-blooded women as those from my desert country. *Mís amigas femeninas de Mexico* would curl your toes, Señor Gibson.

38

Trip said, "I fear I'm not up to the challenge."

Frida said, "What? Are you saying you are too weak for a strong woman?"

Trip laughed, and soon, so did Frida.

Frida Kahlo, world-famous artist and despite her heavy looks, an astoundingly sexy woman, stood and said, *"Buenos tardes, Señor Gibson. I wish you well. You will need all the luck in the coming war."*

Trip said, "I don't think there will be a war."

Frida said, "Oh, yes, there will be a war, and I fear you will be in it. *Buena suerte."*

Trip watched her walk away. She swung her hips, mocking him.

~~<>~~

The afternoon wore on into the evening, and dinner loomed.

Trip looked at the menu posted in the grill room. The cassoulet had set heavily on his stomach, so he decided on poached salmon and asparagus. Perhaps he would make an early evening of it.

Despite his best intentions, after his light dinner Trip stayed in the salon to enjoy the quintet. Tonight was as good as the last night, suggesting the quintet were not just professional musicians, but they played together all the time. One of Trip's musician friends from Atlanta would say the five were 'tight,' meaning they played well together. Trip could not argue.

The Django set was excellent tonight. They played *Minor Swing* and *Dinah*, both lively tunes. The almost sad *Sunshine of Your Smile* reminded Trip of happy days in Paris before he headed south to Spain and war. Trip smiled broadly as the group suddenly broke into a bouncy Gypsy Jazz improvisation, with each player taking the lead and then deftly handing off to the next player. The tune had some familiar melodies and demonstrated beyond doubt that the musicians were virtuosos.

Too soon, the evening ended, and Trip made his way to his cabin. He had not been in the room more than five minutes when there was a light tap on the door. Trip opened it to find Mildred Wright holding a bottle of champagne and two glasses.

"Aren't you going to invite me in?"

Trip stepped aside and said, "Of course. Please join me."

He opened the champagne and poured the two glasses.

Trip thought, *Delicious, both the wine and the woman.*

~~<>~~

The next two days were similar: pleasant meals, delightful music and dancing, and time with an attentive, beautiful woman. Trip woke early on the fourth day of the crossing to the sounds of machinery and the ship's horn announcing the arrival in New York. It was no surprise that Mildred had left while he slept.

Trip darted into the bathroom to shave and shower. He quickly dressed in his fresh suit, crisp white shirt, and dark blue tie. Five minutes and his leather suitcase was packed with his worldly possessions.

He stepped into the passageway to find a porter. He handed the porter his suitcase and a crisp dollar bill. The porter gave him a green claim check and wished him a safe journey.

Trip walked through the corridor past Mildred's room to note the door was ajar and the room empty. Mildred must already be on deck to enjoy the arrival.

Trip continued through the passageway and up to the sundeck to see New York Harbor on all sides. A fire boat sprayed water in tall columns in a welcome salute to the *Normandie*. The last days of

March 1939 in New York were brisk, with temperatures in the mid-40s. Today there was no rain. Trip was surprised at the catch in his throat when he saw the Statue of Liberty off the port rail, near amidships.

The tugs were soon alongside to guide the massive ship into the Marine Terminal Pier 88 on the West Side of Manhattan Island. Trip spotted Mildred standing along the rail looking intently toward the dock and the large crowd gathered there.

He leaned on the rail beside her and said, "Good morning."

Mildred said, "Oh, hello."

Lighting a cigarette, Trip looked out toward the pier. "Quite a crowd."

"Yes."

The tugs were nudging the ship into place when Mildred waved frantically and threw kisses toward someone on the pier.

"Someone picking you up?"

"Yes. My fiancé."

Trip smiled a sad smile. "Your fiancé?"

"Yes, dear. I've had a lovely time with you on this voyage. I hope you're not hurt."

Trip said, "Not at all. I had hoped we might have a couple of days in New York, but I completely understand. I wish you well in your marriage."

He reached into his pocket and pulled out a small notepad. He jotted on it for a moment. "Please send me an invitation to the wedding. If I can't come, I'll surely send a gift."

Mildred was momentarily speechless. "Really?"

"Of course. Your fiancé is a lucky stiff if I ever saw one."

Mildred put the note in her handbag. "You are truly a gallant Southern gentleman, Trip. Most men would be furious."

With his best Clark Gable grin, Trip said, "Oh, I'm ready to bite nails in half right now, but I know when I'm licked."

Mildred turned serious. She said, "Trip, there will be a terrible war soon. Please be careful and know that I will be thinking about you."

Trip grinned, "I'm a hard man to kill, and doubly hard if I know that a beautiful woman like you is pulling for me."

Mildred turned to go. She paused and looked back, her face in the shadow of her hat. She quietly said, "Farewell. I wish I had met you sooner."

Not waiting for an answer, Mildred Wright turned and walked toward the gangplank, her back straight and head held high.

Three hours and a slow cab ride later, Trip walked through Pennsylvania Station and boarded the train for Atlanta. It would be a long ride going away from Mildred and New York City. Trip booked a stateroom. While he was sad about the outcome of his shipboard romance, he would at least arrive refreshed at Brookwood Station in Atlanta. As the train jerked into motion, he thought of Mildred for a final time. At least he told himself that he would not think of her again.

Trip looked out at the platform slowly moving by. He muttered, "Now that, my friend, is the one that got away."

Chapter 7 – Atlanta

Trip stepped off the train in Atlanta's Brookwood Station to Kathy's shriek. "Trip! I'm so glad you're home."

Trip's sister raced to him and threw her arms around him in a giant bear hug. Well, as big a bear hug as Kathy's 5'2" frame could inflict.

"Hahahaha, Sis. Yes, I'm alive."

Kathy leaned back to look at him. "Your face has some cuts."

"Yes. Windscreen glass."

"Windscreen glass?"

"Yep, That's what happens when a bullet hits it."

"Oh, Jesus. Don't tell Mother."

They turned and quickly walked, arm-in-arm, toward Trip's parents, who stood thirty feet away. R.H. Gibson, Jr., wore a fine-quality suit with a thin pinstripe and a perfectly blocked Homburg. His wife, Edith Burke Gibson, wore a dark gray dress with a mink jacket around her shoulders. Her hat matched the gray dress with a spray of baby's breath across the crown. R.H. and Edith did not do public demonstrations of affection. They waited in reserved silence, but Trip knew they were bursting to welcome him home. Then they would scold him for going to war without even a brief telegram.

The family emerged from the station and walked toward the R.H.'s 1938 Buick Roadmaster. The maroon car was magnificent; this was the first time Trip saw it.

"Golly, this is a beautiful car!"

His father said, "She's powerful, too. Got the *Dynaflash* engine. Purrs like a kitten. It's the *Limited* model."

Trip said, "She sure is keen!"

Edith examined Trip's face. "You've been injured!"

"Yes, Mom. A bullet went through the windscreen on my plane. Lots of little pieces of glass flew around, and some of them scratched my face."

Mom gasped, "Oh, MY GOD! A bullet?!"

Trip said, "Why, yes, Mom. It was a war, and the enemy was shooting at me."

"You're just so matter of fact! They were trying to KILL you!"

Trip grinned, "Well, the Messerschmitt was trying to shoot me down, Mom. But we went head-to-head, and I shot him up as much as he did me."

R.H. blanched. "You were shooting at each other? Isn't that a little like an Old West gunfight?"

Trip said, "Well, it was certainly a shootout, Pop. He jumped me, and I dived away. But he was so much faster than my little Russian I-16. He'd have run me down from behind and shot me to pieces if I ran. So, I hauled the *Mosca* around to face him, and we shot it out. I hit him a bunch, but he hit me too. I last saw him diving away, streaming smoke and coolant. I like to think I shot him down. My engine quit, so I glided to France and put it down in a farm field."

Kathy asked, "*Mosca*?"

"Yes, the I-16 is so small that we called it *Mosca*, Spanish for *fly*. The Nationalists called it *Rata*. You can guess what that means."

Kathy grinned. "I like *Rata* better for you, Trip."

Trip poked her playfully in the ribs.

The discussion raged all the way home, with R.H. and Edith asking question after question about Trip's experience walking away from the belly landing.

Trip tried to soft-pedal the experience of the Argelès Concentration Camp. "It wasn't so bad. There was not much food, but I was only there for four days."

Mom said, "What about the poor people still there?"

Trip's eyes went to the far distance, not truly seeing, "I don't know, Mom. I hope La Calle is all right. But I don't know. It was pretty bad. I hope they let them go. But I fear they are still there."

It was Saturday, April 1, 1939. Trip wished he could yell, "April Fool!" but the Argelès Concentration Camp was all too real. Trip did not mention the piles of dead bodies rotting in the sun and rain.

~~<>~~

The Gibsons arrived at their home off Paces Ferry. It was a two-story mansion with tall white columns hinting at money and reflecting its southern locale. R.H. guided the big Buick around the house into an extensive carport that was more of a 19th Century carriage house. Servants quarters – two Negro maids – were upstairs over the carport.

Trip looked around the place. It was unchanged. Four large bedrooms in the main house and chef's private quarters attached behind the kitchen. The large, rectangular swimming pool between the carport and the main house was sparkling clean. The water was inviting, even though it was early Spring, and a chill was still in the air.

Trip grinned when he saw his Dusty Gray 1936 Pontiac Deluxe 8 Cabriolet sitting in one of the four carport slots. He walked over and ran his hand over the fender. *What a great-looking car,* he thought. The swooping tail was the perfect counterpoint to the long straight hood with chrome accents on the sides. The straight-eight engine was smooth and powerful. During his time in Europe, Trip had missed driving the Pontiac.

Kathy walked over and leaned against the front fender. Trip realized she had turned 20 this year. Looking at her leaning against the car, he realized how beautiful his sister was. Her good looks were like Trip's, wavy dark hair, almond-shaped blue eyes, high cheekbones, defined jawline, and dimples when she smiled. What made Trip masculine was softened by Kathy's femininity.

Kathy said, "I've been driving her some. Daddy says it keeps the gaskets and seals from rotting."

Trip put his arm around her shoulder. "She looks great. So do you. You still dating Reb?"

Kathy nodded. She murmured, "Don't mention it to Daddy and Mama. They disapprove of Sid."

Albert Sidney Johnston Clayton – Reb to his friends; Sidney or Sid to Kathy – was brilliant but somewhat coarse. His family had farmland and pine plantations in Berrien County, south of Macon in the middle of the state. Reb Clayton came from backwoods people who worked with their hands. Trip couldn't wait to see Reb and the other two members of his gang of four: Hank and Al.

"I'm glad you and Reb are still together."

Kathy's face clouded.

Kathy said, "Mama and Daddy think he's crude. But Sid is a kind-hearted, gentle soul until you rile him up. Then it's hell to pay. Except with me, of course."

"Y'all getting married?"

"He hasn't asked yet."

"Want me to tell him to?"

Kathy poked Trip in the ribs. "Leave it alone, OK?"

Trip grinned as they walked into the house. It was dinner time.

46

Edith had asked Max, the Negro chef, to prepare a special meal of meatloaf, potatoes, butter beans, collard greens, and Carolina rice, all Trip's favorites. The family sat down to eat and celebrate Trip's safe return.

R. H. spoke finally. "You'll be going back to Tech, then?"

Trip grinned, "Yes, Pop. I think it's time I completed my degree and got on with my life."

R. H. looked satisfied, "Good. When the time comes, I can speak to the director about a place for you at Westinghouse. I can get you a job this summer. You can start in May, if you like. A little extra money, you know."

Trip said, "That sounds good. I need money to keep the Jenny flying. I was paid $1500 a month for flying for Spain. I was there from June to February. They were scrupulous about putting it into a French bank. I also got a bounty of $1000 for shooting down the Bf-109 last year. I won't see anything for the last fight, so I'll have to take surviving as a bounty. I have about $14,500 in the Banque du Nord du Paris. The Embassy wouldn't let me out of the compound when I was in Paris waiting to be thrown out of the country. I'd appreciate help in getting that money, Pop. Also, I'll pay you back for my fare on the *Normandie*."

R.H.'s face reflected surprise and a newfound respect for Trip. He said, "I have plenty of contacts in Paris. I'll get that money wired into the Southern Bank and Trust this week. With that kind of money, you don't need a job."

Trip nodded, but said, "I'd value the job just to learn how to work as an engineer." He didn't mention that the money would allow him great independence and that he could easily move out of the house.

Edith said, "I think you should sell the plane."

Trip looked stricken, "The Jenny? Sell it? No, Mom. You know how much I love flying, and the Jenny is inexpensive and fun."

Edith said, "Still, I think you should have flying out of your system now."

"On the contrary, Mother. Flying is more deeply ingrained in my soul. I'm thinking about trading the Jenny for something more powerful. The Cessna Airmaster looks like a good airplane. I was looking at Popular Aviation on the train and I saw one for sale in Macon."

R.H. glanced at Edith and then at Trip. He said, "We'll discuss this later after you've had time to settle in."

Kathy said, "Trip, will you take me flying?"

Edith said, "Absolutely NOT!"

Trip grinned and winked at Kathy. Now was not the moment to tell the family he was planning to move to the Biltmore Apartments in Midtown Atlanta. It would be convenient when he reenrolled at Georgia Tech.

~~<>~~

The next morning the family all motored to St Luke's Cathedral. After the Episcopal service, the rector, The Reverend John Walker, shook Trip's hand enthusiastically.

"I'm happy to see the Lord has returned you to us safely, Trip. Your parents were quite worried. They visited me on several occasions after you disappeared into Spain last year. In the future, you should write to them more often when you are away."

Trip said, "Yes, Sir. I would have written from Spain, but there was a war on. No one seemed to be getting letters in or out."

Walker nodded, "Still, you must make the attempt. Remember the commandments: Honor Thy Father and Thy Mother."

"Yes, Sir."

Trip was a little sober when the family got back into the Roadmaster. Pop had a surprise for everyone. They were going to *The Colonnade* for Sunday Dinner.

The Colonnade was Trip's favorite since childhood. It was at the corner of Lindbergh and Piedmont, a short drive from the Cathedral on Peachtree Street.

Pop said, "We better hurry. Want to get there before the Baptists!"

This brought gales of laughter from the Gibsons. Pop always said he wanted to beat the Baptists when going anywhere on Sunday. Fortunately, the Baptists were not always prompt about getting out of church at noon, so if the family did not dally, they usually beat the Baptists to the door of the Colonnade.

~~<>~~

Sated with fried chicken, warm yeast rolls with butter and an array of vegetables, the family was sitting in the living room. The radio played softly in the corner. R. H. liked listening to Arthur Godfrey and Jack Benny.

It was 2 p.m., and everyone seemed ready for a nap.

Trip asked, "Do y'all mind if I take the car down to the campus and try to catch up with Reb, Hank, and Al?"

Edith said, "Oh, I wish you wouldn't associate with that Sidney!"

"Mom! He's my friend. Got me out of a couple scrapes, too."

"What!? What kind of scrapes?"

"Oh, you know, broke down car. That kind of thing."

Edith snorted, "I don't believe that broken down car stuff. I'll bet he had you hanging out at that Blue Lantern on Ponce de Leon. It's a terrible dive. I'll bet you were playing dice with the colored people in the parking lot. Why, you could get knifed doing that."

"Aw, Mom. We don't do that," Trip lied. "Besides, they don't play dice there that I know of. Blind Willie McTell plays his guitar out there for tips. He sure is good, too."

Edith harrumphed, "Where there's a minstrel playing, there's drinking, carousing, and dice games."

Trip rose to leave, "I'll be sure to avoid the Blue Lantern, Mom. Besides, we go to classy places like the Ansley Hotel, The Biltmore Ballroom, and the Georgian Terrace."

Edith Burke Gibson, DAR, President of the Paces Garden Club, snorted, "Uh, huh. You be back by suppertime."

Chapter 8 – The Gang

Trip delighted in his faithful little Pontiac. Its straight eight-cylinder engine had a powerful rumble, and the responsiveness to Trip's touch was like a fighter plane. Despite the cool temperatures in the low 60s, he put the top down and enjoyed the open-air ride down Howell Mill Road until he reached 10th Street. He puttered along 10th until he reached Fowler and turned into the familiar outer edges of Georgia Tech. He knew he was truly home when he hit Ferst Street and Techwood Drive. In moments he parked the Pontiac beside Grant Field across from Harris Dorm.

Trip left the top down and sauntered across the street to the knee wall in front of Brittain Dining Hall. Brittain looked the same: medieval red brick, a cloister running left and right from the imposing main doors, stained glass reflecting Tech's various fields of study. Trip smiled, *Never really liked the food.*

He walked quickly to the entrance to Harris Dorm, just beside Brittain. He took the stairs two at a time to the third floor. The interior was warm, with the stairwells getting only a little air from the small windows. Trip grinned to himself, *Won't be long until this place is sweltering.*

He was walking down the hall toward Rooms 307 and 309 when Reb Clayton, Civil Engineering, Class of 1940, stepped out of his door carrying a shaving kit and wearing nothing but a white towel around his waist.

Clayton shifted his tobacco chaw from one side to the other and regarded Trip with a squinting eye, "Son-of-a-*bitch*. Look who tha' Goddamn cat drug in. Kathy tol' me you wuz comin' home, but I didn't believe it 'til jes now."

Trip gripped Reb's hand and felt his eyes sting with unexpected tears. "How you doin' Reb?"

"I'm passable fair. Wait'll tha' others see yore sorry ass. Git in here! I'll be back from tha' shower in a minute."

Al Norham, Commerce, Class of 1940 and Reb's next-door neighbor, was sitting at the desk looking at Reb's *Popular Aviation* magazine. This issue had a photo on the cover of an Army Air Corps cadet climbing into the cockpit of a Vultee BT-13.

Al's face lit up with surprise and pleasure, "Trip! Welcome home!"

He jumped up and stuck out his hand. Trip and Al shook hands and slapped each other's backs.

Trip said, "You look good!"

Al said, "I guess I'm doing ok. Gotta get this quarter over so I can get to workin' full time for that asshole Mortimer. I need to make a buck to pay for the Fall."

Trip didn't comment other than to ask, "Still at the bank, huh?"

"Yep. I'm still behind the eight-ball on that. But I'll get out when I finish this degree."

The door banged, and Hank Overton burst into the room. Hank said, "Damned if it ain't true! You *are* alive!"

Trip grinned as he shook Overton's hand. "In the flesh, my good man. In the flesh!"

Hank Overton, Aeronautical Engineering, Class of 1940, and Reb's roommate, was a flying fanatic and kept a Piper Cub at the Atlanta Municipal Airport. His Cub was hangared with Trip's Jenny. The Cub was almost new, and its first owner had gone bankrupt. Hank got it for $500 and sold a well-used six-year-old Taylor Cub to pay for it.

The four boys had become acquainted through Army ROTC. ROTC was a compulsory requirement for all Tech men. At the time, Trip was a junior, while the others were freshmen.

Trip had given them all a hard time because, as Rats – freshmen at Georgia Tech – they were subject to all manner of hazing from upperclassmen. Rats were easily identified by the required wear of a gold-colored college beanie cap with the brim turned up to display the word RAT written in bold, black letters. Trip had gleefully participated in the hazing. Despite the years of age difference, flying had bonded the four boys in their time together.

Trip decided to leave school for a year and went on the Grand Tour of Europe. While Trip would be a junior, the other three would soon be rising seniors. The wheel of life was moving on, and Trip needed to catch up. He was, after all, 23 and not getting younger.

Trip asked what had been happening at Tech over the two years since Trip had been gone. The boys chatted about the most important things: football, school, girls, flying.

Hank said, "Last year's football season was miserable. Only three wins!"

Al said, "Yep. Add four losses and three ties to that sparkling record, and you have a terrible year on the gridiron for Tech."

Trip said, "I hope this coming year is better."

Reb walked back in, his hair damp. He wore boxers, and his towel was around his neck. He said, "Cain't get no worse. Say, I got some bootleg hooch, it bein' Sunday, an' all. Y'all want a taste?"

After nods all around, the talk turned to flying. Al said, "We've been taking care of your Jenny, Trip."

Trip said, "Thanks for doing that. I hope you've been flying her some."

Al said, "Yes, I've got nearly 50 hours now. We changed the oil last weekend, and I found a mechanic who tightened the flying wires. She should be good to go."

Trip picked up the magazine and waved it around. He asked, "Any of y'all going to go in the Army Air Corps? It's a good way to get hours in fast airplanes."

Hank said, "I can't qualify. We all have the required two years of college, but my eyesight is actually 20/40. I wear glasses and have my private pilot's license, but the Army won't touch me."

Trip said, "Seems dumb. You got, what, 300 hours flying time?"

"Yes, but the Air Corps is very picky. They have only so many spaces in their training school in Texas, and that's it. Cadets have to be perfect, or they go home."

Al said, "I'd kill for a chance to be in the Air Corps, but I want to finish this degree and get moving on a career somewhere. My Commerce degree may not land me in the Air Corps anyway. I don't know about those physical requirements."

Trip said, "Hell, Commerce was good enough for Arthur Murray. He's running all those dance studios and got that mail-order business. All courtesy of Tech."

Al grinned. "I spin records, I don't dance worth a flip."

Al Norham broadcast the dances at the Ansley Hotel on WGST for extra money. He introduced the band's numbers and spun records when there wasn't a live orchestra. Al had no money and was making starvation wages working for a jerk named Mortimer at the Southern Bank and Trust. The other guys avoided ribbing him about being poor.

Reb snorted, "Hell with joining the Army. I keep flyin' because it'll be useful in South America. I'm plannin' to use my Civil Engineering degree to build roads and other public works down there. I reckon bein' able to fly is a good skill to have fer that kinda work. I ain't interested in gettin' in no war. Don't get me wrong, I hate them Goddamn Nazis. They's wors' than tha' Goddamn Yankees!"

Everyone snickered. Reb was named for Confederate General Albert Sidney Johnston. Reb's entire family line had been staunchly rebel. At Tech football games, when the band started the rumble of drums that signaled the playing of Dixie, Reb Clayton was first on his feet, hat doffed and waving his arms at the crowd, shouting, "Git up, Goddamnit! They's playin' tha' National Anthem!"

Al said quietly, "You look like you got some injuries there, Trip. What happened?"

Trip said, "I got talked into going to Spain and signing up to fly fighter planes."

The room went silent. Reb poured another shot for each man. "Well, tell it, brother. What happened?"

Trip told them, including the Argelès Concentration Camp.

Hank whistled softly, "Bodies piled up? Really?"

"Yep. They were bloated and rotting. The place stank so badly that you got used to it finally. Either that, or your nose just got used to it. Don't tell Kathy about it. It'll get back to Mom."

Reb nodded

Al asked, "How did you get out?"

Trip explained about being taken out of the camp after four days and then his trip to Paris and the U.S. "I don't really know who told the Embassy about me, but whoever it was has a drink coming when I meet them."

Hank asked, "So you shot down a German plane?"

"Yes. One that I'm sure of. Felt bad about it because I'm sure the pilot didn't get out. It hit the ground with tremendous force, too. The other one was streaming smoke and coolant as he went by me. I was going about 120 kph – 75 miles per hour – and he was probably going about 250 miles per hour, so the closure rate was very fast. We were probably at about 7000 feet, and he was pointed at the ground. I didn't see him pull out. I was too busy trying not to stall and spin myself."

Al said, "Jesus. That's a scary story."

Trip grinned with false bravado, "Should have been there. It was even more scary."

Changing the subject, Trip asked Reb, "So, now that you're a senior, are you thinking about marriage?"

"Why, do you know an eligible girl?"

Trip belly laughed. "Yep, I got a cute sister."

Reb deadpanned, "Never met her."

Al and Hank rolled their eyes.

Reb sobered a bit and said, "Yore Maw and Paw ain't enamored of me."

Trip snorted, "Enamored is a big word for you, Reb. They just plain don't like you. But when did that stop the Confederate Cavalry from charging into the Union positions?"

Reb snickered, "I don't need my saber dulled."

All four boys roared at this double-entendre. Reb poured the last of the whiskey.

Al said, "I have no money to date anyone, so I remain celibate."

Reb snorted, "Yore right-hand damn shore ain't celibate. Ol' Rosie Palm is 'bout wore out from yore amorous attentions."

Al blushed and said, "I'd love to have a girlfriend like Leona."

Hank said, "Now, now. Leona Woodson is studious and never would consider premarital sex."

Reb smirked, "Bullshit. Leona is in love with yore ass, and no two ways about it. You ortta marry her and set up house keepin', as often as you lock my ass out of this here room of a weekend."

It was Hank's turn to blush. "What about you, Trip? Are you going to take up with Ellie now that you're back?"

Trip looked up at the ceiling, "Dunno. I just got back yesterday. Guess I'll call her."

Al said, "That sounds a little tentative, old boy."

"Yeah, I kinda met someone on the ship. Mildred Wright of New York. Silly girl's marrying some lucky stiff up there. She's clever and a very good conversationalist."

Reb leaned back and squinted at Trip. "You wus a-sleepin' with her, weren't ye?"

Trip said, "Well..."

Hank said, "Of course he was, him being a worldly soldier of fortune and all. I'm sure she fell for his manly charms."

Trip said, "Something like that." He paused, "More like she was using me for a last fling before marrying that bumpkin in New York."

Reb said, "Aw, hell. Go ahead and call up ol' Ellie and get over that Yankee gal."

Al said, "I gotta study for an accounting test."

Trip snickered, "I forgot about y'all being in school. Guess I better let everyone get back to their studies."

Hank said, "You'll be back to it yourself soon enough."

Trip stood up to leave. He looked around the gang. "It's good to be back, fellas. Are we going flying this week?"

Nods all around. Hank said, "Wednesday afternoons have been our flying days."

Trip said, "Good. I'll be here on Wednesday at about 11. We'll figure out who's riding together."

Chapter 9 – New Digs

Atlanta sweltered in May 1939. The thermometer frequently hit in the 90's. The evenings were not much better.

R.H. was good to his word on getting Trip a summer job and getting Trip's money moved from France. Trip worked at the Westinghouse building on Northside Drive. It was very convenient to the Gibson residence, and some days R.H. and Trip rode to work together in the Roadmaster.

Because he did not yet have an engineering degree, his munificent pay was 35 cents an hour. Trip learned engineering drawing and helped design a large power plant generator. It was excellent experience, and Trip was cautious not to let on that he had over $14,000 on account at the Southern Bank and Trust Company.

While driving home one day, Trip said, "Pop, would you like to stop for a drink before we go home?"

R.H. looked at Trip with a startled expression. "You mean a drink of whiskey?"

"Yes, Sir."

"Your mother won't approve, but yes. Is a beer ok with you? I don't know of a good bar."

Trip grinned. Alcohol was not permitted in the Gibson household. For Trip, this had been an adjustment after two years abroad, where wine, champagne, whiskey, and cocktails had been the norm rather than the exception. "Beer's fine."

R.H. drove over to Buckhead to Harry's Delicatessen. As he parked in front of the building faced with Stone Mountain granite, R.H. said, "Best I can do on short notice, Son."

Trip grinned. "I always wanted to see what's inside here."

They sat in the corner at a chrome and gray Formica-topped table, and Trip saluted his Pop with his beer. R.H. clinked his beer glass. They both drank.

Trip said, "It's time I move out and live on my own."

R.H. said, "I kind of thought that's what this conversation would be about. Of course, I completely agree with you, Trip. Mother's a different story, I suspect."

Trip said, "Indeed. This is why we're sitting here. I've rented an apartment at the Biltmore and have applied for re-admission to Tech in the fall. I thought the Biltmore would be better than the dorms. I always thought the dorms were miserable, and this hot summer has confirmed that."

R.H. said, "They didn't have too many dorms when I was at Tech. I lived in a rooming house. That was plenty miserable, too. I can see you'd want to live in a nice place like the Biltmore."

Trip nodded. "Yes, Sir. And it's a short walk to campus. Won't have to move the car."

R.H. said, "I imagine we'll have to present a united front to Mother. I feel a little dishonest planning that, but it will have to be done."

Trip waved at a waiter. To his father he said, "Another beer, Pop?"

R.H. nodded, "We'll need the fortification for the coming joust."

~~<>~~

Edith had faced the news with surprising stoicism. "Of course, you must do what you must do. It's just that you're my baby boy, and you ran off and were nearly killed, not to mention being thrown into a concentration camp on top of it all."

"Aw, Mom, that's all behind us now."

Edith said, "I should hope so, but I fear the news. I can't look at a newspaper or turn on the radio for fear of hearing about some new affront from Hitler. He's a maniac, and I worry that he'll get worse before this ends."

Trip said, "Mom, all of Europe is hanging by a thread. I have friends I'm sure are either dead or being shot at. Those rumors you hear about the Jews are true. France is no better to them than the Germans. But I'm not in the Army, and I'm getting too old to fly for the Air Corps. I think it will all pass me by."

Trip hated himself for lying, but discretion seemed the better part of valor.

Edith said, "Do you think so?"

R.H. said, "My Dear, our son is a man and a damn fine one at that."

Edith sputtered, "R.H.! Language! Have you been drinking?"

R.H. Gibson, JR., drew himself to his full 5 feet 11 and ½ inches and said, "My son bought me a beer on the way home. And yes, I'm feeling a tiny bit tipsy."

Edith tried to be stern, but she began to snicker. She put her arms around R.H.'s neck. "I should scold you both, but the world has turned. You bad boys. Today is the servants' day off. You must take me out to a ridiculously expensive dinner for which our rich son will pay. Perhaps I shall have a glass of champagne or two."

R.H. raised an eyebrow behind Edith's back and winked at Trip.

Trip moved into the Biltmore on the first of June. He was surprised and pleased when Edith helped by making a tablecloth and scouring the Gibson's kitchen for some cast-off plates, an old pan or two, and mismatched silverware. She also found sufficient linens for his bed and towels for the bath.

The apartment was on the east corner of the 6th Floor and got nice cross breezes. The apartment had a 12x12 living room, a complete kitchen, a full bath with blue and white tile, and a shower over the tub. The 10X12 bedroom had windows on two sides and was very pleasant for sleeping, even on a warm night. The apartment came furnished with couch, easy chair, bed, and various tables. Trip's rent was $40 per month. Quite expensive, but Trip considered it reasonable.

Trip splurged and had a telephone installed. He passed his new phone number, ATwood 5191, to his friends at school and, of course, to Kathy and his parents.

Trip smiled. No school just yet. Interesting job. Nice digs; even got a phone. Short walk to the Biltmore Ballroom or to the Ansley. Not much farther to the Georgian Terrace.

Trip thought, *Nice setup. Things are going well. I just wish I could quit dreaming about the concentration camp. I hope La Calle survived. I also wish Mildred would stop haunting my dreams.*

Chapter 10 – Lena

Trip coasted into the ballroom at the Biltmore Hotel. The march of the sparkling white columns with gold accents gave an optical illusion of a much larger room. Still, the ballroom at the Biltmore was spacious.

The orchestra was in full Friday-night swing. They were already roaring with *Sing, Sing, Sing (With a Swing)*, the Benny Goodman version that featured Gene Krupa. The orchestra's drummer was hitting a tom-tom beat that thumped in Trip's chest.

The Maître d' led Trip to a dance floor-side table. The little chairs at the table reminded Trip of those small chairs in an ice cream shop. *Good thing I'm planning to dance some. This chair would kill me to sit on it all night.*

The band kicked into *Moonlight Serenade* followed by Glenn Miller's version of *Little Brown Jug*. Trip smiled and tapped his right toe. He liked these tunes. *Too bad the other fellows had schoolwork. This looks like a good evening.*

A lovely young woman with light brown hair and wearing a shimmering white dress with a pleated skirt came over to his table. "Got a light?"

Trip quickly stood and smiled as he dipped into his coat pocket and pulled out his Zippo. A quick snap-flick and the girl's cigarette was glowing. Trip said, "Like to sit down?"

The girl sat and dragged hard on the cigarette. She huffed smoke toward the ceiling. "My name's Lena. What's yours, handsome?"

Trip told her. He said, "You're not from Atlanta."

"Nope. Jersey. Just came down here to go to school at Massey."

Trip grinned, "Business girl, eh?"

"Plan to be. I'm going back to New York and get a job. Make some bucks. You?"

Trip said, "I'm a mechanical engineering student at Georgia Tech."

Lena said, "Helluva, helluva, helluva..."

Trip grinned, "Something like that. Wanna dance?"

"I thought you'd never ask."

Lena turned out to be a great dancer and light on her feet. She smiled a lot. Her bright red lipstick accentuated her white teeth and dark eyes. Her short, light brown hair snapped when she spun. She swung her hips, and her spraddle-footed Lindy hop was both excellent and slightly suggestive.

When they took a break for a drink at the table, Trip noticed a sparkling drop of sweat running down the side of her neck. He offered his handkerchief, and she smiled her acceptance.

Toward eleven o'clock the band was clearly winding down their contract. Trip asked, "Can I see you home?"

Lena looked at him appraisingly, "Sure. I walked here."

Trip said, "I'll be happy to walk you. This part of town is mostly safe, but you never know these days."

They walked out the back of the Biltmore, across Peachtree, and down 5th Street into a quiet neighborhood.

Trip said, "Nice you found a place here. Massey is not too far, easy bus ride, and this is a safe neighborhood."

Lena nodded and put her arm through Trip's as they walked in companionable silence.

Soon, they reached a corner. Lena said, "It's just down there. My landlady might be difficult about you coming in. But I have a private entrance, and if we're quiet, she won't know."

Trip nodded. They walked along, and just after they stepped out of the pool of light from a streetlamp, Lena tugged his arm and led him up a darkened walk along the side of a two-story bungalow. They reached a set of steps.

Lena touched Trip's lips and made a quiet *Shsss* noise. She tiptoed up the stairs, and Trip followed just as quietly.

Lena quietly put her key in the door and gingerly turned it so as not to make a sound. The door swung open silently, and they stepped into Lena's small apartment. It had a small living room, and Trip could see a bath to the left and a small kitchen to the right. A bedroom was just beyond the living room.

Lena said, "I gotta get out of these shoes. Be right back. Grab something to drink in the kitchen and have a seat."

Trip cracked an ice tray he found in the tiny freezer of the Crosley refrigerator. He remembered to close the heavy refrigerator door quietly. He put tap water over the ice enjoying the crackling as the water hit the ice. He had just settled into the sole easy chair and loosened his tie when Lena stepped into the room from the bedroom. She wore a thin gossamer robe and a pair of puffy slippers with tiny heels. Her make-up was refreshed, and she smelled of perfume.

"Want something stronger?"

Trip shook his head. "Nope. You look very nice. Refreshed from a hard night of dancing."

She walked over to a table with a radio and tuned in to WSB's late music program. Soft jazz filled the room.

Lena turned from the radio and said, "Sorry there's only the one chair. Maybe we can share?"

Trip said, "Sure, I'll move over to make room."

Lena said, "How about I sit on your lap?"

Trip said, "Sure."

Lena walked over and stood in front of Trip. She cocked her head to the side and smiled.

Trip grinned back. Lena was very likable for a Yankee girl. He didn't mean that like it sounded in his head.

She pulled at the tie around the waist of the robe and shrugged. The garment fell to the floor, leaving Lena naked before him.

Trip took in her long, slim legs and hard stomach. He did not fail to notice her dark nipples and equally dark pubic thatch. He said, "You gonna sit on my lap like that?"

Lena said in a slightly challenging voice, "That's the plan. You gonna keep those pants on or what?"

Trip quickly stood, kicked off his shoes, dragged off his jacket, and stepped out of his pants.

He was about to take off his shirt and tie when Lena nudged him back into the chair. Her voice shuddered as she breathed in his ear, "I can't wait."

With that, she put a knee on the left side of his legs and the other knee on the right. She leaned forward and kissed him hard. She tugged his tie down and unbuttoned his shirt. "Are you just going to sit there, or are you going to take advantage of me?"

Trip grinned to himself. *Two Yankee girls this year, and neither one was shy.*

~~<>~~

Two hours later, Trip stood beside Lena's bed. "Damn, girl. You about wore me out."

Lena stretched. "Likewise, I'm sure. I don't have school tomorrow, and it's a good thing. I'd ask you to stay, but Old Lady Chalmers would take a dim view of a man leaving my apartment in the morning."

Trip grinned and said, "I'll be very discrete as I leave. I'll be at the Biltmore tomorrow night."

Lena said, "Maybe I'll see you there, Trippy."

Trip leaned over and kissed her goodnight. "It was a lovely time, Lena."

Lena was already dozing off. "Yeah, me too."

Trip quietly let himself out of Lena's apartment, making sure the door was locked behind him. Twenty minutes later, an exhausted Trip Gibson was asleep in his own bed at the Biltmore.

Old Lady Chalmers was none the wiser.

For once, Trip did not dream about the camp.

Chapter 11 – Ellie

I t was a warm day in June. After considerable thought, Trip sat on the brown chenille couch and picked up the telephone.

The phone rang twice before a voice said, "Peabody residence."

Trip said, "Ellie?"

"Trip? Is that you?"

"Yes."

"You bastard! Where have you been? I thought you were dead!"

Trip said, "It's nice to talk to you, too. Want to have dinner Saturday?"

"I'm furious with you."

"I'm sorry. If it makes you feel better, I thought of you often this past two years."

"Well, it doesn't. Ok, maybe a little. Pick me up at 5?"

"Ok. Can't wait to see you."

Eleanor Crawford Peabody said, "I'll bet, bye."

Trip drove up to the front door of Angus R. "Buddy" Peabody and his wife, Evelyn Crawford Peabody's stately home in Decatur, Georgia. It was precisely 5 p.m. He walked briskly around the Pontiac, flicked a non-existent piece of lint off his dark blue double-breasted suit, and rang the bell.

A negro servant answered the door. "Good evening, Mr. Gibson."

Trip said, "Good evening, Charles. It's nice to see you again."

Charles said, "I'm glad to see you, too, Sir. We all thought you must be dead."

Trip grinned, "'The report of my death was an exaggeration. I was merely abroad.' Mark Twain said that under similar circumstances."

Charles laughed softly, "You always make me smile, Mr. Gibson. Please be seated in the living room, and I'll announce you to Miss Eleanor."

~~<>~~

Eleanor Peabody swept into the room, and Trip stood quickly.

"Hello, Ellie. You look so lovely."

Ellie wore a lightweight dress of patterned sheer netting over a waisted black silk sheath that flared at the knee. The hem came within two inches of the floor. Her black silk heels had small bows and rhinestone buckles at the toe. The black dress perfectly complemented Ellie's blonde locks. A splash of red lipstick matched her nails. A red beaded choker completed her ensemble. In all, Ellie Peabody made a powerful statement that commanded the room.

"Hello, Trip. I'm so glad you are back. I understand you've been back for two months. I'm honored you finally got around to calling."

Trip stuttered, "I'm sorry. It took a little time to get my life together. I called as soon as I was settled."

Ellie said, "I forgive you. You look very handsome. Where are you taking me?"

"I thought the Terrace? I made reservations."

Ellie smiled, "That sounds wonderful. I'll get my wrap."

~~<>~~

Trip drove West on Ponce de Leon from Decatur toward the Georgian Terrace Hotel.

70

Ellie said, "I have my own place now. It's a little apartment in Druid Hills. Mama and Daddy don't expect me back to the house."

Trip nodded at this interesting piece of information. "Congratulations on being on your own."

~~<>~~

The corner turrets and other architecture of the Georgian Terrace Hotel reminded Trip of the corner buildings in Paris. The butter-colored brick and limestone corniche were familiar from his earlier days at Georgia Tech. Rounding the corner onto Peachtree Street, Trip wheeled into the columned ladies' carriage entrance, a remnant of the Gilded Age of the early 1900s.

An attendant snapped to attention and rushed to get Trip's door. As Trip got out, another attendant quickly opened Ellie's door and assisted her to exit the low car. As Trip and Ellie turned toward the entrance, Trip flicked a half-dollar coin to each attendant. They walked through the entrance and headed toward the Terrace Restaurant Grill Room.

Trip said, "The interior areas look like a street in Paris, complete with little shops and bistros. There, the trees are not potted, though."

Ellie said, "I hope that Hitler won't destroy all of that."

Trip said, "I doubt he'll ever get that far."

"Oh, and you're an expert?"

"Uh, in a general sense, yes."

"I can't wait to hear your analysis."

Soon they were seated at a wonderful corner table, well away from the kitchen and not near the door. Linen tablecloths and napkins made for a first-class table.

Trip spoke quietly with the maître d' about which champagne to serve. Soon, the sommelier arrived and removed the cork. Trip approved the champagne. The waiter poured the wine and discretely left.

Ellie said, "Well, at least your time in France resulted in excellent taste in champagne."

Trip looked at Ellie's high cheekbones and alabaster skin. She was flawless at age 23. He asked, "What have you been doing these last two years?"

Ellie said, "I finished my degree at the University of Georgia and got hired by the DeKalb County School System. I have been teaching at the Druid Hills School. It is wonderful to teach young minds. The school was founded in 1911, so we have a little tradition."

Trip said, "Sounds like you're satisfied, then."

Ellie said, "I have meaningful work, Trip. But you left me behind. Where have you been? You have several small scars on your face. How did you get those?"

Trip told her. He left out much of the concentration camp experience other than to say it was wet and cold and he was hungry.

"Did many people die in that camp, Trip?"

"Yes, but I don't really want to talk about it."

"I understand. Maybe you'll tell me someday. So, now what?"

Trip said, "Well, I am returning to Tech in the fall, and I've taken an apartment at the Biltmore."

Ellie said, "My, but your parents are indulgent to pay for that!"

Trip said, "On the contrary, I was well paid for fighting for Spain. I'm on my own now."

Ellie said, "Well paid. My goodness. I imagined you had lived on a shoestring in France and were made a pauper by the experience."

Trip said, "Well, I came away with over $14,000. So, hardly a pauper."

Ellie's cheeks turned pink. "I'm embarrassed for having a low opinion."

Trip said, "Not at all. Do you like the salmon?"

They chit-chatted for an hour as dinner of cold tomato aspic, poached salmon, duchess potatoes, and asparagus was served. Capping off the meal was a dessert of pears poached in red wine.

They sat quietly, satisfied by the food and the company.

Trip brightened, "Want to go dancing?"

Ellie grinned, "I wore this dress with the flounce with just that in mind."

They collected the car and roared up Peachtree Street for the five-minute trip to 5th Street, where they turned and motored to the Ansley Hotel at the corner of 5th and Spring Streets. Trip repeated the process of leaving the car with valets, again with a half-dollar for their trouble.

They walked around to the main entrance. The lobby's red marble columns and white marble floors, complemented by dark woodwork, welcomed Atlanta's elite. Trip guided Ellie to the sweeping staircase down to the ballroom. He and Ellie strode into the Ansley Hotel Ballroom just as the orchestra started their first set.

The Ansley Hotel Ballroom was as Trip remembered it. Orchestra to the right as he and Ellie entered. The parquet dance floor immediately in front of the orchestra looked inviting. Only a few patrons were dancing this early.

Trip got a small table, ordered a drink, and, leaving Ellie's wrap over a chair, took her to the dance floor. They danced and chatted over the sound of the orchestra. After three dances, they took a break and went to sit at their table. The place was beginning to get busy.

Trip spotted Al Norham in the radio booth and walked over. Al clicked off the mike and looked at Trip. "I see you're back with Ellie."

Trip said, "Who knows? It's a pleasant evening, but she's still quite angry that I've been gone."

Al smirked, "Can't blame her for that. Hell, your buddies all thought you dead and gone."

Trip said, "I'm glad you're still announcing for WGST."

Al said, "I like it, but all I do is work."

Trip said, "Yeah, I know it's hard. School is expensive as hell. I'm sure you'll do well, though."

Al said, "Trying. Oops...got to get back. Are we going to fly this week?"

Trip said, "Yup. Wednesday?"

Al nodded.

~~<>~~

It was 9:30 pm when Trip looked at Ellie. "Want to see my new place?"

Ellie said, "Sure."

Ten minutes later, Trip and Ellie pulled up at the Biltmore. A repeat of the valet parking drill followed. Soon, Trip and Ellie Peabody stepped out of the elevator on Trip's 6th Floor and walked to his apartment.

Trip opened the door, and Ellie stepped in. "This is very nice, Trip."

Trip said, "I need to get a couple of paintings to hang on the walls. I have champagne in the refrigerator."

74

Ellie said, "That sounds wonderful. The dancing left me thirsty."

Trip poured the champagne while Ellie tuned the radio to WGST where they heard Al Norham's voice announcing the next number from the orchestra. Soon, quiet jazz music floated around the apartment.

Trip handed Ellie her champagne and sat on the couch beside her. He loosened his tie and kicked off his shoes. Ellie did the same, and soon, they sat in companionable silence. They listened to the smooth jazz and swing music on the radio.

Ellie moved closer and put her head on Trip's shoulder. "I'm glad you're back. I'm terribly angry with you for leaving me behind."

Trip nuzzled her hair. It smelled of floral shampoo. Something in his heart stirred. He said, "You would not have wanted to be with me, especially in Spain."

The orchestra on WGST launched into a credible version of Glenn Miller's *In the Mood*. Trip quietly whispered into Ellie's hair, "Are you?"

"Am I what?"

"Are you in the mood?"

"Yes, damn you."

Chapter 12 – Teruel

Trip settled into a comfortable routine. Work, flying the Jenny a couple of times a week, beers with the gang, and occasional dinner with his parents. He even dusted off a math book and refreshed a bit.

He saw Ellie frequently. With her school schedule, Fridays and Saturdays worked out for them. He had not seen Lena again, and that was good. That might have been uncomfortable if Ellie were with him. Still, Lena was a pleasant memory.

It was a Saturday afternoon in May. The boys sat in Trip's apartment, smoking, drinking beer, and listening to the radio. A light breeze drifted through, washing the cigarette smoke out. A tune came on that everyone knew. *Patrulla Americana*. The Glenn Miller swing version. It had a syncopated military beat, and the boys tapped their feet in rhythm.

Al asked, "Weren't you in the Patrulla Americana, Trip?"

Trip looked pensive, "Yes, what was left of it. Frank Tinker and three others, including a fellow named Ajax Baumler, were the original Patrulla. Salty Tinker was leaving Spain as I got there. Ajax, too. So, it wasn't the same."

Al said, "Tinker was an ace, right?"

Trip said, "Yeah, Tinker had as many as 19 victories over the Nationalists – many Germans. The Spanish cut him out of some of those, and he was credited with only eight confirmed. Ajax shot down at least four."

Rep asked, "Y'all flew them Commie airplanes?"

Trip said, "Yes, we were flying Polikarpov I-15s when I arrived. The I-15s – *Chatos* – were biplanes and very agile. They were pretty good against the Fiat CR-32s. The Fiats were very fast and maneuverable – at least they were fast for biplanes."

Trip was far away as he lit a cigarette and continued, "Then we got Polikarpov I-16s. Monoplanes: heavy, sturdy, and powerful. They had essentially the same engine as the *Chato*, but it felt more powerful. They had retractable landing gear, so they were very clean. Modern, too. The 16s were called *Mosca* – fly. We used to laugh because the enemy – the Nationalists- called the 16 '*Rata*.'"

Trip had a sip of beer and dragged on his cigarette. The smoke popped out in little bursts as he talked, "Those Russian airplanes were not the most beautiful aircraft ever made, but they were utilitarian."

Hank opened another beer. "What was it like being there?"

Trip looked off into the distance as though once again seeing Spain's Dun-colored hills and hot, dry plains. "Miserable."

"Really?"

Trip said, "Oh, it was miserable, all right. The food was whatever we could get, and home was mostly in a tent. We were lucky that the Republicans still held Madrid. We could get to Madrid occasionally and stay at the *Hotel Florida*. Plenty of booze, women, and – best of all – hot baths."

Hank said, "Must be grimy sleeping in a tent and no running water."

Trip nodded, "It wasn't all bad, though. When we could get into Madrid, it was mostly a party. Ernest Hemingway was a resident of the *La Florida* Hotel, and he was always good for a drink and a story."

"One of the other American pilots was a guy named Whitey Dahl. His hair was almost white, so that's where he got the nickname. He had eight or nine victories. His wife was a singer named Edith Rogers. At least, I think she was his wife. Anyway, we all hung around in the bar at *La Florida*. Damn if Hemingway couldn't drink us all under the table."

Hank said, "You seem to collect some famous people, Trip."

"Who, me? I don't think so. Hemingway is about the only famous person I can think of. Well, him and his buddy named John Dos Passos. Dos Passos was probably a commie. He sure seemed to be in love with the Communists. He wrote some novels that Hemingway liked. But they had a falling out over some movie they were supposed to be writing."

Hank pursued the subject, "Didn't you have a fling with that Mexican artist on the ship?"

"Frida Kahlo? I had dinner with her, is all. She was kind of a mess. Pissed off about everything."

Hank said, "I thought you got her in the sack."

"Noooooo! Not on your life. Probably could have, but she might have killed me in my sleep. There was a young lady named Mildred who is quite beautiful and very good company."

Reb said, "Now we're talking!"

Trip said, "A gentleman never tells."

Reb snorted, "Bullshit."

Trip turned a little pink, "Let's just say that I had a pleasant voyage."

The other three roared with laughter.

Al said, "Tell us about flying and fighting."

Reb said, "He damn sure ain't gonna tell us about flirtin' an' fuckin'!"

Hank said, "Damn, Reb. You can say some crude stuff."

Reb snorted, "I only say tha' shit thet yore a-thinkin'."

Dismissing this line of chatter, Trip said, "The Germans were flying some of their newest airplanes, Stuka dive bombers and Messerschmitt Bf-109s. Heinkel 111 bombers. Of course, they were marked with Nationalist markings. Overall painted gray with a white tail and a black X on it. Black dot on the fuselage and wings. Our planes had red wing tips and the Spanish flag – red, yellow, purple – on the rudder."

"The Battle of Teruel was terrible. The Republicans were desperate to take that city. It's north of Madrid, and they surrounded it on three sides. The Nationalists holding Teruel amounted to a bulge in our lines. It looked like a finger stuck in the lines pointing at the Mediterranean. The Nationalists threatened to break out and go to the coast, cutting Republican holdings in half."

"Artillery and aerial bombardment of the Republican forces was constant. By the time I got there, the Nationalists had held Teruel and were expanding toward the sea. The air battles were constant."

Al asked, "What did you do?"

Trip said, "One day, just after I got to Spain, Germans launched a bombing raid on our lines outside Teruel. We were at an airfield outside Madrid. We were alerted and rushed to climb to about 15,000 feet. I was number two in a formation of four. La Calle was leading, and I was on his wing. We reached altitude and turned toward the front lines. There was no real information other than reports from the battlefront that airplanes were bombing."

"We turned northerly and quickly saw the brown and black smoke over the front. We bored in on that smoke. La Calle waggled his wings and waved a hand signal meaning to follow him. We had no radios, so hand signals had to do."

"We turned and throttled up, hoping to catch the German bombers. Soon, I saw glints of sunlight reflecting on the cockpit glass of bombers. La Calle knew to watch high above the bombers for Condor Legion fighters."

"La Calle was not mistaken. They came roaring down at us as we closed with the bombers. La Calle waggled his wings and signaled the second section to engage the German fighters while we went after the bombers. Le Calle bored in on the Heinkels, and I hung onto his wing for dear life."

"I lined up on one of the bombers head-on. From about 500 yards out, I opened fire and held the gun button down for the 5 seconds it took to pass the bombers. The one I was shooting at was shooting back, but I was going really fast, and the closure rate was almost 500 miles per hour."

Trip dragged on his Camel and continued, "They missed, but I didn't. I saw sparkles all over their cockpit and engines. A couple of pieces of metal flew off him. The only way to attack a bomber is head-on. If you try to chase it from behind, you are slow, and they have lots of guns to shoot at you."

Al said, "So you shot that bomber down?"

Trip snorted, "Hell, I don't know. I pulled up into a chandelle – a climbing turn – intending to come back down at the Heinkels. But the Messerschmitts came flashing down and got between us and the bombers."

Reb said, "I hope you shot one of them Nazi bastards down."

Trip said, "Well, I tried. One of them came at me head-on, and I got a shot at him. They flashed by us, and La Calle and I turned to chase them. They were going too fast and quickly gained altitude. I knew they would come back down at us. La Calle knew that too, and we started a dive to build up speed and make it hard for the Germans to catch us."

Hank said, "Did you end up in a dogfight?"

Trip said, "Yeah, they dived at us, building up a hell of a lot of speed, but we were going fast from our own dive. We pulled a punishing six-G 180-degree turn to face them and met them head-on. When we passed through each other, everyone turned 180 degrees again, another crushing six-G's. Now we were in a turning fight. The Germans didn't like that because the *Mosca* could turn tighter than the 109."

Trip lit another Camel and said, "One came at me, and I pulled a hard turn to starboard. I don't know how many G's I pulled, but it was a lot. Everything got dark when I was about halfway around the turn. I had to let off back pressure on the stick to keep from passing out. The 109 was about a quarter of the way around his turn. I pulled hard into a loop, and on my way down, he was dead in my sights. So, I let loose on him with about a four-second burst. I saw a few strikes, and smoke shot out of his engine. He rolled on his back and dived out of the fight."

Al was on the edge of his seat, "What happened then?"

"Well, I'd had enough of that nonsense, and La Calle was nowhere to be seen. I was alone, and that was not safe. I pulled a Split-S – that's where you roll inverted and then pull into a dive – to get out of there. I headed toward Madrid and our home field. When I landed, La Calle was already on the ground talking to the intelligence people. My airplane had several small holes in it, but no major damage. I left the *Mosca* with the ground crew and went to join La Calle."

Reb said, "That sounds like a hell of a lot of fun. Kind of like a quail hunt in South Georgia. You're walking along, and it's quiet. Then suddenly, a covey flies up, and you try to shoot a couple. I almost always miss. Too nervous, I guess. Mostly I try not to piss my pants from the shock."

Trip said, "Yeah, it's a lot like that, except these birds shoot back."

Chapter 13 – Summer of '39

Trip and Al Norham rode along on Whitehall Avenue, heading south to Stewart Avenue and Hapeville. From Hapeville, it was only a mile to the Atlanta Municipal Airport. The boys' hair blew in the wind with the top down on the Cabriolet. The mid-June weather was clear and warm.

Trip looked west and said, "Clouding up out toward Carrolton. We'll have to get the flying in quickly before those storms get here."

Al said, "Speaking of storms, did you see where Hitler and Mussolini signed a ten-year alliance last month? Now I saw where Germany signed non-aggression pacts with Latvia and Estonia the other day."

Trip said, "Yeah. I hope those keep down the chances of war."

Al snorted, "I think it increases the likelihood. It's getting stranger all the time. Hell, Hitler took the Sudetenland last year, and right before you came home, he finally took Czechoslovakia. Now, we're seeing these alliances and non-aggression pacts."

Trip said, "War is not a good thing, and I hope cooler heads prevail on this. I didn't like the invasions of Sudetenland and Czechoslovakia, but there was not much anyone could do about those. I hear Britain and France are not putting up with Hitler's talk about Poland."

Al said, "I don't know how scary that is for the Germans. Hitler keeps talking about Polish aggression. Hell, I think the Poles are too busy trying to survive being between Russia and Germany. Do you think the French can take on Hitler?"

"Absolutely! The French have quite an army. Bigger than the German Army. They have more tanks and plenty of planes. They also have the Maginot Line of forts all along the border with Germany."

Al said, "What did you think of the German planes?"

"Oh, now there, the Germans have something. The Bf-109 and the Stuka dive bomber are both very good airplanes. The 109 is probably the best fighter plane in the world. The Stuka puts fear in the hearts of the people on the ground. It has built-in sirens to add an alarming wail as it screams down in a dive. People panic at that sound. The Germans also have some good bombers – the He-111, for example."

"And you don't think they can defeat the French?"

"Naw! The French have a very good air force."

Al looked at Trip from the side, "So did the Spanish."

Trip said, "Different situation, Al."

~~<>~~

The old JN-4D Jenny purred like a kitten, and Trip delighted in flinging the little airplane around the sky. The Cessna tempted him, but that airplane was more of an airborne passenger car. At least with the Jenny, Trip could do rolls, spins, climbs, and dives. Loops were possible but required precise speeds and careful control to avoid stalling at the top and falling into a spin.

Certainly, the Jenny was not the powerful fighter plane that the *Mosca* was. Trip's Jenny had the 180 horsepower Hispano-Suiza engine. The *Mosca* was powered by a license-built 720 horsepower Wright 1830 engine. The difference in performance was startling, but Trip decided the Jenny was great fun to fly.

Wednesdays turned out to be good days to fly when the weather cooperated. The boys would all work to be free that afternoon. Even Al Norham managed Wednesday afternoons because the Bank was closed on Wednesdays and he worked with the station manager at WGST to have Wednesday as his day off.

Occasionally, Trip would bring Ellie or Kathy to the airport and take them flying. Kathy loved it, and Ellie shrieked with delight. On the days that Trip brought Kathy, Reb would get free and come down. Trip would get out of the cockpit and let Reb take Kathy for a ride.

Trip would head home and let Reb bring Kathy home later. Trip thought the hanger was a love nest for Reb and Kathy when no one was around. There was a small office that was largely unoccupied. The office had a small desk, some maintenance logs on the Jenny and Hank's Cub, a locked cabinet with tools and spare parts, a couple of chairs, and a rickety twin bed pushed against the wall. Trip smiled when he thought that Kathy and Reb, two complete opposites, might occupy the bed, making it squeak uncontrollably.

On the days Ellie joined him, Trip would take her back to his apartment and fry a steak in the old cast iron pan Edith had donated to his household goods. A baked potato in the oven and an Aviator Salad rounded out the meal.

Trip had read an article that Alex Cardini, an Italian flying ace of the Great War, invented a dressing of prepared mustard, egg yoke, oil, garlic, anchovies, lemon juice, Worcestershire Sauce, parmesan cheese, and salt and pepper. The *Maitre d'* at the Ansley Hotel restaurant told Trip that the Aviator Salad dressing was now called Caesar Dressing after Julius Caesar. No matter, Trip liked the idea that a flying ace had invented the dressing.

Trip and Ellie relished the steak, potato, and Aviator Salad with a bottle of burgundy. Then they made love. Ellie often said that flying both scared and excited her. She admitted to being quite randy on the way to Trip's apartment. Sometimes, she was ready to play before Trip could consider dinner. Trip never objected. The afternoon's romp in bed just added to their hunger at the table.

~~<>~~

The Summer of '39 wore on in the same pattern, and Trip was happy. He had a lovely woman, money, a productive job, a nice place to live, and no one was shooting at him. Nightmares of the concentration camp had faded, and Ellie had pushed Mildred Wright aside in Trip's heart. Still, Mildred would occasionally creep back into a dream and command Trip's attention.

The pattern only changed when the heat got so high that flying in the afternoon was impossible. The boys shifted to what they jokingly called the Dawn Patrol, after the movie released just a year earlier. Flying early in the day avoided the powerful thermals that developed later and would toss the Jenny and Cub around uncomfortably. Worse were the afternoon winds and thunderstorms that could be utterly disastrous for a small plane.

The Jenny carried 24 gallons of fuel; at 65 mph, she had an endurance of about two hours. But the Jenny was a handful of airplane, and the boys were usually ready to land after an hour.

Trip's logbook, one of the few things he salvaged from his exit from France, now reflected some 850 hours of flying time. A little over 350 of those hours were combat flying in Spain. Trip reflected on his nine months in Spain. It had not been hard to get the 350 hours of combat. Each mission was about one hour. He calculated that some 270 days of combat at one mission, often two per day, quickly rolled up that kind of record.

Trip was, by any account, an experienced combat flyer. He sometimes wondered if the U.S. Army Air Corps would be interested in him. It was something to consider. Although he was intent on completing his mechanical engineering degree, Trip often returned to the thought that the sky was truly his home. That, too, was something to consider.

~~<>~~

One Wednesday evening in early August, the four boys hung around at Trip's apartment after flying. They were drinking beer and joking around. Trip had two roasted chickens in the refrigerator and a big bowl of potato salad he bought at Harry's Delicatessen. Trip had made some Aviator Salad. The gang would have a feast. A poker game was likely the late-evening entertainment.

Reb said, "I heard they're making a movie of *Gone With the Wind*. I saw in the paper that they's gonna have the premier downtown sometime this fall. I hope them Hollywood assholes don't make out the South as a bunch o' dumbasses. We shoulda' won."

Hank grinned, "Hell, Reb. You think the South should be its own country, still. But I don't think it would have worked out. We don't have diddly for industry. Ain't nobody makin' money from farmin', either. Shoot, 'bout half the farms around Macon clear cut the fields and let the rain wash off all the soil nutrients. Ain't much cotton growin' these days."

Reb said, "Shoot, I know. But it weren't right, them Damn Yankees comin' down here and stealin' our silverware."

Al said, "The bank doesn't really have much money to lend, especially not to farmers. We wouldn't do much of that anyway; the banks down toward Macon are more farm banks. But times are still hard after the Depression."

Trip said, "What do you mean, "after." I think the Depression is still going on. I see lots of people out of work. The coloreds, especially."

Reb started to say something, but Trip cut him off. "They need work, too, Reb. We don't need more problems, and the Negroes shouldn't starve any more than the rest of us."

Reb said, "I don't want nobody to starve. It's jes they's lots o' white boys hurtin' for work, too."

Trip said, "It's a damn good thing slavery ended. Bad as farming is now, and with the depression, we'd have millions of slaves wandering the streets. We need to figure out how to get everybody a job."

Al said, "Virginia is no better. Norfolk is hurting because the war worries have reduced shipping."

Reb said, "That Goddamn Roosevelt! He's done give away ever' damn thang. An' now he's makin' war preparations. He got tha' Navy increased again last year. I saw that the Navy is gonna buy 3000 airplanes. Y'all want to fly, Navy's the place to go."

Al said, "Norfolk has a bunch of Navy bases. My Ma hasn't said anything about that growing. I think it's all on the West Coast."

Hank said, "I heard they moved the Pacific Fleet out to Hawaii."

Trip said, "I saw where the Nazis stopped all the Jewish doctors from getting licenses. Lots of doctors in Europe are Jews."

Hank said, "That's pretty stupid. But who knows? Maybe the Nazis got something with wanting to rebuild Germany."

Trip said, "Here's what you need to know about the Goddamn fascists. Yesterday that bastard Franco had thirteen women – *Las Trece Rosas* – executed. Their crime was aiding a military rebellion. Jesus! Franco is afraid of thirteen women?"

Reb said, "Wal, they's got a bunch o' stuff going on between them Pollocks and the Germans. That shit could turn into a fight."

Trip said, "Never underestimate fascists – Nazis – in what they might do. I got run out of France because the Franco government was looking to prosecute me as a war criminal."

Reb said, "Them Nazis is wors' than the Goddamn Yankees. I reckon they'll take over all of Europe if tha' Frenchies can't beat 'em."

Trip said, "I think the French can beat them.

Al said, "You know, I read the other day that as soon as Germany and Italy signed that alliance, Hitler said he wanted Poland.

Hank snorted, "I was in the Library the other day and saw in Collier's Magazine that Churchill thinks there'll be a war this year.

Trip said, "Please, God! Let that not come true."

Hank said, "Amen!"

Trip brightened, "Y'all ready for some chicken?"

Chapter 14 – War Winds

The heat pounded Atlanta unmercifully in the last week of August 1939. The boys didn't fly on Wednesday but went to the Varsity for dogs and fries.

The Varsity was as it had been since its founding ten years earlier, a small red brick building with a few stools and car service out back. The guys all laughed at Flossie Mae, the flamboyant car hop. Flossie May was a black man who wore insane hats and sang the menu.

Al said, "He sure is a hoot. He's been doing this ever since I got here."

Stuffed with dogs and fries, they walked to the Blue Lantern. Blind Willie McTell was still playing in the parking lot. A group of Negroes played craps in the alley just off the parking lot. The breeze moved the air but failed to cool anything off. The Lantern's interior was air-conditioned, and they sat at the Bar drinking beers and chatting.

The radio was blaring in the corner. Duke Ellington's new tune *The Sergeant Was Shy* was playing.

Hank said, "Damn if that tune doesn't sound like an Army bugle call. We're hearing nothing but military stuff these days."

Ray Lee, the owner of the Lantern, was tending bar. "Y'all better get used to it. The radio was saying Hitler's gonna invade Poland any day now. The French and English have said they won't put up with that shit."

Reb rolled his eyes, "Does anybody really give a damn about Poland?"

Al said, "Guess the French and British do."

Trip said, "Y'all have no idea how the Europeans get fired up about Germany. We can hope Hitler doesn't go into Poland, but it probably won't help. I'm pretty sure that if Hitler invades, the French will go to war immediately."

Two days later, Hitler's Wehrmacht charged into Poland. The invasion, supported by the German Air Force, the Luftwaffe, raced across Poland. The newspapers called it Blitzkrieg – Lightning War. The invasion of Poland on September 1st rushed the world toward war.

It was a harbinger of things. Two days later, Sunday the 3rd of September, Trip awoke to the radio blaring that Britain and France had declared war on Germany. He was depressed by this news but had a date with Ellie, so he showered and dressed. The Cabriolet purred all the way out to Ellie's apartment in Druid Hills.

Ellie answered the door. "My God, Trip, the news is terrible! The whole world will be at war. I heard someone say it will be called the Second World War. Do you think we'll get in it?"

Trip said, "I doubt it. The Neutrality Act is pretty strong about not getting involved."

Ellie's brow furrowed, "I don't know. It seems scary and inevitable."

Trip said, "Let's not worry about things that have not happened, Sweetheart. I thought we'd go to the Colonnade."

Ellie said, "That would be wonderful, but I think we should go to church, first. I'd like to pray for all those poor people in Poland."

Trip said, "Ok. Reverend Walker will be thrilled to see us."

Ellie asked, "Do you think he'll know we're, uh...I mean..."

Trip said, "Making love?"

Ellie nodded.

Trip joked, "It's written all over you, Sweetie."

Ellie looked stricken, "Really?"

"NO! I was just kidding. You look as pure as the driven snow, darling."

Church was the usual liturgical service, and the Colonnade was as near to heaven as food can get. Trip and Ellie went to Piedmont Park and walked a little way, but it was too hot to walk very far. So, they went to Trip's air-conditioned apartment, where they spent the afternoon listening to the radio and languidly making love.

Trip had some leftover beef in the refrigerator and made sandwiches. They sat on the couch and tuned the radio to hear the President's Fireside Chat. After some preliminaries, Roosevelt said,

> *You must master at the outset a simple but unalterable fact in modern foreign relations between nations. When peace has been broken anywhere, the peace of all countries everywhere is in danger.*
>
> *It is easy for you and for me to shrug our shoulders and to say that conflicts taking place thousands of miles from the continental United States, and, indeed, thousands of miles from the whole American Hemisphere, do not seriously affect the Americas-and that all the United States has to do is to ignore them and go about its own business. Passionately though we may desire detachment, we are forced to realize that every word that comes through the air, every ship that sails the sea, every battle that is fought, does affect the Americana future. Let no man or woman thoughtlessly or falsely talk of America sending its armies to European fields. At this moment there is being prepared a proclamation of American neutrality. This would have been done even if there had been no neutrality statute on the books, for this proclamation is in accordance with international law and in accordance with American policy.*

Later in the speech, Roosevelt said,

> *This nation will remain a neutral nation, but I cannot ask that every American remain neutral in thought as well. Even*

a neutral has a right to take account of facts. Even a neutral cannot be asked to close his mind or his conscience.

Trip said, "There, you see? We won't be getting involved with this."

Ellie said, "I don't trust him. That part about not asking that everyone remain neutral in thought scares me. It sounds like he's planning to get involved."

Trip said, "I think they're going to have a hard time repealing the neutrality laws, Sweetie."

"Huh! I'll bet that won't stop Roosevelt. I think he's devious."

Running his hand up her thigh, Trip said, "Hmm, I'm devious too. I think it's time for another invasion."

Ellie half-heartedly swatted at his hand. She turned and kissed him with unusual passion.

~~<>~~

It was 9 p.m. when Trip saw Ellie to her door. Tomorrow was the first day of school for each of them. Trip would start classes at Tech, and Ellie's school year would be starting.

Driving back to the Biltmore, Trip wondered about the president's speech. He thought that Ellie might be right, Roosevelt seemed to create an opportunity for the United States to enter the war.

Trip lay in his bed and smelled Ellie's hair on the pillow. The bed was still warm from her body. He smiled as he thought of her. He was in love with her. He wondered if he loved her enough to be with her for the rest of their lives.

His mind ranged to the days in Spain. Those days were filled with danger and frantic activity, but the thrill of air combat was undeniable. Trip admitted to himself that he would go back to combat flying if he could.

He lay considering these weighty matters a thought surfaced, *God help me, but I loved flying fighter planes in combat. Even when I thought I would die, I loved it.*

As sleep pulled him down into the depths, Robert Harney Gibson, III, realized that war was inevitable for the United States. It was a strangely comforting thought.

Chapter 15 – Georgia School of Technology

Trip parked his Cabriolet by Grant Field and glanced up at Harris' third floor. No lights on. He figured the guys were all gone to class. He was due for his first class in an hour, so he went to the small café in the base of the Tech Tower – the main administrative building of the Georgia School of Technology. As he walked up to the building he glanced up at the tower and grinned. One side still read "ECH", the T having been stolen some time past and never replaced.

The little café, called The Robbery by one and all, was a good place to grab a breakfast of eggs, bacon, grits (or hashbrown potatoes for the Yankees), and coffee. The entire meal was 40 cents, and worth every penny.

Breakfast done, Trip lit a cigarette and sat back to look at his schedule. Thank God he had dodged Saturday classes, but his schedule was packed. He ran his eye down the list of classes:

      EE   225 – Electrical Circuits and Fields

      ESM   308 – Dynamics

      ME   322 – Thermodynamics

      ME   342 – Transport Phenomena I

      ME   312 – Materials Technology

With the associated laboratory classes, he would be taking 18 credits. That was a respectable load. Trip knew he'd have to buckle down and study for a change. This would be a challenging quarter for a man who had been away from mathematics and science for a couple of years.

He reflected that he was adaptable to stress after changing airfields every other day and flying combat against professional killers day-in, day-out, not to mention spending time in French jails and a concentration camp. Nonetheless, he would have to dig deep to make at least a B in these courses. A's were desirable, but every Tech Man knew that a B was highly respectable.

He crushed out his cigarette and left the Robbery, heading toward the Mechanical Engineering building. His first class was Thermodynamics – all about heat, work, and temperature. As he walked the short distance, he thought, *I'd rather be flying.*

Hank Overton was lounging in one of the utterly uncomfortable desks, his legs sprawled in the aisle. "Look who made it to class!"

Trip said, "Jesus, I drank too much wine last night. I ate something at the Robbery but still feel like hell."

Reb Clayton walked in and dropped his book on a desk, "You look it, boy. We flyin' on Wednesday?"

Trip's eyes went into the distance, "Hell, no. I got classes until two o'clock. The storms will be brewing by the time we get out and drive down there. Can't go on Saturdays with the football games coming up. Probably have to plan on Sundays, now."

Hank said, "Dang, that'll slow me down on chasing Leona."

Trip snorted, "I'm sure you'll figure it out."

Reb said, "I'll refrain from mentioning chasing your sister around."

Trip grinned, "Thanks. Saves me the effort of whuppin' your ass."

Reb said, "Shiiiiiit, boy. You'd have to work out for a year first."

Hank said, "Don't know about that. He's a seasoned warrior of the skies."

Reb shifted his tobacco chaw and smirked, "Requires an airplane for that, my boy."

~~<>~~

96

The war news was a constant drumbeat of Nazi victories. September 4th the Netherlands and Belgium declared neutrality. The radio announcer on WSB excitedly reported that the British Royal Air Force had bombed German warships off the Northern Coast of Germany.

The announcer turned more somber when reported the sinking of the *SS Athena*, a passenger liner bound from England to the United States, Many Americans had been lost at sea. Many European refugees were among the passengers, and the death toll was yet to be fully counted.

On September 6th, South Africa rejected neutrality and declared war on Germany. Egypt followed suit in declaring war on Germany on the same day.

Sunday, September 17th, Trip, Reb, and Hank were all studying for a Thermodynamics test – a quiz, in Georgia Tech slang. They should have been studying, but war news dominated the conversation.

Reb said, "I jes heard them Nazis sank a British aircraft carrier. HMS Courageous, I think."

Trip's heart sank. He said, "Air power is critical to the British. I hope the Germans don't start bombing cities. I saw the remnants after the bombing of Guernica and Barcelona. Those were both terrible, murderous attacks. And the damned Nazis did both of those."

Hank said, "I saw something in the paper a couple days ago about the Germans killing Jews in Poland."

Reb said, "Lak Ah said, them Nazis is worse' than the damn Yankees. At least the damn Yankees weren't shooting us."

On the 27th, the Luftwaffe firebombed Warsaw, and the city surrendered. To round out a stressful month of terrible news, on September 30th, the British started evacuating citizens from London in anticipation of war.

Trip saw this as an ominous sign. He didn't know any British people, but his experience of Spain said there would be years of misery for them. He had an impulse to go to England and volunteer. He knew it was futile. He glumly thought, *I'd probably be arrested if I tried to go.*

On Friday, October 6th Hitler denied he would go to war against England and France. Hitler threatened a solution to what he called the Jewish Problem. The day brought the sad news that the last Polish Army units had surrendered. The war in Poland was over. Trip thought, *Yeah, and if it wasn't bad enough already, now the hell begins for the Polish people.*

~~<>~~

Trip took Ellie to the Georgian Terrace for a casual dinner and then to the Ansley Hotel Ballroom for dancing.

During one of the orchestra breaks, Ellie said, "You seem subdued tonight, Trip."

Trip looked into the distance, "Aw, I'm ok. It's just that the war news bothers me. I saw where the British were beginning evacuations. I'd hate to see London bombed like Guernica or Barcelona."

Ellie looked stricken, "You're thinking about going back and fighting again, aren't you."

"Some. But I'd get arrested. So, no sense even considering it."

A tear streaked down Ellie's face, leaving a track in her carefully applied makeup. "For a moment there, I thought you were going to say you didn't want to leave me."

Trip was lost in thought. "Oh, I don't want to leave you. I've had the best few months. It's just that sometimes I feel kind of selfish having a good time when I know good people are standing up to Hitler."

Ellie's face fell, and her eyes locked on her little clutch bag on the table. "But, Trip...I...uh, I've committed to you. I'm afraid you'll leave me and never come back."

Trip looked across the dance floor, "Sometimes, I miss flying and the excitement of combat."

Ellie raised her voice, "The *excitement* of combat?!"

Trip had a far-away look. "Yeah."

"Yeah? Yeah? That's all you can say. Getting shot at and maybe killed excites you? Jesus, Trip! I have this empty place in my stomach right now."

Trip came back from wherever it was, "Huh? Are you feeling all right, Sweetheart?"

"I'm fine. You're the one who's sick! Take me home."

It was a quiet ride out Ponce de Leon Avenue to Decatur and Ellie's apartment. Trip parked and got out to walk Ellie to the door.

Ellie looked at him hard, "You don't care about me. You don't care about anything, including yourself. All you want to do is to fly airplanes and let the excitement wash over you every time you cheat death! You say you care about the people on the ground in England. I think that's just an excuse."

Trip said, "I...uh, I love you, Ellie."

"No, you don't. You love flying."

"Well, I do love flying, but it's not the same as how I feel about you."

Ellie stuck her key in the door, "That's absolutely right. It's not the same. You love flying more than anything. Good night, Trip."

Trip stood in front of the now-closed door to Ellie's apartment. Feeling forlorn, Trip thought, *I hope she didn't just close the door to us.*

~~<>~~

October 7th brought an infuriating defeat of Georgia Tech by Notre Dame. The game was broadcast on WGST, and the four boys sat around Reb's dorm room listening.

The announcer was running down the last moments of the game. "Aannnd, that's it Ladies and Gentlemen. The game is over with the score Notre Dame 17- Tech 14. Today's game has been brought to you by Barbasol..."

Hank snapped off the radio in disgust.

Reb boiled over, "God DAMN it! I hate them damn Yankees from Notre Dame. They's always badmouthin' us, an' talkin' about how they's all Knute Rockne and all that about Tha' Gipper. Whoever heard a' anybody called Tha' Gipper?"

Al said, "Coulda' won, too. I hate losing by a field goal."

Trip said, "I think Ellie broke up with me last night."

In unison, the other three boys said, "What?!"

"Yep. She said I love flying more than I love her."

Hank said, "That's not true, its it? I mean, you love flying, but that's different."

"I tried to tell her that, but she was having none of it. Truthfully, I've been a little distracted since Hitler invaded Poland. I keep thinking about how the people on the ground are being bombed and strafed. Their homes destroyed, loved ones killed..." He trailed off.

Al asked, "You thinking about going back to Europe and flyin' for France or Britain?"

"Truth? I'd go in an instant. But with the neutrality laws, I'd probably just get arrested. I tried to tell Ellie that."

Reb said, "Jesus, son, that's not sufficiently sensitive." His mouth made a little bow, indicating mockery of the word sensitive. "You gotta let yore woman think she's tha' center o' yore universe, boy. You done let Ellie think she's number two to a damn airplane."

Trip was miserable. "I suppose so. Maybe I ought to drive out there and tell her she's number one."

Hank quietly said, "Only if it's true, Trip. If it's not, she'll know and she'll hate you for it."

Chapter 16 – Fall and Rise Again

Fall Quarter plodded along with classes, quizzes, football games, and flying.

Tech surprised everyone by having a championship season. After the first game's ignominious loss to Notre Dame, Trip and the boys delighted in victories throughout October. They went to every game in Grant Field, watching the Yellow Jackets beat Howard, Vanderbilt, and Auburn in succession.

October turned out to be a good month. The Jackets were winning, Trip was making a solid A in Electrical Circuits and Fields, courtesy of his summer at Westinghouse. He was looking at solid A's in the Materials Technology and Thermodynamics classes. The others were at least B's.

Trip's loss of Ellie remained a cloud over him. The cloud was darkened by the news that a German U-Boat had torpedoed and sunk the HMS Royal Oak. Trip was alarmed by the loss of another British aircraft carrier.

November 4th brought a one-point loss to Duke, made more painful by being at home in Grant Field. After the 7-6 disappointment, the gang walked across the street to Reb's room and had an illicit drink of whiskey made all the sweeter because the dorm counselors were oblivious.

Reb said, "I done said this before, but we ain't shit when it comes to kickin' a field goal!"

Al repeated his lament from the Notre Dame game, "I hate to lose by a field goal!"

Trip sat in the corner sipping his straight liquor in a glass, ice being an impossible commodity in the dorms. "This Four Roses is damn good Bourbon, Reb."

Reb smirked, "O' course it's damn good. We Son's of the Confederacy don't drank none of that Yankee piss. I damn shore ain't drankin' that Limey scotch. That stuff tastes like somebody's dirty ol' dishrag."

Hank said, "You've been pretty quiet lately, Trip."

"Sorry. I've been kinda low since Ellie dumped me."

Hank asked, "Did you go talk to her?"

"No. You said don't go lie to her that she's number one if she isn't. I have been over that a thousand times, and I think we wouldn't ever get beyond my love for flying."

Reb said, "Waal, get over it then, and move on, boy."

Trip said, "Did y'all see where the Royal Oak was sunk? That's another British aircraft carrier gone." He glumly looked out the window at the lawn in front of Brittain Dining Hall. The grass had gone brown from the cold nights, and the trees were now leafless sticks, rattling in the breeze. The view matched his mood.

~~<>~~

The next week, the Yellow Jackets started a streak that included beating Kentucky at home, Alabama in Birmingham, and the Gators at Florida Field in Gainesville, Florida.

Thanksgiving was quite a feast at the Gibson home, and Al was invited to join in because he couldn't afford the train ticket to Norfolk.

Two days later, the year's big game was, of course, against the University of Georgia. Trip was sad because he would have enjoyed teasing Ellie about her school, even if she didn't care a thing about football. But she was not present. The other fellows all had their girlfriends to the game. Al was too poor to afford a girlfriend, so he and Trip sat slightly apart while Reb and Kathy sat with Hank and Leona.

They all sang *I'm a Ramblin' Wreck from Georgia Tech* at the top of their lungs with every score and whenever the band drum major decided the crowd needed to be pepped up. That was often, and the group all were hoarse by the end of the game.

At least twice, George P. Burdell, a fictitious Georgia Tech student, was paged over the loudspeaker. This brought peals of laughter from everyone in the Tech bleachers. Georgia went down to defeat, 13-0, and every Tech man was delighted to yell, "To Hell with Georgia!"

The group went to the Varsity with about 20,000 other Tech fans who traveled from around the south. At the Varsity, everyone sang *Ramblin' Wreck* more or less on key. Getting a hot dog that day took forever, but no one cared. Trip knew he would remember this day for the rest of his life. Little did he know that the winds of war were blowing his way, and sooner than for others.

~~<>~~

Trip went to the Airport the first week in December and tooled around the sky in his Jenny. It was great fun, and Trip felt free. These past several months "free" was not a word Trip used about himself.

But today, he felt free. His exams were done, and he knew he had done well. He thought, *At least a 3.5, maybe better*.

And he was flying his airplane which always made him feel unfettered. He pulled some Gs going up and over the top in a loop, stood the little plane on its wingtip, and roared in a wild turn. He rolled the little Jenny, tossing and playing with her like making love to the airplane. Too soon, it was time to land and put his faithful companion away. Trip realized that Jenny was a true love. A tiny note of sadness crept in as Trip went about his post-flight check.

He also admitted to himself that he was free of Ellie. She had dumped him because she knew he loved flying, and she was jealous of Jenny, the airplane. Or maybe she was afraid he would leave her for flying. He still had pangs of sadness and self-loathing for not doing more to keep Ellie happy.

After he rolled the faithful little airplane into the hangar, he went by the main operations building to pay his hangar rent. He was idly reading announcements on the bulletin board when he saw this small posting:

> *Pilots with at least 300 hours, a CAA Pilot's Rating, and a sense of adventure are requested to contact Clyde Pangborn, Oakland, California. KEllog 3300.*

Trip stood transfixed, looking at the bulletin board. *Clyde Pangborn! Sense of adventure...wonder what this is about?*

Trip had no paper, but he used his pen to write on the back of his hand, "Pangborn, KEllog 3300, Oakland." Trip ran upstairs and paid a full year's rent on the hangar. At $15 per month, it was the tidy sum of $180. Trip did not care. His mind was racing. *Wonder what Clyde Pangborn might want.*

Trip was excited that he might be able to speak to *the* Clyde Pangborn, the man who barnstormed at the Atlanta Airport when Trip was about 10. Clyde Pangborn, the man who gave Trip his first ride in an airplane. Pop had paid $10 for that privilege. Clyde Pangborn, the man who had inspired Trip's love of flying ever since that magical day in 1926.

Trip drove the Deluxe Eight all the way to the Biltmore without noticing the traffic. He tossed the keys to the valet in the parking garage and pushed the elevator button six or eight times, impatient to get to his apartment.

~~<>~~

Once inside the apartment door, Trip slowed down. *Calm down, Trip! Wash your face. Pour yourself a drink. Gather your wits.*

He did things in reverse order. Four Roses Bourbon on the Rocks: *Check.* Face washed: *Check.* Wits gathered: *Check.* Well, not really, but close. Deep breath: *Check.* Calm. *Not really, but better than when I walked in the door.*

Trip sat on the brown chenille sofa and picked up the phone. Sticking his finger in the "O", he dragged the dial all the way around and let it go.

The dial made a Zizzzzz sound as it whirled around and stopped.

A nasal voice in Trip's ear said, "Operator"

Trip said, "Yes, Operator. Long distance. Oakland, California. KEllog 3300."

Nasal twang, "One moment, ple-uzz."

Trip fidgeted as a full minute passed. Then, brrrrp, brrrrp, brrrrp.

"Clyde Pangborn."

Trip almost couldn't speak, "Uh, h..hello, Mr. Pangborn? This is Robert Gibson."

Pangborn's voice had a note of impatience, "And..."

"Uh, well, I'm in Atlanta, and I saw your posting at the Municipal Airport. I think I meet the requirements."

"You say your name is Gibson?"

"Yes, Sir. Robert, uh Trip, Gibson."

"Wait, did you say Trip Gibson?"

"Yes."

"I'll be damned. Is this the Trip Gibson that was in Spain?"

Trip was a little wary. "Maybe. Why do you ask?"

Pangborn said, "Don't worry. I'm not a Fed, and I'm buying that this is really Trip Gibson."

"Ok. How do you know about me?"

"Hell, Son. Salty Tinker told me about you. Said you got out of Spain just ahead of being put up against a wall."

Trip said, "I hadn't thought of Salty for a while. I assume he got out because you've talked to him, too."

Pangborn said, "Oh, I talked to him all right. He got out of Spain about the time you were getting in. Had lots of bad nightmares and other shell-shock kinds of things. He was getting over that. Wrote some articles that got published. Tried to get into the Navy or the Army. Got rejected."

Trip said, "What's he doing now?"

"Pushing up daisies in a cemetery in Arkansas. Blew his brains out in a hotel room in Little Rock last June."

Trip couldn't breathe. It felt like an elephant was sitting on his chest. "Why would he do that?"

"Good question, Kid. The FBI was hounding him about neutrality and such. Haven't they been after you?"

"No, but the U.S. Embassy got me out of a French concentration camp and got me back here. So, maybe the Feds are not interested in me. Salty was a big celebrity, I guess."

Pangborn said, "Yeah, I guess. Sorry I was the guy to hit you with that."

Trip said, "I'm sorry to hear it. We weren't really friends. As you said, he was leaving Spain about the time I got there."

Pangborn said, "Look, I can't say a lot on the phone. I work for the Sweeny organization. Colonel Charles Sweeny's group are doing some interviews in Chicago. If you're interested, bring your passport, birth certificate, pilots license, and logbooks to the Chicago Navy Pier next Wednesday at 3 pm. Look for a guy in a white fedora. Say Clyde sent you."

Trip said, "OK."

"And Kid, pack for a long trip if you want to do what you were doing in Spain. Keep it to one suitcase, no steamer trunks. Don't say nothin' to nobody. The Feds are all over this kind of shit. Got it?"

"Yep. Got it. And, Mr. Pangborn, thank you. You took me for a ride in 1926, it's why I love to fly."

"Yeah, Kid. I'd say I remember, but I've flown a lot of snot-nose kids in my time. Remember, Wednesday, the 13th. White fedora. Mum's the word."

Trip said, "Thanks," but the line was dead.

~~<>~~

Trip went down to the school and found that Hank and Reb had left for the Christmas break. Al was still there, but he was packing.

"Where are you going?"

Al said, "I don't know, exactly. Gotta move out of the dorms because I'm not enrolled in the Winter quarter. I gotta work and make money."

Trip said, "Today's your lucky day."

Al said, "Huh?"

Trip said, "I'm going away. I've paid a year's rent. You can live in my place."

Al said, "Uh, thanks. I'm a little concerned about you going away. You're not coming back?"

Trip said, "Best I don't tell you too much. I'm taking my passport and logbook, if you get my drift. I want you to take care of the Jenny."

Al said, "Jesus, Trip. You're going to get killed."

"Not if I see them first."

Chapter 17 – Chicago

Trip was glad he brought his heavy dark blue overcoat. Atlanta rarely called for such heavy winter wear. The wind off Lake Michigan at the Navy Pier was making a 26-degree day even colder, and Trip thought his eyelids might freeze shut. He jammed a pair of Ray-Ban aviator sunglasses on and pulled his gold wool muffler up so that a tiny slit showed in front of his eyes. The Ray Bans started to fog up, so he pulled the muffler open a tad. He smiled to himself. *Good thing the muffler was on the hanger with this coat!*

Trip was also delighted to find a pair of rabbit fur-lined gloves in the coat pockets. The soft-as-butter pigskin gloves with the rabbit lining were almost too warm, even in this weather. He last wore this ensemble during a freezing-cold football game at Grant Field in 1936. Still, from his knees to his ankles, he was cold. So much for the lightweight French wool suit.

The late afternoon was already getting dark as Trip walked down the pier looking for a man in a white Fedora. The brim of his brown fedora fluttered in the wind off the lake, and the hat threatened to blow away. Trip had his suitcase in one hand and held his hat in place with the other.

He tromped along, every step colder as the wind cut under his coat and crept up toward his thighs. His eyes teared a little, and he hoped the cold air wouldn't freeze the tears. As he walked, he reflected on the past few days.

The phone call to Clyde Pangborn was a lark, but Trip realized he called because he was truly interested in adventure. School proved as dull as it had been two years before. Sure, a degree was important, but it seemed not so critical just now. Maybe later...if there was a later.

Trip packed everything he thought he might need, but nothing he would miss if it were lost. His last valise, with his few scraps of clothing, a couple of letters, a carton of cigarettes, and a few toiletries, had been confiscated and not returned. That experience reminded him to carry his passport, money, and flying logbook on his person. These items were in a money belt under his shirt and in his pockets as he clomped along on the Navy Pier.

He was happy that Al could stay in his apartment at the Biltmore. This was a small kindness to his perennially broke friend, and it was a good deal for Trip. No need to go through the rigamarole paying for breaking a lease. Nope. Al would live there for a year, rent-free. Trip paid ahead.

In return, Trip asked Al three favors. First: he was to wire $1500 from the Trip's account at the Southern Bank and Trust to the Chicago National Bank in care of Robert Harney Gibson, III. Second, Al was to call Kathy Gibson and invite her to meet him at the Biltmore on December 14th, where he would give her the keys to Trip's car. He was to tell her that Trip had gone to war and not to worry. Al was to give her a letter from Trip to her and her parents. Aside from telling the fellows that Trip was gone, Al's final favor, and the most difficult one, was to ask Kathy to drive him out to Druid Hills where he would deliver Trip's letter to Ellie. Trip knew that Al was an absolutely loyal friend and would do these three tasks or die trying.

He spent Saturday planning his trip and packing a single suitcase. He had his birth certificate from his last trip to Europe along with his passport. He reviewed his logbook showing almost 850 hours of flying time, over 350 as a combat pilot in Spain. He made sure to include his certificate as a pilot qualified to fly a two-seat airplane.

He went to Union Station a couple blocks west of Five Points and bought his ticket on the Dixie Flyer. One-way, Atlanta to Chicago. First Class. Sleeper.

Monday, December 11, 1939, was a momentous day for Trip. He arrived via taxi at Union Station at 8 a.m. and walked casually toward the platform, suitcase in hand, overcoat over his arm.

The Dixie Flyer chugged into the station at 8:50 a.m. and stopped with a loud hiss. The Pullman porter showed Trip to his stateroom, placed his suitcase in the small closet and accepted a quarter for his trouble. Trip settled into his sumptuous, polished oak paneled accommodation and opened the morning paper – the Atlanta Constitution. On the outside, Trip was studied calm; inside, he quaked with anticipation, sadness, joy, and a little fear.

At precisely 9 a.m., Trip flicked down the page he was reading and watched Union Station, Platform 7, begin slowly moving by. Trip glanced at the Atlanta cityscape as the train smoothly headed from the Southland to America's Second City. Trip Gibson was on his way back to combat flying, and he smiled for the first time in weeks.

Trip enjoyed the service on the *Dixie Flyer*. The dining car had excellent food. Trip enjoyed the roast beef hash with a poached egg (65¢), asparagus (15¢), and green goddess salad (10¢). Lunch added up to a dollar with Trip's 10-cent tip.

The *Flyer* rumbled north through Chattanooga and Nashville where the *Dixie Flyer* Pullmans were sidetracked briefly as the North Carolina and St Louis Railway company's locomotives picked them up for the next leg of the trip. The day wore on as the *Flyer* chugged toward St Louis, Missouri, where yet another locomotive change was required.

Dinner was reasonably priced with a broiled tenderloin steak, potato, small salad, and dessert. Red wine was expensive at 70¢. Trip thought the 70¢ was well spent and bought the bottle for $3.00. It was an extravagance.

Trip thought, *What the hell? Why not? 'We who are about to die, salute you.' Isn't that what the Roman gladiators all said?*

A few minutes later, Trip quietly murmured, "Goodbye, Ellie. I do love you. I'm so sorry."

In St Louis, Trip got an evening paper and read it thoroughly. It got dark early, and Trip went to bed. He slept until about 5 a.m. when the porter passed in the corridor announcing the time. Trip washed his face, shaved, changed his underwear, and donned a fresh shirt.

Trip took breakfast in the dining car. He was delighted with a half-dozen fried oysters (40¢), bacon, and eggs (60¢), plain toast (10¢), and coffee (10¢). The eggs were perfectly cooked to over medium, and the bacon was not overdone like razor blades. The oysters were his splurge, and Trip thought that $1.40 with tip was a very fair price for such an excellent breakfast. *Who knows when I'll see oysters again?*

Trip sorted his suitcase and was ready to leave when the train pulled into Chicago's Dearborn Station very close to the scheduled 7:45 a.m. arrival time. A taxi deposited Trip at the Drake Hotel, one of Chicago's finest. Trip thought, *What the hell? May as well stay at the best place. If my time in Spain is any indication, I may not see a decent place to sleep for several months.*

Trip rang the bellman and asked for a map of the city. While he rested from the journey, Trip checked the map and learned that the Chicago National Bank was only two blocks away. The Navy Pier, built in 1916 for recreation and shipping, was a beautiful Beaux Arts structure only about a mile from the Drake. Now, Trip had his bearings.

At Noon, Trip went to the Drake's dining room where he was impressed with the extensive menu. Not hungry after his breakfast and feeling a bit low after leaving Atlanta without saying goodbye to his sister, parents, or Ellie, he picked at a small piece of salmon on a bed of lettuce with some kind of sauce.

Trip visited the bank and picked up his money. $1500 in large bills, which he carefully secreted in several places on his person. He had wired the funds to avoid traveling on a public conveyance with a large sum of cash. He thought this especially true if one planned to sleep on said conveyance.

Even though it was only two blocks, Trip took a taxi back to the Drake. He thought, *Best not walk around with that kind of cash.*

Once in his room, Trip put fourteen $100 bills into his money belt. He put the other $100 in smaller bills in a couple of pockets and rolled up a $20 bill in each sock.

He kept to his room the rest of the day, only venturing out to take a cab ride to the Navy Pier long enough to know the layout. Trip trusted Clyde Pangborn but was concerned that perhaps not everyone involved in this enterprise would be as forthright.

Trip ate a solid lunch and rested until 2:30 p.m. on the 13th, when he checked out and took a cab to the Pier.

Chapter 18 – Canada

Trip lit a cigarette and got his bearings. He walked along the frigid, nearly deserted Navy Pier looking for a man in a white fedora. Some mist was forming from where the warmth of heat vents met the cold, moist air. It was from such a misty corner that the man in the white fedora materialized.

Trip paused and looked around. There was no one else.

White Fedora said, "You Gibson?"

Trip nodded.

"Come with me."

Trip's heart was pounding as they walked down the pier to a building that backed up to pilings and a dock.

White Fedora said, "There's a boat just down there. Please go aboard."

Trip asked, "Where's it going?"

Fedora said, "Canada. Best you don't know details. The Feds are all over the place watching for Americans going to Canada to join up and fight. They take a dim view of that. If you get arrested, best you don't know much."

Trip nodded. "Thanks."

White Fedora said, "Hope you survive. This ain't fun and games."

Trip nodded and followed Fedora's directions to find a good-sized Great Lakes turtleback tugboat. It had an enclosed cabin over a powerful, 70-foot steel hull designed to break the pack ice on Lake Michigan.

Mindful that sound carries over water, Trip quietly said, "Ahoy, the boat."

An equally quiet voice said, "Please come aboard."

Trip walked down a gangway and then into the passenger cabin of the tug. He was delighted to be out of the wind.

The man who had invited him aboard said, "Name?"

"Robert Gibson."

The man jerked his head at what might loosely be termed a lounge. It was a small space with a few chairs bolted to the deck. Two other men were already sitting there. One was tall and slim with a Clark Gable mustache and dark wavy hair. The other was very small, with a shock of sandy hair and a sharp face. Trip thought the little one could easily be a jockey. Trip nodded a greeting to the two and immediately thought, *Mutt and Jeff.*

When neither rose nor spoke, Trip let it go and sat down. He lit another cigarette and leaned back. Exhaling the unfiltered smoke, Trip tried to relax. His fingers shook slightly.

A fourth man clambered down the gangway and into the cabin. The mate at the end of the cabin said, "Let's keep it quiet, eh?"

Trip overheard the name: Tobin.

Tobin walked to a chair, and Mutt said, "Hey, Red."

Tobin grinned, "Good to see you got here, too, Andy."

The boat rocked slightly as a deckhand ran around, untying the lines. The engine suddenly sounded louder, and the boat lurched as it pulled away from the pier. The engine rumbled, and Trip felt the surge as the boat headed into Lake Michigan.

White Fedora came down the gangway and into the cabin.

Mutt asked, "Where are we going?"

Fedora said, "I will let you know when we're out of range of being stopped by the Coast Guard. Meanwhile, there are some bunks

118

through the passageway there. We have a long trip of about 20 hours, maybe more. So, enjoy the ride and rest when you want."

Trip was happy that he had a magazine in his suitcase. At least he wouldn't be bored. He lit a third cigarette in the last half hour, let the pungent smoke trickle out of his nose, and opened the magazine. He tried to ignore the tug's rumble and wallow.

After a solid hour of swaying and bucking in the swell, the engine sound changed to a more insistent, muted roar, and the boat smoothed out. Everyone looked up with alarm when an occasional loud clang resonated through the boat. The mate at the end of the cabin said, "Ice floes."

Jeff, the smaller man said in a distinctly New Jersey accent, "Ain't that what sank the Titanic?"

The mate said, "The Titanic hit an iceberg. These are just chunks of ice about the size of a car. The bow is heavily reinforced. They are no problem for this boat."

Jeff looked dubious but didn't say anything else.

~~<>~~

The hours wore on, and finally, the tall one – Mutt – stood up and said, "I'm Andy Mamedoff. This is Shorty Keough."

Trip stood, "Trip Gibson."

The third man stood, "Gene Tobin. Everybody calls me Red."

That was obvious to Trip – Gene Tobin was quite a ginger with florid skin to match the red hair.

They all shook hands and grinned sheepishly at one another.

Trip smirked, "Don't know what all the secrecy is about."

Mamedoff said, "This is our third try, me and Red. Got turned around at the border over toward Toronto last month. FBI was there."

Keough said, "Tricky bastards, too. When I went over the first time, one of them welcomed us to Canada and the RCAF. When I said thanks, they piped up and said, "This is still the USA," and that I needed to turn my ass right around and go back where I came from."

Mamedoff said, "Of course, Shorty being the banty rooster, said, "Who the hell are you?""

Keough laughed. "They told me they were FBI, and if they ever saw me again, I was going straight to jail. I'm kind of recognizable, ya' know?"

Everyone had a laugh at that. Vernon Keough was maybe five feet tall, thus the nickname Shorty.

Soon, they were swapping life stories. Gene Tobin and Andy Mamedoff had been flying buddies in Southern California. Shorty Keough had been doing barnstorming, mostly parachuting, to make a buck. All three of them had hundreds of flying hours.

Mamedoff turned to look at Trip. "What about you, Trip?"

Trip gave them a brief history.

"Spain, eh? What was that like?"

Trip said, "It all seems great fun until two things happen. First, your airplane – and maybe you – get hit. Second, one of your squadron mates gets killed."

They all nodded, but Trip could see they didn't understand. *Hell, why not? Nobody knows what it's like until they hear the sound of gravel being thrown at a metal roof and realize that's the sound of machine gun bullets hitting their airplane. They'll find out.*

Trip said, "Getting shot at is part of the bargain. So are aircraft accidents. People forget to fly the airplane because they're too busy trying not to get killed or to kill the other guy. Then, they hit the ground. Lots of stuff happening at once."

Again, the other three nodded. Trip thought, *They'll get it.*

Trip said, "I'm glad to be with the group here. Y'all have plenty more flying hours than I do."

Andy Mamedoff said, "Yeah, but that's no substitute for being there."

Trip said, "I hope we get there before the French beat the Germans and end this thing. This sounds funny, but I've missed flying a fighter plane in combat."

Tobin said, "I don't know how I feel about combat. I just want to fly, and that's where the flying is."

Shorty Keough nodded, "I'd still be in Southern California, but one of my friends wrecked my plane, and I'm broke as hell. On my last try to get into Canada, they gave me a train ticket and $5. That wasn't bad, but five bucks don't go far nowadays."

Trip grinned; he didn't mention that he had money.

~~<>~~

The tugboat rode on, occasionally clanging against an ice floe. The wind whistled around the deck house that sat above the turtle back Trip finished his magazine and handed it to Red Tobin, who nodded his thanks.

They extinguished their cigarettes one by one and went down the corridor to find a bunk. Trip grinned when he got there to see that at least Keough had taken a top bunk, leaving the slightly roomier bottom bunks for Mamedoff and Trip. Tobin was last in, and had to suffer with the other top bunk.

There was a small washroom, and Trip urinated for the first time in hours, brushed his teeth, and washed his face. He didn't like the look of his eyes in the dim light. Trip settled into the bunk and found that the buck and jerk of the boat were easier to tolerate while horizontal. He drifted off to sleep.

121

~~<>~~

Trip jerked awake to the change in vibration as the tug's engine slowed and the boat took on a different wallow and dip motion. The others woke and sat up, Tobin banging his head on the overhead. Trip jammed his feet into his shoes and went to the main cabin to tie them. He lit a cigarette and waited in case there was some news. He didn't have to wait long.

The mate came into the cabin and said, "We're turning to go through the Mackinac Straits and into Lake Huron. Won't be long before we're in Canadian waters, eh."

The boat maneuvered, perhaps avoiding shoals, before making a discernable turn to port and resuming the steady engine roar that lulled Trip to sleep several hours earlier. The others came into the lounge, lighting cigarettes and flopping into chairs.

Mamedoff snorted, "Damn long ride, this."

White Fedora came into the lounge and said, "There are some sandwiches in the refrige in the galley just through this passageway. It'll probably be about three more hours of riding this delightful bucket, and we'll dock in Sault Ste Marie. Well, near it anyway. From there, you'll take a train to Ottawa and then to Montreal. After that, I don't know. You'll check into the Mount Royal Hotel and await instructions."

Everyone nodded. They were more than ready to get off the tug and get on dry land that didn't wallow, swing, plunge, and clang into ice floes.

Trip ate a stale ham and cheese sandwich. A bottle of beer from the refrigerator washed the dry bread down. He smiled to himself, *Not bad. Beats the rotted swill at Argelès.*

~~<>~~

The train chugged into Ottawa Union Station at midnight, and four very tired aviators searched for a grill room or some kind of food.

They were delighted to find a small grill that was still open. Trip ordered *poutine* and was delighted with the gravy-covered French fries and cheese curds. He got a cup of strong coffee.

The other fellows ordered burgers or fish and chips. The burgers looked excellent, and the fish and chips were fried cod with excellent French fries. Trip thought it odd that a brown malt vinegar was served with the fries. He'd seen plenty of mayonnaise and fries in France, but malt vinegar?

They all brought their feasts with them to the train.

The Sweeny organization had paid for second-class seats, but Trip slipped the porter a buck to get them a private room with a table in the middle. The four men sat around the table and ate as the train chugged forward, started, and stopped several times.

Trip was not surprised at the delays, the waitress in the grill had commented that there were dozens of train lines crisscrossing Ottawa and traffic was always a problem. *Guess so, this is the capital of Canada.*

With the traffic behind them, the train speeded up, and two hours later chuffed sedately into Montreal's Tunnel Terminal. The men gathered their things and stumbled onto the platform to see considerable construction all around. Trip thought, *This place must be growing. Plus, the Canadians are at war with Germany, so lots of troops will be moving through here.*

The men put on coats and started a short walk to the Mount Royal Hotel, just a couple of blocks from the station. Trip was glad of this because it was frigid in Montreal. In less than ten minutes of very cold walking, they arrived to learn they were expected, even in the middle of the night. It was close to 3 a.m. when Trip collapsed into his bed in a beautiful room in a truly opulent hotel.

The men had agreed to meet for breakfast in the Mount Royal dining room at 9 a.m. They were drinking coffee and smoking after a solid breakfast when a well-dressed man exited the coat room and walked over.

Uninvited, he pulled over a chair to their table and, without preamble, said: "Take the night train to Halifax tonight. Once there, remain in the station until all the other passengers have left. Once they are gone, discuss flying among yourselves in loud enough voices to be overheard. A man will approach you and guide you to your next stop."

The well-dressed messenger stood, and discretely dropped a white envelope on the table. He said, "Good luck, Gentlemen." With that, he casually strolled toward the coat room.

Shorty picked up the envelope and peeked inside. He glanced around the table, "It's four train tickets and four ten-dollar bills."

Trip smirked, "Guess that's our passage to Halifax and money to pay for this sumptuous meal."

~~<>~~

The train to Halifax seemed to take forever. But Trip was not complaining. He and the others had successfully crossed into Canada without being arrested. They had ridden two trains across half a continent and were rolling into the coastal town of Halifax, Nova Scotia.

Trip mused that he'd never been to Canada and would have enjoyed the trip had he seen any of it. All he had seen was the inside of a train and pitch-black countryside. Oh, and a delightful old-world hotel in Montreal. By now, his folks and Ellie would have received their letters and were probably frantic. He would not have been surprised if his father had notified the FBI to turn him around. Trip smiled to himself. He had told no one of his destination to Chicago and then the obscure little dock outside Sault Ste. Marie on the Canadian side of Lake Huron.

He was sure that Ellie was furious and somewhat satisfied that she had been right, he loved flying combat more than he loved her. He hoped she was not so furious that she would never forgive him.

Dearest Ellie

By the time you get this, I will be well on my way to either France or England. I don't know which. We have a war to win, even though we're not in it officially, just yet. Soon, I fear, there will be thousands of Americans following me to fight against tyranny and injustice.

I am so sorry for how I've treated you. I do love you. I know you think I love flying more than I love you. But that's not true. Why couldn't it be both? Why couldn't I go fly and come home to only you? Please wish me well and think of me often. When the time comes, and it will, please see me in every boy who marches off to war.

I hope you know that I think of you often. I will write again when I get to a place where letters can be sent. I hope to come home in one piece, but if not, I want you to know that my last thought will be of you.

All my love,

Trip

His letters to his parents and Kathy had been similar, with references to his love of flying and the need to defend freedom. He thanked them all for their love and assured them of his undying love for them. He thanked Kathy for taking care of his car. He admonished her to take care of Reb and not let their Mother and Father dissuade her from her love for Reb.

Trip was roused from his reverie as the train chuffed into the station at Halifax. With a squeal of metal wheels on rails and a hiss of air brakes the train came to a shuddering halt.

Trip and the other flyers quietly gathered their personal effects and stepped out onto the platform. The frigid, sea-damp air chilled them all instantly, and they quickly walked into the dimly lit waiting room. Trip glanced around and saw that the station was old and well-used. Thousands of hands had polished the doorknobs and armrests on the church-pew-style seats. Thousands of butts had similarly polished the finish off the pews in half-moon shapes where countless passengers

125

had awaited a ride to joy or pain. Trip quietly prayed that his was not a ride to pain but to the thrilling joy of defending freedom and cheating death in the sunlit silence of the sky.

They gathered in a corner, pretending to look at a posted schedule behind the glass of a locked bulletin board. The other passengers streamed out of the station into the cold Canadian night. Vernon Keough glanced around and noticed the place was deserted.

"Do you think they do much flying around here?" he asked out loud.

Andy Mamedoff said equally loudly, "Don't know! Pretty cold for flying."

Trip joined in, "Aside from keeping the engine warm, I think it would be good for flying if it's cold."

A voice from the shadows across the waiting room said, "Would you gentlemen join me?"

The boys followed the voice to a small luggage storeroom off the main waiting area. The voice belonged to a tall, cadaverous man with hollow, gray eyes and a hooked nose.

"My name is irrelevant but call me Mr. Hoskins. It is too late in the year for you to get on a ship immediately. The ships will not depart until after Christmas, possibly not until January. Meanwhile, we have booked rooms for you in the Nova Scotian Hotel, just down the block. Enjoy a stay there, but please do not speak of your mission and don't engage in idle chatter with other guests. Enjoy food at the hotel dining room, but please do not wander outside the hotel. If asked, you are American businessmen looking to capitalize on the war by setting up a shipping concern in Halifax. You will be contacted about the next steps."

Hoskins handed each man a $20 bill and said, "Happy Christmas. Thank you for what you do for England, Canada, and the rest of the Commonwealth. If you have trouble or need to contact me, ask the concierge at the hotel to ring Mr. Hoskins.

Hoskins looked at each flyer with his strange, coffin eyes. "Please give me a few moments to exit before you leave the station to go to the hotel."

~~<>~~

The next seven days seemed to drag by, and Trip used one of the afternoons to sit at the small desk in his room and write a letter to Al Norham at Trip's old apartment address in Atlanta. Trip did not elaborate on his journey, considering that such elaboration might imperil the operation. He explained to Al that the trip was safe and to look in the kitchen drawer of the apartment for a paper with contact information for Clyde Pangborn. He said to pass that along to the gang should they wish to follow Trip to war. He also included a letter to the Fulton County Draft Board stating that he had gone to England to join the RAF. He asked Al to mail that letter after January 15th, 1940. He sealed the envelope and bought a stamp from the desk clerk. Placing the envelope in his jacket pocket, he resolved to mail the letter on the way to the ship, whenever that might occur.

Two days after Christmas, the pilots were eating breakfast in the hotel dining room. Hoskins walked past the table, paused, and bent as if to tie his shoe. He said in a quiet voice, "Get plenty of rest and be ready to go tonight after supper."

Hoskins straightened and walked straight ahead with a skeletal, gangling stride. His back was straight, and his bony shoulders were square. Trip thought, *Takes all kinds to win a war*.

~~<>~~

Dinner was a subdued affair, and the pilots all went to their respective rooms to wash, brush, and finish packing. As he packed Trip realized he had no time to mail the letter to Al.

The boys quietly gathered in a corner of the lobby. Trip walked over to the concierge and handed him the letter and a one-dollar bill. "Please mail this tomorrow."

The concierge slipped the letter in his pocket and nodded. The concierge said, "*Bon chance*, my friend. Good luck. All Canada thanks you."

Trip returned to the small group just as Hoskins walked from the offices behind the desk area and strode in his jangling way toward the flyers. "Let's go, Gentlemen."

They walked through back alleys, dodging frozen puddles and garbage cans. A startled cat squalled and knocked over a bucket of unknown slop as it streaked to climb a fence. Somewhere a dog barked. Otherwise, Halifax was silent under a blanket of wintry darkness.

Ten minutes later, Hoskins darted into a deserted building and led the way up several flights of stairs to a candle-lit room with no windows.

A medium-height man with a round face wearing a heavy coat sat at a small desk. Despite the cold, the round-faced man sweated. He had pink cards and a pen. A register book and a small stack of cash was next to the pink cards. No words were spoken. Hoskins nodded at Andy Mamedoff, who stepped in front of the little man.

The man said, "Name?"

"Andrew Beck Mamedoff"

"Hometown?"

"Thompson, Connecticut, but I was born in Warsaw, Poland."

The man made a notation on the pink card and in a small logbook. The discussion continued for another minute and included height, weight, eye, and hair color. Next of kin name and address.

The pink-faced man said, "Sign here...and here." One signature on the pink card, one in the register. He handed Andy the pink identification card and $50 in Canadian currency. He nodded. "Good luck to you."

Trip learned that Shorty Keough's middle name was Charles, and he was from Elizabeth, New Jersey. He was only 4' 10" tall.

Similarly, Red Tobin's full name was Eugene Quimby Tobin, and that he was from Los Angeles, California. Everyone called him "Red," and it was easy to forget he had a real name.

Soon Trip had added his information to the register and to a pink identity card, both of which he signed with a small flourish. Pocketing his $50, Canadian, he turned to the group and Hoskins only to see Hoskins leading the way out the door and down the stairs.

As Trip went out the door, the round-faced man in the heavy coat was packing his register and remaining pink cards. Without looking up he said, "Good luck, and fly safe."

Trip said, "Thank you."

~~<>~~

The four flyers followed Hoskins for several blocks to the harbor where several ships were docked. Hoskins briefly spoke to a guard who turned his back and busied himself with paperwork as the pilots quietly walked by the guard shack and followed Hoskins down the wharf. At a gangway in the gloom, Hoskins paused and made a hand motion to climb the gangway. Hoskins stood and solemnly shook each man's hand as he boarded the ship. As the pilots walked up the gangway and onto the ship, just loud enough to be heard, Hoskins said, "Good luck and Godspeed."

Trip was last in line to mount the gangway. Hoskins said, "Not you. Come with me."

Trip looked at Hoskins hard in the gloom. Hoskins said, "Different ship, eh?"

They walked quietly down the wharf with Hoskins leading the way. Hoskins' almost comical skeletal walk made Trip's bones hurt. The cold did not help.

They passed two ships, one of which stank of animals. Trip began to wonder which ship was his. *Please, God, don't put me on some animal stock boat.*

A gangway was just visible in the gloom and Hoskins stopped. "This one for you, Mr. Gibson."

Trip nodded and put a foot on the gangway.

Hoskins' voice floated, "Good luck and Godspeed. Thank you for your service."

Trip turned to thank Hoskins, but he was gone.

~~<>~~

Trip saw the name of the ship: *Rhéa.*

A man in a naval officer's coat waited at the top of the gangway. "Welcome aboard, Monsieur...ah...Gibson."

Trip said, "Yes. Thank you."

The man said, "I am First Mate Pierre Drappier. Please come with me."

Drappier led Trip through a hatch and along a companionway. They went up a couple of ladders to some nicely furnished staterooms. Drappier tapped on the door to a stateroom and waited. A voice said, "Come in."

Drappier pushed open the door and said, "Monsieur Donaldson? This is your new bunkmate, Monsieur Gibson."

Donaldson was sitting at the desk. He stood up and stuck out his hand, "Herb Donaldson."

Trip grinned at a fellow aviator, "Trip Gibson. Where are you from?"

"California, like a lot of the other guys."

Trip said, "Yeah, I called Clyde Pangborn in Oakland. I spotted the notice on the bulletin board in the Atlanta Municipal Airport."

"Southern boy, huh?"

"Yep."

Trip threw his valise on the unused bed. He looked over the 8'X8' stateroom. There were two wooden bunks with a set of drawers beneath each bunk and a desk at the far end where Herb Donaldson sat. A tiny lavatory hung from the bulkhead on the side of the room opposite the desk. Trip thought *This is cozy.*

A steward walked down the companionway. "*Messieurs, ze Captaine* wishes you to join him on ze Bridge."

~~<>~~

The Master, a Frenchman named Antoine Bensusan, looked at the group of flyers. "I know you're going to France to fight the Germans. I am grateful for your service. All France celebrates you!"

"During your time on the *Rhéa*, please help by standing watch for submarines, as assigned. My first mate, M Drappier, will instruct you. Please be aware that this is a dangerous voyage. The U-Boat danger is real. There will be frequent lifeboat drills. Please attend the drills and be very attentive to the procedures. It may save your life."

Capitaine Bensusan looked each man in the eye before continuing.

"The average time across the *Océan Atlantique* is some 17 days due to zig-zag course changes to throw off U-Boats. I hope you become comfortable with life aboard ship. Please enjoy the comforts of this deck, use the wardroom as you wish, and enjoy the voyage to the extent possible.

Donaldson asked, "When do we leave?"

Captain Bensusan said, "I do not know. We're still loading. Our Cargo is crude oil. Once we finish loading, we will stand out into Bedford

Basin and await the convoy's assembly. It might be a week to ten days, perhaps longer, before the convoy is assembled and sorties out into the Atlantic."

Trip resolved to always wear his money belt. A submarine attack and the order to abandon ship could happen anytime. He also resolved to keep his heavy overcoat close at hand. That decision made, Trip and Donaldson stepped into the wardroom to receive instructions from the ascetic Monsieur Drappier, First Mate of the *Rhéa*.

M. Drappier acquainted the flyers with the customs of the wardroom, where only officers and guests were allowed. A small coffee fund assured the pot was always full, and Trip donated $2.00 – 400 Francs - for the voyage. Wine was available at a small charge of 100 Francs or 50¢.

Trip decided that the French knew how to fight a war. At least they knew how to travel to one.

Drappier showed them the ship's complement of books, magazines, and other reading material in the small library beside the captain's cabin. There were two easy chairs in the tiny library. Trip realized there would be no current newspapers, and most of the books and magazines were in French. Trip spoke some French from his time in France, but the others might not.

M. Drappier explained that the *Capitaine* had bought a stack of American and Canadian publications. These were in a cabinet reserved for American and Canadian volunteers.

M. Drappier commented that the ship's radio could be tuned to broadcasts and get news that way. There was a radio speaker in the tiny library. Drappier said the radio was not always highly reliable, but the Master had authorized the radioman to tune the radio to commercial stations and pipe the program in whenever other traffic permitted. Drappier said the captain was sensitive to the language needs of the brave volunteers who would fight for France. Therefore, when possible, the radio would be tuned to English broadcasts.

Fifteen days later, the *Rhéa* took up station in the departing 31-ship convoy. Atlantic Convoy HX-16 stood out into the freezing, windswept North Atlantic. It was January 14th, 1940.

Trip stood at the rail looking at the rolling waves, some twenty feet high and breaking over the bow of the *Rhéa*. He was lost in thought.

What a different situation from just last year on the Normandie. This will be a much less pleasant voyage, not least because Mildred is not here. I hope she is well.

Chapter 19 – North Atlantic

Trip gained his sea legs on the second day out of Halifax, Nova Scotia. The relatively steady rhythm of the buck, plunge, wallow, buck of the *Rhéa* became predictable. Trip stood a watch at 2 p.m. – four bells of the afternoon watch. The zigzag complicated the ship's motion with turns, one every 1 minute and 46 seconds for this day, as dictated by the HX-16's Commodore in the morning signal.

Capitaine Bensusan and First Mate Drappier explained that the rules for a submarine attack included the ship's 5-inch gun deck firing at any submarine spotted, regardless of any danger to a convoy surface ship. This meant it did not matter if the submarine was inside the convoy's destroyer screen, even if the shells fired might potentially impact a friendly ship. The 5-inch gun was mounted in a hastily welded steel tub on the forward deck of the *Rhéa*.

The *Rhéa* mounted four double .50 caliber machine guns as an anti-aircraft defense. The machine guns were mounted in welded steel tubs on the superstructure. The .50s could be depressed to fire in defense against any surface threat, including a submarine. Drappier told the flyers that the captain had forbidden firing the .50 calibers at a surface threat because such a threat would be very close to the *Rhéa*. Opening fire with a machine gun would be a needless provocation that would most likely result in unnecessary loss of life when the submarine retaliated.

Twice daily, the ship went into a frantic anti-submarine drill. The ship usually followed the anti-submarine drill with a lifeboat drill. Trip worked hard to learn to launch his assigned lifeboat. He was willing to risk his life in air combat. Freezing in the frigid North Atlantic water was not on his list of acceptable ways to die.

A full week passed, and Trip and the other pilots were becoming comfortable with the ship's daily routine. It was surprising, then, when the ship went to general quarters at 3 a.m. – six bells of the middle watch – on the 22nd of January 1940. The insistent gong made its bong, bong, bong sound. Nearby destroyers' sirens made loud whoop, whoop, whoop sounds while the WWI-era four-stack destroyers searched for a submarine.

Trip stood at the rail and strained his eyes, looking for a white streak of phosphorescence indicating the wake of a submarine's periscope. He saw nothing until the streak of white foam announced an incoming torpedo.

Trip turned and screamed, "Torpedo off the starboard bow! Torpedo! Torpedo!"

BOOOOOOM!

The *Rhéa* lurched hard and instantaneously lost way, causing Trip to stumble. Looking up, Trip saw steam shoot out of the funnel and instantly knew the tanker was doomed. The steam meant seawater had invaded the ship's boiler.

Trip looked over the side and saw the ship settling by the bow where the torpedo had struck.

Shit! This won't do!

Trip took two steps, opened the hatch to the companionway, and saw that the emergency lights were on. He took ten steps to his cabin. Donaldson was not there.

In the gloom of the weak emergency lights, Trip grabbed his heavy coat and still-packed suitcase. He touched his money belt and went back to the hatch.

He glanced at the ship's radio room as he stepped through the hatch. In the gloom, Trip saw the ship's radio operator sitting at his transmitter. The man was rapidly tapping his Morse key. Trip thought, *There's a brave man. Sitting there calmly sending an SOS and our position despite the almost certainty that the ship will go down quickly.*

Trip's lifeboat station was twenty feet down the rail. Sailors were already gathering at the davits. As Trip arrived, one sailor pulled the cover off the lifeboat and threw it against the bulkhead.

Trip tossed his valise and coat aboard the lifeboat and manned one of the davits.

Allez! Allez! Allons-y! Merde! Mon Dieu! Hâte, hâte!

Trip knew these words meant 'let's go' and 'hurry.' He needed no encouragement to hurry. Trip cranked as quickly as he could but not so fast as to cause the lifeboat to tip.

The *Rhéa* started to list, complicating launching the lifeboat. The list made it very difficult to stand and manage the davit. The lifeboat swayed well away from the side of the ship as the list added to the gap between the ship and the lifeboat. That gap was now a yawning chasm of black night all the way to the water.

A French sailor leaned over the rail to catch a line to steady the lifeboat. The sailor lost his balance and his feet scrabbled momentarily before he plunged headlong into the roiling sea. In moments the only thing to be seen was his white sailor's hat, its red pompom looking black in the dark.

The men grabbed the launching lines and began to descend into the lifeboat, and Trip followed suit. It was much farther down to the boat than Trip had imagined. He inched his way down and down, hands burning despite wearing his rabbit-lined gloves against the friction of the line. Despite the cold, Trip's hands started to sweat.

Halfway down the line, Trip heard the *Rhéa* make a strange groaning sound. *Please, God, don't let the ship sink yet. She'll suck me down with her!*

Trip's arms screamed from the strain of inching down the rope, and he thought he might have to let go. At that moment, his feet hit the bottom of the boat, and he sat in a hurry. He was shaking all over, but he dragged his suitcase over and put it beneath his feet.

One of the sailors muttered something in French. Trip stared at him. *Tough titty, sport. I wasn't leaving my stuff just to satisfy you.*

The sailors quickly unshipped the oars and began frantically rowing away from the stricken *Rhéa*. Trip got on an oar and kept time, pulling hard. The ocean was already thick with crude oil, making each pull of the oar an agony of muscle-wrenching effort.

Trip looked around. *Son-of-a-bitch! This oil might catch fire at any moment.*

As the lifeboat made its way through the gloppy mess, Trip could see the U-Boat's silhouette as it surfaced. The German crew raced onto the submarine's deck and unlimbered the 88-millimeter gun. Other crew members quickly manned the 20-millimeter gun next to the conning tower.

Trip watched in horror as the gun crew quickly spun the wheels at the base of the gun mount, training the 88-millimeter gun on the *Rhéa*. The deck gun flashed and made a hard BAM! followed by a clang indicating *Rhéa* had been hit.

Flash, BAM! Clang!

Flash, BAM! Clang!

Fire blossomed on *Rhéa* and ran down the ship's oil-coated sides. The fire spread to the oil on the water.

Trip looked at the submarine, now more visible in the red glow of the firelight. A man in a heavy coat wearing a dirty white naval officer's cap and smoking a bent pipe watched impassively. The German U-Boat commander glanced at the lifeboat, shrugged, and turned his back.

Flash, BAM! Clang!

The lifeboat crew rowed desperately to escape the oil fire that spread further every second.

Rhéa made loud groaning sounds followed by a series of cracks and bangs as her deck plates popped. Trip watched with deep sadness as the *Rhéa* suddenly stood on her bow and disappeared beneath the waves. The salvation of *Rhéa's* sinking was that the oil fire was quickly extinguished, leaving the lifeboat in utter blackness.

In the near distance, Trip heard the submarine's diesel engine roar as the boat moved off in search of another target.

Later, Trip realized that the entire episode took less than five minutes.

~~<>~~

Trip pulled on his heavy coat and lit a cigarette.

One of the sailors started shouting at him. Trip replied in his little French, "What does it matter now? That U-Boat is long gone."

He shook the pack toward everyone else, and they ignored the man who had complained. Soon, everyone's nerves were settled by the smoke, and they looked around. One man summed up the situation: *"Merde. Nous sommes baisés!"*

Trip couldn't help but grin. *The Frenchman is right, we're screwed.*

~~<>~~

Dawn broke, everyone was soaked, and several sailors were sick from being tossed by twenty-foot swells. Worse, some had swallowed oil-laden seawater and were suffering the effects.

Trip helped to rig a sea anchor to help keep the lifeboat pointed into the swells and to stop the boat from having such wild plunges. Two sailors stepped the mast and were rigging a sail. At least they were out of the oil slick from the sunken *Rhéa*.

Trip remembered a prayer from his Sunday School days. He knew these were not the exact words, but he muttered them anyway: *The Atlantic is vast, o lord, and my boat is small.*

The little boat and its 20 forlorn passengers rode the swells and plunged into the troughs, stopped only by the sea anchor from plunging into the depths of the icy cold water. Each time the boat crested a swell, Trip peered into the distance, hoping to see a ship or evidence of life in the vastness.

The hours wore on, and Trip began to believe the situation was hopeless. The boat crested another swell, and though he thought it futile, he looked around the horizon in the weak light. Just before the boat plunged into the next trough, Trip thought he saw a smudge of smoke nearly due west of their position. The next crest showed the black smoke closer.

Trip shouted, *"Allons! Allons!"* and pointed.

Three sailors jumped to their feet, causing the lifeboat to tip sickeningly. The Chief Boatswains' mate, at least that's what Trip thought he was, shouted them down.

The boatswain's mate crawled and staggered to the mast. He held on as the lifeboat made another sickening plunge into the freezing black water.

Alor's! Cést un bateau! Un bateau! Mon Dieu!

The Chief fumbled with a box bolted to the hull and pulled out a flare pistol. He looped the lanyard over his head and put a shell in the gun. At the next wave crest, he fired the shell straight up.

Trip watched the flare's arc as it streaked red against the gray sky. *Please, God, let them see it!*

~~<>~~

In minutes, the occupants of the little craft heard the Whoop! Whoop! of a destroyer's siren. And in a few more minutes, an ancient British destroyer left over from the Great War came alongside the lifeboat about 50 yards away and slowed perceptibly. A sailor fired a launching gun that paid out a long line that draped over the lifeboat. Trip thought, *Damn fine shot, that.*

The man in the bow of the lifeboat quickly secured the line, and waved at the ship. The destroyer's engine note changed as the ship increased revolutions and pulled away, towing the lifeboat. This created an immediate emergency for the survivors. The sea anchor was jerking the lifeboat as it began to skim the crests. The boatswain's mate shouted to a man in the stern who whipped a knife across the line to the sea anchor. As the lifeboat settled down, Trip noticed they were getting closer to the destroyer. *They're winching us up to the ship.*

~~<>~~

Trip stood shivering, waiting to be hauled to the deck of *HMS Windsor*. Trip had seen D-42 painted on her bow. She was old but well-maintained, and she saved Trip Gibson's life. He was forced to leave his heavy coat behind. His trousers and shirt were oil spattered, but he was uninjured.

Knowing he would have to leave the suitcase, he put on his pullover sweater. His suit jacket went over the top of these. In every pocket, he stuffed a pair of boxers or an undershirt. Two pairs of socks were jammed into his jacket pockets, and his carton of cigarettes was crammed into the waistband of his trousers. He looped his belt through the handle of his shaving kit. Trip removed his oil-sodden shoes, tied the laces together, and looped the shoes around his neck.

As the British sailors hauled him aboard *Windsor*, one of them said, "Blimey! This one looks like bloody *Bibendum*, 'e dos'."

The others laughed.

Trip stood, hands on knees getting his breath back from being hauled aboard the bounding destroyer. "Bibendum?"

"Aye, tha' Bluudy Michelin Man, mate."

Trip started laughing, imagining himself as the Michelin Man. Soon the entire crowd was laughing hysterically.

"'Ere, now! Wot's this? You bluudy 'tars got nowt better to do than laugh at a bluddy over-dressed Yank?" The British Chief Petty Officer desperately tried not to smile.

Trip recovered his breath and said, "Thank you all. I'd bow, but my current dress does not permit it."

To peals of laughter from the ship's crew, the Chief snorted, "Bluudy 'ell! Get 'im below before I frow him to the bluudy sharks."

~~<>~~

Two days later, *HMS Windsor* pulled alongside a French *escorteur, The Volontaire*. A breeches buoy was rigged between the ships without slowing the two fast-moving craft. Trip was unceremoniously put into the harness and flung over the side. The French sailors hauled away on the line, quickly reeling Trip across the gap between the racing ships.

An astonished Trip Gibson stood on the deck of the *Volontaire*. He was completely dry except for a few drops of water splashed at the last moment before being hauled aboard.

An impeccably dressed French naval *lieutenant de vaisseau* saluted and said, "Welcome to France, Monsieur Gibson."

Trip grinned and said, "Thanks, it's nice to be back."

The Frenchman looked puzzled. "You 'ave been to France?"

"*Oui*. Just last year."

"Ah. Well, zen. We shall 'ave much to discuss."

Chapter 20 – France, Again

Trip watched the foaming sea flash by as the *Volontaire* crashed through the rolling swells. They were on station out from the convoy as the coast of Ireland passed on their port beam. The morning would bring the South Coast of England and a hard turn toward Liverpool and safety.

Still, *Volontaire* and other escort ships were vigilant. U-Boats, and now E-Boats, were in the area. E-Boats were high-speed motor torpedo boats lurking near the coast of France. They could sink a major ship in a twinkling, boring in at high speed to launch a brace of very effective torpedoes. Doubling the lookouts and putting on extra revolutions, the diminutive *Volontaire* plowed ahead with all the *elán* the French could muster.

Trip smiled at the verve shown by his French friends. He and the French officer had briefly chatted about Paris and the Jazz Clubs, Django, the champagne, and women.

The Frenchman said, "And now, *mon ami,* you return to France to fly and fight against *Les Boches! Mon Dieu!* You Americans are wonderful allies."

Trip said, "I wish the entire American nation was behind this."

The French officer said, "I know you could be arrested for coming to 'elp."

Trip snorted, "Hell, I had to get out of France to avoid being arrested by your government."

The officer said, "*Mon Dieu,* we should have given you a medal for fighting *Les Boches!* I regret all we can do is replace your oil-soaked clothes with a pair of naval trousers and a shirt. I see the British gave you a good coat."

Trip smiled. The British peacoat was, indeed, a very good coat.

~~<>~~

The *Volontaier* escorted the remaining ships of Convoy HX-16 into St Georges Channel and then into the Irish Sea. The convoy began to disperse and proceed to various docks of Liverpool Harbor along the Mersey River.

The *Volontaire* sheared off as the convoy fully entered the roads before the harbor. The captain of the *Volontaire* saluted the convoy with his ship's whistle. The ships of the convoy hooted back with their powerful horns.

Trip heard the salutes as he drank strong French coffee in the tiny wardroom. The *lieutenant de vaisseau* who had welcomed Trip aboard, came in, and a steward rushed to get him a cup of coffee to his liking. Trip had learned that the lieutenant was the ship's executive officer and was to be addressed as *Capitaine*. The lieutenant sat opposite Trip.

"*Bonjour, Monsieur* Gibson. We will arrive in Le Havre in a few hours. We will travel quickly around the coast of England and race toward Cherbourg before following the coast to Le Havre. This part of the journey is well within the range of the Luftwaffe. We will continue to mount double lookouts and remain at general quarters until we reach Le Havre."

Trip grinned ruefully, "I look forward to reaching Le Havre. I certainly need a tailor to replace my clothes."

The lieutenant said, "You had to leave your clothing behind?"

Trip smiled, "*Oui*. The clothes you gave me are all I have. My shoes are sticky with crude oil."

The executive officer pulled out a small notepad and jotted on it. He smiled as he handed the paper to Trip, "This is the name of my tailor. I also wrote the name of the best hotel. I'm sure you can find your way from Le Havre to Paris."

Trip smiled his thanks. "*Merci.* I hope you have great success and this war ends quickly."

"Oh, we shall surely beat *Les Boches*. France is not Poland, *Monsieur*. *Les Boches* are all bluster and strut."

The Frenchman finished his coffee. "I must return to my duties. *Bon chance, Monsieur* Gibson. France thanks you."

Trip smiled, *"Merci. Bon chance, mon Capitaine."*

~~<>~~

Trip walked down the gangway leaving the *Volontaire* and walked with purpose toward the address of the French Lieutenant's tailor. It was freezing cold and the wind and damp from the sea made it even colder.

The tailor's lip curled at the sorry state of Trip's clothing. "*Mon Dieu, Monsieur*, you are *l' accident!*"

Trip explained and flashed a $100 bill.

The tailor snatched the money and shrugged, "But we have fabric and time. I shall make two suits for you. They will be ready in two days."

The tailor pointed across the narrow street. "Your shoes are terrible. The cobbler is just there. I'm sure he has something suitable."

Trip bought a pair of trousers, three shirts, underwear, a tie, and socks from the haberdasher next door to the tailor. He clomped across the street to the cobbler and bought two pair of shoes. One was a pair of cap-toe oxfords, and the other a pair of ankle-high boots.

Trip took no pleasure in trashing his oily shoes. They were Florsheim's and had cost a pretty penny just a few months ago in Atlanta.

He stood holding his purchases in an unwieldy box. The cobbler had no English, and Trip's limited French would not do.

Trip looked down at the box and raised an eyebrow. He mimicked carrying a suitcase.

The cobbler looked puzzled momentarily and then said, "Ah!" He pointed down the street and said, *"Un valise! Va là-bas. Numéro trois."*

Trip nodded his understanding. A suitcase could be had at the store at Number 3, *Rue de Paris*.

Not standing on ceremony, Trip selected a nice high-end leather backpack instead of a valise. *Maybe I'll have to do some walking…*

Trip checked in at a beautiful turn-of-the-century hotel rivaling Paris' best. He asked for a hot bath. After one such bath, he called for a second and mused: *This is the second time I've cleaned off filth in France. Hope it's the last!*

Dressed in his new clothes, Trip put his oil-stained garments and shoes in the box and called for a bellman to dispose of them. Until his suits were ready, at least he had clean, new shoes, clean trousers, a fresh shirt, and a tie. He considered replacing the heavy British naval peacoat but decided it was warm and dry and didn't cost him anything. He would keep it. He asked the bellman to have the peacoat cleaned.

He ate a wonderful meal in the hotel dining room and went to the smoking lounge to relax and consider his next moves.

Suitably dressed, Trip found a bank and exchanged $200 for French francs. It made quite a wad of dough. Le Havre being a port city, his dollars had been accepted for the clothing and shoes, but elsewhere that might not be the case.

~~<>~~

That afternoon, Trip looked for the address printed on a card Hoskins had given each flier: *20 Avenue Foch*. There was no name, just a pen and ink scrawl on the opposite side: *Hoskins*. Each flier was to report to *20 Avenue Foch* and hand the card to the woman inside the door.

The hotel was near *Avenue Foch*, and the weather had warmed into the mid-40s. Trip walked comfortably, enjoying the sunshine. A fortnight aboard a ship plunging across the Atlantic made Trip most appreciative of the solid earth under his feet. The shoes pinched but would soon break in.

A short, harsh-favored woman with chopped-off red-dyed hair and the aroma of a lifetime of eating garlic glanced at the card and said, *"Un moment."*

The red-haired woman was back in 30 seconds. *"Allons-y."*

She quickly turned and marched up the stairs. Trip followed her noticing that she was mostly diminutive but sported an outsized stern. She led Trip into a room on the second floor and beckoned to a chair.

Five minutes later, a man stepped through the door. He wore what Trip considered a banker's suit with a high, hard collar and a formal tie.

"Bonjour. Monsieur...."

"Gibson. Robert H. Gibson, III." Trip extended his hand, and the banker shook it briefly, his face reflecting distaste at having to touch a foreigner.

The banker did not give a name. "*Monsieur* Gibson, please come with me."

The banker opened a door, and Trip stepped into a room with large windows, several chairs, a map of France on the wall, and a stand-up desk. In the chairs sat Shorty Keough, Red Tobin, and Andy Mamedoff.

The three men jumped to their feet. They all shouted at once, "Trip! We thought you were dead! My God, it's good to see you."

Trip said, "I'm glad you all made it."

Shorty said, "The trip was miserable. We were behind a boat carrying mules. My God the stink! But our trip was not as bad as yours, I'll bet. We saw your ship hit and start sinking. Then, it was behind us, and we had no more information. We heard some gunfire. Of course, that was not promising."

Trip said, "I was lucky to get into a lifeboat, and we got away from the ship before it sank. The U-boat surfaced and shelled the ship until it stood on its bow and sank like a rock. The ship was full of crude oil, so we were covered in that gunk. I just washed the last of it off today."

The banker was looking impatient. "*Messieurs*, if I may interrupt zis 'appy *réunion*, we must discuss business."

The pilots sat and looked at the banker, who did not mince words. "We are at war. Ze French people are, of course, grateful for your service. You must not be er...forthcoming...about your mission. Rather memorize these directions and avoid too much conversation. Take the morning train to *Paris, Gare de Lyon*. Go to the *Hôtel des Grandes Ecoles,* near *Notre-Dame*. Present this card to the concierge."

He handed each man a white engraved card that bore only the words, *Vive le France* in script.

The hotel stay will be free, and the concierge will give you instructions about where to go to officially volunteer to join the *Armee de l'air. Vive le France! Vive l'Amerique! Bon chance, mes amis.*"

~~<>~~

As they walked out of the building at 20 Avenue Foch, Trip said, "I hear there are some great watering holes hereabouts."

Andy said, "I knew I liked you."

Shorty and Red looked at each other. "Lead on."

The men wandered to the center of the old city of *Le Havre* and quickly identified several candidates as bar of the evening. After careful consideration, they decided to visit them all.

They visited, sampled, rated, and re-sampled the *Guillaume Tell,* the *Grosse Tonne,* and the *Normandie.* Trip smiled, remembering his voyage on the *Normandie* just last year. He wondered if his fond memory of the *SS Normandie* was because of the luxury of the ship or because of the luxury of Mildred Wright's bed. Perhaps it was both.

The final stop was *La Lune*, a turn-of-the-century mixture of bar and brothel. In both regards, it was a mixture of the highest order, it's amenities were untrammeled by the ravages of time.

Trip drank but did not partake of the other services. Shorty was wretchedly poor and refused the services of a spectacular *putain* who, at six-feet tall, entreated him with the suggestion that the two would make a most interesting *tableau.*

The others enthusiastically darted for the darker recesses of *La Lune*, leaving Trip and Shorty to stagger back to their respective hotels.

Alone in his quiet room, Trip undressed and crawled into bed. His mind flashed to the near-death experience of being torpedoed in the North Atlantic. He was quite blotto, but his mind ran to Mildred, then Ellie. His eyes closed, and he saw Mildred, her dark locks spilling into her face. Her look of utter concentration as she reached her climax under him made his heart pound. Then, it was Ellie's turn to arch her neck and make soft sounds. Trip had an insistent erection, and he masturbated to these memories. Trip's ejaculation was life-affirming, taking him over the edge into an exhausted, drunken sleep.

Chapter 21 – Le Havre

On February 6th, 1940, a well-rested Trip Gibson donned one of his new suits and went to the Le Havre train station. He enjoyed the short walk on such a crisp Winter's morning. He joined Shorty, Red, and Andy for the trip to Paris and Destiny.

The train chugged across the countryside at a sedate 50 kph, Trip reckoned. *Well, that's fine. It's at least 240 kilometers, so the announced arrival time of 3 p.m. – five hours – is accurate.*

The train chugged out of the station very nearly on time. Arrival at *Gare de Lyon* was a different matter entirely. Several times the train stopped inside a tunnel sheltering from an air raid alert. No such air raid materialized, but everyone was on edge. Every time the train stopped inside a tunnel, the passengers were inundated with the acrid stink of trapped smoke. A few people, Trip included, detrained and walked to the tunnel entrance. This avoided the smoke and offered a chance to see if there was actually an air raid.

Shorty lit a cigarette and said, "Huh! This is what the papers back home have been calling Phoney War."

Andy said, "Sitzkrieg."

Red and Trip guffawed.

Trip sobered, "It wasn't a Sitzkrieg when that torpedo hit the *Rhéa*. I had a cabin mate named Herb Donaldson. Dunno if he made it. If I had to guess, I'd say no. That's because when the sun came up, there were no other lifeboats to be seen, and nobody survived in that freezing water."

Shorty said, "That's true. The North Atlantic is quite a war zone. But we've seen nothing here that looks like a war."

Red snorted, "I hear only a few scattered air engagements are happening. I hope I haven't come all this way for nothing."

Nods all around the group confirmed similar feelings.

Trip said, "I wonder how long this Phoney War will last?"

Shrugs.

Andy said, "I joined up to go to Finland to fight the Soviets. I was born in Poland and thought that would be the right thing to do. But I learned that it's almost impossible to get to Finland. The newspapers say that the Finns are about done, too. Maybe another month before the Russians have them beaten. Rather not go get in the middle of a losing proposition."

~~<>~~

The train arrived about two hours late at *Gare de Lyon*, and the fliers taxied to the *Hôtel des Grandes Ecoles*.

Trip smiled at the sight of *Notre Dame*. Plenty of jazz clubs were nearby, and Trip was excited to be back in Paris without being cooped up in the U.S. Embassy.

After checking into their rooms, Trip sauntered next door and said, "I'm going to see if I can find Django Reinhardt playing somewhere."

Andy said, "Who's that?"

Trip said, "Greatest jazz guitarist that ever lived."

~~<>~~

The morning dawned to four splitting headaches. The fliers stumbled into the hotel dining room one by one, only to feel sick when soft-scrambled – and still-wet – French eggs were rolled to the table on a cart.

Shorty asked for toast and received a piece of hard baguette that was cut into slices and toasted. His face said it was not what he had planned. He muttered, "Damn hard to chew on top of a hangover!"

Andy said, "Oh, God, I'm afraid to order bacon."

Trip said, "Wise beyond your years, m'boy. Bacon here's usually not smoked and often a bit limp."

Andy looked green.

Red ate with gusto. "I'd rather have something to puke up than the dry heaves."

Trip said, "I'm having French Onion Soup."

Red asked, "That any good?"

Trip replied, "The French swear by it. I'm getting some champagne, too."

Shorty muttered, "Please, God, take me from this den of iniquity."

Andy breathed, "Please, God, let there be room for two. Hell can't possibly be worse than I feel right now."

The breakfast hour restored the men's spirits, if not their flesh.

Andy perked up, "That guy, Django, really is the best guitarist I've ever heard."

Shorty said, "Never seen anything like that."

Trip said, "I heard a fellow at a jazz club a couple of years ago say that Django Reinhardt has re-invented the guitar. Seems like it."

Red changed the subject. "Did you get anything from the concierge when we got here about what to do? I handed him my card. He said some stuff about *merci* for volunteering and so on. That was it."

The other three shook their heads. Trip said, "How about I mosey over and ask what's going on?"

The other three nodded. Trip stood, straightened his only tie, and casually walked out of the dining room.

Five minutes later, he was back. Flopping into his seat, he said, "I'd have been back sooner but visited the men's room. The concierge said we'll be contacted. That's it."

Shorty said, "Well, maybe the Phoney War will stay phony, and we won't be needed. That'd be a hell of a note to come all this way for nothing. Funny how the Brits spell Phony with an 'e'."

Andy said, "This may be the calm before the storm, fellas."

~~<>~~

Trip looked at the calendar in his room and saw that the fliers had been guests of someone unknown for over a week. Nine days to be exact: today was February 15th.

He went to the hotel desk and asked, "Where can I send a telegram to the United States?"

"*Ici, Monsieur.* Here. We will be 'appy to send ze telegram."

Trip said, "Somewhere else, perhaps? It's private, and I don't want my friends to know."

"*Ah. Un femme, non?*"

"*Oui, exactement.*"

The clerk said, "The *Hôtel Monde* is just down the street. They can 'elp you, *Monsieur.*"

Trip walked down the street in the direction of the *Hôtel Monde*, but kept going to the next hotel, the *Hôtel Daphné*. He entered and spoke briefly with the concierge who accepted three 100 franc notes to send the following telegram.

TO: CLYDE PANGBORN, OAKLAND, CA, USA

FROM: R. H. GIBSON, PARIS

WE ARE HERE. WAITING. NO CONTACT. PLEASE ADVISE, CARE OF HOTEL DAPHNE, PARIS.

TRIP GIBSON

Trip paid the cost of the telegram to the concierge and wandered back to the hotel, stopping along the way to buy a new fedora.

He walked into the dining room, where three bored fliers sat drinking coffee.

Andy said, "Nice hat. New?"

Trip leaned into the table and said quietly, "I sent Pangborn a telegram asking what's up. Bought the hat on the way back."

The others looked surprised. Shorty said, "Must be nice to be rich and can send telegrams."

Trip said, "This waiting is killing me."

Red glanced around the room. "Well, we're not getting any answers here, so why not?"

〈〉~~

A week passed with no answer from Pangborn.

Soon the fliers were into March, heading for the 15th. Trip grinned to himself, *Beware the ides of March. I think they told Caesar that.*

Trip gave the concierge at *Hôtel Daphné* another 500 francs to have a porter deliver any reply to Trip at the *Hôtel des Grandes Ecoles*.

Trip told the others that there had been no replies. The four young men decided to enjoy Paris while carefully watching the war news.

Shorty said, "Aside from Trip getting sunk, the last exciting thing to happen in this war was the Graf Spee sinking in South America."

Trip flopped a month-old American newspaper on the table. "Bought this at the *Hôtel Daphné*. Probably more information in this."

The boys pounced on the paper, splitting out the sections and digging through them with almost frantic interest.

Andy said, "Canadian troops have landed in England, and the Brits are evacuating school children. Guess they're taking the kids north in England somewhere."

Red asked, "You do know there are more countries on the Island of Britain than just England, right?"

Andy looked hurt. "Yes. I guess there's Scotland."

"Yep, and Wales."

"Huh. I thought Whales and Ireland were together."

"It's Wales, you moron."

"Nice. Thanks. I feel so much better about myself now."

Trip said, "Heeeeeyyyy! My Georgia Tech Yellow Jackets beat Missouri in the Orange Bowl!"

Red asked, "Is Georgia Tech a school?"

Trip started singing, "I'm a Ramblin' Wreck from Georgia Tech and a helluva engineer. A helluva, helluva, helluva engineer! Like all the other good felloooows, I drink my whiskey clear...."

Andy invoked the deity, "Jesus. Can't anyone shut him up?"

Trip roared on, "If I had a daughter, Sir, I'd dress her in white and gold..."

Red snorted, "I think we're gonna have to learn this song in self-defense."

Shorty said over Trip's singing, "At least he's not singing that sickening Boola, Boola song."

And so it went: idle chit-chat filled the days. Jazz clubs, poker games, booze, and cigarettes filled the nights. Hangovers abounded.

Trip ran into Madame Allard at a club and disappeared. As Trip and Louise left, he told Shorty to reassure the others that nothing was amiss.

Two days later, Trip returned to the hotel via the Hôtel Daphné.

Flopping in a chair with the other fliers, Trip said, "No answer from Pangborn, yet."

Shorty smirked, "Took you two days to check on a telegram?"

"I'm a slow reader."

Andy and Red snickered.

Red said, "That Frenchwoman appears to have gotten the better of you, my good man. You look rather exhausted."

Trip snorted, "We better get some movement soon, or I'll be dead. Her husband is a *Commandant* in the French Army and is at the Maginot Line nearly 100 percent of the time. Louise damn near wore me to the bone."

~~<>~~

On March 10th, a porter from Hôtel Daphné came through the door and handed the concierge and envelope. It was a telegram for Trip from Clyde Pangborn. It consisted of two words: SIT TIGHT. PANGBORN.

Trip snorted and crumpled the yellow Western Union paper. He arced it toward a trash can but missed. That made him even more angry.

Trip spat, "God DAMN it!"

Shorty asked, "Madame Allard tired of you?"

Trip looked disgusted. "Nope. Pangborn says to sit tight. We've been sitting so tight, my asshole is puckered."

~~<>~~

All four pilots champed at the bit for several days, but mid-March brought no further activity. And no information.

Trip saw in a French newspaper that there had been a brief but bloody air battle over the Maginot Line.

He showed the paper to the others.

Trip said, "The Germans got the better of that fight."

Andy said, "But it says here that French pilots and Ack-Ack shot down dozens of German airplanes."

Trip smirked, "Yeah, that's what the Republicans in Spain always said when we got our asses whipped."

Shorty said, "Seems to me the French need more pilots."

Trip nodded, "Let's go to the French Ministry of Defense and offer our services."

The other three looked at one another.

Andy said, "Can't hurt."

Chapter 22 – *Non!*

Andy dug up a map of Paris and was pouring over it. Red walked over and said, "The desk clerk said he thinks the Ministry of Defense is at a chateau at Montry. That's outside the city to the east."

Trip grinned, "Perfect. We can go there first thing tomorrow."

Shorty said, "What happens if they say, 'welcome', and haul us off?"

Andy said, "We'll tell them we'll return in the morning and come get our stuff. That'll let us have another evening in the jazz clubs and report in fine fettle."

Trip grinned, "I like the way you think. *Le Club Jardin* tonight?"

~~<>~~

The morning dawned bright and clear, a unique late-winter phenomenon for France. The clear weather brought an even harsher, dry-edged cold to the coldest European winter in years. The men gathered for breakfast and plotted strategy.

Trip said, "Let's take the train out there. It can't be much more than a couple of hours."

Nods all around led to a festive atmosphere for the rest of breakfast. The French thought *les Américains* were insane when they asked for sausage, fried eggs, finely chopped fried potatoes they called hashbrowns, and toast for breakfast. But, in the spirit of *Bonhomme,* the chef did a very credible job. The pilots had a delightful feast.

By this time, most hotel staff knew the crazed *Américains* were here to volunteer to fight for France. So what? If they ate like barbarians, so much the better. They would be barbarians in a fight!

The four pilots – they now called themselves the *Four Horsemen* – trooped out of the hotel and down to the train station.

The train ran on time and chugged along out to Montry. Trip watched the landscape go by and wondered what the day would bring.

~~<>~~

The men walked into the main hall of the train station at Montry. Trip used his limited French to ask a porter pushing a heavily laden baggage cart for directions to the chateau.

Moments later, the pilots were crammed into a tiny taxi and bucking along cobbled streets. The taxi driver mentioned that the Rothchild family owned the chateau.

Immediately, Trip wondered if some of the wonderful Rothchild wines were available in this quaint old village.

The taxi pulled up in front of the sprawling, ancient building with turrets abounding. The pilots disembarked from the crowded taxi.

Trip leaned in the window and handed the driver five 100-franc notes. "Please wait."

The driver shrugged. *"Dix minutes."*

Trip said, *"Oui. Merci bien."*

~~<>~~

Trip and the others walked up to a sentry. Trip spoke his limited French to say, "We are American pilots who wish to fight for France. Could you please ask your officer to speak to us?"

The sentry goggled at Trip. He looked the others over from head to toe. After a moment, the sentry called out a question in rapid-fire French. There was no reply.

Trip and the others waited patiently.

An immaculately turned-out French officer marched out of the office adjoining the guard station. He was delicately dabbing his lips with a checkered cloth napkin.

"What is the meaning of this interruption of my morning?"

Trip said, "Good morning. We are American pilots who want to volunteer to fly and fight for France."

The officer looked at Trip like he had been dropped from another planet.

Trip asked, "Is there someone here we might speak to?"

The officer smirked, "Oh, I'm certain General Gamelin has time to receive you immediately."

The lieutenant said, "You must leave immediately. I have had people shot for less."

Trip paused a moment. He looked up toward the roof of the ancient chateau. Leveling his gaze at the Frenchman, he said through clenched teeth. "Let me tell you something, you jumped-up little garlic-eating Frog asshole. I paid my way to get here. To do so, required sneaking past our FBI. I'm sure you've heard of them. J. Edgar Hoover? Those guys? If they had caught us, they would have thrown us under the jail. I was torpedoed on a French ship in the middle of the North Atlantic Ocean and spent hours in a freezing lifeboat in the middle of a giant oil slick. That oil was coming to Le Havre to support your fight against the Nazis. My friends here were in the same convoy risking their lives to come and try to help France. They lived with the stink of mules for 2500 miles across the Atlantic. The four of us have hundreds of hours flying airplanes. We are skilled pilots. I have over 350 hours in combat against the Germans in Spain. We have done nothing but try to find a way to fly and fight for France. And now I get here, and you threaten to have us shot because we interrupted your fucking croissant?"

The Frenchman was bright red.

Trip turned to leave. He glanced over his shoulder at the French officer and said, "If France should win this fight, it won't be because of idiots like you. I have shit bigger than you."

161

The four Americans walked away from the chateau without looking back. They got in the taxi. Trip said, "Train station, please."

The taxi driver flicked his Gauloise cigarette out the window, let out the clutch, and rattled down the 15th-century cobblestones, jarring everyone's teeth.

After a long minute, Shorty said, "I think you should have let him have a piece of your mind."

~~<>~~

The four men paused at a little bistro outside the train station. They had a croissant and a cup of coffee.

Andy asked, "What now?"

Trip said, "I think maybe we find a French *Armée de l'Air* recruiting office."

Andy said, "I saw something about the French army headquarters being at Chateau de Vincennes. That's a different place than this, I think."

Red said, "There was something in a French newspaper about that. I can't read French, but that name sounds familiar."

They bought tickets to the nearest station to *Chateau de Vincennes*. The train was not far from the chateau, so the flyers walked. They approached a sentry and asked to see the officer of the guard.

This time a pleasant young man stepped out of an office under the entrance to what looked like a medieval castle. "May I be of assistance?"

Trip looked at the others and realized he had been appointed spokesman. "Good morning. We are American pilots who wish to volunteer to fly and fight for France."

The young lieutenant's mouth dropped open. "*Mon Dieu*. But are all *Américains* flocking to France? Just last week, two other men came here with the same offer."

Trip said, "I think there's quite a recruiting effort. These two fellows are from California. This one is from New Jersey. I'm from Georgia."

"Pardon, but I am not familiar with your country, *Monsieur*. Please come into my office. Coffee?"

Shorty muttered, "That's better."

Soon, the Americans sat in chairs before the lieutenant's desk. They told their stories to the attentive young Frenchman.

The lieutenant finally spoke, "*Mon Dieu*, but you are determined. I must say, I admire you, but nothing can be done to assist you in joining the *Armée de l'Air*. You see, I made inquiries last week when your compatriots offered their services. The answer from my commanders is that we have no room to add people, and there are no plans to accept foreign volunteers. I am deeply sorry that I can do nothing for you.

Trip looked at the others. "Well, fella's at least he's polite about it."

The Frenchman smiled, but it was clear he didn't understand. "*Merci, mes amis.* You do us great honor. I wish you *bon chance*."

The Americans rose to leave. Trip said, "*Bon chance, mon ami.* With the people leading your forces, you'll need it."

Chapter 23 – Frustration

Trip stomped into the lounge at the hotel. He paused at the concierge desk to receive the expected news that there were no new messages.

Trip flopped in a chair next to Andy. "I wasn't expecting to hear anything, anyway."

Red said, "Drink heavily. Then go to England. At least they speak the language."

Trip grinned at the three other pilots. "*Maxim's*, then, and then the clubs. We'll celebrate our lack of success – I refuse to call it a failure!"

Maxim's was magnificent and expensive. Albert, the portly and gracious *Maitrê d'*, led the four to a pleasant table in the center of the room. The sun's last light peaked through screened windows to add a little illumination to the darkly furnished room. Mirrors and dark wood played to create a rich atmosphere that had no equal.

The flyers had a variety of excellent dishes.

> Jambon de Bayonne (600 Francs)
>
> Grapefruit Cocktail (400 Francs)
>
> Crêpes Maxim's (450 Francs)
>
> Rissoles de Foie-gras (650 Francs)
>
> Coquille St Jacques (600 Francs)
>
> Filets de Sole Tout Paris (700 Francs)
>
> Rouget Gilée Ceurre d'Anchois (600 Francs)
>
> Steak and Kidney Pie (700 Francs)
>
> Terrine de Canard (700 Francs)

Maxim's Pommes Dauphine (500 Francs)

Asperges Vertes de Sauvés (650 Francs)

Cougettes Niçoise (300 Francs)

Bananas Orientale (400 Francs)

Soufflé Rothschild (400 Francs).

The tab for this astounding meal for four came to 7650 Francs. Trip did a quick mental calculation and concluded that this was about $150.

Trip grinned when he saw the wine and cocktail tab was also about 7000 Francs – another $140. *What the Hell. I got money, and who knows what's going to happen next?*

Trip had no problem picking up that tab. After weeks of no contact from the Sweeny organization that got them to Paris, the others ran short of cash. After paying the tab, Trip still had over $800 in his money belt. That was enough to get him to England. It remained to be seen exactly how.

Sated with fine food and wine, the flyers marched smartly to *Chez George*, a venerable drinking location in the 6th Arrondissement. It was a bit of a walk past the *Jardin de Tuileries*, across the Seine, and down a wide boulevard. But the walk served to settle the dinner and make room for some serious drinking.

Arriving at *George's* they went immediately to The Cave – the cellar where raucous entertainment was the norm. As they entered, a piano player banged out a popular tune and sang, *"We'll hang out our laundry on the Siegfried Line..."*

Two women danced on tables, their stocking tops showing as they tried to shag without falling.

Andy found a table in the corner. As they were sitting down, Trip grinned at the fellows.

He angled his chin at the dancing women, "Look at those fools."

Andy shouted over the music and other hubbub, "It'll soon be April Fool's Day, and we're the bigger fools for accepting Colonel Sweeny's offer to join the French Air Force!"

The others all nodded vigorously, conversation being somewhat difficult in the din.

An RAF Pilot Officer sat at the next table with three women, another RAF officer, and a French Air Force pilot. He was half drunk and was keeping time to the music. A small quintet was setting up in the opposite corner, the better to take over from the execrable banging on the piano.

He leaned over to the flyers' small corner table. He said to Andy, "Couldn't help overhearing, old boy. Flyers, are you?"

Andy said, "Yes. We were recruited by a man named Sweeny, who arranged transport and so on. We've been here for several weeks without contact from anyone. We've been to the French military headquarters. Got insulted there."

The Flying Officer turned to his companions and briefly conversed with the Frenchman. The Frenchman became animated.

The British officer turned back to Andy and said, "Sorry to be rude, Old Boy. My name is Paul Richey, Number One Squadron, RAF. Hurricanes. This is my friend, Flying Officer Les Clisby. He's Australian, so he doesn't speak English. And the Frog is *Capitaine* Jean-Pièrre Maréchal of the French Air Force."

Andy introduced himself and the others. "You gentlemen are the first fighter pilots we've met since getting to Paris nearly two months ago."

Richey said, "The Bomber types get free more often and come to Paris. We don't get here as often, being on alert and whatnot. We get into Nancy more often. Metz, occasionally. Paris is downright infrequent."

Andy asked, "Seen any Germans?"

"Oh, yes. We've had a go at a few. Have to be vigilant, you know. As they said in the Great War, 'Beware the Hun in the sun.'"

Red said, "Trip here has been shot at."

Richey and Clisby leaned forward. Richey said, "I say, shot at? By Jerry?"

Trip nodded. "Seems I was briefly an international criminal for volunteering to fly for the Republicans in Spain. Got out just in time."

"Fought the Jerrys, did you?"

Trip said, "Damaged a couple of Heinkel-111s and shot down a 109. Probably shot down the 109 that also shot me down as I was getting out of Spain during the last days."

Clisby exclaimed, "Stone tha' fucking crows, mate! Shot down a bloody 109!"

Trip said, "One that I'm sure of. The other is very likely. When I last saw him, he was streaming black smoke and coolant and in a dive at about 3000 feet. My *Mosca* was damaged, and the engine quit, so I was a bit busy."

The Frenchman raised an eyebrow, not really understanding the discussion.

Richey turned to the Capitaine Maréchal and spoke briefly.

The Frenchman rose from his chair. He saluted, *"Mon Dieu! Héros Américains!"*

Andy said to Richey, "Please ask him why the *Armee de l'Air* won't accept volunteers like us."

Richey spoke to the Frenchman for a moment. Jean-Pièrre's face fell. Rapid-fire French with a hint of disgust followed.

Richey turned back to Trip and said, "He regrets that the *Armée de l'Air* is undermanned to spend time and other resources to train flyers from other nations. The language barrier and other aspects are just too hard. Several of your countrymen have been turned away. They accepted some Czechoslovaks who were already flying in their own air force and escaped Hitler. It hurts Jean-Pièrre's soul to tell you that."

Trip said, "Thank you, and thank him for us. At least we have a straight answer. Now we will go to England and try there."

Richey's face became solemn. "Afraid it's most likely the same story, old boy. Then, there's the natural English proclivity to distrust anyone from anywhere else. Foolish. But there it is."

Clisby snorted, "Bloody fucking English. None of us are good enough for them."

Richey said, "Now, Les. You know that's not true."

"Right, well, I know we Aussies seem to be considered Englishmen for the duration."

Richey looked at Trip and the other Americans. "Later, we're going to the ANPA. It's the French Aviators' Association. Care to come along?"

Andy said, "We're in! But first, can you tell us how to get to England without being arrested?"

Chapter 24 – Vassincourt

On April 1st a telegram arrived at the hotel.

MONSEIUR GIBSON

HOTEL GRANDE DES ECOLES, PARIS

PLEASE JOIN US AT THE 1 SQDN MESS AT VASSINCOURT. FRIDAY 5 APRIL, 1700 HRS. BRING YOUR FRIENDS.

RICHEY

pilots across the breakfast table. "Looks like we're going to a party. Maybe we can get someone to help us join the RAF. The French are damn-sure no help."

Andy said, "I thought the night we met those fellows was supposed to be our last night in Paris. Aren't we heading for the channel coast and trying to catch a ride to England?"

Trip said, "That was the plan, but with Richey we have a definite contact in the RAF. Maybe we can hitch a ride on a transport to England."

Shorty said, "Worth a try."

Red nodded.

Andy said, "OK. Might as well. Hope it's not an April Fool's joke."

~~<>~~

Friday, April 5th dawned with pleasant weather, and the pilots dressed in good clothes. They each took an overnight bag; it would be late when the dinner was over. Trip thought that the worst that would happen was they would sleep in a tent.

The train ride to the small village of Vassincourt was not difficult. A taxi took the pilots down the *Grandes Boulevards* to the *Gare St*

Lazare. Several brief stops later, they arrived at Revigny-sur-Ornain, a medium-sized village north of Vassincourt.

Red rubbed his shoulders, which were achy from sitting on hard, wooden train benches. "You'd think with all the trains they have in this country, one would go the 30 miles from Paris to this little berg without stopping every 10 feet!"

Trip saw a man in an RAF uniform with three stripes on the sleeve. "Excuse me, Sir. One of the pilots from 1 Squadron invited us to join him at the mess tonight. Can you tell us how to get there?"

The sergeant stopped and looked at Trip goggle-eyed. "'Ere, now. Oi ain't tellin' you nothin' about the location of our unit. You moight be a bluudy spoi or a saboteur."

Trip reached in his pocket, "Here's the telegram. Do you know Pilot Officer Richey."

The sergeant examined the telegram closely. "Aye. Oi knows 'im."

Trip said, "Well, Sir, it would be helpful if you can point us in the right direction."

The sergeant drew himself up to his full height and looked down his nose at Trip. "First, don't call me Sir. Oi works for a bluudy livin'! Second, that lorry is going to the field. I reckon you can 'ave a roid. Oi can allus shoot yer if an officer objects."

Trip grinned at the others and jerked his head toward the RAF truck.

After several miles of bouncing on a dusty country road east of Vassincourt, the lorry suddenly slowed and turned right onto another narrow track. After another two minutes of bouncing and grinding gears, the lorry abruptly stopped.

"Right! Out *Gentlemen*." The sergeant's voice dripped with sarcasm. "Oi don't know if yer allowed 'ere, but 'ere we are. Flying Officer Richey will be found in that building. The tent is the ready area for

172

the pilots. The officers' mess and billets are in town. It's a quarter-mile walk down the 'ill."

Trip said, "Thank you, Sergeant."

"Flight Sergeant."

Trip said, "Ah, yes. Sorry. Afraid I don't know RAF ranks just yet. Again, our thanks. I hope to volunteer to join the RAF. Perhaps we will meet again."

The flight sergeant made a face that might have been considered a smile and said, "Oi doubt it, Sor. But should that 'appen, it will be moi pleasure."

The pilots instantly dismissed, the flight sergeant turned on his heel and marched toward a group of airmen. He shouted, "Oi, you lot! Be careful with that bluudy box! I'll 'ave you on a bluddy fizzer!"

Trip grinned at the others as they turned and walked toward the building.

Paul Richey burst out the door. "Trip, Andy, Shorty, Red! Welcome to our humble home."

~~<>~~

The group sat in the shade of the ready tent. The smell of hot canvas permeated the air. The ready tent would have been hot, but the April weather and a light breeze cutting under the rolled-up sides of the tent made the gathering pleasant.

A pair of Hurricanes roared by at 100 feet before pitching up individually to join the circuit around the field. Trip heard the engine note change as the Hurricanes settled onto the downwind leg. He watched as the landing gear came out of the wheel wells and the engine note changed again. In moments the Hurricanes rolled off a perch adjacent to the end of the runway and began their final turns, one after the other. The group paused to watch the two airplanes touch down in sequence.

Richey said, "They've fired their guns. Hope they bagged a couple of Jerries."

As the Hurricanes trundled to the parking area under the trees, Trip could see red tape shreds hanging off the airplanes' eight gunports. Black cordite smoke had smudged the gunports.

Richey said, "Care to see a Hurricane?"

All four Americans chorused, "You bet!"

They walked out to the recently landed airplanes. Les Clisby was climbing out of his Hurricane. "Stone the bloody crows! Welcome, Yanks!"

Richey said, "Hello, Les. Have any luck?"

"Had a go at a Dornier, but only knocked some pieces off it."

Richey said, "Les knocked down a Messerschmitt 110 on Monday. April Fool's joke for Jerry, what? Shot down a 109 on the 2nd. They've been menacing the French at the line."

Trip took 'the line' to mean the Maginot Line. The newspapers were full of stories of the valiant French beating the Germans at the front lines, and victory was imminent. Of course, it was propaganda.

Richey said, "I say, Les, would you show Red and Shorty the cockpit of your kite? I'll show Trip and Andy."

"No worries. Climb up, Mates."

Richey climbed up on the left side of the other Hurricane and said, "Trip, foot in the stirrup, hand in the handhold, and foot on the wing. Andy, same thing on the other side."

Trip was up first, and Richey indicated a pop-in panel, "Left foot in here, swing your right leg up and into the seat. Left leg in...and now grab the windscreen frame and step down into those troughs."

Trip said, "The Polikarpov had a similar layout. Not really luxurious, but got the job done."

Richey said, "I'd love to fly that little beast."

Trip said, "No, you wouldn't. Beast is right. Nasty center of gravity. Huge engine in front. A bitch to land. Had to fly the final turn nose high and hope not to get slow."

Richey said, "The Hurricane – he pronounced it Hurr-i-c'n – is docile. Flies the final turn a bit flatter with full flaps. Flaps don't add to lift, they're more like brakes. Keep the revs up, what?'

Trip nodded. "Horsepower?"

Paul Richey grinned. "Bit over a thousand, old boy. She'll get airborne in a trice. Have to hold the tail on the ground when you start her up. Stick right back for that. The clamp on the grip is the brake. Need both. A bit dodgy, first time."

Trip looked around the cockpit. Throttle – check. Same location as the *Mosca*, same function. The prop control was something new.

Richey said, "Constant speed propeller, old boy. Set it, and it will stay at the same RPM. Absolute must in combat. Variable pitch from about 6 degrees to about 35 degrees. Some of our kites have them. My machine still has the old Watts wooden two-blade prop."

Trip examined the landing gear lever. It was on the right side of the cockpit. The flap handle was just below that. "I'll bet that's a challenge on takeoff."

"Right-o. Have to get airborne, check for a good rate of climb, set the throttle and check prop control, and then change hands on the stick. Then you can flick off the down lock lever and crank the gear up. Some chaps have pranged trying to do too much."

Trip nodded. "The I-16 had manual gear. I always waited until I had a couple hundred feet before goofing around with the landing gear."

Richey said, "Yes. Only have to worry about overspeeding the undercart."

Trip nodded, "Interesting stick. The *Mosca* had a spade grip as well."

Richie nodded, "The control column goes back and forth for elevator control. This top section rotates right/left for roll control."

Pointing at the round, leather-covered spade grip, Richey said, "Already showed you the brake handle. This brass button is the gun switch, old man. Of course, please don't touch it on the ground. Safety, you understand. You'll note it rotates from 'safe' to 'fire.'"

Andy asked, "Is this a standard layout of the instruments for British airplanes?"

Richey said, "Regret to say, old boy, no. The layout is the whim of some boffin at Hawkers. I've seen a Spitfire. Similar, but not exact. Bloody well have to learn every airplane, what?"

As Richey was talking, Trip ran his eye over the instruments. Magnetos on the left – seemed standard. There was a separate magneto switch. He looked at Richey and raised an eyebrow.

Richey said, "Starting mag, Trip. It's that or one of the Erks will have to wind 'er up with a crank."

Andy said, "Erks?"

Richey grinned, "Ground crew, Mate. Best friends of a fighter pilot."

Trip asked, "You say wind it up. There's a hand crank?"

"Aye. Crank goes in a hole under the exhausts. The Erk turns it, actuating a sprocket and bicycle chain arrangement that starts the engine rotating. Hit the mags, crack the throttle, and – Bob's your uncle – off she goes."

Trip nodded his understanding.

He ran his eyes over the rest of the instruments. Gear-up indicator lights, magnetic compass. Trip smiled, he always called it a whiskey compass after early versions had the compass suspended in an alcohol-based liquid. Artificial horizon – a new thing for Trip, but one he had read about.

A gyro compass was in a gimbaled mount on the center bottom of the instrument panel. Trip was impressed with this new innovation but considered it a difficult location. The pilot would have to look around the control column.

He looked at the rest of the instruments. Turn and bank indicator – the old, but effective, needle and ball. A vertical velocity indicator and altimeter rounded out the flying instruments.

The engine instruments on the right were familiar: a tachometer, oil pressure, oil temperature, coolant temperature, oxygen pressure, and flow gauges.

He looked down and saw the fuel controls. "Is this the primer?"

Richey said, "Right again. Couple good shots and no more, else you flood her out."

Trip asked, "Wobble pump?"

"Right. If the fuel pump goes out, the wobble pump is the way to keep flying."

Trip said, "But the fuel selector is on the left."

Richey said, "Right. Bloody pain to remember switching tanks."

Trip climbed out. "Want to sit in her, Andy?"

Andy said, "Hell yes!"

Andy asked, "Is this an escape hatch on the right side?"

Richey said, "Right. If you had to get out in a scrape, pull the latches. Hood open first, of course."

The men walked around the airplane.

Richey pointed out the eight .303 Browning machine guns. "Reliable, but a bit light on hitting power. Jerry's got cannon, don't ye know?"

Trip said, "I've been hit by those cannon."

"Unpleasant, what?"

Trip nodded.

The four American pilots stood in front of the two Hurricanes, chatting with Paul Richey and Les Clisby. They watched as the Erks refueled the machines, the armorers reloaded the guns, and the other ground crew went about preparing the airplanes for the next sortie.

Trip looked across the field toward a line of wheat growing in the early spring sun. A Hurricane sat there looking forlorn.

"What's the story with that airplane, Paul?"

"Ah. Early Mark I. Shattered propellor. Derelict, I'm afraid."

"Shattered propellor?"

"Yes. It was one of those early Mark I's with a wooden two-blade airscrew. The airscrew hit a lorry that got too close as the engine was winding down. Bloody airman driving the lorry got fizzed right well. Not enough Rotol's to go around, have to have a new propeller shaft for that, anyway. We have no extra Watts propellers. They were all hauled off somewhere when the Rotols came in. We'll have to burn it one day soon if this keeps going as badly, as I think it will."

Trip said, "Damn shame."

Richey nodded. "Yes, well, fortunes of war, what?"

Andy said, "Paul, Les, this has been the most interesting hour."

Clisby said, "Bloody fucking Jerries are out to kill us all. I wish the bloody RAF would wake up and accept you blokes. This one – pointing to Trip – has proved he's mad enough to shoot it out with the bloody Jerries. I'm sure the rest of you are just as keen."

Andy asked, "I suppose taking one of these kites up for a go is out of the question?"

Richey said, "If it were up to me, we'd be flying now. But The Bull would have my guts for garters if we did that."

Andy asked, "The Bull?"

Clisby said, "Best CO in the RAF. Squadron Leader P. H. Halahan. The Bull. You'll see why he's called that when you meet him."

~~<>~~

Dinner in the No. 1 Squadron Officers' Mess was elegant, but spartan. It was also subdued.

Number 1 Squadron's commander, "The Bull," welcomed the Americans. "We wish you all could fight with us. Delighted to welcome you to the squadron." His Irish accent was thick, and with his massive shoulders and neck, Trip could see where he got the nickname.

Then The Bull turned somber; one of the squadron pilots had crashed and died. As the British said, Pilot Officer D. M. Smithers had "Bought the Farm." A brief prayer and a tribute to Smithers' bravery and flying acumen closed out the serious part of the evening.

The menu was roasted chicken, *haricots verts*, boiled potatoes, and baked apples. Scotch whiskey flowed like a river. Scotch was simply 'whiskey' to the Brits, for to them there was no other liquor.

Despite recently supping at *Maxim's*, Trip thought the meal wonderful. He sat quietly and drank in the atmosphere of the officers' mess. It reminded him of his time in Spain.

After the meal, the officers stood for a toast to Pilot Officer Smithers.

Trip found he had tears in his eyes.

Chapter 25 – April

Threalthe flyers reached *Gare St. Lazare* at about 2 pm on April 6th. They went straight to the hotel.

Trip checked messages and walked slowly back from the Concierge's desk.

"Well, fellows, we finally got a message. He handed it to Shorty, who read it and passed it on.

NO LUCK WITH FRENCH. MAKE YOUR WAY TO ENGLAND.

FUNDS ON DEPOSIT IN YOUR NAME AT BANQUE DU NORD DE PARIS.

REGRET UNABLE TO DO MORE.

SWEENY.

Andy sat and lit a cigarette. The others flopped in chairs. Andy said, "What now?"

Shorty said, "I'm short of cash, so first thing Monday, I need to go to that bank."

Red said, "I'd say that's our first stop. I hope there's enough money to get us out of France before the shit hits the fan."

Andy looked at Trip, who nodded. He said, "Guess that's settled, we go to the bank Monday, bright and early. Then we figure it out. I think we should all try to get to England. The good reception we received from the British was encouraging."

~~<>~~

The flyers spent a nervous day on Sunday, April 7, and ate a quiet meal in the hotel dining room. Each man was introspective about his future and what might be the amount of the funds at the bank. Would the funds be sufficient to get to England? Was that the right course? They discussed the possibility of going south to Spain and then Portugal.

Trip said, "Going South is not an option for me. I'm sure I'd be arrested and shot. For me, England is the answer. Either that or I somehow finagle getting into the French *Armée de l'Air*."

On Monday, the papers all reported an increasing drumbeat of war, and an invasion of France was on everyone's lips. The flyers had to contend with many patrons at the bank waiting to withdraw funds. It was not precisely a panic, but the fears of a German invasion stoked citizen concerns, and they were stockpiling money to be ready to flee.

Tall, with movie-star good looks, Andy Mamedoff was appointed spokesman. He straightened his tie and approached the bank manager. The others stood aside and waited nervously.

Trip noticed two similarly aged men with European-cut suits sitting on hard chairs outside the manager's office. He overheard them speaking in a strange, guttural language. Not German, but Eastern European. Trip wondered what they were doing but dismissed it when Andy returned.

Andy walked up and said, "He wants to see our identification. Your passport will do."

They returned with Andy and provided their passports. The manager went to the back of the bank for a brief time. He returned with four envelopes and asked each pilot to sign a receipt for 5000 francs - $100.

Walking out of the bank, Shorty said, "I'm going to England. Not sure how I'm going to get there, though. I guess a hundred bucks is enough to get me there."

Red said, "I think the Concierge at the hotel will know how to do that."

A moment later, a voice behind them called, "Hallo? Hallo?"

The flyers stopped and turned. It was the two Eastern Europeans from the bank.

Warily, Trip said, "Yes?"

The two men walked up, took off their hats, smiled, and bowed slightly. The blonde one said, "We hear you talk. We also pilot to fly for France, England...any but Russia. My friend has no English. You American, yes?"

Trip asked, "Where are you from?"

The men looked at one another, puzzled. "Yes?"

"What is your country?"

"Ah. We Czech. Hitler take our country. We come here to fight Nazi bastard Hitler."

Andy said, "Let's get out of the street and have some coffee."

The Czech said, "Coffee? Yes. Good."

The six men walked a block to a small bistro and took seats. With all the panicky citizens going to and fro, the bistro owner was delighted to have customers. He quickly brought coffee and some complimentary biscuits with jam.

The Czechs fell on the biscuits with vigor.

Trip asked, "When did you last eat?"

The blonde looked up, embarrassed. "We eat? Two days. We go bank to get money. We have money Czechoslovakia. Bank no give money. Bank also say France no take volunteers."

Red said, "We've been here for two months and no luck."

The blonde Czech pointed to himself. He said, "Jan Ruzicka."

The dark-haired Czech said, "Tomas Beneš."

The Americans introduced themselves.

Broken English and sign language established that Jan and Tomas were Czech Air Force pilots who fled Czechoslovakia after Hitler's takeover. Their commander, Major Alexander Hess, bade them farewell, reminding them of their oath saying they would meet again.

Jan said, "We have hope!"

Trip said, "We are going to England. You can go, too. But you'll need money."

He handed Jan his envelope of francs. "I don't need this money, so you can have it."

Jan and Tomas exchanged rapid-fire Czech. Jan looked at Trip, "This is loan. We pay back."

Trip said, "Don't worry about it."

Tomas spoke Czech to Trip. Tomas' eyebrows knit together, his mouth was turned down at the corners. It was a very sincere speech.

Jan said, "Tomas says he kill many Nazis. Every success yours because you kind to us. He thank you. I thank you. Americans, you are all the time wiz gas the cooking!"

~~<>~~

The six pilots walked to the *Hôtel Grandes des Ecoles* where Trip spoke with the concierge and asked about their stay.

"Your stay is paid through April 15th, Monsieur Gibson."

Trip smiled at the Concierge, "We have two new friends who are Czechoslovak pilots. They are passing through Paris on the way to England. Is there a room they can share? I'll pay for it."

"*Oui*. Will zey be saying long?"

Trip said, "I think we're all leaving on April 16th."

184

"Very well, *Monsieur* Gibson. We shall arrange a room for your friends."

Trip wandered back to the table where the five others sat. "Got a room for you, Jan and Tomas. We leave 16th April."

The group looked around at one another.

Shorty grinned, "Can't come too soon!"

Andy said, "We've been talking about going to Spain and getting on a boat to England. Either that or steal an airplane and fly to England."

Trip said, "I can't go to Spain. I also don't think stealing a plane is a good idea. You could get shot doing that."

Jan said, "You no go to Spain, Trip?"

Trip grinned, "Wore out my welcome there last year."

Jan looked puzzled.

Trip explained, "I flew for the Spanish Republican Air Force. I'm now under a death threat from the Spanish."

Jan looked disgusted, "Ah. Well, we all under fucking death threat from fucking Hitler!" He made a spitting sound.

Trip said, "I'm not a communist, but I flew Russian airplanes against Hitler's Messerschmitts. Now Spain would just love to put me against a wall."

Andy said, "Aw, shit! The best way out of here is through Spain. What are we going to do, then?"

Trip said, "Y'all are going through Spain. I'm going to see if I can't get our new British friends to let me hitch a ride on one of their transports."

Shorty said, "But, we'd be splitting up. Shouldn't we stick together?"

185

Trip said, "Shorty, there's too much going on for us to worry about things like that. I'd love to go with you, but Spain is too big a threat for me. So, y'all go. We'll plan to beat it out of here on the 16th."

Red said, "Damned if that's not good thinking, but I think we've kind of become the *Four Horsemen*, you know?"

Trip said, "I do too, but this will not get better. I think the Nazis are coming over the border any day now. When that happens, all bets are off. Best y'all get going before the border to Spain closes, and you get trapped."

Andy said, "That settles it. Jan and Tomas will go with us. We'll meet you in London. Ever been there?"

Trip said, "Yeah, last year for a week. Leave a message at the RAF Club. It's in Piccadilly. If I get there first, I'll do the same."

Andy looked around the table, "That leaves us one week to get maps, make plans, get train tickets, settle finances, and so on. Agreed?"

Chapter 26 – Madame Allard

Trip sat in his room writing. The late afternoon sun cast shadows across the small desk.

Hotel des Grandes Ecoles, Paris   *April 8, 1940*

Dearest Ellie

I hope this finds you well and happy.

I am still in Paris. Three other volunteers and I have had no luck volunteering for the French Armée de l'Air. I have a friend who might help. Otherwise, I will try the Royal Air Force. I have another friend who might help.

I will do what I can to stop the Nazis, Ellie. I hope you can see that is necessary.

Know that I am safe and well. I think of you often.

Wish me luck?

All my love,

Trip

Trip wrote similar letters to his parents and Kathy. Then he wrote a single letter to Al Norham at his old apartment. It was for all his friends at Georgia Tech. This letter closed with a postscript encouraging them to consider going through Canada and volunteering for the RAF. He reminded Al of the contact information in the kitchen drawer. He said he hoped to see them all in England soon.

Trip sealed the letters and took them downstairs to the concierge. He paid for the postage and left 200 francs for the concierge's trouble.

~~<>~~

Trip put on his hat and naval peacoat against the harsh chill of the waning, bitter 1940 winter and left the hotel. He sauntered along the street to the Seine and then along the left bank. It was now dusk, and the shadows were lengthening as the sky became more gray than blue.

An alert sounded, and the few strollers scattered. Trip didn't bother. So far, the Luftwaffe had not attacked Paris. At least Trip had not heard of bombs falling on Paris. Who would attack such a beautiful place?

Trip lived through several bombings in Madrid. He and Hemingway, sometimes Dos Passos, and occasionally Martha Gellhorn, sat drinking, listening to the whistle of falling bombs. They grinned at one another as they estimated the distance of the ensuing blast from the *Hotel La Florida*. Dos Passos and Gellhorn would seek shelter. Neither Trip nor Hemingway would move. To do so was, in Hemingway's estimation, unmanly. On one occasion, Trip accused Hemingway of trying to be Teddy Roosevelt in proving his manliness. Hemingway snorted and poured another drink, proving Trip's point.

While Trip didn't cower in fear of a Nazi bomb as he walked the *Rive Gauche*, he did pick up the pace. It was more a case of wanting to catch Louise Allard at home before the supper hour. He hoped she was alone.

He darted off the river to her street, an address he knew without looking. He hustled up three treacherously narrow flights of winding stairs to the third floor. There were two glossy black doors. The one on the left was Louise's flat with a balcony that looked out toward the Eiffel Tower. Tapping on Louise's door, Trip reflected that the rent must be astronomical.

Trip waited as he heard heels on the hard floor. The door opened a crack. "Trip! *Mon Dieu!* I wondered 'oo could be knocking. Come in."

Louise was ten years older but looked younger than Trip. Her skin was tight, and her blonde hair was styled in a short, shaggy cut with wings framing her face and complementing her square jawline. Her blue eyes were young and, at the same time, watchful like a much older woman's.

Louise was spare, perhaps 100 pounds. She had dancer's legs and sculpted buttocks. Her shoulders were square, and her posture was erect. She wore casual clothes in a way that made them look like they were from the most elegant designer in all of Paris. Perhaps they were.

Louise grabbed Trip's lapels and shoved him against the wall. She kicked the door closed and kissed him, her tongue darting and her breath coming in hurried gasps.

She leaned back to look into Trip's eyes. "Damn you! You pop up at ze oddest times. Thank God Marcel isn't here. But then, he's never here, even when there's not a war. He tires of me, I sink."

Trip said, "It is impossible to tire of you, Louise."

"*Non? Non?* You do not come often. Is there not a younger, more beautiful, more … accommodating … young woman in your bed? Does she use her mouth on you? You bastard!" She shoved him away.

Trip said, "Honestly, there is no one else, Louise. I came to ask a couple of favors."

"Oh, and now you want somesink. Well, we'll talk about that after." Louise grabbed Trip's hand and started dragging him toward the bedroom."

"Shouldn't I take my coat off."

"*Oui*! By all means. Let me 'elp you wiz your coat."

Louise grabbed his lapels and dragged the coat from his shoulders.

"I'll just 'ang eet up." She dropped the coat on the floor. She turned and said, *"Allons-y!"*

She kicked off her shoes and headed toward the bedroom. As she walked, she was unbuttoning her dress. She reached the bedroom door, turned, and appraised Trip.

"You 'ave too much clothes, Trip."

Her dress was open down the front, and she was tugging at the last buttons. One breast was out of her chemise.

Trip paused and kicked off his shoes. He shucked his jacket and tie and, undoing his belt, let his trousers drop in a puddle. He quickly unbuttoned his shirt and followed Louise into her bedroom.

Louise was already on the bed wearing only her wine-colored chemise and a pair of stockings held up by a garter belt. Her underwear was missing. Perhaps she had not worn any.

~~<>~~

Trip's stomach growled. It was nearing 8 p.m. He rolled up on an elbow and looked at Louise. Perhaps a tiny bit of age was beginning to show on her face. A tiny line or two. No matter. Louise Allard was stunning.

Trip asked, "Do you want to get food?"

"Oui. Ze bistro in ze next street is open."

They dressed quickly and walked down the narrow stair, Trip held onto the handrail for dear life lest he miss a step and end up in a pile at the bottom. He did not worry about Louise. She navigated these steps daily.

They walked to the smoky bistro. The clink of glasses and the murmur of dozens of patrons created a soft backdrop to the red leather of the chairs and the dark wood paneling. The smell of fresh bread broke through the pungent cigarette smoke.

The owner spotted Louise through the dim light. "*Bonjour, Madame Allard*. I see you 'ave brought your cousin from the *États-Unis*."

Trip said, "*Bonjour, Alphonse*. Nice to see you again."

Alphonse quickly seated them at the best corner table and brought Louise's usual robust red vintage.

Out of *Gauloises*, Trip lit a *Gitane* and looked out at the busy bistro. Several tables of patrons were eating, drinking, and smoking. A car roared by on the street only feet from their table. Its lights were on full bright. It was difficult to tell there was a war.

Glasses poured, and Alphonse at a discrete distance, Trip said, "I need your help. I need to reach André Malraux."

"And why do you need to reach Malraux?"

"I'm trying to join the French *Armée de l'Air*."

"I am aware zat ze *Armée de l'Air* is French, Trip. And why do you think Malraux can 'elp you?"

"I, that is, we – several other Americans – are here to volunteer. We have tried through official channels. I want to fly and fight the Nazis."

"*Mon Dieu!* But you are crazy. America has not, 'ow you say, a horse in zis race."

"We will soon enough, Louise."

"Ah, well...perhaps. But you are unlucky. Malraux is gone to ze Army. I do not know where he is."

Trip's face fell. "Goddamn it."

"What? You are now sorry zat we fuck like *Lapine* – ze rabbits?"

Trip said, "Not at all. I'm quite enamored of you, *Ma Cher*."

191

She smiled at him, a tinge of sadness in her eyes, "Don't say zat. You don't care for Louise. You use me."

Trip grinned, "Hmmm...I think perhaps it was I who got used."

Louise's mouth turned down, and her chin quivered. "Trip, I am old. I'm saggy. My *seins* droop. My *cul* is saggy. Marcel does not care for me. I ache for attention, and there is none."

Trip smiled gently, "Louise, you are spectacularly beautiful. You move with dancer's grace. Your *cul* is hard as a rock, like an *adolescente*. Yet, you are soft and feminine. If Marcel ignores you, then find another."

"Ah, Trip. You are the nicest man. Are all *Amis* as kind and gentle?"

"I don't know. It's just that you are far more beautiful than I deserve."

"*Hein*, you are full of shit. But I love you, Trip. I can 'elp you get in ze *Armée de l'Air*."

"You can?"

"*Oui*. Now feed me *un petit steak et pommes frites*. I want ze steak bloody. Then we will return to my little flat, where I shall attempt to render you unconscious."

Chapter 27 – The General

Afrigid morning wind prickled Trip's skin as he walked to a newsstand near the Seine. The spring thaw had not yet arrived and the wind off the Seine was biting. The trees had not yet budded, and the bare branches rattled in the breeze.

Trip bought an English-language newspaper and a copy of Life Magazine. The latest issue of Life available was dated April 1st. Trip thought it was a bit out of date being two weeks old at this point, but better than nothing. He hoped some pictures of normal American life might counter his mild homesickness now that the others were gone.

Trip walked back toward the *Hôtel Grandes des Ecoles*. The wind was now in his face and seemed even colder now that he was alone. The others left yesterday. The night before was quite a party of booze and women, some were from jazz clubs, and a couple were whores. Trip didn't care. He was still exhausted from his romp with Madame Allard, so he drank, laughed, and watched as the others cavorted.

The hotel staff had become friends with the pilots and indulged the crazy *Amis* as they goofed around in the bar and spilled out into the lobby. The night manager set up free drinks and toasted the airmen as they headed off to seek glory as soldiers of fortune.

Morning came, and the three Americans and two Czechs, bleary from a lack of sleep, solemnly shook Trip's hand and bade him farewell.

Trip grinned at the lot and said, "Be careful crossing the border into Spain. You'll probably be okay flashing your passports. Neither the U.S. nor Czechoslovakia are at war with Germany, so the Spaniards aren't likely to give you a hard time. Just remember to keep your mouths shut while in Spain. They're mostly Nazis these days, I hear."

Andy spoke up, "We'll see you in England. I bet we'll beat you there. We'll leave a message for you at the RAF Club in Piccadilly."

Trip nodded. "I'm still going to try to get into the French Air Force. I'd like to fly that Curtiss Hawk 75. Seems a modern airplane."

Shorty said, "I'll fly anything they give me."

Red grinned, "We'll get you some extra seat cushions, Shorty."

Shorty smirked, "I'll fly the son-of-a-bitch standing up if I have to!"

Everyone, including the Czechs, laughed.

Jan and Thomas each made a short speech that amounted to sincere thanks for the money and the chance to go kill Nazis.

Trip reminded them that the money was a gift, not a loan, and to use it wisely.

Trip looked at each face as if memorizing it. "Good luck! I'll see you in England."

~~<>~~

Now, Trip was waiting for something. He was not sure what, exactly. But the air crackled with tension. A few days ago, the Nazis invaded Norway and kicked off what Trip thought was the end of the Phoney War. The British were frantically moving troops toward Norway and landing them on beaches along the West Coast. Places like Trondheim, Narvik, and Oslo were in the news.

Trip slumped in a chair in the lobby and looked at the newspaper. The newspaper column mentioned German concerns about keeping access to Norway's Iron Ore through the port of Narvik. There had been a couple of naval engagements, and Narvik was a major strategic objective.

The English-language newspapers were uniformly outraged that Germany had invaded a neutral nation. The newspapers were also outspoken in condemning a man named Vidkun Quisling, a minor Norwegian official who collaborated with the Germans to facilitate their takeover. Already, *quisling* had become a widely used word for traitor.

The Germans countered that they had long feared a British takeover of Norway to deny the Germans use of the desperately needed iron ore. They insisted they took Norway in response to the clear intent of the British to invade Norway. The Germans insisted that the Norwegians were, after all, Germanic Peoples, and Germany was merely protecting their native relations against the avaricious Britons.

Of course, the British insisted that this was all Nazi propaganda. Britain would never violate another nation's avowed neutrality. Norway was yet another victim of Hitler's design of world domination.

Trip tossed the paper on a table for others who might speak English. Terrible news all around, yet he knew his countrymen at home were disinterested in the war in Europe. For that matter, they didn't care about Japan's mistreatment of China.

~~<>~~

Trip leafed through the Life Magazine. The cover featured Johnny Rucker, the New York Yankees' rookie Centerfielder. Trip grinned: *Another Georgia Boy. Hope he does well.*

He flicked through. Saw an ad for *Lucky Strike Cigarettes*. He lit a Gauloise, which tasted harsh from the heavy Turkish tobacco. They were the best cigarettes you could get in France and available everywhere. Trip had become accustomed to the harsh bite of the Turkish tobacco. He often tried to chew some Juicy Fruit to cut the bite, but gum was not as popular in France as it was in the U.S., and it was hard to find.

Trip was pissed off to the gills at Life Magazine's pandering to the Nazis. One photo was of a young German aircraftsman draped in machinegun bullet bandoliers. *Nice! That little bastard is arming Nazi planes to kill Frenchmen!*

What really incensed Trip was the fawning article on Colonel-General von Brauchitsch, Commander of the German Army. *Wonderful! This* nice Nazi *was raised a Prussian, which excuses his unfeeling persecution of any population named an enemy by Hitler.*

Trip thought the crowning glory of Life's descent into absurdity was a friendly article about the meeting among Hitler, Mussolini, Chamberlain, and Lebrun. Trip snorted, *Ridiculous! Old news, and just look at that pompous little shit, Mussolini!*

He threw the magazine on the table in disgust. The only rational, true thing in the entire book was a shot of two girls jitterbugging, their faces animated by the great fun of moving in rhythm to some swing tune. The ignorant laughing faces and the fawning treatment of people whom Trip was sure would become America's enemies reflected the desperation of the intelligentsia to keep the U.S. neutral in a conflict that would certainly spread. Trip scowled, *It'll be our war soon.*

~~<>~~

A messenger came into the lobby area and conferred with the Concierge. The Concierge pointed toward Trip, who perked up at this interest.

The messenger walked quickly over to Trip and said, *"Monsieur Gibson?"*

Trip said, *"Oui."*

The messenger wordlessly handed over an envelope and paused.

Fishing out a ten-franc coin and flicking it to the messenger, Trip said, *"Merci."*

The messenger smirked, *"Merci bien."*

Trip thought *Huh, guess he wanted more.*

The messenger departed without looking around the lobby.

Trip popped open the message.

MONSIEUR R. GIBSON

HÔTEL GRANDES DES ECOLES, PARIS

CONTACT GENERAL D'ASTIER DE LA VIGERIE. NORTHERN ARMY ZONE. TOUL-CROIX DE METZ. SHOW HIM THIS MESSAGE.

MON GENERAL SE PORTER GARANT DE ROBERT GIBSON UN INTREPIDE AVIATEUR AMÉRICAIN. RECOMMANDE.

LOUISE ALLARD

Trip sat back and re-read the message. *Well, now. This is a twist.*

That afternoon Trip packed his backpack. He smiled as he did this. *I'm glad I ditched a suitcase.*

He also checked his money belt. In addition to his carefully folded birth certificate and U.S. Passport, he had nearly $600. He extracted $100 to convert to Francs. *Hope that's enough walking around money.*

Trip spoke with the Concierge about settling the bill. He owed less than 100 Francs which he paid, and informed the Concierge that he would leave in the morning.

~~<>~~

April winds blew cold from the East that day, and Trip felt the need to hurry. The Nazis were blowing an ill wind from the East. Trip squinted against the chill breeze. *Maybe they're preoccupied with Norway, and there's time for me to get into the action, after all.*

He walked briskly to *Gare St. Lazare* and booked a train ticket to Nancy through Metz.

~~<>~~

Things were not going well in Norway. This added to the already twitchy mood in France. The twitch was clearly stronger as the train went farther East of Paris.

Trip saw a good many people heading West on the main roads. Some people were in crowded passenger cars. Trip saw trucks and mule- or horse-drawn wagons piled high with possessions. Many families were on foot with hobo-sacks over their shoulders or pushing wheelbarrows. *Good thing I got this pack. Might need it.*

After four hours, several delays, and a transfer in Metz, Trip stepped off the train in Nancy. The wind blew even colder from the East. Hunkering into his peacoat, Trip hustled to find a taxi. This was no mean feat considering the jittery mood of the public. Many taxi drivers were ill-disposed to leaving their homes for more than a few minutes. Evacuation might come at any moment. Their taxicab might be their salvation.

The taxi bucked and swayed, avoiding refugees plodding along the road from Nancy to Toul. An hour later, the taxi arrived at the Toul-Croix de Metz Airdrome gate. Trip gave the driver an extra 250 Francs for his trouble.

It was a $5 tip, and the driver grinned. *"Merci bien. Bon chance, Monsieur."*

Trip walked to the sentry at the gate and asked in his best French to speak to the *capitaine* of the guard. The sentry looked bored and inclined his head toward a small building beside the gate.

Trip walked to the building and opened the door.

A rough voice said, *"Oui? Entré."*

The voice belonged to a slightly portly French lieutenant.

Trip stepped into the office and stood at what he hoped might look like the position of attention. Handing the lieutenant his passport and birth certificate, Trip said, *"Monsieur, je suis Robert Gibson, aviateur Américain volontaire pour le Armée de l'Air."*

The lieutenant's eyes popped wide open, *"Tu me chies! Uh...en Anglais..."* The lieutenant drummed his finger on the desk, momentarily lost in thought. He hit on the phrase."You shit me."

Trip grinned. *"Non.* I'm not shitting you. I want to fly fighters against *les Boches."*

The lieutenant looked Trip over from head to toe. He scowled and said, "Come."

~~<>~~

The chubby lieutenant, whose name Trip never got, walked with a purpose across a dusty parade ground to a permanent building made of red brick and native stone.

They went inside, and the lieutenant pointed to a seat. "Sit."

The lieutenant stepped into an office and closed the door. Trip was left cooling his heels, looking out a dirty window at the northeast/southwest grass runway. He idly watched a flight of four Curtiss Hawk 75s take off. The throaty roar of their Pratt and Whitney Twin Wasp 1830s reminded him of the *Mosca's* rumble. Trip grinned to himself, *It should; the engines are similar.*

The lieutenant stepped out of the office and jerked his head, indicating Trip should enter the office. The lieutenant left, a confused scowl still etched on his chubby face.

A *commandant* sat behind an imposing mahogany desk looking at Trip's passport and birth certificate.

The *commandant* looked up at Trip with narrowed eyes, "Who the hell are you, exactly?"

Trip was at a bit of a loss. "Uh, my name is Robert H. Gibson, III. My friends call me Trip, *Monsieur Commandant.* I have nearly 850 flying hours, including 350 combat hours flying against the Nationalists in Spain last year. I believe I can help beat the Nazis. Here is my flying logbook."

Trip handed over his logbook and the telegram from Louise.

"Also, this is a telegram from a friend. She is acquainted with General de la Vigerie. The telegram vouches for me."

The commandant sat back in his chair. "Most *inhabituel*, Monsieur Gibson. Most irregular."

Trip said, "I want to help stop *les Boches*."

The commandant, whose name appeared to be Desrosiers, said, "I will take you to the general. He will decide. I must warn you, you may face a firing squad for being a potential quisling."

Trip swallowed hard. "I'm no quisling. I'm here to help."

"We shall see."

~~<>~~

General de la Vigerie steepled his fingers. "What am I to do with you? I know Madame Allard. Beautiful and pleasant lady. She is most reliable. But, then, you may have seduced her to gain her confidence."

Trip said, "Don't you think a fifth columnist would be more direct than to enlist a beautiful Parisian woman to infiltrate a small, out-of-the-way aerodrome like this?"

The general smirked, "Just so...or maybe it is a subtle ploy. Mata Hari was shot in the moat at Le Chateau Vincennes. She was equally subtle. Perhaps Madame Allard has turned to *les Boches*, and you are in league with her. Her husband ignores her at his peril, I think."

Trip couldn't help laughing. "Jesus, *Mon General*! Not everyone is against France."

"You laugh at me?"

"Yes. I'm sorry. But, yes."

The general harrumphed, "I am not accustomed to ridicule, Monsieur."

Trip said, "You know Malraux? The writer?"

"*Oui*. Everyone knows zat tiresome little man. Why do you ask?"

"Malraux recruited me to go to Spain and fight the Nationalists. You could check with him. I hope he doesn't ridicule you."

"Oh, *oui*, I of course 'ave time to 'unt down Monsieur Malraux and ask about some unimportant *pilote Américain*. *Non*, I 'ave un better idea. We shall give you a flying test. Fail and be shot. Succeed and...we shall consider your request."

Vigerie pushed a button on his desk, and a lieutenant instantly appeared in the door. Orders in rapid-fire French went completely over Trip's head, but the next thing he knew the lieutenant beckoned, and the general sat back with an enigmatic smile.

Trip reached for his papers. The general said, "I shall keep these. We may need to provide them to the *l'Ambassade des Etats-Unis* with proof of your execution."

As the door closed, Trip heard the general say, *"Mon Dieu. Où va le monde?"*

~~<>~~

The lieutenant escorted Trip out of the building and marched him toward the flight line.

The lieutenant wore a pilot's badge and steered Trip toward a Curtiss H-75. It was painted light blue-gray on the undersurfaces. Part way up the side of the fuselage the blue-gray blended into random dark green, brown, and medium gray patches that covered the upper surfaces of the trim little airplane.

The lieutenant said, "I am Edmond Marin la Meslée."

Trip said, "I'm Robert Gibson, my friends call me Trip."

"Well, Trip, please climb up on the wing and into the cockpit."

Trip sat looking at the instrument panel. It was his first time seeing an American-built fighter plane this close-up. The instrument panel reminded him of the Hawker Hurricane.

"I've never managed a constant-speed propeller before."

The lieutenant smirked, "But you are an aviator, *non*? It should be simple. You set ze revolutions and control ze throttle. Ze manifold pressure should not exceed 100 cm."

Trip looked over the instruments. Nothing overly complicated and not terribly different from the *Mosca*. Maybe more sophisticated instruments, where the *Mosca* was more primitive.

Meslée said, "Let us learn the cockpit of zis machine. One point: ze throttle operates in reverse. You must pull to go faster."

Trip said, "Wow. That's a surprise."

Meslée went over several instruments, and discussed the start sequence. He finished the discussion with, "Zis lever is ze landing wheels...*trois lumiéres verts* is down and locked, *non*? Zis lever is ze flaps. Remember throttle back means faster."

Trip said, "Ok. Now what?"

Meslée grinned, "Now we fly. I will be in zat Curtiss, you in zis one. We will see if you can fly ze airplane."

Trip grinned, "And?"

"And if you cannot, you will be shot. Assuming you can land. If not, I shall shoot you down. If you run, I shall shoot you down."

Trip grinned at Meslée. He liked him immensely. "What if I shoot *you* down?"

"I 'ave bullets, you do not."

Chapter 28 – Flight Check

Trip remembered the lessons from Meslée. Once the ground crew pulled the propellor through a few times on the engine to clear the oil sump, start the engine.

Suck in twice on the primer, pushing slowly to load the carburetor with fuel, but not too much. Magnetos on - check. Starter switch— hold until the prop slowly turns over and then faster until a couple coughs from the engine and the prop catches. Quickly crack the throttle (remember to pull back!).

Thram, bam, thram, bam, brrrrram, brrrrram! Smoke popped from the twin exhausts under the engine.

Trip gently nudged the throttle. Brrrrrammmm....Brooooorrrrrrr!

The engine settled into a thrashing bang, pop, bam, bang rhythm. Trip cracked the throttle more, and the engine settled into a smooth rumble.

He looked across to Meslée, who moved a finger in a circle in the air. Meslée's dappled blue, green, and gray Curtiss moved forward slowly and then a bit faster. The rudder on Meslée's Curtiss wiggled to the right as the airplane's nose swung toward the southeast end of the wide grass strip. Trip followed Meslée, his Curtiss bucking in the rutted grass of the flying field.

They reached what looked to Trip like the runway. Meslée turned left onto the wide strip of grass that ran Northeast. Approximate heading 020 degrees. Trip followed Meslée's lead, staying to Meslée's left and dropping his flaps for takeoff.

Trip moved the control stick fore-aft, right, left. He danced on the rudders to assure the controls were fully operable.

Meslée left his canopy open, and so did Trip. Didn't matter to Trip; he was used to flying in an open cockpit.

Trip watched Meslée as he put on his oxygen mask and followed suit. He looked at the oxygen regulator and decided that the switch was in the right place. He could taste dry, cold air, so oxygen must be flowing. He hoped so. Succumbing to hypoxia and auguring into the ground would be an ignominious death.

Meslée looked over to Trip and made a circular motion with his index finger. Trip saw his engine run-up. Smoke popped from the exhausts, and the prop went from ticking over to a blur.

Trip pulled the throttle back until it reached the stop. His engine was straining at a smooth roar. He was standing on the tops of the rudder pedals, holding the brakes as the engine strained to make the plane move forward.

Meslée was clearly standing on the brakes, but suddenly his airplane jolted forward.

Trip could taste a little exhaust in the back of his throat. When Meslée moved forward, Trip dropped his feet off the brakes, and his Curtiss jolted forward.

Trip danced on the rudders and worked the control stick to stay on Meslée's left wing. He kept a line from his windshield frame to Meslée's windshield frame. He remained on that line as the airplanes gained speed, bouncing and jarring on the turf of the runway.

In no time, Trip felt the landing gear leave the grass. Watching Meslée's plane, Trip saw the landing gear start to retract. He hit the brakes and jerked the lever for the landing gear. When he saw Meslée's flaps start to move, he hit the flap lever to the up position.

They climbed. Trip was unsure of the exact settings because he adjusted the throttle and pitch to remain on the imaginary line from his cockpit to Meslée's. When the control stick became heavy, Trip reached down with his left hand to rotate the trim wheel backward until it required minimal pressure to keep the stick in one place. Still, Trip clung to the imaginary line to Meslée's cockpit.

Five minutes later, Trip stole a glance at the altimeter. They were passing 4000 meters. Trip calculated this to be about 13,000 feet. Glancing beyond Meslée Trip could see the ground receding, confirming this altitude. He also confirmed that Meslée had slowly turned left to a heading of about 270° - West toward Paris. They were still climbing.

Soon, Meslée made a hand motion indicating leveling off. Trip watched closely as Meslée's Curtiss changed attitude to comfortably settle at 4500 meters. Cutting the throttle somewhat, Trip felt his Curtiss settle into level flight.

We're at 15,000 feet. Now what?

Meslée made a hand signal indicating Trip was to take the lead. Trip nudged the throttle to slightly increase airspeed while Meslée extended the formation somewhat to the right and settled onto Trip's right wing.

Trip looked over his right shoulder at Meslée, who dropped his oxygen mask and grinned. He twirled a finger and dipped a wing to the left, indicating he wanted Trip to pitch hard left, and the mock dogfight would be on.

Trip pulled the throttle to fully open, shooting forward quickly. Trip also dumped the nose a few degrees, rapidly building airspeed. Glancing at Meslée to be sure he was well aft, Trip shoved the stick forward and hauled it right. He roared under Meslée's airplane by a few feet, reversed his turn, and swung onto Meslée's tail. He backed off the throttle.

"Tat, tat, tat, tat." Trip radioed.

Meslée snatched the Curtiss into a hard right turn, and Trip pulled the throttle to 100% as he pitched up, stood on his right wing, and kicked right rudder to swing the nose down onto Meslée.

"Tat, tat, tat, tat." Trip radioed, again.

Meslée instantly rolled inverted and Split-S'ed toward the ground. Trip held his altitude and airspeed as he watched.

Meslée was screaming at the ground, perhaps 500 kph, when he pulled up into a zoom climb, hoping to catch Trip unaware.

Trip rolled off his high perch and half-rolled to wings level in a dive at half throttle. Meslée flew right into Trip's sights.

"Tat, tat, tat, tat." Trip radioed again.

Meslée flew up to Trip's altitude and made a hand signal to rejoin.

Trip coasted into easy formation and settled onto Meslée's wing. Meslée dipped a wing to the east, indicating to return to base. Trip nodded, and they turned smoothly toward Toul-Croix de Metz.

~~<>~~

As the two Curtiss' rolled out on a heading of 090° - due East – Trip's old air combat habits were functioning just like in Spain. His head was on a constant swivel, an uncomfortable feeling while wearing a starched civilian shirt. He loosened his tie and popped open his top button.

In the high distance Trip saw some dots. Aircraft? Maybe 20? He was not sure.

He pulled more throttle and moved ahead some so Meslée could see him. He pointed and made a hand signal indicating 20.

Meslée shrugged. He pointed at Trip's guns and made a hand signal indicating zero. No shells in Trip's guns.

Trip held his hand out, palms up, in the universal language of "who knows." He then swung on a left heading of about 030° and pushed up his throttle a bit. He began a climb to get above the dots that he thought must be enemy aircraft. Glancing right he could see Meslée hanging on his wing.

I must be out of my mind. I got no shells in my guns, and he does. I'm leading this, but we should be rat-racing back to the base to put these airplanes on the ground.

Trip considered the situation. He glanced around the cockpit and spotted a small panel with six switches with counters next to them. *Huh, those must be the gun switches. Funny, the round counters all register 500.*

Trip thought for a moment, *What the hell.*

He reached down below the throttle quadrant on his left and turned on the reflector gun sight. The electric ring popped up on the combining glass in front of him, and he looked at the gun switches again.

He hit the trigger on the control stick. Nothing. He looked at the various switches, all marked in French. He reached over and flicked each gun switch. Then he hit the trigger on the control stick.

Brrrammm! All six guns fired, startling Trip. *Why, that lying son-of-a-bitch! These guns are loaded!*

Trip waggled his wings and pointed to the dots. Meslée nodded. He grinned as he put his oxygen mask back on.

Trip pulled the throttle to fully open and raised the nose of the Curtiss to increase their climb. Unsure of the best climb speed, Trip used the 200 kph of the Mosca. *That ought to be close enough.*

He looked to see that the afternoon sun was behind him and maneuvered slightly to put it more so. Trip started into an upward spiral, he did not want to close with the oncoming aircraft until he had the height advantage.

Trip and Meslée climbed hard, and still, the dots were above them. The dots were now resolving into airplanes, not that this was a surprise.

Trip strained to climb. He wanted the altitude advantage over the other airplanes. Trip was now convinced the dots were German. The French would not fly in a large formation on an easterly heading. No, these were Huns.

The cockpit was getting quite cold, so Trip rolled the canopy closed. He deciphered that a handle on the lower right of the instrument panel was the heater control. He cranked that open and instantly felt welcome heat pouring out near his icy feet. He grinned a rueful grin. He was wearing his cap-toe oxfords and thin dress socks.

~~<>~~

Trip glanced at the altimeter and airspeed indicator. He was at about 6300 meters. He did some mental calculations and realized this amounted to about 22,000 feet. No wonder his bowels were painful with gas. The altitude made his bowel gas expand, and he farted copiously.

Trip leveled off at about 7,500 meters, some 25,000 feet. The climb had stolen much of the airspeed. Trip looked hard for the enemy aircraft. They were nowhere to be seen. He lowered the nose of the Curtiss to build some airspeed. This revealed the enemy formation.

And they were definitely enemies. Trip saw eight twin-engine bombers with thin fuselages and twin tails. Dorniers? They were escorted by another eight Bf-109s with bright yellow noses. These were the familiar E-model Bf-109s. Trip remembered the E-model having two 20-millimeter wing cannon and two 7.92-millimeter nose guns. Lethal.

The bombers were at about 20,000 feet, and the fighter escort was about 2,000 feet higher, four on either side of the bombers' track. Trip and Meslée flew over the top of the enemy formation.

Arcing down in a descending 180° turn, Trip and Meslée roared down on the bombers at nearly 500 kph, about 300 mph. The bombers were the important target. They would kill Frenchmen on the ground.

The two Curtiss fighters flashed past the 109s so fast that there was no reaction. Trip picked out two bombers on the left and expected Meslée to do the same on the right.

Trip throttled back and dumped some flaps to slow down. A quick look over his shoulder told him the Messerschmitt pilots were now aroused and coming to defend the bombers.

Too late.

Trip turned his attention back to the Dornier on the far left and centered it in the reflector sight ring. When the bomber's wing tips touched the edges of the electronic ring, Trip held down the trigger on his control stick's pistol grip, sending thousands of rounds of .30 caliber bullets flying at the hapless Nazi airplane. He later realized he had held the trigger down for a full six seconds. Too long. A waste of ammunition.

Flame immediately licked back from the starboard engine. The gunner on the top of the Dornier fired at Trip, but Trip had already rolled hard right and tacked onto his second target.

The second gray-green Dornier with a prominent swastika on its tail was already shooting at Trip as he rolled out. Trip ignored the defensive fire and centered the bomber in the reflector ring. He hit the trigger a second time.

Brrrrrrraaaaaaammm...the guns hammered for two long seconds and quit. *Damn!* Now he truly was out of ammunition.

Trip saw pieces fly off the Dornier. Then, he was by the bombers, rolling inverted and pulling into a Split-S maneuver. Diving toward the ground, Trip rotated his head in every direction, looking for Bf-109s and Meslée.

Trip spotted Meslée 500 meters to his port side and a hundred meters back. Good.

The angry horde of 109s swarming down and gaining on the Curtiss' was not so good.

Trip pushed the nose more vertically in the dive and opened the throttle to the stop. He checked his flaps closed and looked at the altimeter. It was unwinding rapidly, now passing 5000 meters, about 16,000 feet. Trip thought, *Can't do this for long!*

In no time, Trip saw the altimeter go past 2500 meters. He must pull out of this 600 kph dive soon because he thought he must be approaching the limiting airspeed for the airframe. Too much, and the plane might break apart. Even if it didn't start shedding parts, starting the pull-out too late might result in hitting the ground.

He pushed the throttle to idle and shallowed out his dive. He looked over his shoulder and saw Meslée do the same. The 109s were nowhere to be seen. That would be good, assuming they were truly gone and not just out of Trip's visual range.

He pulled harder and got the nose moving toward the horizon. Now the altimeter read 1000 meters. That ground looked awful close, and Trip was still descending. He also noticed that the airspeed indicator read almost 700 kph. That *had* to be past the limiting airspeed.

Trip pulled hard on the stick, this time with both hands. The little airplane groaned, and Trip saw a rivet pop out of one of the wing panels. He felt at least four G's – he weighed four times his usual gravity weight. But the Curtiss leveled out, still going over 600 kph, even though the throttle was at idle. Trees were alarmingly close and going by with equally alarming speed. He was now at 70 meters.

Trip gently pulled the nose up about 5 degrees above the horizon and shot up to 1000 meters, bleeding off airspeed to level off. He set the power to maintain 300 kph. He rocked his wings and was pleased to see Meslée join formation on his right wing. Meslée's oxygen mask was dangling, and he rolled his cockpit canopy back. Meslée grinned at Trip and made a motion to change leads.

Trip slid left and throttled back slightly. As Meslée moved into the lead, Trip realized he was roasting from the cockpit heat and closed canopy. He rolled the canopy open and cranked the heat vent closed. The cool air was instantly refreshing, but Trip wished he had a drink of water. *Never mind, there will be water on the ground, assuming they don't take me out behind a hangar and shoot me.*

They roared over Toul-Croix de Metz airdrome, where Meslée pitched up from 100 meters to 300 meters while turning 180°. He dropped his gear, chopped his throttle, and turned to final approach. Trip followed him, flying the final turn to land on Meslée's left.

Meslée waited at the end of the grass strip until Trip taxied into position and then the two aviators chugged to their original parking locations.

Trip was unsure of the procedures to shut the engine down in this airplane, but thought, *Can't be that much different from the Mosca.*

With the throttle in idle and the propeller set to fine pitch, he moved the fuel mixture control to what looked like idle/cut-off. The engine quickly slowed to a stop. Trip hit what he figured was the ignition switch to *désactivé*.

A ground crewman with bad skin and the reek of garlic leaned into the cockpit and helped Trip to shut down the rest of the equipment.

Trip popped off the harness, and the ground crewman helped Trip to climb out of the cockpit.

Trip stood holding the wing, his legs were rubbery. *Probably needed to do some practice before getting into a fight.*

He looked up and saw Meslée marching toward him with a serious expression.

Trip told the ground crewman, "Jesus, guess I am going to get shot after all."

Chapter 29 – Welcome

Meslée stomped up to Trip. "You are completely insane! You would attack an *escadrille* of Dorniers with no guns? You are mad!"

Trip grinned, "I thought to break up their formation and force them to jettison their bombs."

"You are a madman! Only I, Marin la Meslée, would think to do such a thing."

Trip said, "Oh, and you're the Roland Garros of this war?"

Meslée's wide forehead wrinkled in concentration. He simply said, "*Oui*. I 'ave been victorious over *les Boches*."

Trip said, with laconic irony in his voice, "Congratulations."

"*Oui*, now you mock me."

"Nope."

"Well, I am taking you to ze General."

Trip said, "Oh, Jesus."

"*Mon Dieu, Jesú* will not 'elp you today, *mon ami. Allons-y*."

~~<>~~

With Meslée in the lead, they walked into the office of General de la Vigerie. Trip stood quietly while Meslée delivered a lengthy report in rapid-fire French. The general occasionally asked a pointed question. Finally, the general said, "*Merci, mon lieutenant*."

Fixing Trip with a hard stare, the General said, "You are dangerous. You fly like a madman with ill-discipline. You attack an enemy with empty guns. You will get my *pilotes* killed, I think. But Meslée believes you are a talented pilot. He says you are either completely mad or

215

among the bravest men 'e 'as ever seen. This means much coming from Meslée, who is, as you impudently put it, the Roland Garros of this war."

Trip started to say something, but the general held up a hand. "I should 'ave you shot and be done with you. But *non*, I will give you a chance. Madame Allard supports you, your logbook is plainly not falsified, and you can truly fly. Your combat experience is invaluable to France. Therefore, against all rules and regulations, I will have you sworn into the *Armée de l'Air*. And may God have mercy on us all."

Trip said, "*Merci, Mon General*. I will serve France as though she is my own country."

"That is what worries me, Monsieur Gibson. You may not serve as an officer as you are not French. Also, you are not to be enlisted in the *Armée de l'Air* as an Américian. You must select a name, *un nom-de-guerre*, that will keep France out of an *incident international*.

I shall issue orders that you are to be enlisted as a *Sergent-chef*. Zis is in recognition of your daring attack against tremendous odds in which you and Lieutenant Meslée damaged at least two enemy bombers. I think it is likely that your first victim crashed, but we 'ave no proof. So, it must remain as 'damaged.' Still, you showed great *élan, Chef*."

Trip grinned, "*Chef*. I like that. I can't cook worth a damn, *Mon General*."

"Out. *Mon Dieu*. Ze insanity of zis war..."

Trip and Meslée walked out of the office.

Meslée said, "Let's find you a bed and get you a uniform."

Trip grinned, "Can I get a drink of water, first?"

"*Oui*. Air combat is most 'eavy labor. Mos' people do not understand zis."

~~<>~~

Their thirst slaked, the two men walked across the airfield to a low barrack made of red brick with a slate roof. This was to be Trip's home.

Meslée spoke to an *aviateur de première classe*, a rank Trip thought of as similar to a private first-class. The *aviateur* stood to rigid attention as Meslée issued instructions, his only response being to roll his eyes at the new *Chef* in his midst.

The *aviateur* spoke rapid French to Trip who said, *"Parlez lentement, s'il vous plait. Je suis Americain."*

"Oui, mon Chef."

The *aviateur* explained in words and gestures that a comfortable room at the end of the barracks was for *le Chef*. The *aviateur* showed Trip the room with a flourish. Trip nodded and smiled his appreciation. Trip said, *"Merci bien."*

The *aviateur* explained that they would visit a supply room for uniform items and flying equipment.

Satisfied that Trip was in good hands, Meslée said, "We will discuss flying, rules, and formations once you 'ave your uniform and have put your things away. Come to the *escadrille* building."

Trip nodded, *"Oui, mon Lieutenant. Merci beaucoup."*

~~<>~~

Suitably attired in his wool *Armée de l'Air* uniform, *Sergent-chef* Tripolitano Beneš, Czech airman in the French Air Force, as Trip was formally enlisted, marched across the airfield and found the *escadrille*. Trip thought that Tomas Beneš would not mind the use of his last name.

The next two days were spent intensely reviewing *Armée de l'Air* tactics, formations, rules, and regulations. Trip was acquainted with customs of military service from his ROTC days at Georgia Tech, so the expectation of salutes, calling senior officers by their rank and last name was familiar. He soon learned that his position as *Sergent-Chef* was privileged, and that the other enlisted personnel treated him with respect. One or two were a bit surly, but Trip did not care. The NCO pilots were uniformly impressed with Trip's flying, combat experience, and leadership qualities.

Meslée also checked Trip out completely on the Curtiss 75. Trip was impressed the day he flew it and was more impressed with it as he learned the details. He learned that he had, in fact, over-speeded the airplane escaping the Germans. The limiting speed in the manual was 648 kph. He had exceeded that speed by about 50 kph, and this concerned him. The rivets that flew off the wing panels suggested damage to the structure. He worried that someone else would fly the Curtiss with the large 8 on its tail and die when the airplane broke apart.

To help with his guilt over this possibility, Trip asked the Mechanical Officer, Lieutenant Conte, that he be assigned to Number 8 when possible.

On the fourth day, April 24th, 1940, Trip was assigned to fly Meslée's wing as a full-fledged GC I/5 – *Groupe de Chasse* I/5 – member.

The commander of the entire wing, *Commandant* Jacques-Louis Murtin, interviewed him and welcomed him to the unit. Murtin warned Trip that he must fly as part of the unit, not as a lone wolf. *Capitaine* Jean-Mary Accart, Commander of GC I/5, welcomed Trip and reminded him of the need to fly as a unit rather than as an individual.

Trip bonded with his mechanic, *Sergent* Jules Giraud. Giraud was always first to be at the flight line and last to leave. Giraud had been the ground crew to help Trip on his first flight and was the man with bad skin and garlic breath. These last two had not changed.

~~<>~~

April 25th dawned bright and sunny. The temperature was 19° Celsius. Beautiful spring weather. *Great for flying*, Trip thought.

The GC I/5 was alerted to intercept any Luftwaffe incursions from Strasbourg north to Saarbrücken. The Curtiss aircraft were fueled and ready. The weapons were loaded with 500 rounds of ammunition per gun. Giraud had started the engine and kept the oil warm by turning the engine over every hour. The petrol bowser trooped the line-topping off the fuel tanks behind the pilots' seats. All was in readiness.

The hours dragged by with the slowness of molasses in winter. Some pilots sat in the shade of their aircraft wings. Those that wanted to smoke, which was most of them, sat in the shade of a large tree just behind the flight line. Trip sat next to Meslée, smoking a Gauloise and drinking a tumbler of red wine. The French had no real concern about alcohol and flying. Everyone joked that there was no smoking within 24 hours of flying and no drinking within 100 feet of the aircraft.

The sun climbed higher, and the temperature rose to around 20° Celsius. The pilots were growing weary of inaction.

Everyone paused at the ring of a telephone in the command center at about noon. In moments, an NCO ran from the command center and shouted, "Alert, Alert!"

The pilots ran to their airplanes. Starter cartridges fired one after the other as the pilots' butts hit seats and the ground crewmen strapped pilots in.

Giraud got Trip settled and grinned at him. He patted Trip on the shoulder, *"Bon chance, Chef!"*

Giraud then slid off the wing to the ground and ran to the front of the Curtiss to wave him out into line as the escadrille taxied to the grass strip and began taking off in groups of four.

Soon it was Trip's turn, and he rolled onto the runway on Meslée's left wing and roared down the strip in seconds. 600 feet of ground run, and the Curtiss broke ground. Trip watched Meslée intently, and as soon as Meslée's landing gear began to move, Trip snatched the landing gear handle and then the flap handle. He closed the cowl flaps and trimmed the elevator to take pressure off the controls.

Heading almost due North and maintaining a climb speed of 200 kph, the escadrille climbed to 6000 meters. The climb took about eight minutes.

The squadron reached 6000 meters and began to patrol along the north-south axis. Each pilot constantly scanned the horizon to the east, looking for hints of enemy airborne activity. They looked for sunlight flashing on aircraft canopies or wings, dark spots against a light sky, and anti-aircraft bursts along the border suggesting aircraft flying.

So far, nothing seemed to be happening.

Then, Trip spotted a canopy flash about 20 miles south of Saarbrücken. "Red leader, Red 4. Possible enemy at 10 o'clock, 30 miles."

Trip's French was execrable, but he had worked on radio calls with Meslée, and this call was quite intelligible.

Capitaine Accart turned the squadron thirty degrees to starboard and began a climb to 7000 meters, pushing up the RPMs.

Trip's bowels began to gripe from the reduced atmospheric pressure at altitude. Sitting back and flying Meslée's wing, Trip checked his oxygen and looked in all directions.

The squadron reached 7000 meters, and Trip looked down at the patchwork quilt that was the earth. Browns, greens, grays, the same colors as splashed on the French Curtiss airplanes.

Trip constantly scanned for further sign of Luftwaffe airplanes. Every pilot was scanning both along the horizon and well above it. The Luftwaffe fighter pilots loved to have altitude advantage. Trip thought it unlikely that the Luftwaffe would be much higher than the current 7000 meters. That was about 23,000 feet, and much above that airplanes didn't perform well. He knew the 109s had a service ceiling of about 33,000 feet – 10,000 meters. But that was a stretch. Still, he wished Accart would take the squadron to 7500 meters for a little insurance.

The sun was almost directly overhead, so there would be no sun advantage unless the Boches were directly overhead. Which is exactly where they were.

Trip saw a shadow flick across the airplane on the other side of Meslée. "Marin! Huns attacking from directly above. Break! Break!"

Meslée jerked the Curtiss hard left, and Trip pushed down to stay with him. Trip kicked the rudder to extend the distance between his plane and Meslée. All the while Trip was looking almost straight up. In two heartbeats, he saw a dark dot appear out of the harsh noon-day sun. The Curtiss to the right of where Meslèe had been blew up in a hail of cannon shells.

Meslée reversed his turn, Trip fading more to the left and then swinging hard to the right to stay with his leader.

A dappled blue, gray, dusty green Bf-109 floated between Trip and Meslèc. Trip shouted, "Marin! Boche on your tail! Break." He nudged stick and rudder as he spoke, and when the 109's wings filled his ring sight, he hit the trigger.

Nothing.

Trip shouted out loud, "Shit! I forgot to turn on the Goddamn gun switches!"

He reached and flicked one, two, three...six switches. Then he concentrated on the 109 in front of him. The 109's wingtips hit the edges of the reflector sight, and Trip hit the trigger.

Brrrrrraaaaammmmmm!

Trip counted two full seconds and let off the trigger. Pieces flew off the 109, but Trip had no time to watch.

He quickly checked his 6 o'clock position – dead astern. A 109 was just settling on his tail, and Trip slammed the control column to the left and stomped hard right rudder. He ignored the prohibition against snap rolls above 225 KPH. He dumped the stick, as he had once done to dodge a 109 over Spain. The Curtiss darted downward hard, and the 109's cannon fire flew harmlessly overhead.

Trip looked frantically for Meslée. There! Marin was in a desperate turning fight with two yellow-nosed 109s. Trip swung his head 180 degrees in all directions; no enemy. He turned hard toward Edmond Marin la Meslée and jerked the throttle back to full RPM. The Curtiss jumped toward Meslée's fight.

In 10 seconds, Trip was closing on one of the two 109s intent on ending Marin la Meslée's life. Because of Trip's rapid overtake the 109's wingtips touched the reflector sight and then quickly filled the windscreen between the two metal wire braces.

Trip hit the trigger at a range of less than 50 yards. The 109 simply disintegrated under the hail of Trip's concentrated fire.

Meslée's other antagonist saw this situation develop and rolled inverted into a Split-S. The yellow-nosed 109 quickly exited the fight in a near-vertical dive.

Trip pushed the throttle to half the RPMs, rolled up on a wing, and scanned all around. The fight was over.

Meslée rocked his wings, and Trip joined up. They headed south toward Toul and the airdrome.

Trip grinned.

He had never felt more alive.

Chapter 30 – The War Becomes Real

May arrived, bringing the quiet glory of early spring. French farmers still plowed, harvested, and brought produce to market. The trees budded bright green, and the fields burst with new crops. Once or twice a week, Trip and other senior NCOs went into Toul to eat at a small café and drink rough red wine.

The citizens of Toul were jittery, and it was obvious that many had evacuated to the West. Many houses were empty. Some stores were shuttered, but many cafés remained open.

Norway was becoming a tedious news story. The British and a few French forces were constantly beleaguered in the still snowy rough country that composed Norway. Although the French papers spread propaganda about how the glorious French troops were beating the Nazis, Trip saw an occasional English-language paper that told a different story. Many units had been withdrawn by May 2nd, and Trip quietly thought, *Norway's done, and we're next.*

GC I/5 flew daily. Often the orders were to penetrate into Germany and attempt to rouse the Luftwaffe into climbing into a dogfight. Trip was surprised that GC I/5 was not called upon to bomb German roads and intersections. It was clear that the Germans would come across the border in the next few weeks. Trip thought it would be sooner. *Shouldn't we be hitting them now?*

The flying weather was good, but the Germans were quiet. The senior officers argued that the Maginot Line was impenetrable and that the Belgians would stymie the Germans should they consider coming toward France through Belgium and Luxembourg.

Trip observed, even when he was in Paris, that the French mobile forces were arrayed along the Belgian and Luxembourg borders. It was clear to Trip that the Maginot line was useless. Thus, GC I/5 was located at Toul to support either an unlikely defense along the

Maginot line or to help blunt a more likely thrust through the Ardennes.

Trip sat with Meslée under the shade of what he considered the alert tree. They smoked and drank the rough red wine that complemented the tobacco burn in their throats from the Gauloises.

Trip said, "So, we're on the defensive and must await *les Boches*."

"*Oui*. But Trip, it is simple. Defense is easier; an enemy often exhausts himself on the defensive walls. Consider the Battle of Fredericksburg in your Civil War. Longstreet occupied a ridge and simply murdered the Union Army as it crossed a river and marched up the hill into the Confederate guns. We studied this *en le école militarie*."

Trip said, "It's true that the Confederates were on the defensive and won many battles. But they lost the war. They ran out of time, money, equipment, and food."

Meslée said, "Zis is true. Ze Union had all ze advantages. But it is filthy expensive to create an attacking army. The logistics – equipment, supply, gasoline, food, you understand – is *simplement énorme*. Ze Union Army was well supplied, but zat was incredibly expensive."

"And you think that same consideration will slow Hitler down?"

"*Oui*. We will let *les Boches* spend their coin on these items and empty their coffers in a futile attempt to conquer France. *Hein?*"

Trip said, "Do you think Belgium and the Netherlands can stop the Germans after what they did in Poland? Don't forget that Belgium declared neutrality a few years ago."

"*Oui, Belgique* is as neutral as Norway was. When *les Boches* marched into Norway zey became not so neutral. *Belgique* has English Hurricanes, and ze army is strong and well-trained. Luxembourg, not so much."

He paused to light a cigarette. Then snorted smoke out his nostrils. "Ze Poles? *Alors!* Zey had nozink but horse cavalry and some miserable little planes. We have thousands of tanks and a much better air force."

Trip said quietly, "Having good equipment and training doesn't make a fighting force."

"*Non*. That is true. We have *élan!*"

Trip grinned as he lit another Gauloise, "They have the blitzkrieg, *mon ami*."

~~<>~~

Trip was frustrated. Flying endless patrols up and down the border between France and Germany was a waste. There was no information about enemy intrusions, so interception was mostly hit or miss. Occasionally, there was a high-altitude bomber that was worth pursuing. Likely any such bomber was taking photographs. Trip never heard anything about bombs being dropped.

~~<>~~

Trip and Meslée rode through the French hedgerows toward a nearby airfield. A Curtiss had an engine failure and landed at the small airfield. Trip and Meslée were going to evaluate the airplane's airworthiness and recommend action. Sergent Giraud rode in the front seat of the car. He was to examine mechanical issues with the grounded Curtiss.

They chatted and smoked as the driver negotiated potholes and washed-out road edges. Giraud, reeking of garlic as usual, sat stoically with the driver; his position was clear. He was the junior member of this small, impromptu team.

The car swung around a hair-pin curve requiring nearly a full stop before driving ahead. The driver said, "Merde!"

Something buzzed loudly and made the sound of a hammer on thin metal. A whiz-chunk sound immediately followed as something hit the metal above Girard's head. Sprang! A piece of metal flew off the rear passenger door next to Trip.

Trip shouted, "Jesus! We're being shot at!"

The driver floored the accelerator, and the car shot forward. A loud PRAAAANG! sound followed the car roaring ahead, bucking on the partially washed-out farm road.

Trip immediately understood that the pranging sound was a bullet hitting the metal of the car. Ditto for all the other odd sounds that preceded it. They were under fire, and there was little to do except run. While the driver had a Berthier carbine and Trip and Meslée had sidearms, the car was essentially defenseless. This ambush had been planned!

The car soon topped a small rise and dropped down into a swale. The shooting stopped.

Trip looked around, "*Mon Dieu!* We're lucky! Is everyone alright?"

Meslée muttered with his typical understatement, "*Jesú.* This was most disconcerting."

The driver and Giraud both had eyes the size of saucers. Giraud said in his native French, "I have many things to do besides being shot at by some traitorous bastard."

The small team arrived at what looked like a large farm field. The Curtiss sat forlornly in a corner of the farm field. Giraud quickly checked the aircraft.

Trip asked Giraud, "Flyable?"

"*Oui, Mon Chef.* Ze fuel line is fouled. I can clean it."

Trip said to Meslée. "You're in command. You want me to fly it back to Toul-Croix de Metz?"

"*Oui*, Trip. If Giraud believes it is flyable, then we must recover this valuable asset. I shall fly it back, and you will command the return of the recovery team."

Trip grinned, "Very well, *Mon Lieutenant*."

Meslée snorted, "Asshole, I know you were thinking you might just hedge-hop over to Germany and see if you could find a fight."

Trip said, "I cannot tell a lie, as George Washington once said."

"*Oui*, I'm sure he said zat same shit to Lafayette."

~~<>~~

Trip and the two junior enlisted men watched Meslée break ground in the repaired Curtiss, suck up the landing gear, and turn south toward Toul-Croix de Metz.

Trip said, "Goddamnit, he'll be on the ground before we can get out of this farmer's field. Guess we better go."

With several bullet holes and one shattered window, the car bucked comfortably, heading away from the airstrip. Trip told the driver to use a different route to get out of the area. Trip doubted their assailants were still there, but there was no sense driving back through the same ambush.

Clearly, the fifth columnists had seen the airplane land and knew that the *Armée de l'Air* would send a recovery team. It was a simple matter to plot an ambush. Trip took comfort that Meslée had left him his pistol. At least the small team had three weapons.

A mile from the airstrip, the road forked, and the driver stopped to consult a map.

Kerrang! A bullet glanced off the hood of the car.

There was a loud smack as the driver's head burst, spraying brain and bone matter all over the car's interior.

Trip said, "Let's get out of here, Giraud!"

He jerked open his car door and rolled out into the dirt, scrambling over a low ditch to get behind a berm. Giraud was right behind him and flopped flat. He had the presence of mind to drag the Berthier Carbine out of the driver's dead hand before he left the car.

Ziiiizzzz, Pow! A bullet flew past Trip and Giraud. The belated "pow" was because the bullet was going much faster than the speed of sound. Trip said aloud, "You won't hear the one that gets you."

"Hein?"

"Never mind. Come on." Trip low-crawled away from the car, staying behind the berm.

Ziiiiizzzz, Pow! This bullet was well behind the two men as they slopped through the mud and muck at the edge of the farmer's field.

They came to an intersection in a hedgerow. Trip pointed and said, "Let's go over to the other side."

Giraud nodded. He had little English but understood Trip's plan.

They found a low spot in the hedgerow and slithered through without rising and risking getting shot.

On the other side of the hedgerow, Trip stood, keeping the berm at the base of the hedge between him and the car, now about 50 meters away.

They watched. Soon, a man stepped out of the bushes 20 meters away from the car on the other side. He wore rough French farmer's clothing and carried a German Mauser rifle.

Trip quietly said, "I'll bet that's a German and not a French farmer."

"Oui," Giraud breathed quietly. "We kill ze *Boche bâtard!*"

Trip handed Giraud the extra pistol and took the Berthier and quietly checked that the chamber held a round. He murmured, "Let's watch a moment."

Soon, the man was at the car. He looked it over carefully and nudged the poor dead driver. A second man rose from the brush.

They spoke unintelligibly. The distance was too far to hear, but Trip believed they planned to search for him and Giraud. That could only lead to one end.

Trip handed the carbine to Giraud and pointed to the second man. He held up Meslée's pistol and pointed at the first man. "*En trois.*"

Giraud understood. "On three."

Trip leaned against the hedgerow and rested the automatic pistol on a fallen limb. Trip knew the *Pistolet Automatique Modèle 1935A* was a fine weapon, akin to the U.S. .45 caliber M1911A1 pistol. Only, it was better because it had a more stable, longer-range cartridge in the 7.65-millimeter longue. Trip knew the pistol had eight rounds, and the extra magazine Meslée had provided held seven more.

Trip didn't know for certain how many rounds were in the Berthier, but thought it was eight. He patted his own *Modèle 1935* in its holster on his hip.

The two enemies soon stood near the car, and the first man leaned over the berm to see the marks in the mud where Trip and Giraud had crawled. He looked directly at the hedgerow.

Trip quietly said, "un, deux, trois," and shot him four times.

Giraud fired twice. Both enemies were down as Trip looked at Giraud. "*Bon!* Stay here, and I'll go check. Shoot them if they move."

"*Hein?*"

Trip pointed to himself and made motions to go look. He pointed to Giraud and made motions to stay and shoot if necessary."

"Ah. Oui, Mon Chef."

Trip quickly left the hedge row and ran, crouching, toward the car. He looked at the second man, who was clearly dead. His head was oddly shaped from Giraud's bullet. The first man was lying on his side, blood drooling from his mouth. Trip kicked his rifle away and looked at him hard. He was still alive.

Trip waved at Giraud. He turned back to the fifth columnist.

"Who are you?"

No answer.

Trip repeated his question as Giraud trotted up. Giraud carried the Berthier carbine at port-arms. His face said, *I will kill you!*

Trip said, "Ask who he is."

"Hein?"

"Ask his name, *nom.*"

Giraud nodded, *"Ah, Oui, Mon Chef."*

Giraud looked at the fifth columnist. He said something in French, then German. There was no answer.

Giraud kicked the fifth columnist in the ribs. Hard. He bent close to the man's face and asked the same question.

No answer.

This time the kick was more vicious and aimed at the enemy's stomach.

The fifth columnist muttered something in German.

Giraud stood, "His name is Fritz Müller. He is a native of Saarbrücken. He refuses to answer any further questions."

Trip shot the German in the head.

Giraud said, "*Mon Dieu, mon Chef!* You scare me."

Trip said, "I don't want to fuck with explanations."

He grabbed the dead man's wrist and dragged him toward the roadside ditch. Giraud grabbed the other wrist. Soon, both fifth columnists were in the ditch, and Trip kicked some sod over their bodies.

Trip paused to look at them. Lighting a Gauloise for himself and one for Giraud, Trip spat, "Bastards."

~~<>~~

They put the driver's body in the trunk of the shot-up car and used the driver's own coat to cover his body. Trip touched the body gently and said, "*Bon homme.*"

They walked to the dead bodies, and Trip tore off a strip of clothing from the second man. He used the torn cloth to wipe the driver's blood and brains from the seat and threw the cloth in the ditch.

Giraud drove back to Toul-Croix de Metz.

The driver's brain-spattered map proved to be quite accurate.

It was May 8th, 1940.

Chapter 31 – Suippes

It was a scheduled day of rest for Trip. He was sleeping hard when frantic activity in the barracks woke him.

An *aviateur* was hurrying down the corridor shouting, "We're moving! Everybody up!"

Trip put his head in the corridor. "Where are we going?"

Suippes, Chef.

Trip turned back into his small room and grabbed his backpack. He had kept it mostly packed against just this possibility. Preparing to leave required no more than stuffing it with his underwear. He had a small diary and a couple of English-language magazines, which went into an outside pocket. There was a small sink in his room. He quickly shaved before dressing and putting his shaving kit in the backpack.

Looking around the room, Trip satisfied himself that he had everything. Having done this innumerable times in Spain, Trip walked out and did not look back.

He stomped into the escadrille offices. Meslée was standing at a counter looking at a map. "Ah, Trip. *Bonjour*. We're off to Suippes. *Les Boches* seem to be about to cross into *Belgique et* Luxembourg."

Trip said, "*Bonjour, mon Lieutenant*. Nothing new to me. We moved nearly every day in Spain. What is my assignment?"

"You will fly Number Eight on my wing. It appears *les Boches* will follow their *Schlieffen Plan* from the Great War. They planned to sweep through Belgique and Luxembourg and past Sedan, then hook south toward Paris. There is no reason to believe they will not do exactly that again."

"We are centering our air elements on Reims. The RAF will remain with us in the *Zone d'Opérations Aériennes Nord*. General de La

Vigerie is moving ZOAN Headquarters to Chauny, a few kilometers West of Reims. Suippes is about 40 kilometers southeast of Reims."

Trip nodded. "We've been expecting something. It has started."

"*Oui, mon ami*, there will be lots of death."

~~<>~~

Trip looked down at Suippes. The Suippes River ran east-west here, then north. Rail lines ran from Paris to the south and bent toward the east at Suippes, along the Suippes River's south side. He could see several military installations. In the distance to the east was Verdun. Sedan was slightly northeast, and beyond Sedan was the Belgian Frontier.

Looking closely at the landscape, Trip could see damage from trenches, artillery, and murderous battles. Trip shook his head, *Jesus, we're back to the Great War!*

Meslée pitched up to the pattern, and after five seconds, Trip followed him. Soon they were on downwind, and Trip hit the landing gear lever and flap lever. Meslée was in the final turn to land as Trip felt the landing gear lock into place and saw three green lights on the instrument panel. The airplane slowed when the flaps reached their limit. Setting the prop and pulling the throttle to set the RPMs and manifold pressure, he caught the airplane at its 120 kph pattern airspeed.

Trip looked for other airplanes before he rolled into the final turn. The other squadron members approached the airfield, but no one was attempting to land. Trip lowered the nose and rolled into the final turn. Moments later, Trip Gibson settled the Curtiss onto the Suippes grass strip and rumbled along, quickly catching up to Meslée and clearing the runway.

They taxied, bumping along the grass-tufted surface. Meslée expertly spun his Curtiss to point it out toward the grass strip, and Trip saw the propeller spin up for the shutdown checks. A moment later, Trip swung his Curtiss into the spot next to Meslée. He raised the RPMs and checked the engine instruments. Then, he moved the mixture control to idle/cutoff, and watched the propeller slowly stop. He hit the switches to *Arrêt* - off.

Giraud ran up the wing and helped Trip with his straps.

It was nice to see Giraud, a friendly face.

Trip had a new home.

~~<>~~

That night the mess tent was in full operation. The squadron's pilots all gathered to hear rousing speeches from senior officers. Soon, red wine was flowing, and the pilots became rowdy. They began singing.

Trip did not know the words, but he joined in. They sang a series of songs *like 'Saint-Cyr Garde à Vous,' 'Les Artilleurs de Metz,' and 'Marche Lorraine.'*

Trip contributed *'Ramblin' Wreck from Georgia Tech.'* The French pilots loved it. They were lusty singers and everyone the world over knew the Georgia Tech fight song, especially the chorus, "...helluva, helluva, helluva, helluva, helluva engineer!"

They sang and tried to ignore the imminent German invasion.

The next morning, Trip nursed a painful head as he sat under what he dubbed the New Alert Tree. He had finished drinking a canteen full of water and smoking his third Gauloise of the morning.

An NCO ran out of the dispersal tent and waved his arms toward the sky. *"Décoller, décoller! Un Boche!"*

Trip stepped into the daylight, squinting hard at the sky directly overhead. He could just make out a vapor trail high in the French spring sky.

Meslée stepped out beside him. *"Merde. Allons-y, Trip.* Let us go shoot him."

Trip followed Meslée to the grass strip and pulled the throttle all the way to the stop. Meslée didn't stand on ceremony but roared down the strip, breaking ground after about 250 meters. Trip did the same and entered the same upwardly-spiraling climb as Meslée.

Trip thought, *Damn! Kick the tires and light the fires. First one in the air is the leader.*

The air was crisp, and the Curtiss 75s climbed quickly. In less than 10 minutes, they were topping 7500 meters – 25,000 feet. All the while in the climb they checked the location of the vapor trail. It pointed to a tiny dot that was their prey.

Trip felt a little giddy. He thought, *Wine and too much food last night.*

A few more moments and Trip thought, *Hmmm...is my oxygen working?*

He watched his hand slowly reach out to the oxygen regulator. He was intensely curious as that hand turned the knob. His head buzzed. His face felt tingly and numb like when he had one brandy too many. Everything seemed sluggish, and he noticed that the edges of his vision were darkened. *Oh, Jesus. I think I'm about to blackout from lack of oxygen.*

Trip rolled to put the nose down and pulled into a steep dive. *Oops. Pretty dopey. Best be careful. Don't want to get into a dive and pass out.*

He cut the dive angle in half and thought he might nap briefly.

Something went BANG, and Trip jerked upright in the seat. He looked in all directions but didn't see any enemy. *Guess I'm not getting shot down. Now what?*

He looked at the altimeter and saw that he was at about 3000 meters, he was in a roaring dive at nearly 450 kph. He could easily reach the limiting speed of the Curtiss. *What am I doing? What was that bang?*

He checked the wings and craned his neck to see if the tail plane was intact. Nothing broken there. He looked at the tachometer and saw the engine RPM was near the redline.

Trip shoved the throttle closed and looked to see the tachometer continue to move higher. *Run-away prop? The dive was so fast that the prop governor failed. It'll tear the engine up if I don't slow it down.*

Trip quickly moved the propeller control to feather the prop and reduce the airplane's forward motion making the prop spin. He also hauled on the control stick to level out and then raise the nose to bleed some airspeed.

Fortunately, he was over the top of Suippes, so he didn't have to find an airfield. He was now at 2500 meters and no engine. The engine was running, but the propeller didn't work, so the engine was useless.

Trip rolled the little Curtiss up on its right wing and began a spiraling descent. His head cleared more and more as the airplane descended. *Gotta time this just right. If I miss, I'll end up in a heap of crushed aluminum.*

As he descended and his vision cleared, he saw Meslée zip down final approach and land in a cloud of fine dust. *Good. He survived.*

Not wanting to wait until the last moment, Trip hit the gear lever down and lowered the flaps. He kept the speed above 140 kph, the stall speed with landing gear and flaps. After what seemed an eternity, the three green lights on the instrument panel lit up, one at a time, as the gear clunked down and locked.

Trip played the turns of the spiral, gauging that he wanted to be about 50 meters above the ground when he hit the final turn of the corkscrewing maneuver. Of course, he muttered silent prayers that this final position would also occur when aligned with the grass strip.

In the last half-turn, Trip realized that this would work out perfectly, and he relaxed a bit. The world around him was deathly quiet, and the wind rushing past the cockpit was oddly comforting. It reminded him of his glide out of Spain and into the grain field in France.

Trip rolled the canopy back in case something happened, and he needed to get out of the airplane. He cut the fuel to the engine and shut off the fuel flow in case the airplane flipped over on landing.

Fifteen seconds later, *Sergent-Chef* Trip Beneš touched down without incident. He rolled as far as momentum would let him and then slowly nudged the airplane toward the parking area. He had no engine to taxi, but at least he'd leave the grass strip clear for the next airplane to land.

When the Curtiss stopped rolling, Trip threw off his seat harness and shrugged out of his parachute. He climbed out of the cockpit and realized his flight coverall was sweat-drenched. He held onto the wing tip and lit a Gauloise with a shaky hand.

Giraud ran up. "What happened, *Mon Chef*?"

"Oxygen."

"*Oui*, zey didn't tell you? We have none. *Pilotes* were supposed to be briefed to avoid high altitudes until we get our oxygen equipment from Toul."

Trip snarled, "Nobody told me a Goddamn thing!"

Giraud was crestfallen, "I should have known."

Trip waved a hand. "No matter. I'm not dead, but you've got a prop to fix, and I'm afraid I might have oversped the engine, too."

Giraud waved over a tow vehicle, and Trip walked shakily toward the New Alert Tree.

Meslée looked up from a newspaper and asked, "What the hell happened to you?"

Trip told him.

Meslée muttered, "Ah, *oui*. I was slightly giddy but did not drink much last night. Still, I could not climb high enough in time to catch that Hun."

Adjutant-chef Louis Bouvard wandered over. "Trip, what 'appened?"

Trip explained, and Bouvard said, "Mon Dieu! I 'ave not checked *mon* oxygen today."

Bouvard turned and walked quickly to his Curtiss.

Trip flopped into a lawn chair next to Sergent Emil Moravek, a Czech pilot who had, like Jan and Tomas, escaped Czechoslovakia to join the squadron.

Lighting a Gauloise, Trip muttered to no one in particular, "God, I need a good night's sleep."

The next day was the end of sleep for many weeks except for those who slept the eternal sleep of death.

Chapter 32 – Rude Awakening

The squadron stood down at dark on May 9th, and Trip found a cot in the corner of a tent reserved for NCOs. He was flat on his face, his boots beside the rickety cot, his flying jacket rolled up for a pillow. It was chilly in the early morning of May 10th, but Trip slept on.

FRAM, FRAM, FRAM, FRAM...FRAM, FRAM, FRAM, FRAM...

Bewildered, Trip sat up.

He said aloud, "What the hell?"

Shoving his feet into his flying boots, he stepped to the tent's open flap. He blurted out to no one present, "Oh, shit! Antiaircraft fire. We're under attack."

Trip threw on his flying jacket as he ran from the tent toward the dispersal area where his Curtiss was parked.

A stick of bombs ran across the field.

BOOOOOM...BOOOOOM...BOOOOOM...BOOOOOM...BOOOOOM ...BOOOOOM!

They sounded like 100-kilogram bombs. Shrapnel and debris spattered all around. There was no trench or other shelter, so Trip kept running. Trip saw a jagged two-meter long board go flying into a tent. *Hope no one got hurt.*

A Curtiss' engine started, and Trip looked to see Meslée taxiing as fast as possible to the strip.

Trip rushed to Number 8 and looked desperately around for Giraud. Ducking under the airplane, Trip snatched away the wheel chocks and darted around the wing. He climbed up and hauled open the canopy. He settled into the seat and hit the switches to energize the battery.

Looking around, he still did not see Giraud or any other ground crew, so he hit the cartridge start button and cracked the throttle.

The shotgun bang of the starter cartridge, followed by the sluggish turns of the prop, worried Trip. *Damn, this thing has not been propped over today. Probably full of oil in the bottom cylinders.*

Blat, blat, blat...blat, blatblatblatblat...brruuuum, brruuuum...and the engine caught. A huge burst of stinking blue oil smoke popped out of the exhausts. Trip thought *That'll damage the engine. Oh, well, too bad. It's running.*

Opening the throttle to start taxiing, Trip shoved his arms into the parachute harness and fastened chest and groin buckles. He grabbed the shoulder harness and latched them into the seat belt. A quick tug satisfied Trip he was sufficiently belted in.

Giraud ran up, but Trip waved him away and opened the throttle to taxi faster.

Another stick of bombs marched across the field. As Trip moved away from the dispersal area, two Curtiss's shattered as 100-kilo bombs and shrapnel burst all around.

The hell with it, I'm taking off!

Trip checked his flaps down and glanced at the engine instruments. The engine oil was still cold. Trip snorted, *Too bad. Sorry, old girl.*

He pointed the nose of the Curtiss at what looked like an undamaged part of the airfield and opened the throttle. *Thank God she's got a short ground run.*

The engine roared, backfired twice, and bogged down. Trip's heart jumped. *Come on, baby. Let's go.*

The engine roared again and settled into its familiar 2550 RPM takeoff setting. Trip noticed immediately that Number 8 was sluggish. He glanced at the throttle. *Jesus...forgot the damned prop.*

He pushed the prop control to low pitch, full RPM, and the little Curtiss jumped forward. Checking the manifold pressure at 100 centimeters of mercury, Trip grinned at his foolishness.

Another stick of bombs tore across the field behind him, the blast wave shoving the Curtiss forward. Trees at the end of Trip's makeshift landing strip were coming up rapidly. The Curtiss bounced once...twice...airborne.

Trip breathed a ragged breath and grabbed the landing gear handle. He snatched it up and prayed for salvation as the trees loomed.

Don't touch the flaps, Trip-boy. Gotta clear those trees. Come on...come on...come on...he saw spring buds on the new growth flash by as Number 8 struggled to climb. Then they were past it.

Whew. Made it. Thank you, Jesus. I swear to God, I will go to church as soon as I can. Flaps up, and now let's go find those Boche bastards.

Trip felt the flaps retract. He settled into a spiraling climb at full throttle. He ran his eyes over the neglected instruments and was relieved to see the cylinder temperature was now registering and the oil pressure was good. Maybe he had not destroyed the engine after all. The fuel gauges indicated full tanks, and Trip rechecked fuel selector set to the main tank. *Good. I've got a couple of hours' worth of gas. I'm going to hunt down those Nazi sons-of-bitches.*

He began to swivel his head, especially behind and up. The bombers had been at least 3000 meters high – 10,000 feet. *More like 4000 meters,* Trip thought.

He knew the Curtiss could make 15,000 feet in about 5 minutes but had lost track of time. He was passing through 1500 meters. Ok, so maybe four minutes to 4000 meters?

Trip thought *They probably are Dornier 217s and going something like 360 kph. That's six kilometers per minute. Hum...in the 5 minutes since they hit us, they'll be 30 kilometers east of here.*

Checking in all directions, Trip rolled out of the spiral climb onto a heading of 090° - due East - and let the little Curtiss climb straight ahead. The Curtiss was climbing at 450 kph, almost eight kilometers per minute. *Can I reach them before they cross back into German-controlled territory? Great. An eighth-grade math word problem. If a train leaves New York and another train leaves Chicago... Christ, but I hated those, and I'm supposed to be an engineer.*

Trip did the math as quickly as he could. *180 kilometers to the German border. At 450 kph, that's about 25 minutes. The Dorniers have to go 150 kilometers at about 360 kph. That's about 25 minutes. Damn. It's going to be close.*

Will I have enough gas to get to them and get home? Who cares? I'll probably have to land somewhere else, anyway. I think our strip is shot.

Trip checked the instruments and scanned the sky. Still, he climbed. *I'm going to catch those bastards.*

Trip grinned to himself. *They're messing with a Georgia Tech engineer...well, almost, anyway. I can do math with the best of them. Just hope all my guesses were right about where they're going and how fast they're getting there.*

~~<>~~

Trip leveled off at 4500 meters. His head was on a constant swivel, but every glance to the east was a brief pause to scan for the bombers. Now he was scanning level and slightly below the horizon. *Come on, come on...I'll take anything, anything that hints that we're converging.*

Trip reassured himself. The Dorniers had to be going back to Germany. Where else would they go?

A flicker of light just below the horizon, about 10 kilometers dead ahead, made Trip sit tall in the seat. He strained to see more. *Come on...come on, you son-of-a-bitch.*

Another flicker. *Yep. Got to be the Boche.*

Trip lowered the nose slightly and checked to see if he had any more throttle to use. No, he was full out. He was burning gas at a high rate, too. He had a 400-liter tank and 115-liter reserve. He was burning about 200 liters per hour at this setting. If the engine didn't blow up from the high RPMs or the propeller didn't shear off, he would have enough gas to catch the Boche and at least find a place to land.

Trip kept his head moving. He looked high and behind constantly. The 109s loved to hang about 1000 meters above the bombers. He saw a dot in the distance. It was just a flicker against a high cumulus cloud top, about 5 miles at his 5 o'clock position, maybe 300 meters higher. *Jesus, I hope that is not a 109. I don't need a dogfight.*

He scanned for the bombers again, spotted them more clearly now. Dorniers. Definitely headed for Germany. He looked back for the dot. It was closer. *Damn! I don't want a fight with a 109. I want to kill the bastards that bombed our base. Worse, they woke me from the first sound sleep in days. Don't know which makes me madder.*

Trip scanned, left, high, low; behind, high, low; ahead, high, low; back to the dot and right high and low. The dot resolved into the definite outlines of a Curtiss. *Good, at least it won't be a fight. Meslée? Nah...couldn't be.*

Trip returned to looking for the bombers. Sudden black puffs of antiaircraft fire burst around where he expected the Dorniers to be. He looked back at the Curtiss and saw Meslée's number 2 on the tail. Trip rocked his wings, and Meslée rocked in response. Trip grinned a fierce snarl. *Now we'll kill them all.*

~~<>~~

Meslée pulled into formation on Trip's right wing. He made hand signals that Trip was lead in this fight. Trip nodded exaggeratedly so Meslée could see.

They both scanned all around and turned their attention to the bombers. Trip saw that the Dorniers had changed altitude to dodge the ack-ack. They were lower. *Good. Now we'll build plenty of airspeed in the diving attack and have plenty of speed to zoom back up and come around on them again.*

Trip dipped his right wing briefly, a signal to Meslée to move out to a wider attack formation preferred by the *Armée de l'Air*. Trip would take the enemy on the left, Meslée on the right.

Scanning the horizon and high above and left, then right and above Meslée and then back to the Dorniers. Trip knew Meslée was doing the same. He flicked the six gun switches on and lowered the nose into a 15° dive. He checked the instruments again. All good.

The rearmost Dornier was quickly growing in Trips sights. He dropped his left hand off the throttle to adjust the rheostat making the sight ring brighter. The Dornier's wingtips touched the ring's edges, and Trip hit the gun trigger on the pistol grip of his control stick.

Brrrrrraaaatttttt...

The stink of gunpowder filled the cockpit, and the flash from the nose guns temporarily obscured the Dornier. When Trip let off the trigger, he could see that his fire was effective. Pieces flew off the Dornier and tumbled back through the slipstream. A stream of yellow lights came floating at him from the Dornier. *Damn, he's shooting back.*

Trip dumped the nose and kicked left rudder. The Dornier gunner adjusted his aim, but Trip was too quick for him. Rolling out of the slight turn to the left, he swung the nose back right toward the bomber and opened fire, continuing the turn as he fired. His shells raked the bomber from its left wingtip all the way across and down the fuselage. The enemy gunner fell silent as the bomber streamed black smoke from the left engine and dropped out of the formation. Trip gave him one more squirt of machinegun fire and turned his attention to the next bomber.

From the corner of his eye, Trip saw a Dornier burst into flame. Meslée had scored.

Trip looked up, back, down, back, scanning right and left for an escort. None. Good.

Trip lined up on the second Dornier in formation. He settled into a near-perfect pursuit curve, rolling out below and behind his target. Raising the nose a bit, he hit the trigger. Six streams of tracer flashed at the Dornier and converged on its right wing root. Trip was so close he could not miss. The bomber did not shoot back. Trip was in the bomber's blind spot. Even when the bomber tried to turn to give his gunners a shot, Trip hung into the blind spot.

The Dornier's right wing flew off, its engine still running full speed, making the airfoil into a dancing, unguided missile. The wing flipped crazily toward Trip. Trip jerked the Curtiss into a 90° bank, lost 200 meters, and rolled out below the bomber formation. He let the airplane accelerate and then hauled the nose up to close on the first bomber in the formation.

Trip glanced at the round counters and saw he had less than 100 rounds per gun. Coming vertically under the Dornier, Trip held the trigger down raking the bomber from nose to tail. The guns quit firing. *Shit. I shouldn't have fired that final burst at the first Dornier.*

Trip rolled inverted and dived out of the formation. He used the Curtiss's momentum to climb back to the altitude of the retreating bombers. He looked for a landmark and also scanned for Meslée and enemy fighters.

In the distance, he saw Meslée shooting at one of the bombers before breaking off just as they reached the Franco-German border. Meslée turned back to Trip and waggled his wings. Trip joined formation as Meslée's number two, and they turned toward Suippes.

Trip glanced at his fuel gauge. He had perhaps 110 liters left in the main tank with the 115-liter reserve. *Won't make Suippes.*

Trip looked over to Meslée and signaled that he had low fuel. Meslée nodded, pointed to himself, and made signals that he was also low.

~~<>~~

247

Fifty kilometers behind the border, they spotted an airfield and set up to land. Meslée waggled his wings and pitched up to land. Trip was right behind him. They touched down and taxied clear of the landing strip.

The field looked familiar to Trip. There was a derelict Hurricane under a tree. It had shattered propeller blades. *Ah...Vassincourt.*

The two flyers climbed out of their Curtiss's and looked around.

A British flight sergeant marched over and stood, arms akimbo. "'Ere, wot's this? You two Froggies just land 'ere wivout permission?"

Meslée looked at Trip to interpret. Trip looked at the flight sergeant, "Remember me?"

The flight sergeant's eyes popped. "You? Wot are *you* doing wearing that Frog uniform."

Trip said, "I joined up. We've been out killing Boches while you and the chaps have been enjoying some tea and biscuits. May I present Lieutenant Edmond Marin la Meslée of the *Armée de l'Air*?"

Meslée said, *"Enchanté, Mon Sergeant."*

The flight sergeant drew himself and said, "The pleasure is mine, I'm sure, Sir. He muttered, "Tea and biscuits, indeed."

Trip said, "Our airfield was bombed at dawn, and we got off and chased the attackers down. We need petrol and would appreciate a drink."

The flight sergeant said, "Please come with me."

~~<>~~

The small entourage walked to the mess tent area, and the flight sergeant asked them to sit while he looked for the commander. Trip helped himself and Meslée to a glass of cold water and sat in the shade.

Two hurricanes roared down the grass strip, pitched for landing, and taxied up to dispersal. The pilots got out and wandered over to the mess tent.

The first one pulled off his flight helmet. It was Paul Richey. "Hullo, Trip. Who's your Froggie friend?"

Les Clisby jumped down from the wing of the other Hurricane. "Stone tha' fuckin' crows, Mate. Wot th' hell are you doin' in that Frog uniform?"

Trip said, "Long story. May I introduce my friend and leader, Lieutenant Edmond Marin la Meslée of the *Armée de l'Air*?"

Clisby said, "Bloody hell. Nice ta' meetcha, mate."

Paul Richey said, "This is a pleasant surprise. *Enchanté, Mon Lieutenant*."

Meslée looked confused but said, *"Enchanté, mes amis."*

Paul smiled at Meslée and then looked at Trip. "Now you really must tell us everything. How did you become a French pilot."

Meslée said, "'E is a mos' insane *pilote*. Eel is *mon honneur* to fly wiz *Sergent-Chef* Gibson."

Clisby said, "So, now you're a chef? What's for dinner?"

Trip grinned, "While you're fucking yourself, Les, is there any chance of some wine?"

Meslée said, "*Mon Dieu*, zeese people are your friends, Trip? Zis explain many zings."

Chapter 33 – Veldwezelt Bridge

Trip and Meslée had sat in the officers' mess in the little town adjacent to the Vassincourt airfield. Trip, Meslée, Paul Richey, and Les Clisby enjoyed ale and rough local red wine and cigarettes.

Richey said, "I'll speak to The Bull about petrol for your kites. Getting a bit late in the day to fly if your field was bombed."

Meslée asked, "Ze Bull?"

"Yes, old boy. Squadron Leader Patrick Halahan. He's called The Bull because he's like a bull and takes no guff. Bloody good leader, too."

Meslée laughed and agreed. "*Oui, et merci.* Perhaps we might sleep 'ere tonight?"

Clisby said, "Too right. Two of our lads won't be using their beds."

Richey looked sad, "Aye, they're buggered. Either dead or in hospital."

Paul Richey had pulled strings with the 1 Squadron commanding officer, Squadron Leader Bull Halahan, and had the French Curtiss fueled. A fitter had looked at the few bullet holes in the airplanes and determined they were flyable. The British could not work on the French airplanes beyond basic maintenance.

The worst news was that 1 Squadron was moving to Barry-ac-Bac, a small airfield not far from Vassincourt. Vassincourt was abuzz with activity, and a small convoy of ground support fitters and armorers was preparing to leave.

An hour later, No. 1 Squadron's Hurricanes began flying out. Two unflyable airplanes were unceremoniously rolled into bomb craters and set ablaze. It hurt Trip's soul to watch such exceptional airplanes be torched.

Richey said, "I'm with the lead element there, so hop on board, and we'll take you to town. I'll have a word with the locals where our chaps were billeted, and you should have no difficulty getting a bed."

Pausing the convoy for a moment, Richey escorted Trip and Meslée to the private home where the two missing fliers were billeted. The French owners were only too happy to invite valiant French flyers to stay.

Richey bid the two *Armée de l'Air* pilots farewell, and the No. 1 Squadron convoy set off for Barry-ac-Bac.

Trip, exhausted from yesterday's flight, slept on a bed belonging to a missing Englishman.

~~<>~~

Morning broke without an attack on the airfield. Trip thought, *Probably noticed there were no airplanes here.*

The French homeowner insisted that Trip and Meslée enjoy a pleasant breakfast before heading to the field to fly their Curtiss's out. Trip discreetly left two 100 Franc notes for the homeowners.

There were no ground crew available, so they propped over the airplanes together to push the oil out of the bottom cylinders of the radial engines. Then, Trip helped Meslée to strap in and get his engine running. Trip pulled Meslée's chocks and hurried to his own airplane. He pulled the chocks aside and climbed in.

He quickly turned on the boost pump and set it to low. Checked the magnetos off. Checked the mixture control to IDLE/CUT-OFF. Then he cracked the throttle and hit the starter cartridge.

The stink of the cartridge gas roiling out of the cowling told him the cartridge had fired, and he watched the prop blades slowly turn. He hit both magnetos to ON and set the prime to ON/STEADY.

BRRRRAMMMM! BAM, BAM, Brrrrraaammmm....

The engine fired. He quickly nudged the throttle, looked for oil pressure to register, and waited for the engine to settle down into the 800-1000 RPM smooth running range.

Unlike the previous morning when hell was breaking loose, Trip took a few moments to let the engine warm before moving the mixture lever to RICH. He let the RPM drop to about 200, then stopped the prime and adjusted the throttle to about 1000 RPM.

Trip grinned at Meslée and gave him a thumbs-up signal.

Meslée taxied straight ahead to the surprisingly undamaged Vassincourt airstrip and turned into the wind. Trip followed closely, checking engine instruments for steady RPM and oil pressure.

Neither Trip nor Meslée had ammunition. Their guns were empty from the fight with the Dorniers. The British .303 ammunition did not fit the French guns. They agreed to fly directly to Suippes and land quickly.

~~<>~~

Meslée landed first, picking his way among the bomb craters along the Suippes landing strip. He taxied to the dispersal area with Trip following closely.

Meslée gave quick instructions to the ground crew to fill the fuel tanks and re-arm the fighters. Then, he led Trip across the pock-marked landscape to find the commander.

Capitaine Jean-Mary Accart was sitting in a lawn chair when Meslée and Trip walked over. He flicked the ash from his Gauloise and glanced up, "I might have known the two of you were together."

Meslée spoke for himself and Trip, "*Oui, Mon Capitaine.*"

There was a rapid-fire exchange of French that Trip barely interpreted. Meslée explained that he and Trip had managed to get airborne despite the bombing. They had individually chased the Dornier 217 bombers that had attacked the airfield. Trip and Meslée had joined formation and attacked the Dorniers that numbered approximately 14. Trip destroyed two and severely damaged a third. Meslée destroyed one bomber and probably destroyed a second. They were out of ammunition and low on fuel after this engagement. They recovered at Vassincourt where the RAF were leaving but provided them shelter, gasoline, and food.

Accart dragged on his cigarette and snorted, "I thought you two were lovers and had absconded to Paris."

Trip said, "*Mon Capitaine*, I have better taste."

Meslée smirked, "This one was sent here by Madame Allard. *She* is ze one wiz ze bad taste."

Accart laughed out loud. Then he became serious.

He dragged on his Gauloise and said, smoke puffs escaping with every word, "We are relocating to Saint-Dizier. This field is too damaged to repair. Also, we started yesterday with 29 aircraft assigned. There were three unflyable. Of the 26 flyable airplanes yesterday, we now have 13. Lieutenant Goupy and Sergent Preux were wounded yesterday and out of action. Preux may be back. Goupy was badly hurt. I believed both of you were dead but didn't report it, yet."

~~<>~~

GC I/5 launched at 0430 to escort a squadron of British Fairey Battle Bombers on an attack mission against bridges across the Meuse River. They would recover at Saint-Dizier.

Trip jacked his seat as high as it would go and craned his neck to see the bombers. No bombers in sight, Trip thought, *Shit. No luck. It's a complete mess.*

But then, so was Spain. No coordination, no control, no planning. Limited support. Trip looked around at the rest of the squadron, keeping perfect formation on the way to nowhere. He thought, *This is a losing proposition. Worse than Spain.*

The squadron landed at Saint-Dizier and taxied to dispersal areas well away from the landing strip. The squadron maintenance units were already in place but operating with no shelters.

Trip was delighted to see Giraud come running to Number 8. "*Alors, Chef.* We thought you were dead."

Trip grinned, "Takes a lot to kill me, Jules. Is the mess tent working? I'm starved."

"*Oui, mon Chef.* The mess tent is cooking. Not *Maxim's,* I'm afraid."

~~<>~~

Trip ate some lamb stew and root vegetables sparingly. He wondered what poor farmer had given up a large chunk of his annual income to feed GC I/5.

En route from Suippes to St-Dizier, Trip saw thousands of people on the road. They were hauling hand carts and driving mules, and riding wagons. The fortunate ones were in cars and trucks. The cars and trucks looked like juicy targets for a Stuka dive-bomber or a strafing attack from fighters.

Trip sat eating his meal which was far better than anything the poor refugees would have for weeks, if not months. He felt guilty. He was hungry, but his heart felt heavy knowing he was privileged. Trip put that suffering out of his mind and forced himself to eat the delicious lamb stew. To ignore the food and let it go to waste was a bigger sin than consuming it when others were going without.

~~<>~~

Trip got four hours of exhausted sleep before someone came through the town banging a dinner gong or some kind of pot. "Alert! Alert. All pilots report to the field."

Trip dragged himself to his feet and looked at his watch. 0400 – four a.m. *Jesus.*

Hustling into his uniform, flight coverall, flying boots, and jacket, Trip rushed downstairs from the aging, rickety hotel in Saint-Dizier. Looking wildly for transportation to the field, Trip snatched a beat-up bicycle leaning against a lamppost. Turning the bike, he pedaled furiously up the long hill to the airfield.

He skidded to a halt in the dispersal area, dropped the bike, and ran into the tent that served as the operations room. Accart was just stepping in front of the assembled squadron.

Accart spoke rapidly in clipped French. "We have been tasked to escort British Battle Bombers from Number 12 Squadron, RAF, in attacking two bridges over the Albert Canal."

"I will lead one flight of six and escort British aircraft attacking the bridge at Vroenhoven. Lieutenant Meslée will lead the second flight of six and escort the attacking aircraft at Veldwezeit."

"We rendezvous with the British at 0600 over *Huy, Belgique.* It is on the Meuse, 20 kilometers west of Liège. Clear?"

"Very well. We take off in one hour. Our initial heading is 005 degrees. The RAF bombers must destroy the bridges over the Albert Canal between the Netherlands and *Belgique.* Failure will allow *les Boches* access to all *Belgique.* If *Belgique* falls, France is next."

The squadron hurried to their airplanes, where ground personnel rushed to prepare them for takeoff. Mechanics were pulling propellers through to clear oil out of the engine cylinders while armorers feverishly loaded ammunition belts into the guns.

Meslée put a hand on Trip's arm. "*Les Boches* 'ave taken the Fortress Eben Emael, south of Maastricht in the Netherlands. Eben Emael's artillery covered the bridges. But now? *Non.* We must destroy the bridges."

Trip stopped and looked at Meslée. "How did the *Boches* take that fort so quickly?"

"It doesn't really matter now, but they landed gliders and parachutists on top of it. I fear the Maginot Line will suffer the same fate."

Trip nodded and turned to head for his airplane. He turned back to Meslée, *"Bon chance, mon ami."*

Meslée grinned, *"Merci bien, et vous."*

Trip stepped up on the wing of Number 8 and then into the cockpit. He snapped his parachute straps into place and started pulling on his harness.

Giraud jumped onto the wing and hurried to help.

Trip nodded. He grinned and shouted, "Welcome to the party, Jules."

Giraud looked at Trip inquiringly, *"Hein?"*

Trip grinned. "Never mind."

A flare flew heavenward to burst and illuminate the field in red light. The signal was to start engines.

Twelve radial engines started in a continuous roar. Ground troops pulled chocks away, and the aircraft began to taxi, following Accart as he swung into the wind on the landing strip.

The squadron was soon airborne, with Trip flying in the number 4 position in the second flight of six. Meslée in Number 2, his usual mount, led the second flight, and they climbed steadily on a heading of 005 degrees. Trip looked at his chart and put a finger on the northern bridge of the two. *That's our target.*

~~<>~~

At precisely 0600 hours, GC I/5 arrived over Huy, Belgium, but the bombers did not. Liège had lights showing, which was a surprise.

Accart led the squadron in a large left circle at 4000 meters. Still, there were no bombers. Accart rocked his wings and drew the squadron onto their original heading of 005 degrees. They would continue to the targets hoping to find the bombers at some point.

The squadron roared along at 4000 meters, and Trip continually searched the sky in every quadrant for potential enemy activity. He also looked for dark specks that might be the British bombers.

The squadron split into two flights with Meslée's Blue Flight to the left on an even more northerly heading. Accart's Red Flight to the right, heading slightly East of North. Radios silenced, they droned on toward Maastricht and the strategically critical Albert Canal.

The ground was still in the somnolent shadow of pre-dawn. But at altitude, the sun was now bright in the east. Trip worried about German fighters coming out of the sun to attack the squadron. Trip continually put a fingertip on the brightest part of the sun and looked to see if the enemy lurked there.

The British bombers were yet to be seen.

A bit bored, Trip cracked open the canopy, shut off his oxygen supply, and lit a Gauloise. The nicotine settled his nerves and he resumed scanning for the British bombers and enemy fighters.

Ahead, Trip could see the dawn breaking on the Albert Canal, a long, straight north-south waterway that branched off the Meuse River. It was a perfect protective ditch but for the two bridges. Near, to the right, Trip could see Fort Eben Emael. He imagined a Nazi flag fluttering atop the ramparts. Then he saw the first bridge – Vroenhoven. Red Flight was to protect bombers there.

Running his eye up the canal to the north, he saw the Veldwezelt Bridge. Its metal girders glinted in the early light. He also saw puffs of antiaircraft fire. *Shit, the bombers are already there.* He took a deeply satisfying drag on his Gauloise made all the more tasty by the knowledge that smoking in the cockpit was against regulations.

He glanced toward Vroenhoven and saw puffs of antiaircraft fire blossom. They were briefly red in the center when the shell went off.

As the explosion faded, the German antiaircraft shells were marked by white puffs. *Where the hell are the bombers if there's all that fire?*

In answer to his question, a huge burst of flame and a streaming fireball identified the death of a British bomber. It splashed across the Belgian landscape in seconds, setting fires and destroying buildings as its bombs detonated. *That's one down. Wonder how many bombers the Brits sent?*

Trip didn't have time to consider this question because in the distance he spotted a formation of enemy aircraft rolling into a dive from about 2000 meters. He quickly calculated the track of the attacking fighters and spotted the British at about 1000 meters altitude. They were boring in on the Veldwezelt Bridge.

Trip hit the microphone switch on his throttle. His French was improving, and he called out, "Blue Flight, Enemy eight kilometers ahead, low. Attacking the bombers."

Meslée replied, "Roger. Blue Flight, combat formation."

Trip edged out from his lead aircraft. He flicked his half-smoked Gauloise into the slipstream. In the same motion, he cranked the canopy back tightly shut. He swept his oxygen mask on and hit the regulator. The mask was less about delivering oxygen at this altitude and more about covering his face in case of fire.

Trip saw black smoke pop from Meslée's exhausts. Following Meslée's lead, Trip was soon at full throttle and the maximum 100 cm of manifold pressure. Wind made whistling noises past the closed canopy of the airplane. The little Curtiss was going as fast as it could go. It would not be enough, because now Trip could see streaks of fire from the attacking fighters. He saw that the fighters were Bf-109s and 110s. Perhaps 30 total.

This is going to be a fight, Trip thought as he tightened his seat harness and checked his parachute buckles.

Meslée's voice crackled, "Blue Flight, five and six, remain as top cover. Blue Flight, attack, Now."

Trip glanced at the two airplanes ordered to remain at altitude to act as high cover for the rest of the flight. One of the pilots, Trip was not sure who it was, waved as Trip rolled into a diving right turn to pursue the enemy.

His job as Number Four in the flight was to spread wide of Number Three and weave right to left watching for any enemies attacking from behind. He edged out some 30 meters and slightly below and behind Number Three.

Meslée was fully engaged in a diving right turn that would roll him out dead astern of the nearest Bf-110. Number Three selected another Bf-110 and rolled out about 100 meters astern of the twin-engine fighter.

A stream of yellow traces arced from the rear gunner on Meslée's 110. Three's target also opened defensive fire, and Trip watched as a lazy stream of yellow death flicked toward Trip's leader.

Number Three dodged down and astern of the 110, and Trip backed off the throttle to stay with him. Trip watched as Number Three opened fire, the still dusky landscape below making the six streams of fire even brighter.

Trip looked left, right, above, behind. Bf-109s were slicing down from a solid 1000 meters height advantage to attack Meslée's Blue Flight. He keyed the mike and shouted, "Blue Flight, Break! Enemy high astern."

Meslée ignored the call long enough to destroy the 110 in his sights. The enemy left a long flaming arrow as it streaked toward the ground. Then, Meslée jerked the Curtiss hard left, reversing turn to face the 109s. It was almost too late.

Trip hauled his faithful little airplane around in a punishingly tight turn, the G forces pulled his oxygen mask down to his chin. He grunted hard, much like trying to breathe against a blocked airway, attempting to overcome the blood draining from his brain under the heavy G turn.

He rolled out and ran his eye over the gun switches. All ON. Good. His left hand went to the gunsight rheostat and adjusted the brightness. He set the diameter to match the 109's 10-meter wingspan.

He checked throttle – full, propeller controls to high RPM, and manifold pressure to 100 cm. Mixture – rich. There would be little time in the fight to worry about these.

Now the 109s were in range, and Trip hit the gun trigger. Simultaneously, two 109s lit up with gunfire. Trip saw tracers arc toward him. He stopped firing and shoved the stick forward, causing the engine to cough when the carburetor was briefly starved of fuel.

Now the 109s were past Blue Flight, and Trip stood the little plane on its wing to follow. His leader Blue Three was nowhere to be seen. Once again, Trip grunted against the G forces and turned the little fighter on a dime.

The 109s, with superior speed from their dive, could not make such a tight turn. Trip rolled out of his turn in time to have a German plane float right into the gunsight reticle. Trip hit the trigger and counted off two seconds. The 109 almost disintegrated. It should have, Trip was within 100 feet by the time he fired, and the concentrated six streams of 7.5-millimeter literally tore the Messerschmitt apart.

Trip shifted his focus to a Bf-110 hustling to catch the last of the British bombers. A glance around the area showed four streaks on the ground burning plus another three or four explosions from crashed airplanes.

The 110 in front of Trip was chasing a single-engine British bomber with a large greenhouse canopy. Trip realized it was a Fairey Battle Bomber. Old, slow, outmoded, and easy prey even for the somewhat cumbersome Bf-110. He could see the white codes on the side of the Fairey: PH-K.

The Fairey's pilot was throwing the bomber left and right, up and down, but it was of little value. The 110 was faster and more maneuverable.

Trip opened fire on the 110 from a great range. He had less intent to destroy the airplane than to distract him, hoping to let the Fairey get to the bridge. A stream of tracer from the 110's rear gunner swept toward Trip's Curtiss.

Kicking left rudder and dipping the left wing, Trip brought the Curtiss dead astern of the twin-tailed 110 and some 50 feet below its altitude. Trip thought, *Careful, Trip-boy. That's the ground just down there.*

He was now within 100 meters of the 110. Trip hit the trigger and walked the tracers from wingtip to wingtip. The 110 rolled into a left turn, hoping to offer the rear gunner a shot at Trip's Curtiss. Trip nudged right rudder and fired a burst that shattered the rear canopy, killing the German gunner.

Continuing to fire, Trip whipsawed the bullets to the 110's left engine and was rewarded with panels flying off and a satisfying lick of flame. More importantly, white coolant streamed from that engine. The 110 was doomed or at least out of the fight.

Looking for the Fairey Battle, Trip saw it hit by groundfire multiple times, yet PH-K continued its attack on the Veldwezelt Bridge.

Trip looked for the enemy antiaircraft batteries and opened fire on the closest one. Satisfied he had suppressed their fire, he shifted to another gun emplacement. These were obviously newly occupied by the Germans and perhaps not as well prepared against attack.

The Fairey Battle pressed the attack and released its stick of six bombs. Then, it seemed to stagger in mid-air. Trip thought, *Jesus, he's been hit badly this time.*

But the Battle's pilot lowered the nose to get some airspeed and flew on, turning short of Maastricht and heading back to the west and home. Trip flew alongside the Fairey and waved at the pilot. The second man in the long greenhouse canopy was slumped against the glass. Toward the rear of the cockpit, the gunner was lying against the cockpit combing, an arm lifelessly dangling in the slipstream. The Battle's engine was streaming oil and glycol coolant. Flames licked out of the panels under the exhausts. The British airplane was doomed.

Trip made hand motions to the pilot to bail out. The pilot shook his head and jerked a thumb behind him. Apparently, the second man was not dead, but badly wounded. The pilot would not leave him. Trip made hand motions to belly land and get out. Again, a head shake.

Trip saluted and maintained an escort for the brave Battle pilot and his injured crew.

It was no use, the Fairey's engine suddenly seized and a gout of flame shot backward from the exhausts, igniting gasoline that was leaking from the fuel tanks. The Fairey was engulfed in flame and streaked at the ground in a blinding flash.

Trip turned for Saint-Dizier, his heart heavy in the knowledge such brave men would die in such a suicidal attack. Yet, PH-K's bombs had taken out a span of the Veldwezelt Bridge.

That was the mission. And the mission came first.

Chapter 34 – Frustration

Trip and the others landed at Saint-Dizier. Not as a formation of 12 Curtiss's, but in ones and twos. Trip was happy to see the large white Number 2 on Meslée's tail as he taxied off the landing strip and into the dispersal area.

Meslée was waiting when Trip walked into the intelligence tent to tell his version of what happened. Already debriefed and drinking a large beaker of rough red, Meslée stood listening to Trip's tale. He occasionally interpreted for the French intelligence officer.

"So, you claim one Bf-109 certainly destroyed, one Bf-110 likely destroyed. Any others? *Non?*"

Trip said, "I fired at several enemy aircraft, but those were the ones I am sure I hit."

The intelligence officer nodded. *"Merci, Chef Beneš."*

They walked out of the intelligence tent. Meslée asked, "Wine?"

"God, yes."

~~<>~~

Meslée said, "That story you told about the bomber and its pilot willingly dying before he would leave his comrades is why we shall win this war."

Trip nodded. "Yeah, but it will take a while."

"Oui. I fear time is not on our side just now. We must endeavor to hold the line and stop the Germans. They will come through that gap at Eben Emael. They will also come through the Ardennes Forest."

Trip looked up, alarmed, "I thought the Ardennes was impenetrable?"

"*Non.* When I was a boy, we often camped there on holiday. There are many roads, and the trees are dense but not so thick as to be a major impediment. The Nazis will come through there soon. They are making noise in front of the Maginot Line but will not attack there. The attack into the Netherlands and Belgique is to pull our forces north. Our generals – and the British – don't see that, Trip. Once we're completely distracted, they will crash through the Ardennes. It will be hell to pay."

Trip looked thoughtful, "Why are you telling me this?"

"Ah, *mon ami,* this is the question. You are an American wearing a French uniform using a false Czechoslovak name. You may be taken prisoner by the Nazis and shot as a spy. Worse, you may be taken prisoner by our own side and shot as a spy. This worries me."

Trip said, "I haven't thought of that."

Meslée said, "I 'ave dictated a letter that should be ready for my signature. It identifies you and explains your situation. Moreover, it tells the reader that you are a brave defender of France and now an ace pilot. I saw you damage that Dornier on our first flight together. There were others over the past months. Yesterday and today, you destroyed at least four enemy aircraft. Add those to your score in Spain, and you have six, perhaps more."

Trip said, "I haven't considered how many enemy airplanes I've damaged or destroyed. I suppose you're right. One for sure in Spain, probably a second one. Then, I think there were four here in France."

Meslée said, "We're down to only a few effective airplanes. Yours is one, but it has bullet holes and requires an inspection before we can fly it again. If it does not pass the inspection, it will be destroyed. This will leave you without an airplane."

Trip said, "I can fly other airplanes."

"Of course, but there's no guarantee we will have another airplane available. Worse, I expect the Germans will push us back. Reims is the main air headquarters. I expect we will be pushed back west of Reims very soon."

"So, what should we do."

"I think when we get pushed back, you can go with the ground element, but then you must make your way to England. You have friends who are Englishmen. They can help you."

"I don't think they can help, Marin. They are already gone from Vassincourt. I know they went to Barry-ac-bac. The next place for them is unknown."

Meslée said, "Let us hope that we can continue fighting."

~~<>~~

Trip's Number 8 passed its inspection and remained airworthy. It had many holes that were repaired with tape. Fortunately, there were no vital parts damaged.

The days passed with alarming rapidity. GC I/5 flew often, mostly patrolling up and down the lines, rarely seeing enemy aircraft. Trip strained to see into the distance, but there was no success.

The 14th of May dawned with German forces on the West side of the Meuse-Albert Canal Line and then in France. They quickly threatened Sedan. GC I/5 was too far south at Saint-Dizier to effectively patrol near Sedan, and so were mostly out of the action.

Meslée was furious, "The Stukas dive bomb relentlessly all over near Sedan, but we do nothing. I understand they have bombed hospitals with red crosses clearly marked. They attack refugee columns to spread terror. Yet, we sit here behind the supposedly impregnable Maginot Line awaiting an attack that does not come."

From May 15th to 17th, Guderian's XIX Panzer Corps burst through the French lines and drove a spear into the Somme River Valley, effectively severing the Allies into two camps. British and Belgians to the North, French to the South.

Meslée and Trip were sitting in the makeshift pilots' ready area drinking the excellent local red wine and smoking.

Meslée said, "The *Boche* assault has been happening for seven days. Seven days! And we're cut in half, the British are dithering near Calais and Dunkirk. Rommel has burst across the lines at Dinant, *Belgique*, and along with the XLI Panzer Corps, is running riot in the open country. They call Rommel's unit the Ghost Division. No one knows where he is. And the worst is that the *Boche* are approaching the other Channel ports near Arras, behind the British. I predict the British are already thinking they must pull out. We shall be left alone."

Trip asked, "Why are we still here when the fighting is North?"

"Ah, *mon ami*, it is because of the Maginot Line. We will defend that relic to the death."

Trip flew every other day, but there was no action to speak of. It was all routine patrols, boring holes in the empty sky.

~~<>~~

Trip and Meslée were chatting, and as usual, nothing was happening. Morale in the unit was at rock bottom. It was May 27th.

Meslée said, "We had a signal from Reims. King Leopold surrendered the entire *Belgique* Army. The British have been pulling out of Dunkirk. There is a massive sealift operation where the Royal Navy and every boat in England are going across the Channel and back picking up British and French troops. The RAF is flying top cover. It appears the Spitfires are giving the 109s a hard time."

Trip snorted, "Great! And here we sit."

"*Oui. Mon ami* I think you should consider what you will do if we must pull out of here. I think France will fall in days, Trip."

"Well, I'm not going over the wall!"

"*Non.* But I can arrange a discharge. Then, you are an *Ami* simply caught in a war zone."

"Can I think about it?"

"But, of course. But don't think too long, *mon ami.*"

Chapter 35 – Last Fight for France

June 1st dawned with clear weather and a quiet rustle of leaves in the trees. The sky was blue with a gray haze that reduced visibility to less than 10 kilometers. Trip and several others sat smoking and reading the same magazines each had read a dozen times. Some dozed in the warmth of the morning sun.

The *escadrille* adjutant rushed into the dispersal area. "Alert! Bombers approaching at 3000 meters from Saarbrucken."

Cups, glasses, magazines, and chairs scattered as the GC I/5 pilots rushed to their airplanes.

Trip climbed up on the wing of Number 8 and settled into the cockpit. Giraud quickly strapped him in. The engine was warm from the morning preflight engine run. Trip hit the switches, held the starter through five blades of the propeller turning, and cracked the throttle. The engine caught and settled into the comforting, steady rumble that only a radial engine can make.

Giraud patted him on the shoulder, jumped down to pull the wheel chocks, and marshal the plane out of its parking spot.

In minutes the *escadrille* was airborne and forming up. There were only eight planes serviceable. Trip was on Meslée's wing.

Capitaine Accart set the *escadrille* climbing in a formation that looked a bit like an arrowhead, pointed straight at Saarbrucken. They passed 2000 meters in less than 5 minutes. Soon, they were at 4000 meters, and Accart kicked his rudder to direct the *escadrille* to spread into combat formation.

Trip checked his gun switches to the on position while constantly scanning for both enemy bombers and fighters. The bombers were prey, the fighters were deadly opponents.

In the distance, Trip saw a flash. Sun on canopy glass or a wing? He looked harder at the area where he saw the flash. There! Another wink of sunlight.

Trip rocked his wings to get Meslée's attention. He pointed.

Meslée nodded and, tugging his throttle open, pulled alongside Accart. They exchanged hand signals, and Accart turned toward the flash.

In less than three minutes, a formation of 12 gray and green German Heinkel 111 bombers materialized from the haze. Trip always marveled at the German camouflage. Light blue undersurfaces were hard to see from below. From above the splinter-pattern gray-green and dark green, almost black, paint scheme was devilishly hard to see against the Continent's farm field colors. Fortunately for the defenders, the Heinkel bombers had a large glass-enclosed cockpit that would reflect the sun.

Accart climbed to gain height advantage. It was clear to Trip that GC I/5 would pass overhead the bombers and sweep around in a diving turn, building speed to slash the bomber formation from dead astern.

With the bombers located, Trip constantly scanned for fighter escorts. He wondered if there were a dozen Bf-109s lurking in the bright rays of the morning sun.

Trip adjusted the throttle to remain in position, and continued moving his head in all directions, attempting to locate enemy fighters.

Now Accart rolled into a left descending turn to attack the bombers. Trip thought four fighters should attack the bombers while four should remain as top cover, but that was not to be. Accart was intent upon killing all 12 bombers and the entire *escadrille* was required for that.

Soon it was Trip's turn to roll left and lower the nose to swing around behind the bombers. As he rolled and turned, he glanced at gun switches, checked prop setting and manifold pressure, and edged the throttle forward to slow the Curtiss a bit and maintain formation position. *God, I hope there are no fighters up there.*

Trip watched Accart pick out a 111 and open fire. In moments, an unscathed 111 was in Trip's sights, its wingtips quickly touching the edges of the sight reticle. Trip hit the gun trigger and focused his fire on the Heinkel's starboard engine. The little Curtiss shook from the recoil of six 7.5-millimeter guns.

Trip saw pieces fly off the Heinkel's right engine and wing. Simultaneously, a stream of yellow tracers flew at him from atop the bomber. The bomber's engine began smoking and streaming white vapor from the coolant tank. *Good. He's badly wounded.*

Bombs fell from the Heinkel in a stream as the crew tried to lighten the load. Trip kicked rudder and dropped his left wing to slide across to the port side of the 111. He fired again, his six streams of tracers raking down the fuselage sides and across to the port engine.

Another stream of tracers came from atop the bomber. *Huh, thought that gunner was dead.*

A hole appeared in Trip's windscreen. The rattling sound of ball bearings hitting a tin roof penetrated Trip's earphones.

Clang, clang! Crash. This last sound accompanied a large hole opening up in his starboard wing. One of his wing guns hung at a crazy angle, its mounts shot away.

Trip dumped the stick to get out of the enemy gunner's sights.

No luck. The Heinkel had a bathtub-like ventral gun position that now came into play. A stream of yellow tracer reached out to Trip's Number 8 with deadly accuracy.

You Nazi son-of-a-bitch. Trip pulled the nose around and fired again. The starboard wing guns fired, but the Curtiss slewed hard into a left skid because the guns were dangling from the wing. This may have saved Trip Gibson's life.

A row of bullets ran across the starboard wing and punched holes in the fuselage. If not for the skid, Trip would have been right in line to be hit all over with the German gunner's fire. As it was, Trip felt a sledgehammer blow to his left leg. *Jesus, I'm hit.*

He reached out and turned off the gun switches for the starboard wing. He saw that his oxygen panel was shattered. *Have to finish him and get down to lower altitude soon.*

He tried to kick left rudder, but his leg would not work. No matter, he rolled the airplane wings level and opened fire with the four guns he had left.

The Heinkel's left landing gear slowly drooped out of the nacelle below the port engine. Then, the bomber rolled slowly into a 90-degree left bank, its nose slicing into a near-vertical death dive. Trip hauled hard on the stick to avoid colliding with the stricken Heinkel.

~~<>~~

Suddenly, the sky was clear. Trip looked around. How did he get to 1000 meters, and where were the others?

Things seemed dream-like to Trip. He was in a slight right turn which he immediately corrected. It was quiet, but his engine was roaring away at full throttle. His ears popped and some of his hearing was restored.

He pushed the throttle closed somewhat to reduce manifold pressure and preserve the engine. Trip looked around. His ears popped again, and he felt lightheaded. He rolled the canopy open. *Maybe cold air rushing in will help.*

Looking down, he saw blood all over the bottom of the cockpit. It was coming from a hole in the left leg of his flight coverall. *Oh, yeah, I got hit back there.*

He drifted along for a moment before jerking alert. *Damn, I think I've lost a lot of blood.*

He looked down and spotted a couple of known landmarks. *I'm about 20 kilometers west of Saint-Dizier. Better turn that way.*

Trip reached down to set the elevator trim and found that the wheel was shot away. He investigated further. No radio controls. No trim controls. Landing gear lever intact, unknown function. *Son-of-a-bitch, I'm in a hell of a pickle.*

His airspeed was holding up at about 340 kph. The airplane landed at about 100 kph, so that was all good. His altimeter appeared to be working. 1000 meters, slight descent. *Fix that.*

He leveled off at 900 meters. The airplane seemed controllable. Trip checked the stick forward and back, left and right. Each direction the airplane responded correctly. He found he could control the rudder by pulling or pushing with his right foot that was under the leather rudder pedal strap.

Trip's left leg began to hurt. It was throbbing with each beat of his heart. He looked down. It was bleeding but not spurting blood. *Good, maybe I won't bleed to death before I land this crate.*

Ahead, Trip could see the field at Saint-Dizier. *Good. Just fly it straight in. Should I lower the landing gear?*

To land wheels up was to write off the airplane at a time when France needed every airframe it could get. *Fuck it, I'm putting down the wheels. I hope the starboard one works.*

Trip backed off the throttle and went through landing checks. He checked the canopy locked open. No sense having it jam closed on landing.

He slowed to about 160 kph and lowered the landing gear lever. Trip prayed for three green lights to show on the instrument panel.

Left gear – OK.

Tail wheel – OK.

Right gear... *Come on!* Trip pushed the light to be sure the bulb was good. The bulp popped on. *Yes, it's working. Damn!*

Right gear... *Come on! Get down and lock.*

Trip feld the right gear clank into position – OK!

Three green lights on the dash shone brightly. *Whew.*

Trip grabbed the flap handle and pulled. The Curtiss slewed hard left as the left flap lowered, but the right flap did not. Putting the stick to the right and pushing on the rudder was agonizing. Trip's left leg screamed from the sudden movement.

Snatching the flaps back up, Trip prayed that he could get the left flap back up. The Curtiss would be impossible to land with combat damage and an asymmetrical flap condition.

The airplane was quite a handful to fly for a few moments until the left flap settled into place fully up. *Thank you, God, for small favors.*

Trip was fully focused on flying the airplane, but a desperate urge for a cigarette kept popping into his mind. His mouth was dry. *Damn, I'd kill for a smoke and a drink of wine.*

Trip crossed the field boundary at about 135 kph, just above no-flap stall speed. He edged the Curtiss down until it was inches off the grass before cutting the throttle.

The little airplane settled onto the turf but rolled like a runaway freight train. Too bad. Trip couldn't apply brakes with his injured leg. Once the Curtiss was below flying speed, Trip hauled on the stick, hoping to keep the tail down.

He hit a couple of bumps in the surface before the airplane settled down and slowly slewed to a stop a few feet before the trees at the far end of the field.

Trip quickly turned off the fuel valves and boost pump. He hit the main battery switch and mags to off.

He popped his harness open and stood up to get out of the airplane. The world spun, and Trip Gibson collapsed over the side of the cockpit into the fresh green grass of France.

~~<>~~

There were some bright lights and a familiar face with a high, wide forehead. Trip felt cool, crisp sheets against his cheek.

Meslée was leaning over Trip. "Ah, you are awake, *mon ami.*"

Trip nodded. "Uh, where am I?"

Meslée said, "You are in *le Hospital Américain* in *Neuilly-sur-Seine.*"

"How did I get here?"

"*Hein.* Zat is ze good question, Trip. Ze *escadrille* doctor bandage your leg. But 'e think you need more care. I think you need *Américain* 'elp. So, we bring you here in Accart's car."

Trip nodded. "Where's Accart?"

"'E was badly wounded. 'E is in hospital near Troyes. We take him zere on ze way to bring you to Paris."

Trip thought a moment. "I hope *Capitaine* Accart recovers. What happened?"

"We shot down many Heinkels. There was no fighter escort and we 'ad what you Ami's call a field day. Damaged all of them. Shot down five, including yours. Accart landed at Saint-Dizier just after you. He was worse shot up than you, but ze doctor say Jean-Mary will recover. You, too."

Trip nodded. He felt woozy. "Good. What now."

Meslée's face became serious. "I am now *Escadrille Commandeur.*"

"Congratulations, *mon ami.*"

Meslée's mouth turned down. "*Merci.* It comes wiz a sad responsibility. Trip, you are my *ami* and my brother. You must go. Here are your discharge papers and ze letter I promised you."

Trip had a hollow place in his gut. He looked at Meslée. "Why?"

"*Hein, mon ami. You are hors de combat.* Your airplane is beyond repair. We shall take from it any parts useful and burn ze hulk. For all ze reasons we talked about, you must make your way out of France."

"I guess you're right. Any idea where I should go?"

"*Non*, but certainly toward England. Your friend Paul Richey is here. 'E was wounded in combat and is recovering. We entrusted 'im wiz your moneybelt."

Trip said, "Thanks for that. The money may be necessary to get me to England."

"*Oui.* Paul may be of assistance."

Trip nodded. "Please give Sergent Giscard my best wishes and *bon chance*. I will miss you and the other members of the *escadrille.*"

"*Oui*, I will tell Giscard. I will miss you. *Bon chance, mon ami.* It will be like ze English song, "We'll meet again."

Chapter 36 – Paris, The American Hospital

A familiar voice said, "Hallo, old boy! I see you're banged up, too. What happened?"

Trip looked up to see Paul Richey slouching against a medical cabinet near his bed.

"Hello, Paul."

Trip told him about the last fight.

"Bloody Hell! The 111's are tough customers, what?"

Trip asked, "What happened to you."

"Shot up by a 111 like you. Took a bullet in the neck. Blood everywhere. Hood was stuck so had to ride it down. Managed to land and get the hood open. Fell out into a heap on the wing and ran. Expected my kite to explode. She didn't, so I ran back, put all the switches off, gathered my maps, and walked to a nearby tree, where I promptly collapsed. Someone brought me here. Miracle, really, I did get three of the blighters before they got me."

Trip nodded. "Well done. I think the He-111 was my sixth, including Spain. Guess I'm an ace now. I don't remember all the details, and I woke up here. What day is it?"

"Ah, it's Monday, June 3rd."

Trip asked, "What about the war?"

Paul said, "Not good news, I'm afraid. We did get about 300,000 troops out at Dunkirk. But Jerry is pressing forward, and things are not looking good. Are you up to going out on the town?"

Trip pulled himself up. "Just have to see if I can get around on this leg."

Paul smiled broadly. "The quacks say the bullet missed bone on your left calf. Hurts like hell, I'm sure. It was bloody just because it punched a hole in the meat of your leg. I'll work on the nurses to get you released. Anyway, the food's better in town."

Trip grinned and said, "In that case, I wouldn't miss it."

"Good. This way, when I spend your money, I won't be stealing."

Trip smirked, "Thanks for taking care of that."

"Not a bit of it, old boy. The Froggies brought along your kit. They tell me you're discharged from the *Armée de l'Air*. They gave you a nice gong – *Croix de Guerre avec Palme*. Gallantry and all that. Citation was in with your discharge papers."

Trip said, "How nice. I didn't know. Meslée was insistent I be discharged because I might otherwise be shot as a spy."

Paul looked thoughtful, "Very well, no more of that uniform wearing. You do have a pair of nice suits and a slightly battered fedora."

Trip said, "It'll be strange wearing civilian clothes again."

Paul said, "Aye, but you cut a good figure. By the by, there are some cracking beautiful American nurses here."

Trip smirked, "It is the American Hospital, after all."

"Right-o."

~~<>~~

The ache in Trip's leg had subsided, and he was dozing. At about 11:30 a.m., sirens began to wail, waking Trip and causing momentary disorientation. Frantic activity all around the ward made the air raid sirens seem serious. The slamming sound of anti-aircraft fire confirmed this was no drill.

Paul stuck his head in the door to Trip's room. "Care to hobble to the roof and watch?"

Trip said, "Hell, yes!"

Paul got on one side of Trip, and a Doctor named Rogers got on the other.

Rogers, a kindly man with a good bedside manner, said, "This is against my better medical judgment, but Paul insists. We must be careful not to reopen your wound. Don't put any weight on that leg."

They hobbled into the hallway and to a modern elevator that went straight to the top floor. The three of them stumped onto the roof, stood under a small concrete shelter, and watched the fireworks.

Trip lit a cigarette and perched his left buttock on a low wall.

Rogers looked at him inquiringly.

Trip lied, "Doesn't hurt a bit."

Rogers looked at Paul. "Do all American's lie as poorly?"

Paul said, "Don't know. Haven't met them all yet. But this one is quite a professional."

Trip snorted, "I should get a certification or some such."

The air battle raged with sirens wailing, anti-aircraft guns cracking, aircraft engines growling, shrapnel spattering, and the crump of bombs blasting away at the City of Light. It appeared that the bombs fell on St Denis, the Seine, and St Germain.

Trip heard the rattle of a Curtiss' guns. "Hope they shoot down the entire *Boche* force."

Dust and smoke filled the air as Paul and Dr. Rogers helped Trip to the elevator and the dining hall.

Paul grinned, "Time for lunch, old boy."

Paul and Rogers made faces at the food as they sat down, but Trip was grinning. "My God, look at this. They've got meatloaf."

Paul said, "My God, what is the world coming to?"

~~<>~~

Despite a very painful leg, Trip got a pass to go into Paris with Paul Richie. Taking readily available cabs everywhere, they hit a couple of cafés and Harry's Bar. Trip had a French 75 that nearly put him under the table. Discretion being the better part of valor, Trip vowed not to drink again until the leg was better.

They cabbed it to *Maxim's*, where Albert, the portly Maître d', bowed them in and graciously led them to the best table. The food was every bit as good as it was before the Battle of France. Trip noticed a complete lack of uniforms among the patrons. He thought, *Guess everybody's at the front.*

~~<>~~

The next few days, Trip alternated between dozing and getting walked around the floor by a pretty American nurse named Alice. She had reddish-brown hair, worn in the latest bob. She was sturdily built, but in a good, corn-fed way. Strong back and tight waist with dancer's legs, she had the strength to prop Trip up as he stomped along the hallway. He called her Alice in Wonderland, and she didn't mind.

Paul arranged a cab to take them to The Ritz for luncheon. The Ritz bar was in full swing, even this early. Trip avoided alcohol, but Paul said, "I need a drink, old boy. I can't stop thinking of the descent to hell in my damaged Hurricane with blood spurting and a stuck hood. Couldn't bail out. Convinced I had bought the farm. Occupies my dreams, what?"

Trip said, "I've had some nightmares. The concentration camp at *Argelès-sur-Mer* wakes me up at night."

Paul said, "I don't know if I mentioned it, but we lost Les Clisby just before I went down. He had 17 Huns shot down. Too aggressive, I think. He is most likely dead. Everyone else shot down on that hop has been accounted for."

Trip raised his water glass. "Sorry, this is not champagne or wine. In Les' honor, 'Stone the fucking crows!'"

Paul said, "Stone the fucking crows!"

It was a fitting tribute to Flying Officer Leslie Clisby, fighter pilot, Australian ace, and good companion. Trip wished he knew him better.

~~<>~~

Trip was still hobbling some, but the wound no longer bled. He was exercising up and down the hall on the arm of Alice in Wonderland when Paul came in.

Trip grinned and said, "Hi, Paul."

Richey jerked his head toward Trip's room. Alice smiled and let Trip walk in on his own.

Paul said, "Doing all right, Trip?"

Trip said, "Yes. A bit stiff is all. It's been ten days. The doctor says it's mostly healed. Just needs therapy to get the muscle tone back."

Paul looked serious, "Can you walk some?"

Trip looked thoughtful, "Yes. I think walking will be good for it."

"Good. We need to leave soon. The Germans are pressing, and I think it won't be long before they are here. Every day we're seeing more Parisians with their belongings strapped to a car and driving West. I saw a car this morning with a mattress tied to the top as protection from strafing or a bomb blast. Silly, that."

Trip said, "I'm surprised it's taken this long."

Paul said, "I'm going to the RAF assistant provost marshal and get a *Ordre de Mission*. I will get you a pass if you let me have your letter from Meslée and your discharge papers. That will get us a train ride to Blois, where the RAF is now headquartered."

283

Trip said, "I'll pack my bag."

~~<>~~

Two hours later, Paul was back. "Success, Old Man. I've got an RAF lorry downstairs. Say your goodbyes."

Trip hobbled down the hall and found the doctor and nurses. He told them he was leaving, and they gave him three changes of dressing and some powder to put on the healing wound. The doctor shook his hand and was pleased to accept 5000 Francs - $100 – as a donation to the hospital.

Alice surprised Trip by stepping into the hall with him. She turned her face to him and kissed him with a passion he'd not experienced since Mildred Wright. "I wish things were different, Trip. I could make you very happy."

Trip said, "I wish things were different, too, Alice. You're lovely and you have been so good to me. Perhaps after this war we will meet again."

Alice's mouth turned down. "Sure, Trip. I don't know where we'll be, but I know you're from Atlanta. Maybe I'll come there."

~~<>~~

Trip's travel papers were in order. Paul helped him climb into the lorry, and they rolled for *Gare de Lyon* only to find a gigantic crowd spilling onto the street. Paul shouted to the driver, "Let's try *Gare d'Austerlitz*."

The crowd at *Gare d'Austerlitz* was at least as big.

After making his way through the crowd to the platform, Paul returned to the lorry. "They're bombing every train. We'll have to go with the provost marshal's convoy to Blois. That's tomorrow."

They returned to the hospital and begged a couple of beds for the night. Another $100 donation didn't hurt their case.

Trip was tired and dozed fitfully. At about midnight he felt his bed shift and smelled a familiar, soft perfume.

Alice whispered, "I'll take you through the looking glass, Trip."

Trip awoke at dawn to a memory and an empty bed. A note on the pillow read,

Think of me when you can.

Alice

Alice Gustafsson

1419 Oak Street

Urbana, Illinois

BAldwin 7131

Trip tucked the note into his backpack, stole a cane from a bin by the door, and quietly stumped out of the hospital.

~~<>~~

Trip made the half-mile walk to the British provost marshal's headquarters to meet Paul at 5 a.m. The cane made walking much easier, but the price was the beginnings of a blister on his left hand and some blood seeping from his wound. He put on a thin leather flying glove, and that helped the hand. There was nothing to be done for the leg.

The air over Paris was a fug of smoke and dust mixed with the stink of something burning blowing from the East. The burning smell was a mixture of wood, metal, gasoline, oil, and explosives.

Paul was fit to be tied over a lengthening delay. One of the PMs men was missing. He was finally located asleep in his bed, oblivious to the danger all around.

The convoy consisted of three vehicles with RAF motorcycle outriders who cleared the traffic. Trip was happy to ride in a lorry carrying 15 RAF policemen. They were a bit hostile until they learned his story. Then, they were friendly. The group rode along in companionable silence, smoking and watching the landscape go by through the open back of the canvas cover. The burning oil in the air left a layer of black grime on everything, getting into the creases on the men's skin and coating their clothing. It left a taste in their mouths that would not soon be forgotten.

The men were bitching about the oil, but he remembered being coated with thick, black-yellow crude and sloshing in an open boat in the freezing Atlantic. Trip grinned. This was terrible, but much better than the North Atlantic.

The roads were clogged, and no surprise. Everyone was going in the same westerly direction, and the RAF motorcycle riders nudged them out of the way efficiently. At Blois, the convoy stopped.

Paul trotted back to the truck. "This is us, Trip."

Trip dismounted with some difficulty and followed Paul to an airfield with Fairey Battle Bombers parked on it. He remembered the brave man who saluted him just before dying because he wouldn't bail out and leave his crewmen behind.

Paul retrieved a pistol from a friend. He and Trip went to see some friends of Paul's at a chateau, where they were feted at a pleasant dinner with an RAF group captain and the French baron who owned the chateau.

After dinner, Paul made Trip's case to the Group Captain, a man named Wann, who said he would look into getting Trip into an RAF uniform once back in England. Trip was invited to share a room with Paul, and they both collapsed in exhaustion.

~~<>~~

Paul and Trip, looking like two vagabonds, walked into No. 1 Squadron RAF's dispersal area at Châteaudun. Paul was received warmly by the remaining squadron members. Squadron Leader Bull Halahan and several original members had rotated back to England, but some were there when Trip visited in the spring. Trip was offered a cot, and he and Paul were present with No. 1 Squadron when the Nazi troops goosestepped into Paris on June 14.

That morning, Paul walked over to where Trip sat in the sun smoking his last Gauloise and rubbing his leg.

"Look here, old boy, I've been offered a ride on the mail plane back to Blighty. Only room for one with the weight. I'll tell 'em no if you want me to stay with you."

Trip said, "Paul, you absolutely must go. I'll find another way out. I'm sure there are still boats to England. As an American, I'm a neutral. I might be able to use that to my advantage. But you should go."

"You're certain?"

"Absolutely. I'd be stuck in Paris if it weren't for you."

Paul stuck out his hand, "Very well, then. I will be certain to see you in England."

Handing Trip a scrap of paper, "Here's my address. Do look in. If I'm not there, someone will know where to find me. Such good luck, old man. Oh, and here's my pistol. Hope you don't need it."

Trip grinned and said, "Thank you for everything, Paul. *Bon chance, mon ami.*"

Chapter 37 – Hurricane

The members of No. 1 Squadron RAF packed swiftly and began leaving as soon as their aircraft could be started. They were covering Operation Aerial, the withdrawal of the remaining British Expeditionary Forces from Western France. No. 1 Squadron's Hurricanes were required on station early in the day to protect the ships departing with RAF personnel. A troop ship, the *SS Lancastria*, had already been sunk with 3000 souls lost.

Trip was politely asked to leave the Squadron area. Security, you understand. He went to the chateau where he and Paul had stayed and asked for shelter for a few nights. The baron and his British wife were happy to oblige.

Trip watched the Hurricanes of No. 1 Squadron depart in groups of four, their Merlin engines making a characteristic smooth roar. He noticed that most No. 1 Squadron Hurricanes were now equipped with Rotol two-speed, three-blade propellers. The older Watts two-blade fixed-pitch wooden propellers were replaced.

Trip considered what to do. The stream of refugees pouring from Eastern France and Paris clogged the roads to impassibility. Fortunately, with the June 17 Armistice, the Stukas were not dive-bombing the poor refugees. Until the armistice, the shrieking Stukas dropped bomb after bomb on the civilian refugees across France. Burning, destroyed vehicles and personal property were scattered everywhere, clogging the roads and adding to the refugees' misery of walking away from their homes. There were horror stories of dismembered bodies and shattered carcasses of horses and people along the roads from the Belgian frontier across France.

Two days after the armistice between the French and the Germans, Trip knew he must make a move. It was high time he left. Vera de Viennay, the baroness, was giving him looks that indicated he might enjoy favored nation status with her at some point, and he did not wish to cuckold his host.

He thanked Baron Pineault de Viennay and his admittedly lovely wife and stumped out to the airfield previously occupied by No. 1 Squadron, RAF. His leg was improving by the day, but Trip knew he could not walk long distances. He still used his cane. There were no cars to steal. The fleeing mobs had taken all bicycles, carts, and even baby carriages.

He saw a barn that he thought must belong to the baron. Perhaps he could sleep there and move on tomorrow.

Trip pushed open the large barn door, and there to his amazement, was a Hawker Hurricane Mark I. It sat, hump-backed and menacing, in the middle of the barn.

He looked over the Hurricane. It seemed intact, except that one of the two-bladed wooden propeller blades was cracked off about ten inches from the end of the blade.

Trip looked at this and shook his head. Trip climbed up on the wing and checked the fuel tank. Full. He checked the coolant tank. Full. He popped open the gun doors and found it completely loaded with shells for all eight of the .303 caliber Browning machine guns.

Damn. I can't fly it like this, even with a full fuel load. The unbalanced propeller would tear the engine out of its mounts.

There were farm tools in the barn and an RAF mechanic's toolbox. A pile of hay in the back offered a place to sleep.

Trip thought, "Perfect. At least I can sleep here."

Trip wondered *Didn't they replace all the two-blade propellers with the Rotols? If so, where were the old two-blade props?*

Trip left his backpack in the barn and wandered the property. No evidence of two-blade propellers. *Probably changed the props out at some other base.*

Trip wandered back to the barn. He sat down on a haybale and looked at the Hurricane. He looked at the broken propeller. He walked over to the propeller and looked at the broken part. The blade was intact except for the last foot. There were no obvious cracks in the remining part of the blade. Perhaps some ground crew had hit it with a truck. If the propeller had been spinning when it hit something, it would have shattered, and both blades would have been broken.

Trip thought, *My kingdom for a new propeller.*

He smirked, *Yeah, well, Shakespeare ain't gonna help you, Trip-boy.*

Trip remembered his last summer's employment. The blades on the turbine he helped to design needed to be the same length, but it was not exactly a requirement that they be some specific length. The decision about the diameter of the turbine blades for the Westinghouse generator was about fitting into a space rather than some efficiency requirement.

Trip thought about the Taylor Cub that his friend Hank owned in Atlanta. Hank had paid an aircraft mechanic to shorten the blades on the two-blade propeller. It made the engine run faster, but the airplane flew. It did take a longer ground run to get airborne.

Trip remembered some general information about the thickness of the blades, blade length, and RPM. *Seems that cutting off a few inches of prop blade is not that big a problem. Maybe.*

Trip thought, *My kingdom for a saw.*

He snickered. *Sure.*

That might actually work.

He glanced around the barn. *Is there a saw in here?*

He looked around the tools in the barn. There was a saw, but it was a two-handed long wood saw that required two people. *Won't work. I need something I can use by myself.*

He dug in the hay at the back of the barn and found an old cross-cut saw. *This might work.*

Trip took a piece of string and found a small, rickety ladder. He climbed on the ladder and removed the propeller spinner. Placing the string at the center of the propeller boss, he dangled the string down the length of the broken blade.

Hmmmm...won't do. Got to cut off those ragged tip pieces.

Trip climbed off the ladder and found a pencil. He found a rusty builder's square and used it to mark a straight line across the broken propeller end.

He began sawing the propeller across the marked line.

It was exhausting. The propeller wood was a variety of very hard maple or something similar. It was laminated in many layers. Trip moved the saw smoothly back and forth.

Of course, the wood is hard. It has to pull an airplane through the air without breaking. It would be easier if this saw were not so dull.

After an hour, he had cut into the propeller wood about ¼ inch.

This is going to take all night. Hope my leg doesn't give out.

Trip doggedly sawed on the propeller for what seemed like hours. He lost track of time. He dozed as he moved the saw back and forth. He came to his senses to notice that he had about ¼ inch left before cutting through the propeller. It was also getting dark.

Rummaging the barn for some kind of light source, Trip found a lantern in a cupboard with a few ounces of kerosene. He put the lantern on a high shelf and lit the wick. It provided dim illumination but enough to work on the propeller.

He grabbed the square, marked a corresponding line on the back of the propeller blade, and began cutting on that side. *I don't want to shatter the wood. I need a clean cut.*

Trip's back and arms ached as he reached the last few thousandths of an inch, and the cracked propeller pieces fell off.

Trip went to the workbench in the barn and searched frantically for a wood rasp.

There! At least this ratty old barn has some woodworking tools.

He grabbed the wood rasp and went to the propeller. Unsure of exactly what he should do to smooth the rough-sawn edge, he took the rasp and rounded off the end of the blade. He tried to bevel the edge to resemble the blade's leading edge.

Trip was bone tired. He wearily climbed the ladder and attached the string to the propeller boss. Returning to the floor, he stretched the string to the new propeller tip. He tied a very precise knot at exactly the leading edge of the cut propeller tip.

Then, he pushed the propeller to swing the good blade from being on the bottom to being on the top. He had to jump to catch the good blade and his leg screamed in protest.

He hobbled as he swung undamaged blade to hang straight down. *Good. Now I can cut this one.*

Tugging the string tight, Trip used the square to precisely mark a cut line at exactly the knot. Then, he went to work, moving the saw back and forth. Slowly at first, then with more authority as he cut a thin line across the width of the Hurricane's propeller.

His wounded leg quivered and ached. His shoulders hurt worse. Seeking relief, Trip dragged over an old workbench and sat on it. He was already exhausted, but sitting on the bench took the weight off his wounded leg and allowed him to rest his aching back. His eye tic came back and annoyed him.

He smoothly slid the dull saw back and forth. Sweat ran down Trip's face and soaked his shirt. He created a sing-song rhythm sliding the saw. An hour passed and then two. Trip had cut a full inch into the propeller blade. He took the square, marked a line on the back of the blade, and worked on that side for an hour.

Back and forth Trip went, working ½ inch at a time until only a thin line of laminated wood remained. Finally, the propeller blade gave way, and 11 inches of blade fell to the floor.

Excited, Trip put the wood rasp on the blade tip and tried replicating the same shape as on the first blade.

Shaping the blade tip, Trip did some mental calculations. The propeller was now 22 inches shorter than the original 11'2" airscrew. Now it measured 9 feet 4 inches. Would the new shorter airscrew produce enough thrust to propel the Hurricane enough to become airborne? Would it allow him to climb and turn?

Will just have to try it.

Near midnight, Trip threw a piece of canvas tarp on the hay pile in the back of the barn and collapsed. *Tomorrow I'm flying out of here. I hope.*

Chapter 38 – Vera

Trip awoke to sunlight streaming through cracks in the barn. The smell of the hay and old wood mingled with the smell of the fresh-cut wood of the propeller reminded Trip of his seventh-grade woodshop class. He had enjoyed that and made a nice bookshelf that Edith still used in the upstairs hallway of the house in Atlanta.

His stomach growled, but he had no food.

All the more reason to get airborne and get to England.

He walked to the door and opened it a crack to see if the field around the barn was unoccupied. He looked left and right. No one. The wind soughed through trees and across the fields. Trip looked down the flying field. He walked up and down the field, looking at the surface. The ground was dry and hard. It would support the Hurricane taking off.

Trip looked for the end of the field and calculated that he must take off on a northerly heading. The wind was from the north, and the field was longest in that direction.

Now to get the airplane started.

~~<>~~

Trip returned to the barn to find Vera de Viennay sitting on a hay bale.

She said in a slightly mocking tone, "Hello, Mr. Gibson."

Trip tried to keep the surprise from his face. "Good morning, Baroness."

"Oh, please, don't be so formal, Trip."

Trip grinned, "I don't usually have the pleasure of associating with nobility."

Vera lit a *Gauloise*, huffed smoke, and propped herself back on one hand, presenting an appealing view of her bustline. She wore a thin white blouse tucked into snug jodhpurs. Her black riding boots had a deep luster that made clear she had servants.

Leaning forward, she waved the pack of *Gauloises* toward Trip.

She said, "I'm not nobility now. I was British aristocracy until I married André. Now I'm a poor French woman with a useless title and an expensive-to-maintain estate. You may call me Lady Vera."

Trip lit one of the *Gauloises* and smiled, "Very well, Lady Vera. Did you ride here?"

"Yes, I saw you walking the field and tied my horse out back. I didn't want to alarm you. And I was joking, I haven't been Lady Vera for several years."

"Funny, you look to be about my age. I'm 24."

Vera threw her head back and laughed. "God! I wish I were just 24. But this war has made us all grow up, hasn't it? With death just around the corner, we're all at an indeterminate age."

Trip said, "Yes. Spain is where I grew up. Flying for the Republicans was an awakening."

Vera stood, crushed out her cigarette on the hard-packed dirt floor, and walked to him. "Trip, you are not a communist. Why the Republicans?"

"Because I wanted to fly fast airplanes, and I don't like Fascists."

Vera stood close. Trip could smell her perfume infused with the harsh tobacco from her cigarette. Her voice was husky, "I think you are an international soldier of fortune, Trip. I've never made love with a soldier of fortune."

Trip said, "I was about to start this airplane and fly to England."

"Oh, my. That is ambitious. Won't you get shot down?"

"Hope not."

"Ummmm...hope is not the best method for success, I think."

She stepped closer and leaned her head back.

Trip kissed her, and she kissed him back. "Take me, Trip. Give me one memory of my soldier of fortune that I can hold onto until this madness is over."

Trip was quite exhausted, but he walked her back to the haystack, and pushed her down onto the canvas.

She snickered, "This canvas is rough."

Trip helped her out of her boots and noticed her toenails were painted bright red.

She unbuttoned her blouse partway and then pulled it over her head. Trip pulled off his jacket, unbuttoned his shirt, and dropped his pants in a pile around his ankles. He grabbed Vera's jodhpurs at the waist and pulled. She wore no underwear.

~~<>~~

An hour later, they lay entangled. Vera said, "My goodness. I should have been romping in the hay all these years. Quite invigorating."

Trip grinned. "I'd offer you a cigarette, but I'm all out, and we'd probably start a fire in this hay. That smoke you gave me was the first I've had in a couple days."

"What will you do, Trip? I mean, when you get to England?"

"I hope to join the RAF and fly fighters. England is going to need fighter pilots."

Vera said, "I would lay here all day with you and see if we could start our own fire in this hay, but André will worry if I'm not home soon. Shall I help you get this machine started?"

Trip grinned, "I thought you'd never ask."

~~<>~~

They dressed quickly, and Vera asked what she could do.

Trip found a hand crank from the RAF toolbox. He showed her how to insert it and how to crank it to get a flywheel and the propeller turning. He showed her how to remove the crank and move away from the propeller once the engine started.

"Those exhaust stacks just above your head might spit flames when the engine starts. They will go out, so don't be alarmed. Above all, don't back into the spinning propeller."

"Once we get it started, I'll give you a signal like this." He held out his fists, thumbs up, and swept them to the sides. "That means to pull the chocks – those wooden blocks on the wheels. Again, don't back into the propeller. Just pull the chocks to the side with that rope and walk to the wingtip."

Vera nodded her understanding. "This is so exciting."

Trip became serious. "Yes. But airplanes can catch fire. If there's a fire, run like hell. This airplane is full of gasoline, and you don't want to be near an explosion."

Vera's eyes were large and wet. "Oh...do be careful, then."

~~<>~~

Trip threw his backpack and walking cane into the radio compartment that doubled as a small baggage hold. He still had his hard French flying helmet. He put the helmet into the cockpit. The French radio connection would not fit the English plug. Neither

298

would the oxygen connections. He would not be flying high enough to require oxygen. He hoped he would not have to talk on the radio.

He leaned into the cockpit and flicked on the battery switch. The instruments popped on, but Trip was unsure if the battery had sufficient power to turn over the engine. He decided to save the battery until he was ready to start the engine, so he turned off the switch.

Vera asked, "Will the engine start?"

Trip said, "Who knows? Maybe this will work. If not, I wasted hours cutting off that propeller."

He put the inertial starter crank into the hole below the exhausts. It fit. He tried turning it and found it was stiff, but not impossible. He heard a flywheel move when he moved the crank. The propeller also moved.

Trip spat, "Damn, I need to put the propeller spinner back on."

He climbed up and reattached the spinner. Its jaunty red tip seemed to taunt him.

Vera gave him a bawdy wink. "That thing looks like a breast."

Trip snickered, "Not as pretty as yours, my dear."

"You know how to charm a girl."

Trip said, "You turn the crank until the flywheel reaches a certain speed, and then I'll hit the battery, mags, especially the starter mag, and crack the throttle. The engine should start. I'll shout a warning just before I start the engine."

Vera nodded.

Trip climbed up on the wing. He reached into the cockpit and pulled and pushed the primer. Nothing.

He climbed in and sat in the seat, his left leg screaming from the effort. He located the wobble pump – the manual fuel pump – and cycled it several times until it seemed to reach pressure. It certainly became stiff, suggesting fuel was in the lines.

Then, Trip loosened the prime plunger and pulled it out, pushing it forward. This time he felt a satisfying resistance of fuel being pushed into the engine. Another primer stroke, and he pushed and turned the primer knob to lock it. That's it, two strokes on the primer. More would flood the carburetor.

He sat for a minute, familiarizing himself with the cockpit. The wooden propeller had a fixed pitch, so his airplane did not have propeller controls. *Good, one less thing to worry about.*

He set the mixture to IDLE/CUT-OFF.

Trip climbed out of the cockpit and arranged the harness so he could put it on. The parachute needed adjustment, so he worked on that. It would not do to have to bail out with a loose-fitting parachute.

Putting the parachute back into the seat pan and arranging the straps so he could easily put those on, he climbed off the wing and walked around to the front of the airplane.

Trip walked over, pushed open the barn doors, and checked the clearance for the Hurricane. The wings would just clear the door jam. He would have to taxi it out because he and Vera alone could not push the plane. Taxiing through the door might present some difficulty.

Trip muttered to himself, "First, we have to get it started."

Rechecking the clearance of the doors a second time, Trip walked back to the Hurricane.

He put on his thin leather flying gloves.

He turned to Vera. "Thank you for helping me."

Vera gave him a hooded look. "I almost hope it doesn't work. But that would be terribly selfish of me. Still, I'd like you to stay a while."

Trip smiled at her. "Thank you for an unexpectedly lovely morning. I hope you are safe from the Germans."

Vera said, "Such good luck, Trip. A kiss for luck?"

Trip kissed her and looked into her eyes, "André is a lucky man. I'll think of you often."

Vera said, "Oh, and here." She reached into her jacket and handed Trip her nearly full packet of *Gauloises*.

Trip grinned, "Oh, God. Thanks!"

He shoved the cigarettes into his pocket and turned to the crank, "Let me get this started moving. Then, you can keep it going."

He began pulling and pushing the crank: up, around, down, up, around, down, up, around, down. He cranked and cranked until he was satisfied that the flywheel was spinning. The propeller was turning, too.

He nodded to Vera, who stepped in, put her hands on the crank, and continued cranking up, around, down.

Trip briefly put his hands on Vera's hips from behind, an affectionate gesture. He kissed her on the side of her lovely neck. Then he hustled around the Hurricane's left wing. He climbed up and vaulted into the cockpit. He quickly sat, and hit the mag switches, especially the starter mag. He remembered Paul Richey telling him to hold the stick back in his lap and squeeze the hand brake to keep the tail from coming up when the engine starts.

He shouted, "CLEAR!"

Vera nodded.

Trip cracked the throttle, remembering that this was an English airplane, and the throttle worked from back to front.

Pap, pap, bam, bam, the prop blades were turning, and the engine caught. Black smoke popped out of the exhaust stacks, creating a choking mist inside the barn. He was unfamiliar with the Rolls-Royce Merlin engines but knew inline aircraft engines from his time with the Jenny. He nudged the throttle, and the engine settled down to a satisfying rumble.

Hay was flying around in the barn; the canvas tarp he and Vera used was floating in the propeller wash. *To hell with it. Too late to think about that now.*

Vera stood at the wingtip holding the hand crank. He gave her the hand signal for chocks-out.

Vera ducked under the left wing. Then she ran around well outside the propeller arc to the right wing and ducked under. She came out and nodded.

Trip gave her a thumbs-up and a smile.

She blew him a kiss.

Trip nudged the throttle and eased off the hand brake.

The Hurricane edged forward. Trip frantically watched the wingtips as the airplane crept forward. He hit the throttle a little harder and felt the tail try to come up. *Whoops. Don't do that.*

The Hurricane moved forward a few more inches, and Trip let the hand brake go. It moved forward, and the wings were clear.

Thank God. Now to taxi to the very end of this field.

As he taxied past the edge of the barn, he saw Vera in the rear-view mirror standing, looking forlorn, her hair disheveled by the wind blast from the chopped-off propeller. She raised a hand in farewell.

Trip stuck his arm outside the cockpit and waved.

And now, for England.

Chapter 39 – Flight to the Future

Trip nudged the throttle a little and soon reached the end of the field. He moved the control column forward and back, looking in the rear-view mirror to see the elevators move up and down. He rotated the top half of the stick left and right checking the ailerons. He pushed the rudder, his left leg aching. The controls were good all around.

He ran through what he thought must be the takeoff checklist. He set the elevator trim to a degree nose-down. Checked the mixture to rich. Starter magneto-off. Mag 1 – off, check. Back on. Mag 2 – the same. The engine instruments were all in the green range and he looked to be sure the gyro compass was aligned with the whiskey compass. The artificial horizon was operating and looked right. He pulled the knob, caging that gyro for takeoff. Fuel Boost Pump-on. Fuel selector set to main. No need to mess with the oxygen. His helmet was familiar, but there were no connections.

Checking the cockpit canopy – the Brits called it a hood – locked open. *If this thing crashes, maybe I can get out.*

Trip tugged on his harness and parachute buckles. *Hope I don't have to use these.*

He spotted a small canvas map case. *Wonder if there's a map in there?*

Trip popped open the snaps and rummaged. He came out with a map of Western France with the Channel and Southern England. English airfields were marked with red Xs. One, Tangmere, was very close to the coast near Portsmouth.

A quick glance suggested a heading of about 350 degrees – just west of North. He saw that he'd have to fly near Le Havre, then cross about 50 miles of Channel and try to hit land near Portsmouth. Flying east from Portsmouth would take him to Tangmere.

He hoped this was right. *Probably should avoid Le Havre. Anti-aircraft guns there. Ditto, Portsmouth.*

~~<>~~

Trip looked at the grass waving in the wind. *Good, I'm pointed into the wind. I hope this thing will fly.*

Trip took one last look around the cockpit. Everything looked good. He advanced the throttle smoothly. *Here goes nothing!*

The Hurricane's tail tried to come up immediately, but Trip held the stick in his lap.

Wow! This thing's got horsepower.

The Hurricane trundled forward slowly and began to build momentum. *Hope I have enough field to get airborne.*

The nose tried to swing with engine torque, but a nudge of the rudder kept the airplane going straight. Trip thought *Bit of a crosswind .*

He felt the controls come to life and nudged the control column to the right, putting a wing down into the crosswind. Left rudder to keep going straight.

The Hurricane began bumping on the slightly uneven surface. *She wants to fly.*

Then the Hurricane was airborne. The ground fell away, but not too fast. *Trees coming up. Let's climb, baby.*

Need to clean it up. Trip held the control column in his left hand as he flicked the landing gear down-lock and pumped up the gear. He jerked the flap handle up.

The airplane felt faster, and Trip could see the ground falling away more as the little airplane speeded up. *Trees still coming at me.*

Trip relaxed the back pressure on the control column and let the airplane settle with no aerodynamic forces on the airframe. The

306

engine RPM was at 2800. *Hell, I don't know the speeds for this thing, but it all seems right.*

Trip watched the airspeed indicator hit 120 mph and pulled the stick back. *Come on, come on. Climb, baby.*

Trading airspeed for altitude, Trip zoomed over the trees at the end of the runway. He quickly let the nose back down at about 300 feet of altitude and breathed a sigh of relief. *No need to get into an accelerated stall.*

He set the trim. He turned without too much bank to a heading of 350 degrees on the large gyro compass and waited for things to settle before comparing the gyro with the whiskey compass. All good.

He uncaged the gyro on the artificial horizon and was happy to see it respond and settle to reflect the actual attitude of the airplane.

His airspeed was now about 200 mph, and he decided to climb. *1000 feet should do it.*

A series of zoom climbs and Trip reached 1000 feet and was settled on a heading of 350°. Throttling back to 180 mph, he fished in his pocket for Vera's *Gauloises* and lit one. He hoped the Hurricane had good fuel tanks because he was desperate for a cigarette but didn't want to explode. *So far, so good.*

The nicotine hit, and Trip began to relax. His left leg ached from the wound. His groin ached from the morning's excess. His back and arms ached from hours of sawing iron-hard propeller material.

He looked down and saw he was following a North-South road. He edged more to the left to still see the road but be less notable to anyone gathered around it. He could see a good many refugees on intersecting East-West roads. Even the smallest pathways seemed jammed.

He looked at the map and decided the first town would be Yévres. It was a major intersection of at least ten roads. *Should be easy to spot. Maybe seven miles?*

He dragged on the Gauloise and remembered to swivel his head in all directions. *Who knows if the Boche are about?*

In about two minutes, Trip saw Yévres. *Good. Looks like 45 miles to L'Aigle. Should be recognizable. Rugles is to the right, about two miles. Fifteen minutes maybe.*

Trip quickly estimated the rest of the route.

Twelve miles from L'Aigle to Orbec – 4 minutes

Ten miles from Orbed to Lisieux – 3 minutes

Fifteen miles from Lisieux to Deauville – 5 minutes

He would hit the coast at Deauville with Le Havre to his right. That would start the most dangerous leg of the flight: 100 miles across the English Channel to Portsmouth and Tangmere Airdrome. 100 miles at about 3 miles per minute means I'll be over the Channel for about 30-35 minutes.

Trip swallowed hard. In less than 30 minutes, he would be over the Channel. He kept his head on a swivel as he contemplated the potential to be shot at from ships in the channel or attacked from the air.

Trip was doing mental math. *The airplane has about a 2-hour endurance at 180 mph. The total flight should take about 75 minutes, give or take. I have maybe 45 minutes of endurance beyond the route.*

Knowing he had a few minutes of extra flying time beyond his planned route, Trip wondered about the airplane's performance.

I don't know if this airplane is maneuverable with this prop.

He pushed the throttle up and lowered the nose to build airspeed. At 300 mph, he pulled back on the stick slightly and executed an aileron roll.

The Hurricane responded with a smooth roll. He rolled into a tight right turn, 60 degrees of bank, and two G's. The little airplane stayed level and made a full 360° circle. Trip rolled out and did the same maneuver to the left. Again, good.

He put the nose down, built up to 300 mph again, and hauled back on the controls. The Hurricane went up, but as speed fell off, so did performance, and the airplane faltered. It rapidly approached a power-on stall, and Trip quickly unloaded the controls rolling wings level and nose down.

He was soon back to about 180 mph and on heading. As predicted, he saw L'Aigle and to its right, Rugles.

This airplane will fly, but dogfighting is not possible. I'll have to do what I can to avoid getting in a fight.

Trip quickly discovered that identifying roads and intersections was not difficult. The roads were clogged with vehicles, many of which were on fire and belching black smoke skyward. The intersections were even worse, creating a torrent of smoke and flame. The people of France were desperately fleeing the Nazis, and the Nazis were making that trip miserable.

Stay away from the roads, Trip-boy. The Boches are out and about and killing the civilians. If there are French military down there, they might shoot at you. If the Boche see you, they'll try to kill you.

~~<>~~

Trip could see Deauville and the Channel coming up in about 5 miles. He offset to avoid overflying Deauville. As he approached the coast, he turned hard left and right. It was good because a stream of orange tracers flew up from the ground and would have bracketed him.

Trip hoped the British paint scheme of one black wing and one white wing on the underside of the airplane would help keep the gunners at bay. He rocked his wings trying to show that recognition paint to the ground gunners.

He turned hard right and then left as he crossed the coast. Again, this was a good idea, as gray puffs of anti-aircraft fire popped to the left. They had orange centers and went off with harsh bangs, leaving a black ball of smoke. Trip was certain there was shrapnel in those bursts.

He dropped 500 feet and angled farther left as he passed Le Havre well to his right. He looked down at Normandy. *Beautiful country. I'd like to see that one day.*

Then, he was well out from the coast. A small ship appeared off the nose. Yellow flashes burst out all over the ship. *Damn, they're shooting at me.*

Trip dodged hard left and dropped to 250 feet. *Maybe they'll have a hard time seeing me this low.*

Gray puffs with orange centers burst at 500 feet, where Trip had just been.

Ahead, about two miles to his left was a smaller ship. Trip hauled hard right and dropped to 100 feet.

A geyser of water shot up followed by another and another. *Damn, they're trying to knock me down with water. Best climb a bit.*

Leveling off at 500 feet, Trip looked all around, especially up and behind. It was midday, and the sun was nearly straight overhead. Hard to hide in there. An enemy would have to match his speed and heading exactly. He looked down at the water. An enemy would leave a shadow.

Trip could see his shadow but no others. *Good.*

He lit another *Gauloise* and tried to relax a little. Still, he kept his head on a swivel and continually checked the sea surface for shadows, his and any others.

He paused for thought. *I guess I've been over water now for about ten minutes. In another ten minutes, I should start to see the English coast.*

He had not seen a ship of any description since the last ones that fired on him. The gray and black antiaircraft puffs were almost certainly British. German Ack-Ack bursts were white.

Soon, Trip estimated he was mid-Channel. *Guess I'll be seeing a lot of this soon. That's if they don't shoot me down first.*

Trip spotted two black dots at 12 o'clock high against the clouds. They were probably over Portsmouth and heading South across the channel toward France. *Hope those are not after me. If they are, I hope they're British.*

Trip turned slightly left and then right. He looked over his shoulder and came back to the high black dots. They were resolving to a pair of elliptical-winged single-engine airplanes. One black wing and one white wing told Trip they were British. This must be the Spitfire that was mentioned in the news and an airplane the French had begged Chamberlain, and then Churchill, to deploy.

Trip continued flying toward Portsmouth and maintained 180 mph.

The two Spitfires rolled over and dove toward Trip. He kept an eye on them as they curved around behind him. *Better make sure they know I'm friendly.*

Trip climbed to 1000 feet and lowered his landing gear. He found the navigation lights switch and turned it to ON. He looked behind and saw the two Spitfires closing, so he rolled gently right so they could see the yellow circle on the outside of the fuselage roundel. He swung back to his heading and rocked his wings vigorously. *Hope they got the message.*

He settled down to wait and very shortly the two Spitfires pulled alongside in formation.

Trip made hand motions that indicated he had no radio. He made another hand motion that indicated he had about 45 minutes of fuel left.

The lead Spitfire pilot made hand signals to follow him. Trip nodded vigorously and pulled into formation with the lead Spitfire and the second Spitfire on his other wing.

Looking ahead he saw the coast and then began to see more details. He could see the coastline and a small city to the left. Further left – West – was almost certainly Portsmouth.

They crossed the coast and flew past an airport. The lead Spitfire turned the small formation 180° and set up on a long final approach to what Trip hoped was RAF Tangmere.

The lead Spitfire lowered landing gear and flaps. Trip's gear was already down, so he lowered flaps. Immediately the Hurricane ballooned up and Trip had to manage the controls to maintain formation.

He settled into a 100-mph approach which seemed to be the Spitfires' preferred speed. The Hurricane seemed all right with the 100-mph approach speed.

Trip continued to be concerned that the prop didn't generate sufficient power for much maneuvering, so going around from a bad approach was probably out of the question.

They crossed the boundary fence and Trip reduced throttle a bit but continued to maintain power through the landing. Once the main wheels touched, he cut the throttle and let the airplane settle. When he was certain he was below flying airspeed, he pulled the control column back into his lap to keep the tail on the ground.

He reached the end of the runway and was about to turn off when several vehicles surrounded the Hurricane.

Trip pulled the throttle all the way back, moved the mixture control to IDLE/CUT-OFF, and turned off the fuel flow and boost pump. The engine sputtered to a stop. He hit all the switches to their off position.

Letting out a sigh of relief, Trip pulled off his helmet, stood in the seat, and raised his hands over his head.

Fifty armed troops surrounded the Hurricane, pointing rifles with fixed bayonets at Trip.

Trip smirked to himself. *Not exactly the reception I'd hoped for.*

Chapter 40 – Salvation

"Right! Let me understand you. You're a Yank 'oo's fought in Spain and France against the Nazis. You escaped France under 'itler's nose and flew here in that Hurricane parked on the field?"

Trip who was handcuffed and sitting on a hard chair at a metal table in a small room with bare brick walls and a concrete floor. His butt hurt, and he said, "Yes. That's about right."

The British Warrant Officer Provost Marshal for Tangmere looked disdainful.

He smirked, "And, we're to believe the moneybelt with a mixture of American dollars and French Francs totaling nearly £200 was your personal funds because you were paid 1500 American dollars a month flying for the communists in Spain."

"Yes."

"And these papers 'ere are from some Frog lieutenant, and this paper says you're all these things and should be welcomed."

"Yes."

"And this bluddy passport wiv your picture purports to be an American passport. And this scrap of paper is your bluddy birth certificate saying you were born in Crawford Long Hospital in Atlanta, Georgia, wherever the bluddy 'ell that is?"

Trip said, "Yes. Best hospital in the Southeast."

The Warrant's voice dripped sarcasm, "Too right. Best there is. Tra-la, tra-la."

"You say you sawed the blades off 'Is Majesty's 'awker 'urricane aircraft with a bluddy 'and saw becos one of the bluddy fucking blades was broken. So you, a fucking brilliant mechanical engineer, bluddy fixed it!"

Trip said, "I'm not a mechanical engineer, yet. But, yes, I fixed it."

The warrant officer's face was nearly purple with indignation, "And you claim to know a Pilot Officer Paul Richey, Number 1 Squadron, RAF. And he gave you this British Military Issue .455 Webley Revolver that you just 'appened to 'ave on your person when captured while attempting to attack 'Is Majesty's Royal Air Force Installation Tangmere?"

"Yes. I gave you Pilot Officer Richey's address."

"Yes, I bluddy see that. Troops are on the way there now to arrest him. Quite obviously, 'e's your English spoi contact."

The Warrant Officer stretched his neck, shoved out his chin, and jerked his tunic down.

"You're a bluddy fucking spoi, an' I'm going to see you shot. As a matter of fact, I shall take personal pleasure in commanding the bluddy firing party, you goddamned Nazi spy!"

Trip started to speak, but the warrant officer said, "Not a bluddy word."

Looking hard at one of the troops who stood, rifle at the ready, the warrant officer said, "Take him to the glasshouse and be quick about it."

~~<>~~

The door clanged behind him, and Trip sat on the hard bunk in a room with beige tile. *I hope they do get hold of Paul. Hope he got back safe.*

Trip ran the last few days through his mind. *Paul left France on the mail plane on June 14th. Today is June 18th. So, it's been four days, perhaps Paul made it back and has had time to reach his home. He was injured and not fully recovered, so a hospital may be involved.*

Trip thought it must be time for supper when he heard some clanging of cell doors. *Do they have a dining hall or some arrangement for prisoners? Wonder how many prisoners they have here?*

A hatch in the solid metal door popped open, and the warrant's face appeared. "'Ere's yer bluddy food, spoi!"

He shoved a plate through the hatch, but it fell on the floor.

"Whoops a daisy."

The hatch slammed shut, and Trip heard the warrant officer whistling as he walked down the corridor.

Trip thought for a moment. *I've eaten worse, and at Argelès-sur-Mer they threw rotting food into the mud next to bloated corpses. A little crud from this floor can't hurt.*

He picked up the plate and scraped the food onto it. He ate silently thinking, *Not bad. Boiled beef, a piece of potato, some kind of beans. A little crunch of dirt. Doesn't matter. I haven't eaten for two days. Quite good, actually.*

The hours wore on. The stuffy cell was about six feet by nine feet. He stood and walked back and forth to get some exercise. There was no window. Trip kept up with time based upon when meals arrived.

The Warrant Officer had not been back, so Trip's food was not corrupted by being thrown on the floor. The guards were wordless and ignored Trip's requests for water.

~~<>~~

There were no further interviews, no contact. *Maybe they will shoot me.*

Breakfast was a hard roll and some tepid tea. *Guess these fellows don't drink coffee.*

Once again, Trip begged for some water. No answer.

By Trip's reckoning it was about noon. He heard clanks indicating food service. *Good. I'm hungry.*

His door burst open and two soldiers with helmets and rifles charged in. Another man wearing sergeant's stripes walked in and slapped handcuffs on Trip's wrists. They put leg irons on him, stood him up, and hustled him down the hall. His feet barely touched the floor.

He was shoved roughly into the same small interrogation room as before.

A man wearing a civilian suit said, "Sit."

Trip said, "Thank you."

The man with a sharp nose and hatchet face said, "Kindly speak when spoken to."

Trip smirked, "I believe you just spoke to me."

Hatchet Face said, "You know what I mean. Punishment for impudence will be dealt with severely."

Trip snickered, "Oh, and this is not severe?"

Hatchet Face leaned back, "I am Deputy Chief Inspector Raphael Wormley. And you are a spy."

Trip looked at him. "So, you're theoretically a smart man, smarter than that moron warrant officer with the bad teeth. Do all Brits have bad teeth? Never mind. Why do you think I'm a spy?"

Wormley, "I'll ask the questions here."

Trip snorted, "Fire away, Sport."

"IIow did you come to have a IIawker IIurricane Aircraft Z1911 in your possession."

"Just lucky I guess."

"Please answer the question. I'm authorized to use force when it comes to enemy agents."

"I'm not an enemy agent. I am a neutral American citizen who was trapped in France after your lot made a complete cock-up of the war. I happen to be a skilled pilot. After being afforded transportation by the RAF Provost Marshall of Paris to Châteaudun, I spent a couple of pleasant days at the country home of Baron Pineault de Viennay. On the 17th, after your valiant army failed miserably at everything except retreat, I decided I needed to make my way to the Channel Coast of France. I stopped at one of Baron Pineault de Viennay's barns, intending to rest. My leg was wounded in combat flying as a French pilot, and it aches when I walk. I wonder if you've seen a German? I certainly have. Makes me better than you, I think."

Trip let that sink in for a moment. He continued, "The Hawker Hurricane had been left in the barn with a toolbox. The airplane had a broken propeller which I cut off cleanly and then cut the other blade to match. I did not know if the airplane would fly with some 22 inches of propeller blade missing, but I thought it was worth trying."

"You see, I wanted to get out of France because I am an American citizen, but I was fighting against the Germans. I suspect when the Germans take over – or is that past tense? – took over, they would brand me a fugitive. Moreover, I am a wanted man in Spain. Fought for the Republicans, you know."

Trip sat back, "But you know all this. Why are we sitting here going back over it?"

Wormley said, "I'll ask the questions."

Trip said, "Ok, so far you've asked the same fucking questions that moron warrant officer asked. So, here's my answer. I want a lawyer.

A barrister. Whatever the hell y'all call 'em. I want one. I also want to speak to someone in the U.S. Embassy."

"In due time."

Trip said, "Due time is now. I highly recommend you don't continue with this bad treatment of me because you are losing this war and don't need a diplomatic incident with the Americans."

Wormley smirked, "Very well. We'll return you to your cell."

Trip smirked back, "Fucking fine! The cell is better than a Nazi concentration camp."

Trip was surprised to be allowed to walk to his familiar cell. The leg irons were uncomfortable, but at least he wasn't manhandled.

~~<>~~

Hours went by. The same routine of no contact beyond the guard delivering food. The same food came at the same intervals.

Trip smelled himself. A bath of some kind would have been acceptable.

Trip heard boots marching down the corridor. *Here we go again. This is getting monotonous.*

Keys clanked in the door, and Trip stood up. *Screw them, I'll go with dignity.*

Wormley stood at the door. "Please come with me, Sir."

Trip goggled at him. "Huh?"

"Do kindly come with me."

Not waiting for a reply, Wormley turned on his heel and walked down the corridor. There were no guards.

Trip looked both ways and followed Wormley.

They walked into the interrogation room to find Bull Halahan, Paul Richey, and two other members of Number 1 Squadron, RAF.

Halahan said, "Damn lad, you stink."

Wormley raised an eyebrow. Halahan said, "Bloody Hell, that's him. He's not a damned spy."

Paul chimed in, "He's all right. I've met him with Lieutenant Marin la Meslée of the *Armée de l'Air*. Meslée spoke highly of him. Plus, you have Meslée's letter."

The other two No. 1 Squadron pilots nodded. The one named Pussy said, "If drinking and carousing is a qualification, this one is an ace."

Wormley looked from one man to the other. "What's to be done with him?"

Halahan said, "Bloody well need to put him in a cockpit. Bugger's here and willing to fight against Jerry. He's welcome in the RAF as far as I'm concerned."

Wormley said, "He's all yours."

Turning to Trip Wormley said, "His Majesty's officials are not used to your cheek."

Trip said, "Yeah. We figured that out in '76."

Chapter 41 – The RAF Club

P aul and Bull invited Trip to the Tangmere Officers' Mess to clean up and change into his other suit. They arranged for one of the mess stewards to send Trip's prison-fouled suit for cleaning.

The station had been built three years earlier and had permanent facilities, including an excellent officers' open mess and accommodations. The bathing facility was modern, with several bathtubs and other modern features.

The bath was most welcome, and Trip luxuriated in the hot water. Trip shaved a week's worth of beard and scrubbed his hair.

Paul arranged for Trip to have a room. Trip was thrilled to learn that No. 1 Squadron was now assigned to Tangmere. *What a coincidence. At least I know some of these fellows.*

Paul explained that he was officially recovering from his wound and no longer assigned to Number 1 Squadron. Bull Halahan had also moved on from command of No. 1. Despite his hard-charging leadership that resulted in the squadron being top-rated against the Germans, The Bull rubbed the stuffed shirts at the Air Ministry the wrong way. One of the pilots commented that it appeared he would be posted to India. *What a waste. They will need good combat leaders.*

As they walked into the mess the wireless was on in the corner. Everyone was listening. Paul and Trip walked over to see what was happening. They heard Winston Churchill saying,

> …What General Weygand called the Battle of France is over. I expect that the battle of Britain is about to begin. Upon this battle depends the survival of Christian civilization. Upon it depends our own British life and the long continuity of our institutions and our Empire. The whole fury and might of the enemy must very soon be turned on us. Hitler knows that he

will have to break us in this island or lose the war. If we can stand up to him, all Europe may be free and the life of the world may move forward into broad, sunlit uplands. But if we fail, then the whole world, including the United States, including all that we have known and cared for, will sink into the abyss of a new Dark Age more sinister, and perhaps more protracted, by the lights of a perverted science. Let us therefore brace ourselves to our duties, and so bear ourselves that, if the British Empire and its Commonwealth last for a thousand years, men will still say, "This was their finest hour."

Trip found he had tears in his eyes. Looking around the group, Trip saw he was not alone.

~~<>~~

Paul said, "I say, old boy, I'm driving back to London tomorrow. Happy to offer you a lift."

Trip jumped at the chance. He checked his backpack. Clean suit, fresh shirt, socks, underwear, toilet kit. Extra tie. His hat was cleaned and reblocked. *At least I'm presentable.*

His other personal effects were in order. Money belt returned with 100 percent of his funds intact. His personal papers were all there: passport, birth certificate, discharge from the *Armée de l'Air,* and surprisingly, the Citation for the *Croix de Guerre avec Palme.*

At about noon, they piled into Paul Richey's MG and roared off down a country lane that Trip thought was just a dirt track, but it turned out to be a major road. *Lot to learn about England.*

They stayed overnight at a small country inn. The blackout made it impossible to drive after dark.

They rolled into London at about 6 p.m. on June 23rd. Paul negotiated the maze of streets and astonished Trip by pulling up in front of an imposing building at 128 Piccadilly. *RAF Club* was emblazoned over the entrance.

They walked into the entrance and the man behind the desk said, "Good evening, Pilot Officer Richey. Welcome."

Paul said, "Nice to see you again, Martin. This is my friend from America, Robert Gibson. I need a special favor..."

Trip and Paul were seated at a pleasant table near a window that looked out onto a large green space that Paul called *The Green Park*. About half an hour later, a distinguished man with a bristling mustache walked up to the table and said, "Mister Gibson?"

Trip stood, "Yes?"

"Sir, it is my pleasure to welcome you to membership at the Royal Air Force Club. Your service with the *Armée de l'Air* is most qualifying. It is an honor to have you as a member. Here is your membership card. The annual dues is five guineas which you can arrange at your convenience, Sir. We also have arranged a room for you. If you'll just sign here and here, we'll get you sorted."

Trip said, "Thank you. I'm deeply honored. I will, of course, maintain the decorum of the club. I'll arrange the dues immediately."

The man left.

Paul grinned, "They were also most impressed with your service in Spain."

Trip said, "There may be a message for me at the main desk. Andy, Shorty, and Red were to leave me a message here if they got here first."

Paul said, "Must run, old boy. You know where I am at hospital. Weekends I'm at Sir Roy Robinson's estate. He is my father-in-law. Do come visit."

Trip thanked Paul Richey and said, "I'm sure we'll meet again."

Richey smiled, "I'm like a bad penny, I have the habit of turning up when you least expect it."

~~<>~~

Trip walked to the front desk and said, "Good evening, Martin."

"Good evening, Mr. Gibson. Welcome to our club. How may I help you?"

Trip said, "I believe I may have a message left by some friends. It may have been a few weeks since they left it."

"One moment, Sir. Allow me to check our files."

Martin stepped into a small area behind the desk. Two minutes later the desk manager stepped around the partition. "No, Sir. There is no note."

Trip was crestfallen, "Thank you. I need to establish an account in a bank. Any recommendations?"

Martin said, "I think you would be very happy at Barclay's, Sir. Many of our members bank there. Of course, there's always Lloyds."

Trip said, "Thank you very much. Is Barclay's nearby?"

"Yes, Sir. Just up to Piccadilly Circus and then down to Jermyn Street."

Trip smiled his thanks. "I will visit there tomorrow morning. May I leave a message for my colleagues who may call here for me?"

"Certainly, Sir."

~~<>~~

Trip made his way to Barclay's the next morning. With $500 U.S. on deposit – some £150 – he was settled in London. He changed his 5000 Francs for English pounds. That put about £25 in his pocket. Trip learned that £25 was a tidy sum.

Back at the RAF Club, he paid his five Guineas dues and had some lunch.

Cane in hand, he went for a walk in the *Green Park* across the street and down by Buckingham Palace. London was on a wartime footing, but the day was pleasant, the breeze cool, and the sun warming but not hot.

Trip stumped along with his cane and considered what to do next. He would need to find a way into the RAF, or the last months would be wasted.

But how?

He walked back into the RAF Club, and the manager at the desk said, "Oh, Sir. Your friends were here. They inquired about you, and I told them you were here. They said they would be at the King and Crown Pub, just down Piccadilly."

~~<>~~

Trip walked into the King and Crown and shouted, "By God! You made it!"

The three rough-looking Americans stood and hurried to Trip. They shook hands all around.

Returning to their table, Andy said, "Yeah, we made it, but not without drama and terrible events."

Trip asked, "What happened?"

Andy said, "We left Paris on April 15th. We were held up outside Paris for a month. The refugees, train schedules, bombings, and so on made it impossible. To save money, we got one small room for all five of us and took turns using the bed."

Shorty said, "The French government fled to Tours, so we went there hoping to have one last shot at joining the *Armée de l'Air*. I don't know why we did that."

Trip said, "About that time, I was told to leave France."

Red said, "We should have. It was a terrible trip with the train full of desperate people. We got off the train at Tours and tried to find the French Air Ministry. It was dark and late. When we got there, we were given the run-around. We slept in a field."

Trip nodded, "Sleeping without any cover in the cold must have been miserable."

Red continued, "We boarded a jam-packed bus for Arcay. The French had no interest in dealing with us. We were ordered to Bordeaux on a train that was bursting with refugees. It was so bad we rode between cars most of the way to avoid the stink of unwashed bodies, cigarette smoke, and the foul latrines."

Andy picked up the story, "At Bordeaux, the Czechs were keen to get to England right away. They saw an airplane sitting in a field. It was a French Potez twin-engine bomber. They insisted we steal it and fly to England."

Andy said, "You know I'm always up for gambling, but not this. They hurried to the airplane with us telling them that we could all get shot. They could not understand English. We had only picked up a little Czech."

Red had tears in his eyes, "Things went bad from the start. The French airfield guards shot Jan and Tomas. We didn't have time to try to save them. The guards were shooting at us as we ran into the woods. We got to a main road, where we hitched a ride to a train station. We hopped a freight heading south. After that, we rode a French Army truck to Bayonne. We walked a great deal of the way, too."

Andy said, "We got to Bayonne trying to see the British consul, but he had already left the country. We went to the American consul in Saint Jean-de-Luz who gave us some money and food. The American consul got us passage on the last ship out. The *Baron-Nairn* was a miserable old ship, but it was beautiful to us. The ship's Master was a man named John Kerr, and he treated us well."

Red said, "We got out on June 22. When the ship landed at Portsmouth, we came straight here."

Shorty said, "You have to tell us your story."

Trip told them.

Andy said, "My God, but that flight in the buggered Hurricane must have been scary."

Trip said, "It was a bit frantic during takeoff. I thought it never would climb. So, I lowered the nose, let it accelerate, and then zoomed over the trees. I almost ran out of airspeed once I cleared the trees, but I kept letting it accelerate and zooming until I reached about 1000 feet."

Trip looked into the distance, not really seeing, "The worst was being arrested as a spy and threatened with being summarily shot. That guy was very serious about shooting me."

Andy said, "We need to figure out how to get into the RAF and get flying."

Trip said, "I hope Paul Richey can help with that."

Chapter 42 – P.O. Gibson

Trip, Andy, Shorty, and Red sat at a table in the King and Crown. Warren Potts, the publican, asked, "Wot do yer gents want fer breakfast?"

Trip looked at the other three. "We're Americans. Breakfast for us is eggs, bacon, toast. We've spent a few months in France where breakfast is a croissant and a cup of coffee. What should we order here?"

"Right, Mate. We have wot we calls 'Full English.' Fried eggs, bacon – t'won't be loike what yer thinkin' – bangers, tomatoes, black pudding, beans, toast."

Trip asked, "Bangers?"

The publican grinned, "Sausages, Mate."

Trip said, "I don't know about these other blokes, but Full English sounds perfect."

"HP Sauce?"

Trip said, "Sure."

Andy said, "I'd eat a horse after the last weeks of starving. Bring on the Full English, Mr. Potts."

The others nodded.

Potts grinned, "You blokes is reg'lars now. Me name is Warren, but me mates calls me Potty."

The Americans laughed among themselves at the double meaning. "Potty it is! The pilots introduced themselves, Trip, Andy, Shorty, and Red."

"I'll get yer Full English out, Mates."

Shorty said, "My God, but I'm stuffed!"

The others nodded. The four pilots were full and sitting quietly indolent with full bellies.

Red said, "Not sure about the black pudding. I'm pretty certain that was blood. Tasted kinda metallic."

Andy snorted, "I don't give a damn. It'll take me a year to gain back the lost pounds from the last couple months."

Trip said, "We need to figure out how to get to the Air Ministry to volunteer."

The others nodded and they all marched down to the RAF Club, and Trip asked the desk manager how to get to the Air Ministry.

"It's not far, Sir. Let me draw you a map."

The pilots cleaned up and checked suit and ties. *Best foot forward.*

Trip smirked. "I'm already talking like a Brit."

They marched up Piccadilly and found their way to Pall Mall. Then, following directions, walked along a pleasant street past some ancient looking buildings.

Trip looked around as the flyers came into a large open area with a tall column in the middle. "This must be Trafalgar Square. I think that's Lord Nelson on the column."

They exited Trafalgar Square and strolled along a street called *The Strand.*

Andy said, "I thought 'the strand' meant something like a beach. This is just a major street."

Soon they found an imposing, oddly shaped white building at 10 Kingsway. There was a guard at the entrance. At least it appeared to be the entrance. The guard stood in front of a small sentry box surrounded by sandbags. In fact, the entire lower floor of the building was bedecked with sandbags, making the white paint disappear behind a towering wall of burlap.

Approaching the Guard, Trip said, "Good morning. I know this will sound odd, but we are American flyers and want to volunteer for service with the RAF. Where might we go to do that?"

The guard, a young man with one stripe on his olive-green sleeve, a flat helmet, rifle and bayonet, and a bag that was clearly a gas mask container, goggled at Trip. "Sir?"

Trip said, "We're Americans who want to fly and fight for England. Where do we go to volunteer?"

"Haven't the foggiest, Sir. Can't leave my post to inquire. You'll have to clear off. Can't 'ave people loitering."

Trip said, "Certainly. How do we contact your superior officer? I'm sure he might help."

"Right. My superior is Sar'nt Major Carstairs. 'E's inside. You can't go in there."

Trip smiled. "I understand completely. Please help us. We will wait under the shade of the tree just across there. At changing the guard, could you please speak to Sergeant Major Carstairs on our behalf? We would be very grateful."

The guard nodded and said, "Right. Now clear off before I get put on a fizzer."

~~<>~~

The flyers walked across the street and found a park bench in the shade of a large tree. They flopped on the bench, and all lit cigarettes. They settled in to wait.

333

Shorty had bought a copy of last week's Life magazine, and they passed it around.

Red said, "Jesus Christ! Everything's going straight to hell in a handbasket! Look at this: 'Americans face choice between democracy and dictatorship at home.' What kind of headline is that? Look at the pictures of the refugees in France. It ain't like we didn't see that. These pictures are cleaner than the real thing. I saw a group of French troops drag women and children out of a shelter just before a bombing. Of course, we had to duck under a shattered building. When we got the all-clear and came out, I saw body parts from those women and children scattered everywhere. Made me sick."

Shorty reached for the magazine. "There's some hope. Look at this about the RAF being the 'cloud cavalry.' That's where we'll be!"

Trip said, "Fellows, there's no cavalry up there. It's all frantic, surprise attacks from faster, better Nazi airplanes. Frankly, their pilots are damn good, and experienced. If you survive five missions, you may live long enough to shoot down a couple of theirs."

Shorty said, "I think we can survive five missions."

Trip said, "Hope so."

Andy said, "Party pooper."

~~<>~~

Two hours later, Trip said, "Looks like they changed the guard. There's a new guy on the sentry box, and our boy just went inside."

A few minutes passed before a tall man with a bristling mustache, erect carriage, and a large wand tucked under his arm marched across the street to where the flyers sat. As he approached, Trip saw a circular insignia on his arm that looked like an English royal seal.

"Right, 'Oo are you lot, and wot do you want?"

The flyers looked at one another, and then Trip spoke, "Sergeant Major Carstairs, I presume?"

The man nodded.

Trip said, "I'll save introductions for later and just say that we are Americans who have traveled here through France. We were trying to volunteer to fly for the French, but they've fallen apart. We've been through hell to get to England and volunteer to fly for the RAF. Today we hope to be directed to the correct office to volunteer."

"Identity papers?"

The flyers handed over their American passports and birth certificates. Trip included his discharge from the *Armée de l'Air* and the letter from Meslée.

The Sergeant Major examined each document in detail. "Well, for what it's worth, I believe these are authentic. I will escort you to the correct Air Ministry office. After that, I'm afraid I have no influence."

The group followed Carstairs across the street and through the door. Carstairs marched along with confidence through a veritable rat maze of corridors. Finally, he paused at a door with opaque glass and said, "Please come in and take a seat."

Carstairs walked into the room and stepped over to speak with a man in a somber black suit sitting at a desk with two telephones. The flyers sat on a hard couch and a side chair.

Carstairs left the flyers' passports and other documents with the man at the desk. He turned to the Americans, said, "Good luck, Gentlemen, I leave you in the charge of Mister Hannant," and stepped out the door.

Trip took the man at the desk to be Mr. Hannant. Hannant had bad skin, a receding chin, and narrow eyes. A greasy shock of black hair hung over his forehead, and he smoked constantly. The black suit made him look like an undertaker.

Fixing the group with a narrow-eyed stare, Hannant said, "May I see your flight logs?"

The boys handed over their logs which Hannant myopically examined, holding them close to his desk lamp.

At length, Hannant looked up and said, "I fail to see how you might help the Royal Air Force. These three are deficient in required flying hours. Flying in air shows is much different from flying in combat. This one – he held up Trip's – seems quite impossible."

Trip said, "May I present you documents from my former commander in the *Armée de l'Air?*"

Hannant made a 'come hither' hand motion, and Trip handed over the documents.

Hannant's shock of hair bobbed and wiggled as he examined Trip's letters.

"Impressive. My command is French is excellent. The letter states you are to be trusted and are an aggressive fighter pilot. This discharge indicates you were wounded."

Trip held up his cane and pointed to his left leg. "Still hurts."

Hannant insincerely said, "Sorry for your pain. This last is a citation for the French *Croix de Guerre avec Palme*. Very nice. Sadly, they seem to give those out with afternoon tea. Also, old chap, it appears it was issued to a fellow named Tripolitano Beneš."

Trip said, "I was surprised to find a medal in those papers when I awoke in the American Hospital in Paris. Too many other things to worry about, I guess. Beneš is my *nom de guerre*.

Hannant said, "Ah, *nom de guerre*. Of course. Froggies love those. Look here, chaps, I can't do much for you. We have a war to fight, and training a group of Yanks, however keen they may be to get at Jerry, is simply not on. Honestly, you should visit the American Embassy

336

and inquire about transportation across the pond. Thank you for coming."

Dismissed, the Americans stood up to leave.

Andy said, "We'll find a way to get into the fight if we have to enlist in the Army."

Shorty said, "Speak for yourself, Andy. I'm going to find a way to fly and fight."

Hannant smirked, "Please, do have your lovers' quarrel elsewhere, chaps."

Trip grinned, "They're very much in love. How do we get out?"

"Ah, it's easy, actually. Out to the left, next corridor on the right. Straight ahead."

Trip said, "Thanks for your time."

"Now what?" Asked Andy as the flyers trooped out past the guard and into busy pedestrian traffic on Kingsway.

Trip said, "I'm calling on Paul Richey. I'm sure he knows someone who can help."

~~<>~~

On Friday, June 28, Trip deciphered the English train system and found his way to Sir Roy Robinson's estate in the countryside. At Robinson's estate, Trip met Richey's wife, Teresa, and her parents, Sir Roy and Charlotte Robinson.

He was invited to stay for the weekend. The men shot grouse on Saturday afternoon. Sir Roy spoke to Trip at length about his experiences in Spain and France. Trip's body hurt from all the effort of the past couple of weeks. Trip relished the feather bed in the guest suite, and returned to the RAF Club refreshed.

~~<>~~

A messenger arrived four days later at the RAF Club with a note for Trip. The messenger accepted a shilling and did not wait for a reply.

Trip opened the sealed note.

The Air Ministry

10 Kingsway, London

1 July 1940

Dear Mr. Gibson

Kindly come to my office on 4th July at Ten O'clock a.m. Bring your documents and your three companions.

Harold
Hannant

~~<>~~

Trip, Andy, Shorty, and Red all walked up to the guard and presented their identification.

This time the guard smiled at them. "Back for more, I see? Carstairs din't thump you enough, then?"

Trip said, "Sarn't Major Carstairs was very nice to us. We're here to see Mr. Hannant."

The guard snickered, "Well, do tell."

Andy said, "We got lucky."

"Right, Mate. Flying against Jerry where blokes is gettin' killed left and right is not my idea of gettin' lucky. But to each 'is own. Do go ahead to Mr. Hannant's office, Gents."

The four young men marched straight ahead, turned left and quickly found Hannant's door. They knocked and entered.

Hannant, still looking funereal, glanced up from some papers. His shock of hair wiggled with each word, "Ah, good morning, gentlemen."

He pointed at the sofa. "Please take a pew. His nibs will be with you shortly."

Wondering exactly who 'his nibs' was, Trip realized that Harold Hannant was not a bad type. He was just beleaguered with work, never saw the sun, ate at his desk, and wished for better days.

Hannant must have pushed a secret button because the door opened and a senior RAF officer in the uniform of a Group Captain beckoned the flyers in. "Come in, Gentlemen."

Once the four men were in the rather cramped office, the Group Captain said, "I am Group Captain Reginald Burton-Owens. It is my duty – and pleasure – to welcome you to the RAF and to administer the oath. Given that you are all Americans, and your government is dodgy about your swearing allegiance to a foreign sovereign, the oath has been modified slightly to avoid that problem. If you will kindly stand in a bit of a line just here and raise your right hands, we'll get on with it."

The flyers lined up and stood attentively and raised their right hands.

Group Captain Burton-Owens said, "Please repeat after me, "I – state your name – do swear that I will obey the orders of His Majesty King George VI, his heirs and successors, and the officers appointed over me, according to law. So help me God."

Burton-Owens stepped back and surveyed the group, "Congratulations, gentlemen. You have taken a big step, and His Majesty's government thanks you for your willingness to serve. It is not lost on me that today is America's Independence Day. I believe we shall make fighter pilots of you. Mr. Hannant has paperwork for you and instructions about where to report and so on. Best of luck, you'll need it. Dismissed."

The flyers grinned and chorused, "Thank you, Sir."

Burton-Owens was already sitting at his desk and looking at his next paper.

Hannant had them sign several documents and gave them directions to a clinic for flight physicals. "Remember, you must pass the physical or you'll be released from duty."

~~<>~~

The flyers walked out of the MOD building, each with a packet of papers. Andy said, "How did you pull this off, Trip?"

Trip grinned, "Well, Paul Richey's father-in-law is a high muckety-muck in the British Forestry Service. He's a knight of something or other. Sir Roy Robinson. Apparently, he knows this or that member of parliament. Phone calls were made, measures were taken, and arrangements were completed."

Then, Trip smirked, "Hell, I don't know. I went to see Paul and met his wife – lovely girl – and her parents. I told Sir Roy about our troubles and, as the Brits say, 'Bob's your uncle, Fanny's your aunt,' and here we are."

Shorty snickered, "I had an aunt with a fanny as wide as a truck."

Trip said, "Used to eat at a place outside Atlanta called Aunt Fanny's Cabin. Great food."

~~<>~~

The flyers walked into the King and Crown and Red spotted Potty right away. "Hello, Potty. Pints all around, old boy."

Potty asked, "Wots the occasion, then?"

Andy said, "We are all now Pilot Officers in His Majesty's Royal Air Force. Heading off to flight physicals and then Number 7 Operational Training Unit at Hawarden in Cheshire."

Potty said, "The pints are on the house, Gents. Thank you, and congratulations. And, er, thot I'd never say this, but 'appy 4th of July."

The Americans all stood and saluted Potty with their pints. "Independence!"

The boys were in high spirits when they boarded the train the next afternoon for Cheshire. They all passed their flight physicals that morning. On the way back to the RAF Club they picked up their RAF uniforms ordered the day before from Moss Brothers in Covent Garden. Trip paid the cost of the uniforms with the promise of repayment when everyone got paid. He did not really care if the others paid him back.

Andy, as usual, offered a bet on who would be the first to shoot down a Jerry. Failing to get a game of poker going, Shorty shuffled a deck of cards and played solitaire.

Red quietly looked out the window at the scenery, he held a newspaper on his lap. He turned to the group. "I was reading Churchill's speech from a month ago, just before France collapsed. Here's what he said:"

> ... we shall defend our Island, whatever the cost may be, we shall fight on the beaches, we shall fight on the landing grounds, we shall fight in the fields and in the streets, we shall fight in the hills; we shall never surrender, and even if, which I do not for a moment believe, this Island or a large part of it were subjugated and starving, then our Empire beyond the seas, armed and guarded by the British Fleet, would carry on the struggle, until, in God's good time, the New World, with all its power and might, steps forth to the rescue and the liberation of the old.

Red said, "The Battle of Britain is about to begin, fellas. Maybe we're part of the New World, with all its power and might, stepping forth."

Trip lit a cigarette and put a foot up on his battered backpack. Catching his reflection in the window, Pilot Officer Robert H. Gibson, III., RAF, smiled to himself.

I made it.

THE END

Look for Book II of The Sunlit Silence Series:

The Shouting Wind

by

Frank A. Mason.

Available Fall 2023 on Amazon.com

Appendix 1 – Recruitment of Americans

U.S. Isolationism and Neutrality Laws

Any examination of the recruitment of Americans to serve in foreign military services must be taken in the context of American neutrality laws of the 1930s. Under the Neutrality Acts, there were provisions to prevent U.S. citizens from getting involved in foreign conflicts as combatants, mercenaries, or volunteers.

The United States Congress was sensitive to the devastating impact of World War I and passed several neutrality laws during the 1930s intended to keep the U.S. out of foreign conflicts. The Neutrality Acts reflected a policy of isolationism, where the U.S. sought to distance itself from international conflicts. While this approach was intended to protect American interests, the U.S. hesitated to engage in international efforts to address aggression.

The **Neutrality Act of 1935** prohibited the sale of arms to any belligerent nation at war and required non-military goods to be sold on a "cash-and-carry" basis. This meant that if a country wanted to buy goods from the U.S., they had to pay in cash and arrange for their own transportation. The goal was to prevent the U.S. from being dragged into conflicts by ensuring it didn't extend credit to warring nations.

The **Neutrality Act of 1936** renewed the 1935 Act's provisions and included a ban on loans or credits to belligerents.

The **Neutrality Act of 1937** extended the provisions of the previous acts and added further restrictions. It included a "cash-and-carry" requirement for all goods, not just military ones. It also allowed the President to declare a "limited national emergency" and provide arms to belligerent nations on a case-by-case basis.

Important to the story of Americans in the RAF, this act prohibited Americans from traveling on belligerent ships. By not allowing U.S.

citizens to travel on ships of warring nations, the U.S. government hoped to keep its citizens safe and prevent any appearance of favoritism toward one side of a conflict.

The Neutrality Acts also made it illegal for U.S. citizens to volunteer for or serve in the armed forces of any foreign belligerent nation. This was meant to prevent American citizens from directly participating in conflicts abroad, which could lead to the U.S. being accused of taking sides and potentially being drawn into the conflict. Violations of these travel and volunteering restrictions could have legal consequences for U.S. citizens. Penalties included fines and imprisonment for those who knowingly violated the provisions of the Neutrality Acts.

In the face of the escalating conflict in Europe and Asia, the U.S. gradually shifted its stance from strict neutrality to supporting the Allied powers. The **Neutrality Act of 1939** ended the munitions embargo, and the **Lend-Lease Act of 1941** allowed the U.S. to lend or lease military equipment to nations deemed vital to American defense.

As the war entered its second year, Germany emerged as a clear enemy of world democracy. The U.S. Government quietly stopped enforcing the neutrality laws' prohibitions on Americans traveling to belligerent nations and on belligerent ships and serving in a foreign military.

Recruitment efforts for foreign militaries

Charles Sweeny

Charles Sweeny was an American soldier of fortune who served in the French Foreign Legion and various other nations' armed forces in the early 1900s. Born into poverty in California in 1882, Sweeny made a fortune in mining. He later contributed considerable funds to recruiting Americans to fly and fight for France and England in WWI's Lafayette Escadrille tradition.

Sweeny's large extended family included cousins in England. Sweeny's nephews, Charles Francis Sweeny and Robert "Bob" Sweeny were active in helping the elder Sweeny with the recruitment of

Americans for the RAF. Ultimately, Sweeny was named an honorary group captain in the RAF and helped found the Eagle Squadrons, units made up entirely of American volunteers.

Charles Sweeny walked a fine line with the U.S. Neutrality Acts. FBI Director J. Edgar Hoover set the FBI to apprehend Sweeny, but they failed. Using word of mouth and posting notices at U.S. airfields, Sweeny recruited 32 flyers for France. Four were killed, 11 were taken prisoner, and five reached England. The other 12 are lost to history. Thus, it is entirely possible that someone like Trip Gibson could have reached France and followed the path outlined in *Sunward I've Climbed*.

One of Sweeny's key recruiters was Clyde Pangborn, a famous barnstormer. Many of his recruits were from California, Pangborn's primary recruiting territory.

Sweeny funded expenses for many of the recruits, but his haphazard approach was seen by some as creating a chaotic situation. The Clayton Knight Committee took over when Sweeny was persuaded to visit England to continue his efforts there.

The Clayton Knight Committee

A major pathway to serving with the Royal Air Force was through Canada and the Royal Canadian Air Force (RCAF). Charles Sweeny certainly funded Americans to travel to and through Canada. He provided funding to support the flyers' needs, accommodations, and passage on convoy ships from Halifax, Nova Scotia, to Great Britain and France. But Sweeny's effort was haphazard and lacked organization.

A more concerted effort was started the day after Britain declared war on Germany. World War I flying ace William "Billy" Bishop, now an Air Marshal in the RCAF, contacted an American named Clayton Knight who had flown for the RAF during WWI.

Knight and Bishop set up the Clayton Knight Committee in the United States with the clear intent to recruit Americans to serve in the RCAF. This contravened U.S. Neutrality laws.

Knight and Homer Smith, another Canadian WWI pilot and heir to a vast oil fortune, set up operations in the Waldorf Hotel in New York City. They opened branch offices in other cities and began assisting volunteers to contact the Dominion Aeronautical Association, a shell organization. Recruits contacted the Association and were immediately referred to the RCAF.

The entry of the United States into the war with the Pearl Harbor attack ended the work of the Clayton Knight Committee. During its short life, the Knight Committee recruited over 2500 Americans for the RCAF and the RAF.

Appendix 2 – People

Paul Richey

Pilot Officer Paul Henry Mills Richey, RAF, DFC and Bar, was assigned with No. 1 Squadron RAF in France during 1939 and 1940. There are several complete biographies of Richey, who reached the rank of Wing Commander in the RAF.

Richey's memoir, *Fighter Pilot* (1941), informed *Sunward I've Climbed* of the feelings and challenges of real pilots serving in the chaotic first year of the Second World War. Trip Gibson becomes Paul Richey's friend, and Richey often helps Trip as he navigates the world of the RAF. They will meet again at RAF Middle Wallop, a fighter station near Portsmouth.

Paul Richey's *Fighter Pilot* is still available. The story is exciting and engaging. Trip participates in some of Richey's experiences as recounted in *Fighter Pilot*.

Edmond Marin la Meslée

Edmond Marin la Meslée was a French fighter pilot and 16-victory ace. His entire service as a pilot in the *Armée de l'Air* was with *Groupe d'Chase* I/5. The Air Order of Battle for the *Armée de l'Air* indicates GC I/5 was stationed at Suippes and Saint-Dizier throughout the Battle of France.

Meslée was well-liked and loyal to France. Upon the fall of France, Meslée evacuated to Rabat, Morocco, where he continued to fly the Curtiss Hawk 75 as commander of the Vichy French Air Force unit GC I/5. Operation Torch, the invasion of North Africa, ended the Vichy air force.

Meslée was made commanding officer of the reconstituted GC I/5 "Champagne" in January 1944. He was killed while flying a Republic P-47D Thunderbolt strafing German forces on February 4, 1945.

Edmond Marin la Meslée led with *élan*, and it is completely within his character to have befriended and mentored a talented fighter pilot such as Trip Gibson.

Leslie Clisby

At once described as courageous and profane, Australian Flying Officer Leslie Redford Clisby, DFC, was a fighter ace during the early days of World War II. He served with No. 1 Squadron RAF and scored 16 victories before being killed in combat on 15 May 1940. Clisby was known as a highly aggressive fighter pilot who disregarded his personal safety and pressed an attack regardless of the odds.

The London Gazette reported Clisby's Citation for the British Distinguished Flying Cross on 14 June 1940:

> Flying Officer Leslie Redford CLISBY (40043) (now reported missing). One day in April 1940, this officer was the pilot of one of three Hurricanes which attacked nine Messerschmitt 109's, one of which he shot down. The following day he destroyed another Messerschmitt 109. In May 1940, this officer was engaged in six combats against the enemy in which he shot down eight enemy aircraft. Flying Officer Clisby has displayed great courage on all occasions.

Clisby's character and "stone the crows" comments are as quoted in Paul Richey's *Fighter Pilot*.

André Malraux

André Malraux was a French novelist and government minister. In the 1930s Malraux was active in the left-wing Popular Front in France. At the beginning of the Spanish Civil War, Malraux joined the Spanish Republican Air Force, and though not a pilot, led the España Squadron made up of the obsolete Potez 540 twin-engine bombers.

Malraux was both an adventurer and a writer. A connoisseur of the arts beyond the written word, Malraux frequented the usual writers' spots in Paris and was a friend and confidant of Ernest Hemingway.

Hc rccruitcd pcoplc to go to Spain and fly combat airplanes for the Republicans.

Andrés García La Calle

Real name: Andrés García Calle. Squadron leader of the 1st Fighter Squadron of the Spanish Republic. Later he was commander of all fighter units of the Spanish Republican Air Force during the Spanish Civil War.

At the end of 1938, La Calle led his few remaining fighters at the Battle of the Ebro against German and Italian aircraft despite 10-to-1 odds.

La Calle was personally successful as a fighter pilot, scoring at least 11 victories against Nationalist Air Force units. His score may have been as high as 21.

In January 1939 La Calle led the very last of the Republican Air Force's fighters from Vilajuïga Airfield to the Francazal aerodrome near Toulouse, France. He was arrested by French authorities and interned in the *Argelès-sur-Mer* concentration camp.

La Calle escaped to Mexico, and died at age 66 in Santo Domingo, Dominican Republic.

La Calle's behavior in *Sunward I've Climbed* is consistent with his known character.

Andy Mamedoff, Red Tobin, Shorty Keough

These three men are integral to the story and deserve mention. More extensive biographies are available online. Like many other Eagle Squadron pilots, they were heroes by merely volunteering and risking all to reach England to fly and fight.

Andrew Beck Mamedoff (1918-1941) was a Polish-born American fighter pilot who was one of the few Americans recruited by Charles Sweeny to fly for France. Initially assigned to No. 609 Squadron at Middle Wallop, he was one of the founding members of the Eagle

Squadrons. Andy Mamedoff followed the path outlined in *Sunward I've Climbed*. He was killed in an aircraft accident on October 8, 1941.

Eugene Quimby "Red" Tobin (1917-1941) was an American fighter pilot who was a friend of Andy Mamedoff. Tobin was recruited by Charles Sweeny to fly for Finland but was diverted to France along with Mamedoff. Their escape from France to England was as described in Sunward I've Climbed. Initially assigned to No. 609 Squadron at Middle Wallop, Tobin was a founding member of the Eagle Squadrons. He was killed in combat with Bf-109s of Jagdgeschwader 26 on September 7, 1941. His path to flying for the RAF was as described in *Sunward I've Climbed*.

Vernon Charles "Shorty" Keough (1911-1941) was an American fighter pilot flying for the RAF. Shorty Keough was one of three Americans who went to France and ultimately escaped the German invasion to Britain. His path to England was as described in *Sunward I've Climbed*. He was a founding member of the Eagle Squadrons.

Shorty Keough was a skilled pilot and barnstormer with over 400 parachute jumps to his credit before volunteering to join the RAF. Keough was killed on 15 February 1941. After a combat chase over the English channel, Keough was seen to spin into the channel. His body was not recovered.

Appendix 3 - The Spanish Civil War

The Spanish Civil War (1936 to 1939) was a struggle between various factions within the country following over 100 years of dissent regarding the monarchy. The elections of 1931, permitted by King Alfonzo XIII, resulted in a Republican victory. While Republicans touted democracy, the election results led to even more strife and a coup. The Second Spanish Republic was declared two days after the elections and Alfonzo went into exile. Tensions between different social classes and regions contributed to the buildup of animosity.

While the Republicans enjoyed wide support among the Spanish population, the Great Depression sparked great dissent. Rural workers were poverty-stricken, and governmental actions did not alleviate this situation. The Republicans were increasingly seen as socialists. The result was a victory for Nationalists, right-wing conservatives, in 1933.

Elections in 1936 did not remedy the problems of a vastly divided nation and a military coup in that year sparked an all-out war.

Thus, the conflict pitted the Republicans, who were composed of a broad coalition of leftist, socialist, communist, and anarchist groups, against the Nationalists, who were led by General Francisco Franco and supported by fascists.

The Republicans received support from the Soviet Union and various international leftist groups, including volunteers worldwide who joined the International Brigades to fight against fascism. The Nationalists, on the other hand, received assistance from Nazi Germany and Fascist Italy.

The air war in Spain attracted international attention and participation. The Spanish Civil War marked one of the first instances of significant air-to-air combat. Fighter aircraft were used to engage enemy aircraft, protect bombers, and gain air superiority. This experience helped refine tactics that would become crucial during World War II.

The bombing of civilian populations, including Barcelona, demonstrated the destructive power of aerial bombing and its impact on civilian morale. The Nationalist bombing of Guernica by Italian forces and the German Condor Legion became a symbol of the indiscriminate destruction of civilian populations.

Various types of aircraft were deployed in the Spanish Civil War, ranging from biplanes to more advanced monoplanes and bombers. Soviet and German military leaders used the war as a testing ground for their new airplanes and tactics. Both sides utilized air power for reconnaissance, ground attack, and strategic bombing missions.

After three years of intense fighting, the Nationalists emerged victorious. General Franco's forces captured Madrid in 1939, effectively ending the war. The Spanish Civil War served as a precursor to World War II, showcasing new technologies and the willingness of governments to intervene in foreign conflicts.

Appendix 4 - The Battle of France

The Battle of France began on May 10, 1940, when German forces launched a surprise invasion of France and the Low Countries (Belgium, the Netherlands, and Luxembourg). The German strategy involved a rapid and highly mobile offensive called the *Blitzkrieg* (lightning war) that had proven effective in Poland. *Blitzkrieg* emphasized the use of combined arms forces – tanks, infantry, and air support – to swiftly penetrate enemy lines and create chaos within their ranks.

The Germans attacked through Belgium and the Netherlands, bypassing the heavily fortified Maginot Line along the French-German border. This approach caught the French and their allies off guard and allowed German forces to rapidly advance deep into France. The German forces surprised the Allies by not driving directly for Paris. Rather, the Germans outmaneuvered and encircled the Allied troops to the north, forcing them to retreat. The culmination of this first phase of the battle was the heroic British evacuation of over 300,000 British and French forces from the beaches of Dunkirk.

Despite the successful evacuation of such a critical number of troops, numerous Allied forces remained in France. The German forces continued to advance and split the French and British forces, isolating pockets of resistance.

Thousands, perhaps millions, of refugees fled the German advance clogging the roads with discarded possessions and broken, destroyed vehicles. In many cases, German aircraft dive-bombed and strafed the civilian refugees, adding thousands of dead humans and draft animals to the already chaotic, impassable roads.

The French leadership was thrown into disarray as they struggled to respond effectively to the speed and intensity of the German offensive. Despite some valiant efforts by French and British forces, they could not halt the German advance.

The French Air Force – the *Armée de l'Air* – and the British Royal Air Force did what they could with their limited number of obsolescent airplanes against the more modern German Luftwaffe. The *Armée de l'Air* suffered many lost aircraft in early German bombing raids. Thus, their effectiveness was reduced in the first days before the battle was fully joined. British aircrews valiantly attempted to blunt the German advance, to no avail.

The German breakthrough at Sedan, where their armored divisions crossed the Meuse River and effectively split the French army in two, spelled the end for France. German forces encircled a large portion of the French army, effectively trapping them. Realizing the dire situation, the French government declared Paris an open city to prevent unnecessary destruction and surrendered on June 22, 1940.

Immediately upon the breakthrough at Sedan and the subsequent rapid advance of the German Army, the British began Operation Aerial, the withdrawal of their remaining forces in France. Coastal ports from Bayonne in the far southwest all the way around to Le Havre on the Channel coast saw hundreds of ships transporting men and equipment to England and Gibraltar. This final battle phase was as stressful and chaotic as the first phase, with overloaded trains moving slowly toward ports. The roads were clogged with burning vehicles, fleeing citizens, and the dead –human and animal.

France's rapid collapse shocked the world and marked a significant success for Nazi Germany. The Battle of France also had long-lasting implications for the rest of World War II, as it isolated Great Britain and set the stage for the Battle of Britain.

While the Battle of France seemed a must-win for the Allies, it became a mere precursor to an even more critical fight.

> ...What General Weygand called the Battle of France is over. I expect that the battle of Britain is about to begin. Upon this battle depends the survival of Christian civilization. Upon it depends our own British life and the long continuity of our institutions and our Empire. The whole fury and might of the enemy must very soon be turned on us. Hitler knows that he

will have to break us in this island or lose the war. If we can stand up to him, all Europe may be free and the life of the world may move forward into broad, sunlit uplands. But if we fail, then the whole world, including the United States, including all that we have known and cared for, will sink into the abyss of a new Dark Age more sinister, and perhaps more protracted, by the lights of a perverted science. Let us therefore brace ourselves to our duties, and so bear ourselves that, if the British Empire and its Commonwealth last for a thousand years, men will still say, "This was their finest hour".

– Winston Churchill,

Appendix 5 – Attack at the Albert Canal

The valiant attack by British Fairey Battle Bombers against the two bridges over the Albert Canal on May 12th, 1940, resulted in only minor damage to the bridges. The Veldwezel and Vreenhoven bridges were the critical link across the otherwise impassible Albert Canal. The mission was to destroy the bridges and deny the advancing Germans an easy crossing. All of the Fairey Battle Bombers were lost in the attack. The lead aircraft, crewed by Flying Officer Donald Garland, Sergeant Thomas Gray, and Leading Aircraftsman Lawrence Reynolds, pressed the attack despite heavy damage. The aircraft crashed shortly after destroying one span of the Veldwezel Bridge.

Trip Gibson's observation in *Sunward I've Climbed* is in consonance with the bravery shown by the Garland and Gray. For their bravery in the face of tremendous odds, Garland and Gray were awarded the Victoria Cross (VC), the United Kingdom's highest award for valor.

Leading Aircraftsman Reynolds did not receive the VC because he was not in a decision-making position.

This is the citation for Garland and Gray's Victoria Cross:

> Air Office, 11th June, 1940
>
> The KING has been graciously pleased to confer the VICTORIA CROSS on the undermentioned officer and non-commissioned officer in recognition of most conspicuous bravery:-
>
> Flying Officer Donald Edward Garland (40105)
>
> 563627 Sergeant Thomas Gray
>
> Flying Officer Garland was the pilot and Sergeant Gray was the observer of the leading aircraft of a formation of five

aircraft that attacked a bridge over the Albert Canal which had not been destroyed and was allowing the enemy to advance into Belgium. All the aircrews of the squadron concerned volunteered for the operation, and, after five crews had been selected by drawing lots, the attack was delivered at low altitude against this vital target. Orders were issued that this bridge was to be destroyed at all costs. As had been expected, exceptionally intense machine-gun and anti-aircraft fire were encountered. Moreover, the bridge area was heavily protected by enemy fighters. In spite of this, the formation successfully delivered a dive-bombing attack from the lowest practicable altitude. British fighters in the vicinity reported that the target was obscured by the bombs bursting on it and near it. Only one of the five aircraft concerned returned from this mission. The pilot of this aircraft reports that besides being subjected to extremely heavy anti-aircraft fire, through which they dived to attack the objective, our aircraft were also attacked by a large number of enemy fighters after they had released their bombs on the target. Much of the success of this vital operation must be attributed to the formation leader, Flying Officer Garland, and to the coolness and resource of Sergeant Gray, who in most difficult conditions navigated Flying Officer Garland's aircraft in such a manner that the whole formation was able successfully to attack the target in spite of subsequent heavy losses. Flying Officer Garland and Sergeant Gray did not return.

Note that Garland was one of four brothers, all of whom were killed during the Second World War. Such was the sacrifice of families in the cause of freedom.

Appendix 6 - Aircraft

While it would be useful to recount all the details of WWII aircraft mentioned in *Sunward I've Climbed*, many sources on the internet offer detailed descriptions of each aircraft. Below, I have provided links to some of these for each of the aircraft types mentioned in the story.

Generally, I provided the Wikipedia listing for each aircraft and then any other interesting webpage, especially those with photos, that might help the reader visualize the action in the story.

Polikarpov I-16

https://en.wikipedia.org/wiki/Polikarpov_I-16

https://www.militaryaviationmuseum.org/aircraft/polikarpov-i-16/

https://www.militaryfactory.com/aircraft/detail.php?aircraft_id=216

http://www.aviation-history.com/polikarpov/i16.html

Curtiss JN-4D Jenny

https://en.wikipedia.org/wiki/Curtiss_JN_Jenny

https://www.nationalmuseum.af.mil/Visit/Museum-Exhibits/Fact-Sheets/Display/Article/197406/curtiss-jn-4d-jenny/

https://airandspace.si.edu/collection-objects/curtiss-jn-4d-jenny/nasm_A19190006000

Curtiss Hawk 75

https://en.wikipedia.org/wiki/Curtiss_P-36_Hawk

https://www.classicwarbirds.co.uk/american-aircraft/curtiss-hawk-75.php

https://www.militaryfactory.com/aircraft/detail.php?aircraft_id=155

Messerschmitt Bf-109E

https://en.wikipedia.org/wiki/Messerschmitt_Bf_109

https://www.rafmuseum.org.uk/research/collections/messerschmitt-bf-109e-3/

https://www.museumofflight.org/exhibits-and-events/aircraft/messerschmitt-bf-109e-3

Messerschmitt Bf-110 Zerstorer

https://en.wikipedia.org/wiki/Messerschmitt_Bf_110

https://www.battleofbritain1940.net/0014.html

https://www.militaryfactory.com/aircraft/detail.php?aircraft_id=96

Dornier Do-17Z and 217

https://en.wikipedia.org/wiki/Dornier_Do_17

https://en.wikipedia.org/wiki/Dornier_Do_217

https://www.militaryfactory.com/aircraft/detail.php?aircraft_id=543

Junker Ju-87 Stuka

https://en.wikipedia.org/wiki/Junkers_Ju_87

http://www.aviation-history.com/junkers/ju87.html

Heinkel He-111

https://en.wikipedia.org/wiki/Heinkel_He_111

https://www.militaryfactory.com/aircraft/detail.php?aircraft_id=99

https://www.battleofbritain1940.net/0017.html

Fairey Battle Bomber

https://en.wikipedia.org/wiki/Fairey_Battle

http://www.historyofwar.org/articles/weapons_fairey_battle.html

http://www.pilotfriend.com/photo_albums/timeline/ww2/Fairey%20Battle.htm

Hawker Hurricane Mark I

https://en.wikipedia.org/wiki/Hawker_Hurricane

https://www.nationalmuseum.af.mil/Visit/Museum-Exhibits/Fact-Sheets/Display/Article/196916/hawker-hurricane-mkiia/

https://www.battleofbritain1940.net/0010.html

Appendix 7 – WWII Fighter Formations

Armée de l'air

The formations used by the *Armée de l'Air* in 1940 were loose, with wide spacing for airplanes. The lead airplane and number 2 flew nearly abreast of one another, separated by 50 to 100 yards. Stacked above and behind by between 50 and 100 yards, Numbers 3 and 4 flew a weaving pattern intended to provide full 360° visual coverage.

Royal Air Force

At this stage of the war, the RAF had three main formations.

The four-ship diamond with the fourth aircraft tucked in tight below and behind lead. The Number 2 and Number 3 aircraft were on either side of lead. This was a very tight formation and was not intended for high maneuverability (although airshow demonstration teams use this formation even today).

The most common formation was a three-ship inverted V referred to by the RAF as a 'Vic.' The lead airplane was at the apex of the inverted V with Numbers 2 and 3 on the legs of the V.

Line astern was what the name implies. As many as eight aircraft would follow the leader. It was a difficult formation to maintain while scanning for enemy aircraft. During the Battle of Britain this formation was used to produce a 'flow' of aircraft attacking German bombers.

Luftwaffe

The Luftwaffe pioneered the fighter formation most often used today. Air Forces the world over now employ the *'finger-four'* formation, but in 1940 this formation was innovative and difficult to beat. The Luftwaffe called this four-ship formation the *schwarm,* and its two-ship components were called *rotten*. Two *rotten* made up a *schwarm*.

This formation was perceived as the most effective and flexible formation for air fighting.

The best way to understand this formation is to look at the fingers of either hand imagining each fingertip as an airplane. Lead is the longest, second, finger. Number 2 is the index finger and flies the relative position of that finger to lead. Number 3 is the ring finger, and Number 4, the wingman for Number 3, is the pinky finger.

The two *rotten* are made up of numbers 1 and 2 and numbers 3 and 4. The functions for the flight positions are 1 and 3 are leaders and engage the enemy, while 2 and 4 are wingmen and work to protect their respective leaders. This is not set in stone. Wingmen and leaders can interchange, allowing the aircraft in the best position to engage the enemy while being protected by the other flight members. (Example: Eagle Squadron members Captains Don Gentile and John Godfrey were lead and wing but exchanged positions when the tactical situation called for it. They were both very successful aces).

WWII Fighter Formations

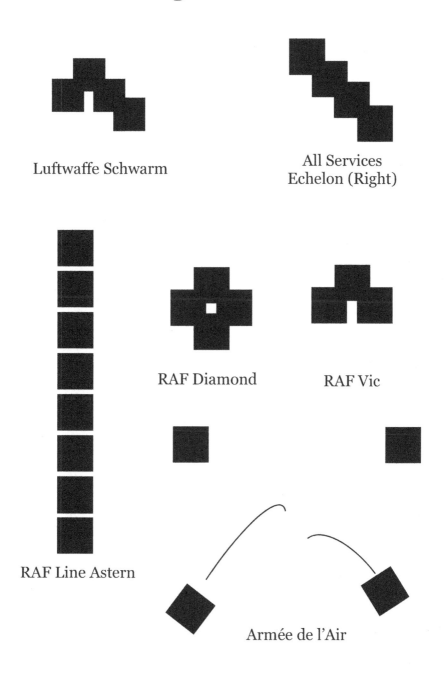

Luftwaffe Schwarm

All Services
Echelon (Right)

RAF Diamond

RAF Vic

RAF Line Astern

Armée de l'Air

References

1939 Georgia Tech Yellow Jackets Schedule and Results. College Football at Sports-Reference.com.

Aerial Warfare and the Spanish Civil War. (n.d.). U.S. Centennial of Flight Commission. https://www.centennialofflight.net/essay/Air_Power/Spansh_CW/AP18.htm

Anonymous. (1940, February 15). Handbook of operation and flight instructions for the Models P-36A and P-36C pursuit airplanes. Dayton, OH: Material Division Chief of the Air Corps.

Anonymous. (1999, 25 February). *Armée de l'Air order of battle, 10th May 1940.* france1940.free.fr/adla/ada_may.html#Fighter ZOAN

Anonymous. (2020, December 4). *Timeline of 1940 events: World War II takes shape.* https://www.historic-newspapers.com/blog/1940-timeline/

Baughen, G. (2016). *The RAF in the Battle of France and The Battle of Britain: A reappraisal of Army and Air policy 1938-1940.* United Kingdom: Fonthill Media.

Brown, C. (n.d.). SS Normandie – too excessive for passengers? *World of Cruising.* https://www.worldofcruising.co.uk/editors-corner/ss-normandie-legacy-passengers-failure

Caine, P. D. (1993). *American pilots in the RAF: The WWII Eagle Squadrons.* New York, NY: Brasseys.

Convoys. (n.d.). Canada in the Second World War. https://www.junobeach.org/canada-in-wwii/articles/convoys/

Cooke, H.D. (1950, August). *The Atlantic convoys.* Annapolis, MD: U.S. Naval Institute Proceedings.

Curtiss Aeroplane Division. (n.d.). *Detail specifications for Curtiss Hawk 75-A Pursuit Airplane.* Curtiss Wright Corporation.

Curtiss Hawk 75A-C1 (France). (n.d.). History of War. www.historyofwar.org/articles/weapons_curtiss_hawk_75.html

Dunkirk Evacuation: May 26-June 4, 1940. (n.d.). Infographic-
Dunkirk-Evacuation-World-War-II-1940.jpg. Encyclopedia
Britanica.

Escorteur le Volontaire Novembre 1944. (n.d.). La Marcophile
Navale Envelopmer.
https://envelopmer.blogspot.com/search/label/Escorteur%
20le%20Volontaire%20novembre%201944

Fitzgerald, C. (2023, March 14). SS Normandie: The French ocean
liner lost to a suspicious fire during World War II. *War
History Online.*
https://www.warhistoryonline.com/ships/ss-
normandie.html

Flyer Menu. (n.d.). flyer menu.png

Goodson, James A. (1983). *Tumult in the clouds: A story of the
Eagle Squadron.* New York: St Martins Press.

Green, William. (1961). *War planes of the second world war.
Volume Two Fighters.* Garden City, New York: Doubleday.

Hague, A., & Kindell, D. (n.d.). HX Convoys 1939-1945 (North
America-U.K.). Convoys HX 1 through HX 50.
http://www.warsailors.com/convoys/hxconvoys.html

Harvey, A.D. (2020). Why did the French Air Force fail in 1940?
History Net. https://www.historynet.com/why-the-french-
air-force-failed-in-1940/

Haughland, V. (1979). *The Eagle Squadrons: Yanks in the RAF
1940-1942.* New York, NY: Ziff-Davis Flying Books.

Hawker Hurricane in Combat. (n.d.). History of War.
www.historyofwar.org/articles/weapons_hawker_hurricane
_combat.html

Hawker Hurricane: The Most Up-to-Date Encyclopedia, News,
Review & Research. (n.d.). https://academic-
accelerator.com/encyclopedia/hawker-hurricane

Hawker Hurricane. (1940). Air Publication 1564B: Pilots Notes.

Hawker Hurricane. (n.d.). Wikipedia: The Free Encyclopedia.

Henry, S. (2019). Timeline: The long, risqué history of Atlanta
nightlife. Atlanta Magazine.
https://www.atlantamagazine.com/news-culture-
articles/timeline-the-long-risque-history-of-atlantas-
nightlife/

History of the Ministry of Defence. (n.d.).
https://assets.publishing.service.gov.uk/government/upload s/system/uploads/attachment_data/file/49053/history_of_ mod.pdf.

HMS Windsor (D42). (n.d.). Wikipedia: The Free Encyclopedia.

Hotel Ansley. (n.d.). Wikipedia: The Free Encyclopedia.

Johnson, D. A. (2015, April). *American Eagles over Dieppe*. Warfare History Network. Retrieved from https://warfarehistorynetwork.com.

Johnson, D. A. (n.d.). *Americans in the Royal Air Force*. Warfare History Network. Retrieved from https://warfarehistorynetwork.com.

Kan, K.C. (2007). *First in the air: The Eagle Squadrons of World War II*. Washington, DC: Air Force History and Museums Program.

King, E. (n.d.). *Atlantic convoys World War II*. Retrieved on March 21, 2023.

Lauher, J.D. (1980). American pilots in the Battle of Britain. [Master's Thesis] U.S. Army Command and General Staff College.

Listemann, P.H. (2018). *The Supermarine Spitfire Mk. V: The Eagle Squadrons. Squadrons No. 25*. Orlando, FL: Listemann.

Listemann, P.H. (2022). *The Hawker Hurricane Mk. I & II: The Eagle Squadrons. Squadrons No. 53*. Orlando, FL: Listemann.

Listemann, P.H. (2022). *The Supermarine Spitfire Mk. II: The Rhodesian, Dominion, & Eagle Squadrons. Squadrons No. 53*. Orlando, FL: Listemann.

Ludikar, M. (2014). *A short history of the Czechoslovak Air Force in WW2 and the post-war period*. https://fcafa.com/2014/09/18/a-short-history-of-the-czechoslovak-air-force-in-ww2-and-the-post-war-period/

Marsh, E. (2020). The Unthinkable: Remembering the Battle of France. The Vintage Aviation Echo. https://vintageaviationecho.com/2020/05/09/battle-of-france/

Mathews, T. (2021, December 14). *A year in history: 1939 Timeline.*
https://www.historic-newspapers.co.uk/blog/a-year-in-history-1939-timeline/

Menu. (n.d.). Maxims 1940s.
https://www.worthpoint.com/worthopedia/maxims-restaurant-dinner-menu-paris-1754383283

Moores, S. (2023). No I Squadron Hurricanes in France 1939-1940 – Sqn Leader 'Bull' Halahan and 'blue 109s'. *Falke Eins – The Luftwaffe Blog.*
https://falkeeins.blogspot.com/2023/04/no-1-squadron-hurricanes-in-france-1939.html

No. 1 Squadron Royal Air Force during the Second World War. (n.d.). The wartime memories project.

Operation Aerial. (n.d.). Wikipedia: The Free Encyclopedia.

Paul Richey. (n.d.). Wikipedia: The Free Encyclopedia.

Persyn, L., Stenman, K., & Thomas, A. (2009). *P-36 Hawk aces of World War 2. Osprey Aircraft of the Aces Number 86.* New York, NY: Osprey.

Posey, C.A. (2009). The war between the wars. *Air & Space Magazine| Smithsonian Magazine.*
https://www.smithsonianmag.com/air-space-magazine/the-war-between-the-wars-57934780/

Richey, P. (1941). Fighter pilot. London, U.K.: B.T. Batsford Ltd.

Scutts, J. (1986). *Hurricane in action.* Carollton, TX: Squadron/Signal.

Ship's Bells Explained. (n.d.). Antique Clock Guy.
https://www.clockguy.com/SiteRelated/SiteReferencePages/ShipsBellsExplained.html

Ships hit by U-boats. (n.d.). Baron-Nairn. British steam merchant.
https://uboat.net/allies/merchants/ship/974.html

Snapper, Red Tobin. (2005). Key Aero.
https://www.key.aero/forum/historic-aviation/50064-snapper-red-tobin

SS Normandie. (n.d.). Wikipedia: The Free Encyclopedia.

Tanner, J. (Ed.). *British aviation colours of World War Two: The official camouflage, colors, and markings of RAF aircraft, 1939-1945.* London, UK: Arms and Armor Press.

Taylor, B. (n.d.). *The Battle of France: Furor Tutonicus & Gallic debacle*. Warfare History Network.

The Brief but Glorious Career of SS Normandie. (n.d.). The History Press. https://www.thehistorypress.co.uk/articles/the-brief-but-glorious-career-of-ss-normandie/

The Dixie Flyer Route to Florida: Schedules corrected to January 1, 1930.
Dixie_Flyer_and_Dixie_Limited_timetables_1930.jpg

Toul-Croix de Metz Airfield (n.d.). Wikipedia: The Free Encyclopedia.

Zahniseer, M.R. (1992, May). Rethinking the significance of disaster: The United States and the fall of France 1940. *The International History Review 14*(2).

Acknowledgments

In any writing project, the author is only one of the players. I am fortunate to have many friends who kindly function as helpers. They all help as beta readers, consultants on history and military operations, consultants on writing, and advisors on the business of being an author.

I extend my sincere thanks to the following people who have been invaluable in my journey as an author.

My wife Deri encourages me daily and serves as my primary beta reader.

Ms. Karen Brady is always willing to edit my books. Her contributions are invaluable.

Ms. Payson Tilden, Museum Director, Ximenez-Fatio House, St. Augustine, Florida. Her facility in French added accuracy to the dialog in *Sunward I've Climbed.*

Mr. Randell Jones, award winning author of several histories of the Revolutionary War era and fellow Georgia Tech grad (we survived!) offered his generous counsel on book design and reference sources. He has made me better at the craft of writing. Visit Randell's webpage at: https://www.randelljones.com/

Mr. Griff Hosker is a renowned English author of historical fiction and a most generous friend in the gift of his time and advice. Griff has kindly given me the value of his counsel on managing the business of being an author. Visit Griff's webpage at: https://www.griffhosker.com/

Danny Morrison at Amazon ProHub, my publisher.

I am sure there are others who deserve thanks. If I missed anyone, please know you are valued and appreciated.

FAM

About the Author

Frank A. Mason is the pen name for retired U.S. Air Force Lieutenant Colonel Bob Amason, PhD, who also served as a college professor for 25 years.

As an officer in the USAF, Mason flew as a crew member on B-52s during the Cold War, served as a flying training instructor, and directed high-level staff organizations over 22 years of his early adult life.

A college professor from the late 1990s to the present, Mason's alter ego earned degrees, including a Ph.D., from two of the nation's top five public institutions. He had the privilege of mentoring hundreds of doctoral students at three institutions. He is a member of the Sons of the American Revolution. Several of his patriot ancestors rode with Francis Marion.

Frank A. Mason is the author of Amazon bestselling *Journeyman Chronicles*, the adventures of Will Yelverton, a young gunsmith caught in the vortex of the American Revolution. Book II of the Journeyman Series, Heart of Tempered Steel, was selected a finalist in the Florida Writers Association Royal Palm Literary Award Competition for 2023.

Mason's *Four Women of the Revolution* is a story of courage and resilience inspired by actual events and is a companion to the *Journeyman Chronicles* series of novels.

Mason's *Sunlit Silence Series* of World War II in the air features the exploits of American pilot Trip Gibson as he flies for Spain, France, England, and the United States. *Sunward I've Climbed* is book one.

Frank A. Mason also is the author of a series of modern suspense novels featuring the reluctant hero, Mac McCall. The Mac McCall novels are available on Amazon.

Books by Frank A. Mason

Journeyman Chronicles Series

Journeyman: The Bridge

Journeyman: Heart of Tempered Steel

Journeyman: Honor Fades Not

Historical Novels

Four Women of the Revolution

Sunlit Silence Series of WWII in the Air

Sunward I've Climbed

The Shouting Wind (Coming 2023)

Mac McCall Suspense Novels

Blue-Green for the Grave

The Bronze-Wound Lament

Frank A. Mason's novels are available on Amazon.com and other booksellers.

Writing as Bob Amason, PhD

"November Wind." Personal story in Randell Jones' Anthology, *Twists and Turns* (2022, Winston-Salem, NC, Daniel Boone Footsteps).

"My Father's Photograph." Personal story in Randell Jones' Anthology, *Lost and Found* (2023, Winston-Salem, NC, Daniel Boone Footsteps).

"My People: Crackers, Cow Hunters, Patriots, and Rebels." Personal story in Randell Jones' Anthology, *Sooner or Later* (2023, Winston-Salem, NC, Daniel Boone Footsteps).

Made in United States
Orlando, FL
30 July 2024

49737133R00212